Heiresses of Russ 2013

Heiresses of Russ 2013

THE YEAR'S BEST LESBIAN SPECULATIVE FICTION

edited by
Tenea D. Johnson
and Steve Berman

Lethe Press
Maple Shade, New Jersey

Heiresses of Russ 2013:
The Year's Best Lesbian Speculative Fiction
Copyright © 2013 Tenea D. Johnson and Steve Berman. ALL RIGHTS RESERVED. No part of this work may be reproduced or utilized in any form or by any means, electronic or mechanical, including photocopying, microfilm, and recording, or by any information storage and retrieval system, without permission in writing from the publisher.

Published in 2013 by Lethe Press, Inc.
118 Heritage Avenue • Maple Shade, NJ 08052-3018
www.lethepressbooks.com • lethepress@aol.com
ISBN: 978-1-59021-072-7 / 1-59021-072-7 (library binding)
ISBN: 978-1-59021-170-0 / 1-59021-170-7 (paperback)
ISBN: 978-1-59021-173-1 / 1-59021-173-1 (e-book)

Credits for first publication appear on page 309, which constitutes an extension of this copyright page.

These stories are works of fiction. Names, characters, places, and incidents are products of the authors' imaginations or are used fictitiously.

Set in Minion and Gondola SD.
Cover and interior design: Alex Jeffers.
Cover image: © Heartland—Fotolia.com.

Introduction
  Tenea D. Johnson ix
One True Love
  Malinda Lo 1
Saint Louis 1990
  Jewelle Gomez 27
Elm
  Jamie Killen 55
Winter Scheming
  Brit Mandelo 79
Reality Girl
  Richard Bowes 99
Oracle Gretel
  Julia Rios 121
Otherwise
  Nisi Shawl 133
Harrowing Emily
  Megan Arkenberg 159
The Witch Sea
  Sarah Diemer 167
Barnstormers
  Wendy N. Wagner 197
Nightfall in the Scent Garden
  Claire Humphrey 211
Beneath Impossible Circumstances
  Andrea Kneeland 221
Feed Me the Bones of Our Saints
  Alex Dally MacFarlane 227
Narrative Only
  Kate Harrad 247

Nine Days and Seven Tears
    JL Merrow   251
Chang'e Dashes from the Moon
    Benjanun Sriduangkaew   259
Astrophilia
    Carrie Vaughn   277

Introduction

TENEA D. JOHNSON

There's nothing like an anthology. Novels are fantastic, book series engrossing, novellas a special kind of magic, but anthologies are somethin' else. Between two covers you can discover a dozen new authors, as well as just as many magazines, presses, and websites you never knew existed and soon find you can't live without. Anthologies are the internet before the internet, but better. They are curated abundance collected and packaged for your pleasure.

I've always gravitated to them—from *Home Girls: A Black Feminist Anthology* and *Does Your Mama Know?* to *The Year's Best Fantasy and Horror*, the *Oxford Book of Science Fiction Stories*, and the problematic but informative Norton Anthologies of

Everything. These were the neighborhoods I frequented as a child, the worlds I visited, the places that I loved, even when they didn't love me back. Rarely though could I find where these groupings met. When I did, they became my favorites: the loveliest edges and corners vibrant with possibility, nuance, and depth.

And here we have one, often longed for and seldom found: lesbian-themed speculative fiction, the best we read that was published in 2012. To be sure, much wonderful work came out last year, but these are the short stories and novelettes we simply could not do without: the fairy tales too long in coming, the re-imagined myths both humorous and dark, the return of a classic vampire and the revenge of a culture, the stories of women back from the dead and into the light, bodies taken and surrendered, the dystopic futures and future returns to the agrarian past that satisfied that deep desire—when only words will do and, for a time, we get to crawl inside their world.

One of the most compelling aspects of speculative fiction is its ability to fulfill otherwise unattainable desires—whether one wants to create a magical society or travel through time, visit an alien civilization or remake history. It also satisfies more mundane reader desires, the ones it would not seem so hard to fulfill. To call a few of these out, I'll willingly step on this mine: the explosion of "should":

It should not be easier to find a zombie apocalypse than it is to find a lesbian protagonist in the aisles of your local bookstore. Falling for werewolves and shape shifters should not be more accepted than a transgendered love affair; marginalized people really will still exist in the future; more folks should know that, and more so create like they know it. Someone then must step into the gap, or to be more accurate the gaping holes in the collective visions of our possibilities as human beings. In these pages, someone has. Seventeen someones to be exact.

And here's one more foray into the embattled Land of Ought: we should blow up the notion of a single literary canon once and for all, and revel in the multiplicity. After all, if a literary canon is central and representative, who does it represent? Where is the center?

Introduction

Perhaps a best-of anthology can be a political act—à la "I'll show you my literary canon if you show me yours" As Joanna Russ tells us in *How to Suppress Women's Writing*, "there is a false center to 'literature.'"

And this is where it gets complicated, that is to say, interesting, in the space where these stories exist, even where this anthology hopes to: in the center of the ever-expanding edges.

Perhaps an anthology can be such an act when the authors have given such great work, such compelling, beautiful, powerful stories. If so, let this third in the *Heiresses of Russ* series burn brightly. Let it be both a comfort and a message.

Tenea D. Johnson
Near the Gulf of Mexico
Spring 2013

One True Love

Malinda Lo

It is never lucky for a child to kill her mother in the course of her own birth. Perhaps for this reason, the soothsayer who attended the naming ceremony for Princess Essylt was not a celebrated one. Haidis had barely finished his own apprenticeship when the summons came. He knew that delivering the prophecy for this princess was a thankless job, because no soothsayer in his right mind would attempt to foretell the life of a girl-child born out of death.

His mentor and former teacher told him to sugarcoat the prophecy as much as possible. "She's unimportant, in the grand scheme of things," said Gerlach. "King Radek needs a son; he'll find a new bride soon enough and the princess will simply be married off when she's older." He gave Haidis a sharp glance. "Make sure your prophecy sounds true enough, but remember that the king doesn't need the truth; he only needs a benediction."

So Haidis went to the naming ceremony prepared to omit any problematic details from the prophecy he would deliver. He planned to stop by the soothsayers' temple afterward, to make an offering to the God of Prophecy to counteract whatever bad luck he might acquire from being in such close proximity to the princess.

It was a small ceremony, as Haidis expected, and the king himself seemed a little bored, his mind likely focused on his next journey to the war front rather than the baby held in the arms of the nursemaid nearby. The child wouldn't stop crying, her voice a thin, angry wail that echoed in the cold, stony throne room. When Haidis approached her with the Water of Prophecy and the Scepter of Truth, she screamed even louder, her mouth stretched open in a tiny O of frustration, her eyes screwed shut. She had wisps of reddish hair on her scalp, and her cheeks were ruddy. He wondered if she would ever grow into a beauty; her mother, the late Queen Lida, had been known for her inheritance, not her looks.

King Radek barked, "Get on with it before the girl makes us all deaf."

"Apologies, Your Majesty," Haidis said. He lifted the pewter bowl containing the Water of Prophecy and dipped his fingers in it, dampening the girl's forehead and cheeks with the liquid. Her squalls stopped as if she was shocked by his touch, and she opened her eyes. They were a vibrant green, as vivid as springtime in the woods outside the castle, and Haidis was as startled by her as she seemed to be by him. She might not become a beauty, he thought, but those eyes were certainly a marvel.

He picked up the Scepter of Truth and held it over the princess as he began the incantation that would bring him into the trancelike state required to foretell her future. He didn't expect to fall deeply into the trance; he was too aware of the king glaring at him, not to mention the princess's luminous green eyes. He kept his own eyes

One True Love

half open, so he saw the moment when the girl reached up with her baby fingers and wrapped them around the Scepter itself.

This was unusual, and Haidis knew it. He knew it because the Scepter changed into a living thing at the princess's touch, and he had to hang on to it with all his might to prevent it from flying out of his hand. His eyes widened, but he did not see the nurse's astonished expression, or the way the king sat up in surprise. He saw, instead, the princess's future, and this vision would remain with him for the rest of his life, for it was the first time he had seen true, and he could not resist speaking it wholly, without any of his mentor's suggested sugarcoating.

"The princess shall grow into a young woman strong and pure," Haidis intoned. "But when she finds her one true love"—the nursemaids standing in the throne room giggled—"she shall be the downfall of the king."

The attendants and guests erupted into shocked whispers. Haidis's vision cleared with a snap, and he saw the baby Princess Essylt gazing up at him with what appeared to be a smile on her face. Terror filled him as he realized what he had said. He pulled the Scepter of Truth away from the princess, and as it left her hands it became ordinary again.

Behind him the king roared, "Take this abomination away! She shall never be the downfall of me! Take her away or I will have her killed, *and she will join her mother in the grave.*"

The nursemaid clutched the Princess Essylt to her breast and fled. Haidis swayed on his feet as he wondered if he had sentenced the baby girl to her death with his careless speaking of the truth.

It was the king's most trusted advisor who devised a solution to the problem of Princess Essylt's prophecy. "We shall simply never allow the princess to find her true love," he told the king, "and so your safety will be assured." Of course, the advisor had ulterior motives—he believed the princess might one day be useful, politically—but he kept that to himself, and the king consented to his plan.

From that day forward, Princess Essylt was restricted to the castle's West Tower under the supervision of her nursemaid, Auda, and was not allowed to see any man except for her father. He visited her rarely, for he had little desire to see the cause of his prophesied doom. The few times he did visit, he glared down at the princess and demanded, "Are you being an obedient little girl?"

She shrank away from him at first, running back to Auda, who would turn her around forcefully and whisper in her ear, "This is your father, the king of Anvarra, and you are his daughter, a princess, and you must behave as such."

As the years passed, Essylt learned to bow to her father, and she came to see him as a sort of duty: one that she had inherited by birth, but not one that she enjoyed. She knew that he did not particularly like her, but she did not know why, for Auda kept the prophecy that had relegated her to the West Tower a secret.

Auda was a skilled and loving nursemaid, and she took her job seriously. She knew that the only way Essylt would be content in the tower was if she thought her life was entirely normal. For several years, Auda was quite successful, for she made the West Tower into everything a little girl could wish for. When Essylt wanted new dolls, Auda ordered them; when she asked for playmates, Auda invited the princess's young female cousins to visit; when she yearned for a pony, Auda convinced the king to deliver one to the gardens adjacent to the West Tower. She even arranged for a female riding instructor to teach Essylt how to ride. Whenever Essylt voiced questions about why she couldn't go through the heavily carved oak door in the hall, Auda said, "We must keep you safe, for you are the princess of Anvarra, and you must be protected."

The only times Essylt left the West Tower were on the occasions of her father's weddings, for it was deemed too unseemly for the princess to remain locked away on such an important day. For those events, Essylt was dressed in veils from head to toe so that no one could see her face. The veils also had the unfortunate—or perhaps intentional—side effect of rendering her mostly blind, so she had to hold Auda's hand the entire time. That meant that Essylt's experience of the greater castle was confined to careful study of the floor, glimpsed in flashes through the gap at the bottom of the veils.

During Essylt's childhood, King Radek married several times, for his wives had a troubling tendency to die. Essylt's mother, of course, had died in childbed, as did the king's second wife. His third wife bore two stillborn children—sons, the king noted in despair—before succumbing to a fever. After that, several years passed before the king decided to marry again. Some believed he worried that he was cursed, but others noted that he was merely distracted by a new war that had broken out between Anvarra and its eastern neighbor, the kingdom of Drasik. This war went on season after season, and Essylt passed her thirteenth and fourteenth and fifteenth birthdays with her father away at battle, and no new bride on the castle threshold to draw her out of the West Tower.

As Essylt grew older, she became increasingly curious about the court and her father and why he did not return except once or twice a year, and Auda reluctantly began to answer her questions. In this way, Essylt learned that King Radek had sought an alliance with the island nation of Nawharla'al, which had once been invaded by Drasik but had successfully driven them out through an ingenious use of poison-tipped arrows that spread plague through the Drasik soldiers. In Essylt's seventeenth year, Anvarra and Nawharla'al fought and won a decisive battle against Drasik. In celebration of victory, the king of Nawharla'al gave his seventeen-year-old daughter Sadiya to King Radek in marriage to further cement their alliance.

Sadiya, like all Nawharla'ali people, had brown skin and black hair, with eyes the color of rich, dark soil. The first time King Radek saw her—in a tent on the side of the road after the last battle—he felt lust stir within him, for he had never seen a girl as beautiful and exotic as she. The king saw the way his attendants looked at her, too, and black jealousy rose within him, even thicker than his lust. He ordered that Sadiya be taken immediately to the West Tower and locked inside until their wedding, which would take place in exactly one fortnight.

Sadiya did not understand what he said, for she had not yet learned the Anvarran language. She only knew that the king's voice was covetous and greedy, and when he lifted her chin with his hand, she could almost smell the desire on his breath. It took all her years of royal training to not spit in his face, and she prayed to her gods that something would come to deliver her from this marriage.

On the day of Sadiya's arrival, Essylt was poring over history books in the West Tower's small library when she heard the heavy oaken doors in the entry hall flung open. Startled, she ran out onto the balcony overlooking the hall and saw a stream of women in strange, colorful clothes entering the tower, bearing a series of curious objects: wooden trunks carved with unfamiliar animals; a golden cage containing a bird with brilliant purple and green feathers; cushions the color of sunsets. Amid all this movement, Essylt saw one girl standing stock-still in the corner, her arms crossed around herself protectively. She was wrapped from head to foot in azure scarves, with only her eyes peering out.

Auda came running into the hall, demanding to know what was going on, and a woman in a plain blue dress detached herself from the entourage of attendants to speak to Auda in low, intense tones.

Essylt came down the stairs. She was drawn to the silent girl in the corner, who looked up at that moment and saw her. A shiver ran down Essylt's spine: quicksilver, insistent. Go to her.

As Essylt approached, the girl unwound the veils from her face to reveal brown skin, full lips, and dark eyes: a beauty unlike that of any Anvarran woman. This girl took a step away from her corner and extended her hands, palms up, toward Essylt. In the center of her palms a design was painted: swirls and loops that connected to form a pattern that was like a flower, but no flower that Essylt knew. Instinctively, Essylt reached out and covered the girl's hands with her own, paler ones, and when their skin touched, a tremor went through Essylt's body. For the first time, she became wholly aware of the way her fingers and toes were connected to the pulsing of her heart, to the breath that fluttered from her lungs to her lips, to the heat that spread over her cheeks.

Behind her, Auda said in a strained tone of voice, "Your Highness, this is the Princess Sadiya of Nawharla'al." There was another round of feverish whispers between Auda and Sadiya's chief attendant, who spoke Anvarran with an accent that Auda had never heard before and thus found difficult to understand.

"Sa-*dee*-ah?" Essylt said uncertainly.

"*Sah*-dee-ya," the girl corrected, and her name sounded like music on her lips.

Sadiya's chief attendant said something to her in Nawharla'ali, and Essylt heard her own name amidst the stream of foreign words. "Ess-*elt*," Sadiya said tentatively, her gaze never leaving Essylt's.

Essylt's heartbeat quickened, and she realized that Sadiya had wrapped her fingers around her own, and it was as if a faint dusting of magic had settled over them, fixing them in place so that they might look at one another for just a bit longer.

It was Auda who broke the spell. "Your Highness," she said, "Princess Sadiya will be staying here in the West Tower until your father returns in ten days. Then they will be married. The princess will be your new stepmother."

"My new stepmother?" Essylt said, and saw Sadiya's attendant whisper something urgently in her ear.

Sadiya pulled her hands away. She knew that her attendants were shocked by how Essylt had touched her and how she had accepted it. The proper greeting would have been for Essylt to hover her hands over Sadiya's and then to incline her head ever so delicately, but of course Essylt did not know Nawharla'ali customs. Her mistake could be excused, but what had caused Sadiya to hold Essylt's hands, as if she were a lover rather than a stranger who would someday become her stepdaughter? Sadiya's face flamed as she realized what a scene she was making.

Essylt did not understand how she had erred, but she saw that Sadiya was uncomfortable, and she regretted it, for already she wanted to ensure that Sadiya was happy. "Welcome," she said, but then her mouth went dry. She could think of nothing more to say except *You are so beautiful*, but even Essylt, unpracticed in courtly manners, sensed that others would find that odd, so she bit her lip and remained silent.

But that was enough, and Sadiya smiled, and her face was so exquisitely shining that Essylt was certain that another sun had burned into being right there in the entry hall to the West Tower.

From that moment on, Essylt and Sadiya were inseparable. Essylt taught Sadiya the words for the flowers and plants that grew in the West Tower's garden, and Sadiya taught Essylt the Nawharla'ali equivalents. Their progress was remarkably fast, for they spent every waking minute together, exclaiming over the sounds of words and the way sentences formed when they spoke them to each other. Essylt learned that Nawharla'al was a kingdom of many islands, and each island was named after a different tropical flower, and each flower was worn by the prince of that island on state occasions. Sadiya learned that summer was short and hot in Anvarra, and she had arrived at its beginning, when the days are long and lush and sometimes so humid that sitting in the shade brought sweat to the skin. Essylt learned that the women of Nawharla'al wore long, loose skirts dyed in shades to match their islands' flowers, and they preferred to leave their arms bare, binding only their breasts in scarves that matched their skirts. Sadiya learned that the women of Anvarra wore layers of undergarments beneath heavy skirts and bodices that gripped their torsos with whalebone, and she wrinkled her nose at these gowns and said, "I will not wear those," and Essylt laughed at the expression on Sadiya's face.

The days they spent together seemed to stretch out luxuriously in the peaceful isolation of the West Tower, but as the fortnight drew to a close, neither girl could avoid the increasing sensation of impending doom, for soon Sadiya would marry Essylt's father. The night before the wedding, they walked the garden together in silence, as if not speaking would stave off the future. When they parted to sleep in their separate chambers, Essylt held her hands out, palms upward, in the way Sadiya had upon her arrival. Sadiya was surprised, but she hovered her hands over Essylt's unmarked ones, a bittersweet sadness sweeping through her.

Then, as if she were a knight in a storybook, Essylt raised Sadiya's hands to her mouth and kissed the knuckles, her lips brushing soft and quick over Sadiya's skin. A flush spread across Sadiya's face, and she saw an answering emotion in Essylt's green eyes.

"Sleep well," Essylt whispered, and she wished she could sleep beside Sadiya and guard her against any nightmares that might slip into her mind that night.

"A blessing upon you," Sadiya said in Nawharla'ali, and then backed away before the tears could slip from her eyes. Essylt watched her go, her scarves fluttering in the dim evening light.

The wedding was held in the castle's Great Hall, which was hung with golden ropes in honor of the God of Matrimony and wreaths of snowbell flowers for the Goddess of Fertility. The morning before the ceremony, which was to take place at noon, Sadiya's attendants bathed and scented and dressed her in the Nawharla'ali bridal finery they had brought with them. They wrapped her body in fine white linen, and then draped her with scarves the color of the sea in every shade from deepest blue to azure and aquamarine. They hung jewels from her ears and twisted them around her bare arms and throat, and when she stepped into the sunlight she glittered with reflected light. Her lustrous black hair was brushed out and woven with the little white flowers plucked from the gardens around the West Tower, and though they were not the tropical blossoms of Nawharla'al, they served well enough. Essylt especially liked to see the flowers she loved in Sadiya's hair.

Auda had taken care while dressing Essylt that morning, as well, though Essylt's gown was much plainer so that she would not outshine the bride—and so that she would draw no man's eye. Essylt did not like the way the tight stays cut off her breath; she found the layers of skirts confining; and she thought the dove gray of the gown itself was ugly in comparison to the brilliant colors of Sadiya's clothes. But the thing she hated most was the gray linen veil she was forced to wear, obscuring her hair and face and swathing the whole world in dimness. As they left the West Tower, Essylt followed in Sadiya's perfumed wake with Auda's guiding hand on her arm. She felt suffocated and suppressed, each layer of clothing like a hand over her mouth.

In every Anvarran wedding ceremony, a series of customs is dutifully followed in order to ensure that the union is a fertile one. As with every naming ceremony, a prophecy is given, and to be chosen to deliver the prophecy at a royal wedding is a high honor. Haidis, the hapless soothsayer who had presided over Essylt's naming ceremony, was present at King Radek's marriage to Princess Sadiya of Nawharla'al, but Haidis had not been chosen to officiate. He came as a guest of his mentor Gerlach, who was prepared to deliver a prophetic benediction on the king's marriage to the exotic foreign princess if he had to lie to do it.

The wedding prophecy, however, would not take place until after the initial prayers to the God of Matrimony and Goddess of Fertility, led by a high-ranking priest, who intoned the traditional phrases in a voice devoid of emotion. Sadiya was expected to kneel on a cushion at the feet of King Radek during the prayers, and though she did as requested, she refused to lower her gaze, for she did not believe in these gods. To her right, seated in the first row of ornate wooden benches, she could just make out the corner of Essylt's veil, shroudlike in comparison to the bright colors worn by Sadiya and her attendants.

Essylt did not need to bow her head, for no one could tell if she participated in the prayers at all. Instead, she clenched her hands into fists and hid them beneath the voluminous folds of her hot, scratchy gown. A deep ache began to spread in her, from belly to chest to throat, until she felt as if she might choke from it. She heard the priest ending his series of prayers, and she knew that after this would come the ceremony itself, when Sadiya's hands would be bound with golden rope to the King's left wrist, and from that moment on, Sadiya would be her stepmother.

One True Love

Essylt watched through her veil as the priest picked up the rope and approached Sadiya, still chanting the blessings for matrimony. The rope dangled over Sadiya's head like a snake uncoiling to strike. The ache that gripped Essylt hardened. A desperate anger galvanized her. She lurched to her feet and felt Auda's hand reaching for hers, but she shook it away. She ripped off her veil and cried, "*No! Please, no.* Sadiya, you must not marry him."

Essylt lunged for the rope and tore it out of the priest's hands, throwing it behind him onto the stone floor.

Sadiya stood, astonished and terrified and hopeful.

At first everyone in the Great Hall was simply too startled to move, for none could remember a time when a royal wedding had been disrupted in such a manner. In that moment of stunned immobility, Essylt took Sadiya's hands in hers and pulled her away from the king. Sadiya said to her in Nawharla'ali, "You are mad, my love," and Essylt responded in the same tongue, "I am mad with love."

Haidis had watched in shock from his seat as Essylt leapt to her feet, jerking away the marriage rope. As she clutched the hands of the foreign bride, Haidis realized that the prophecy he had delivered on Essylt's naming day was coming to pass. He stood up—he was the first among the audience to do so—and said under his breath, "*The princess shall grow into a young woman strong and pure, but when she finds her one true love—*"

Gerlach's hand gripped his arm. "Do not speak any more!" he hissed, and Haidis's mouth shut tight in fear as the Great Hall exploded into shouts.

King Radek's thick, strong hand clamped down on his bride's shoulder, and as Sadiya winced in pain, he dragged her from his daughter. "What perversity have you wrought on my bride?" he demanded of Essylt, who tried to reach for Sadiya again but was wrenched back by the hands of the king's soldiers, who had leapt forward at his command. "What damnation are you bringing upon my kingdom? You have been cursed since you killed your own mother, and it was only my mercy that kept you alive." The king would not take his hands off Sadiya, whom he held near him like a plaything. He growled to his soldiers, "Take Essylt away to the farthest reaches of the darkest forests of the north, and abandon her to the wolves. She is no longer my daughter. May she die alone."

Essylt heard the words as if from a distance, for all she could focus on was the look of terror in Sadiya's face. As the soldiers dragged Essylt from the Great Hall, she tried to struggle but her skirts were too heavy and her bodice too tight, and then someone struck her across the face. Pain burst in her cheek and nose. She screamed and lunged away from the soldiers, but they grabbed her and hit her again and again. The last thing she saw before she fainted from the pain was the glimmer of blue in the jewels around Sadiya's neck, liquid as the faraway sea.

Essylt awoke in a cage on a moving wagon. She winced as the wagon jolted over a bump and caused her hip to bang against the wooden floor. Outside the bars she saw green fields rolling past beneath a clear late afternoon sky.

She was outside the castle.

This fact alone overwhelmed her. She had never been outside the castle, and her heart began to race as she sat up, hands gripping the bars. She drank in the unfamiliar landscape: stone walls rising and falling over the fields; solitary trees standing watch in the distance; an occasional farmhouse or barn, with horses grazing nearby. It was almost dark before she realized that a man was riding behind the cage, watching her.

A soldier.

She shrank away from the bars, and everything that had happened rushed back to her: Sadiya and her father's wedding, the marriage rope hanging like a noose above Sadiya's head, her father's words. *May she die alone.*

As the sun set she wondered whether it was still the day of the wedding. Was this the wedding night? Her stomach twisted. When she had first begun her monthly bleeding, Auda had told her what it meant, and Essylt knew very well what her father desired from his wives: sons. There was a chance that her father had not gone through with the wedding, but the way he had treated Sadiya made Essylt doubt that he would give her up. No, he would take Sadiya as his bride regardless of how perverse he thought his daughter was.

Essylt wanted to throw up, but she hadn't eaten all day, and she could only cough up bile, bitter and acidic.

The soldier behind the cage rode closer and banged his sword on the bars. "Don't choke to death, Princess, we've a long way to go yet."

The journey to the wild forests of the north took a week. There were two soldiers: one who drove the wagon, and one who rode behind. They gave her a bowl of water every night that she had to lap up like a dog, and once or twice the driver slipped her a piece of dried beef out of pity, but she was given no other food. Neither of the soldiers ever let her out, so Essylt was forced to relieve herself in one corner, humiliated by the stench that began to rise from her body.

She watched the countryside when she was awake, but as the days passed and she grew weaker, she slid into a half-sleeping doze in which she saw Sadiya's face hovering over her, radiant and beautiful. She clung to those visions as tightly as she could, the memory of the last words that Sadiya had said echoing in her mind: *You are mad, my love. Mad, my love. Mad.*

Finally, they reached the pine-forested border of Anvarra. The driver drew the wagon to a halt in a small clearing in the woods and climbed down from his seat. The soldier riding behind dismounted, pulling a black iron key from the chain attached to his swordbelt. Inside the cage, Essylt sat stiffly with her arms around her knees, her bright green eyes wide in her pale face. The soldier unlocked the cage door, which groaned open on its hinges.

"Welcome to your new home," he said, and laughed. "Time to get out."

Essylt didn't move until the soldier reached inside and clamped one hand on her ankle. Frightened, she kicked him in the face. He cursed as blood spurted from his nose, then grabbed both of her ankles, his nails digging into her skin, and dragged her out until she landed with a bruising thump on the ground.

"Never seen a man except your father, eh?" he said, and the tone in his voice made her skin crawl. He began to unbuckle his belt.

Essylt tried to scramble away, but she only banged into the wagon wheel behind her.

"There's a reason you turned out wrong," the soldier was saying, a horrible grin on his face. "You need to learn what's right—"

"Shut up," said the driver. He smashed a wooden staff into the side of the soldier's head, knocking him to ground, unconscious. The driver shook his head and looked down at the princess. He had a sister her age, and he would never forgive himself if he let the soldier have his way with her. Even if she was perverse. He jerked his head toward the woods. "You'd better run for it, Princess. You're on your own now."

Essylt didn't hesitate. She jumped up, her legs tingling as she stood for the first time in seven days, and she fled.

She ran over unbroken forest ground, her thin-soled court shoes doing little to cushion her feet from fallen twigs and upturned stones. She ran as the daylight faded and turned the forest into a land of murky shadows, and she slowed down only enough to prevent herself from tripping on the uneven ground. She found a riverbed where the trees parted to reveal a sliver of black night sky strewn with stars, and she knelt down and drank the water from her cupped and dirty hands, and then she kept going.

At some point she removed her whalebone corset so that she could breathe more freely. She stripped off her encumbering underskirts and wrapped her torn shoes in the cloth to cushion her feet. When she was too tired to walk any farther, she made a nest for herself in a bed of fallen pine needles and slept with her head resting on her arms. When she awoke, she continued. She saw no one.

She was hungry, but she did not know what she could eat in the forest, and her book learning had taught her to be wary of unfamiliar plants. A few times she thought she glimpsed the shadowy movement of wolves nearby, and she prayed to the God of Safe Passage to watch over her. She did not know where she was going, but she knew she had a destination. With every step she took, even though her body felt weaker and weaker, she was more and more certain that she had something to live for. Sadiya. *Sadiya.* Someday, she vowed, she would go back for her. She would return to Anvarra City and save her, and King Radek would pay for what he had done.

⁓

One morning, after Essylt had walked in a stubborn, starving daze for hours through the dark night, she stumbled through the last of the pine trees into a clearing where she saw a little cottage built of logs. Smoke curled out of the chimney, and the windows were hung with cheerful plaid curtains. She dragged herself the last few steps into the clearing before she collapsed, her body giving up at last.

The cottage belonged to a retired knight named Bowen, who lived there with his wife, Nell. It was Nell who discovered Essylt later that morning, lying in a crumpled heap at the edge of their garden, and it was Bowen who lifted the princess in his burly arms and carried her inside, laying her down on their bed.

Essylt did not wake until evening, and the first thing she saw was an older woman rocking in a chair nearby, knitting. Essylt was not frightened, for the woman had a kind face and reminded her of Auda, but she was disoriented, and she pushed herself up and asked, "Where am I?"

Nell put down her knitting and studied the girl, whose eyes were a remarkable shade of green. Her reddish-gold hair was disheveled and knotted up, and her face was dirty. In fact, all of her was so dirty that she smelled rather unpleasant, but neither Nell nor Bowen would turn away a girl who so obviously needed their help simply because she also needed a bath.

"You're in the village of Pine Rest," Nell told her, speaking with an unfamiliar accent. "I found you in our garden this morning. I am Nell, and my husband's name is Bowen. He is outside. What is your name?"

Essylt stared at the woman, whose gray hair was wound up in braids coiled at the nape of her neck. She seemed kind, and Essylt wanted to trust her, but a knot of fear still held tight within her, and she did not wish to reveal her true identity. "My name is Auda," Essylt said, and flushed slightly at the lie.

Nell nodded. "You must be hungry."

Essylt's stomach awoke at those words and growled so loudly that it embarrassed her. But Nell only smiled and got up from her chair. She left the little room and came back a few minutes later with a bowl of soup. "Something gentle for you," she said, "while you regain your strength."

Essylt took the bowl from Nell's outstretched hands and inhaled the fragrant scent of broth and herbs. She drank every last delicious drop, and then lay down again in Nell and Bowen's bed and fell asleep instantly, feeling safe at last.

In the morning she met Bowen, who was large and gentle and had lost all his hair except for the bushy white eyebrows that seemed to speak long sentences on their own. She learned that the village of Pine Rest was just over the border from Anvarra in the neighboring kingdom of Ferronia. Essylt remembered from Auda's geography lessons that Ferronia was rarely concerned with Anvarran politics because the Black Forest that separated the two countries was mostly impassable—and this Essylt could now attest to personally, having crossed it herself on foot. Bowen had been a knight serving the king of Ferronia, but after many years of service he had retired to the village where he had been born. Bowen and Nell's son, Petra, was a swordsmith whose forge was in Pine Rest, and Petra drew much of his business from Bowen's old knightly acquaintances.

As the days passed, Essylt regained her strength while Bowen and Nell fussed over her as if she were their long-lost daughter. They set up a pallet for her in the loft over the main room of the cottage, and Essylt began to help out with the chores. She grew strong from tending the garden with Nell and learning how to chop wood with Bowen's hatchet. And though she came to know the other villagers and to love Bowen and Nell, she kept her secret. Pine Rest might be far from Anvarra City, but the news of Princess Essylt's depravity had reached Ferronia via traveling minstrels who sang of her tragic lust for the queen. Essylt worried that Bowen and Nell would turn their backs on her in disgust if they knew who she was, so she grew accustomed to being called Auda, and swallowed her own feelings of shame and sorrow. Every day, she thought of Sadiya and her vow to return for her. Every night before she slept, she whispered Sadiya's name to herself so that she might never forget how to pronounce it.

She spoke with Petra, who had traveled to Anvarra because of his skill as a swordsmith, and began to plot her own return journey. She laid aside a store of food, stealing as little as she could. From the old trunks in the loft where she slept, she discovered a cloak that was moth-eaten but could still keep her warm at night. She felt guilty for taking these things from Nell and Bowen, but she promised herself she would return one day and pay them back if she could. She did not let herself think of where she and Sadiya might go. Was there a place in this world that would have them? She did not know, and it was easier to accept the emptiness of not knowing than to face the fact that she might rescue Sadiya and still fail in giving her a happy life.

One morning she awoke and her body felt ready. She was strong and healthy again, and she had finally stocked enough provisions to last for the several weeks' journey to Anvarra. But when she went outside to pump water as usual, snow was falling from the sky. She stood on the doorstep in shock as white flakes tumbled down, thick and fast, from iron-gray clouds. How had the summer passed so quickly? She hoped that the snowfall was an early anomaly and that it would only delay her journey by a day or two.

But the snow continued to fall, and it stuck to the ground, and the air became colder and colder until, weeks later, Essylt had to admit that winter had come early and hard, and she would not be able to journey to Anvarra until spring.

It was Nell who found her, weeping silently at the woodpile, her tears turning to ice crystals on her cheeks. "My dear," Nell said, "whatever is the matter? Come inside and be warm."

That night, exhausted from the subterfuge, Essylt told her the truth. "I am Essylt," she said, and speaking her own name out loud broke a dam inside her and she sobbed. Nell gathered her into her arms and stroked her hair and rocked her back and forth as if she were a baby. "I am Essylt," she said again and again. When at last her tears were spent, she told them of growing up in the West Tower, and the unexpected joy she had felt when she met Sadiya, and the anguish of being forced apart. She told them of her plan to rescue Sadiya, and finally, her voice diminished to a tentative whisper, she said, "I will leave if you will not have me here any longer. You have been so kind to me, and I have only defiled your home."

Bowen had sat silently in the corner as Essylt confessed her truth, but as Nell's hands stilled on Essylt's hair, he said, "It is never a crime to love someone."

Essylt looked at him in surprise.

Anger darkened Bowen's face. "The king of Anvarra is a bastard. In the spring you shall ride to Anvarra City and save your true love, and we will help you."

"But—but why?" Essylt asked.

Nell had drawn back a little, and Essylt saw that tears streaked down Nell's face as well. She shook her head. "My dear, we love you like a daughter. That is why."

As Essylt looked from Nell to Bowen, she felt as if her heart might overflow with gratitude and love for them. "I have never felt like anyone's daughter," she said, "but I will do my best to make you proud."

༄

All winter, Essylt trained with Bowen. "You will need to learn to fight," he said to her, "for the king will not give up his wife without a battle."

Bowen took down the old tools of his trade from the attic: his broadsword, which was so big that Essylt had to carry it with two hands, and his armor, which was now darkened with rust. During the days, he forced her to run through snowdrifts with the sword strapped to her back until sweat streamed down her face. At night, she helped him polish the armor until it gleamed. It was too large for her, but Bowen said that Petra could adjust it to her size. And so she began to visit Petra at the forge, where he fitted various pieces of steel to her, muttering under his breath about fashioning a special breastplate.

Essylt could not understand why Petra was willing to do this for her. She knew that he knew who she was now, for he called her Essylt instead of Auda. She thought perhaps he was simply his father's son, and would not speak out against anyone his father loved. It wasn't until well past midwinter when she noticed the way Petra spoke to the blacksmith who shared the forge with him: Markus, a broad-shouldered, black-bearded man who sometimes came to supper at Nell and Bowen's home. There was a certain angle to Petra's body as he approached Markus, and then Essylt saw him reach out and smooth his hand gently over the man's shoulder: a caress. Essylt realized with a jolt that Petra did not merely share the forge with the smith; he shared a life with him. She felt a great sense of wonder steal over her, and she had to turn away as tears came to her eyes.

From that day on, she felt as if she had found her family. She would hate to leave them in the spring, but she could come back. She could come back with Sadiya, and they could be happy here.

Petra finished the full suit of armor in late winter. It was light and well balanced, but when Essylt put it on she felt the strength of the steel close against her muscles, and she knew that it would protect her. To her surprise, Petra also presented her with a sword, forged specially for her height and weight, and the first time she swung it in an arc, it sang in the cold winter air.

She spent the last month of winter parrying with Bowen, and sometimes with Markus, who had been a knight's squire in his boyhood. She learned how to ride a horse in full armor, her red-gold hair braided and coiled beneath her helm. She learned how to force back a man twice her size with her sleek, elegant sword, her gauntleted hands gripping the beautiful hilt that Petra had designed. And she thought of Sadiya, as she always did, keeping her face alive in her memory, as fresh as the first day she had seen her, standing behind the oak door to the West Tower, swathed in azure scarves.

The news came before she was entirely ready to go, but as soon as she heard it from the mouth of the traveling minstrel at the tavern in Pine Rest, Essylt left to pack her supplies. The Anvarran king had discovered that his island-born wife had been drinking a concoction she had brought from Nawharla'al to prevent herself from conceiving a child. This, King Radek said, was treason. He sentenced Sadiya to die by beheading on the first day of summer, which gave his people time to travel from their villages to witness her public execution.

When this news reached Pine Rest, the last of the winter snow had barely melted, even though the first day of summer was less than one month away. Essylt decided to ride directly through the Black Forest to Anvarra instead of following the highway south. It was dangerous, but it would cut two weeks from her journey.

"There are wolves," objected Nell, worried.

"They didn't kill me before," Essylt said. "They won't kill me now."

Bowen and Petra wanted to go with her, but she refused to allow them to come.

"It is my task, and my choice," she told them. They relented, for they saw the determination in her eyes.

She departed at dawn, riding Markus's white mare—a horse he insisted she take—with her saddlebags full of food that Nell had prepared. The forest was quiet as she rode south, with only the sound of her horse's passage to accompany her. Petra's armor sat lightly on her shoulders, and already she was so familiar with her sword that when she slept, she rested her hands upon it. She did not feel threatened by the wolves she glimpsed sometimes at night, their eyes reflecting the light from her campfire. They saw her weapons, and they left her alone.

She emerged from the Black Forest two weeks later, and struck out on the hard-packed dirt road that led southeast toward Anvarra City. At first she was alone on the highway, but as she drew closer to Anvarra City, other travelers joined her, all on their way to the execution. At night, she camped as far from the other travelers as she could. She kept her armor covered with her long brown cloak, and she did not remove her helm in the daylight. She could not reveal who she was, for the Princess Essylt was supposed to be dead.

She arrived on the eve of the execution, and though she could have ridden into the city and bought herself a room at an inn, she could not bring herself to pass through the gates. In the distance she saw the West Tower—her old home—and now she recognized it as a prison. She wondered what had happened to Auda, and her gut

One True Love

wrenched, for though Auda had always maintained a certain formal distance from her, she was the one who had raised her.

All night, Essylt lay awake beneath a spreading oak tree on the side of the highway, watching the silhouette of the castle on the hill. When dawn broke, Essylt was already mounted on her horse and waiting outside the city gates. Hundreds of other people surged around her, eager to view the death of the traitorous foreign queen. Their jubilation made Essylt sick with rage, and her fingers trembled as she curled them into fists on her thighs.

A stage had been erected at the northern edge of the central square, and on that stage the executioner's block was waiting. Essylt rode into the square, surrounded by the crowd and unnoticed by the soldiers who stood guard along the perimeter. She found a place near the stage, beside a fountain that shot cool water up into the warm summer morning. The scent of snowbell blossoms hung thick in the air, sweet and cloying. The people in the square chattered about the coming event, but Essylt paid no attention to them. Her entire body was tense and alert, her heart beating a war drum in her chest. She could sense Sadiya approaching—as if they were connected, flesh and bone drawn together—and when the murmur of the crowd crescendoed, she looked to the north and saw the king riding into the square on a black stallion.

He was flanked by soldiers and followed by a wagon with a cage strapped onto it—the same kind of cage that Essylt herself had been locked into. Within the cage, Sadiya was seated with her hands bound behind her back.

The crowd exclaimed at its first glimpse of her: hair loose and tangled, a rough sackcloth dress draped over her body, her face bruised but defiant.

Essylt felt as if an arrow had torn into her belly. She had to suck in the muggy air to calm herself down, for her mare sensed her nerves and began to prance in place. Essylt wanted to rush forward at that very moment and seize Sadiya from the soldiers, but she remembered what Bowen had taught her, and she forced herself to wait.

She waited as the executioner mounted the stage, his black cowl hiding his face from the crowd, the sun glinting on the blade of his axe. She waited as the king, resplendent in purple robes, joined the executioner. She waited as the cage door was unlocked and Sadiya was pulled out, barefoot, onto the cobblestones of the square. She waited as Sadiya was hauled onto the stage by two soldiers who bent her arms back at an angle that made Essylt wince to see it.

She waited until the king said: "For betraying me, and by extension, your people; for dishonoring me, and by extension, your people; for murdering before birth my very own children and heirs; for all this, you are sentenced to death."

Then—and only then—Essylt threw off her cloak. Her armor shone silver-bright in the sun, and her white horse leapt through the crowd that parted before her, their mouths agape in excitement. Everyone on the stage turned to see a knight riding toward them, sword raised in the air. From the margins of the square, the king's soldiers raised their bows and shot, their arrows flying toward the rider.

Essylt felt an arrow slam against her back, but Petra's armor held. Then she was at the edge of the stage and the archers had to stop shooting, because the soldiers were in their line of sight. She pulled herself onto the stage and met the first soldier with her sword raised. She shoved him back with all her strength, her steel blade screaming against his. The soldier stumbled, startled by her assault, but he had a second to back him up, and then Essylt had to fight two of them.

But the soldiers wore standard-issue armor, not nearly as well crafted as hers. She could slice their breastplates off with ease, and beneath that, they weren't even wearing chain mail. No one had expected an attack at the queen's execution. Essylt disarmed one and slashed open his side. He yelped and fell off the stage into the crowd. The other came at her with his broadsword, but she used his momentum against him and flipped him onto his back, knocking his weapon out of his hands and tipping the point of her sword against his throat. His eyes bulged up at her and for an instant she hesitated—was she going to kill a man?—but out of the corner of her eye she saw him pull a dagger from his boot and ready it to throw at her. Before his weapon left his hand, she cut his throat.

She looked up and across the stage, her heart pounding, and called, "Sadiya!"

Sadiya had watched the knight beat back the king's soldiers with a rising sense of hope, and when she heard the voice behind the helm, she knew who it was, and hope exploded into joy. She tried to run to her, but the king grabbed her arm, yanking her back. He shouted, "Who would dare to act against me?"

Essylt took off her helm. The long braid of her red-gold hair fell out over her shoulder, and she said, "Father, I dare."

The king's face was a mask of fury as he beheld his daughter standing before him—his daughter who should be dead, and yet she was alive and breathing, her green eyes glinting like emeralds as she raised a sword against him, and he unarmed.

"Give me a weapon!" the king cried. The executioner stepped forward and handed the king his axe.

The king swung it in an arc, and Essylt met the axe handle with her sword. The thunk of metal meeting wood rang through the square. She jerked the sword back and leapt away as the king advanced, his eyes wild with anger. She parried him again, and this time the handle of the axe broke as the sword cleaved through it. The axe head clattered onto the stage.

"A weapon!" the king shouted again. A soldier in the crowd tried to shove his way through to give the king his sword, but the crowd—riveted by the spectacle before them—would not let him pass.

"I will not kill you unarmed," Essylt called. "Let us go and you will never see us again."

"Never," the king snarled. "You will die. Both of you will die here today."

Suddenly Sadiya stepped over the body of the dead soldier and said, "She may not kill you unarmed, but I will." She lunged toward the king and shoved the soldier's dagger into the king's chest, thrusting it straight through the rich purple velvet, and the king fell, howling, to the wooden boards of the stage.

Sadiya stood above him, gasping, her hands bloody, and spit on his face.

The crowd roared.

Essylt saw the hatred in her father's eyes swept away by fear and bewilderment as his hands scrabbled furiously at the dagger. Sadiya turned to Essylt, wiping her bloodied hands on the ruins of her dress. Essylt reached for her and crushed her into her arms, and Sadiya's body shook against Essylt's armor. All around them the crowd murmured. Those who had been close to the stage had heard Essylt declare who she was, and now they passed that knowledge back across the square, until all who had gathered for Sadiya's execution understood that Princess Essylt was not dead—she was alive—and the words of her naming-day prophecy were repeated until it became a slow and steady hum.

The princess shall grow into a young woman strong and pure, but when she finds her one true love, she shall be the downfall of the king.

Prophecies, the people said, were not always straightforward, but if they were real, they were true. None who saw the way that Essylt and Sadiya held each other that day could deny the strength of their love. But for many years to come, they debated whether it was Essylt or Sadiya who had been the downfall of the king.

No one stopped Essylt and Sadiya as they left the city. No soldier lifted a weapon to harm them; no man or woman shouted a curse. They rode as far as they could before stopping to rest their horse. They found a sweet little spring bubbling out of a rocky cleft in a hill near the road, and dismounted to allow the mare to drink.

Then Essylt took off her armor, and Sadiya peeled off her soiled dress, and they waded into the water and scrubbed the dried blood and sweat and dirt from their skin. When they emerged from the spring, naked and wet in the warm evening air, they saw each other as if for the first time: one woman dark and slender; one woman fair and muscular. Essylt took Sadiya's hands in her own and pulled her close, their breasts and hips sliding together, slick and soft, and her breath caught in her throat as Sadiya whispered, "You are my one true love."

One True Love

Essylt wrapped her arms around Sadiya's waist. Her fingers found the hollow of Sadiya's lower back, her spine like a string of jewels, and she leaned in, pausing to remember this moment always, and kissed her.

JEWELLE GOMEZ

Saint Louis 1990

Gilda was more than alive. The hundred fifty years she carried were flung casually around her shoulders, an intricately knit shawl handed down from previous generations, yet distinctly her own. Her legs were smooth and mocha brown, unscarred by the knife-edge years spent on a Mississippi plantation, and strengthened by more recent nights dancing in speakeasies and then discos. The paradox did not escape Gilda: her power was forged by deprivation and decadence, and the preternatural endurance that had been thrust upon her unexpectedly. Her grip could snap bone and bend metal, and when she ran she was the wind, she was invincible and alone.

Tonight, hurrying toward home to Effie, she walked anxiously, gazing at the evening skyline. It sparkled like Effie's favorite necklace, which plunged liquid silver between her dark breasts. The image pushed Gilda faster through the tree-shrouded park. She glanced over her shoulder at the shadowed sidewalk behind her, where the light from the street lamps was cast through shifting leaves. Little moved on the Manhattan avenue at this late hour but Gilda knew danger was not far behind her.

Gilda had not seen any of her siblings since she'd escaped slavery more than one hundred years before. Their loss was so remote; Gilda was always surprised when an image of them arose in her mind. It was the same with Samuel, whose face she could not banish now. Not a relative, but a blood relation, Samuel had haunted her path since they'd met in Yerba Buena just before the turn of the century. The town had been exploding with prosperity, much like New York now. Gold almost coursed down the hills into the pockets of seamen, traders, bankers and speculators, until its pursuit became a contagion.

Gilda easily remembered her first impressions when she'd met Samuel: greed, selfishness, fear and jealousy. That volatile blend had swirled through Samuel's eyes like mist from the Bay. Even when he'd smiled, Gilda knew he despised her. Her femaleness and her blackness were an outrage in his eyes. It was this peculiar amalgamation of feelings that turned Samuel into a dangerous man. The surprise of seeing him again tonight had left Gilda feeling chilled and sluggish. She walked slowly turning over in her mind every word he'd said in that angry encounter, trying not to let his sudden appearance alarm her.

When he'd stepped from the darkened doorway on upper Broadway Gilda had been preoccupied with getting home. Samuel appeared abruptly in front of her, giving an elaborate bow as if it were still 1890.

"The not-so-fair Gilda lives, I see," Samuel had intoned, the taut agitation of his voice unchanged after almost one hundred years.

Saint Louis 1990

"Samuel," Gilda answered simply, as if she were greeting him in one of the Yerba Buena salons they used to frequent. She said no more but shifted her weight in preparation for his attack.

"Gilda, why so pugnacious? I'm only looking up an old friend."

"What do you want Samuel?"

"I've just stated my intention. One would think you'd be more solicitous of past acquaintances."

Remembering how Samuel had tried to choke the life from her the last time they'd seen each other, Gilda only replied evenly: "As I recall our last encounter was less than friendly."

"Those of our blood are fewer than used to be, Gilda. We must learn to make peace with each other. We greeted the turning of this century in each other's company; I thought perhaps we might do the same for this millennium which is on everyone's lips."

Gilda had watched his eyes as he spoke. They still glittered with the sullen anger he'd always harbored. Samuel's dark blond hair was masked almost completely by a narrow-brimmed hat which he wore at a rakish tilt. His wiry build rippled with tension beneath a raincoat with a short cape. The affectation made his shoulders appear much broader than Gilda knew them to be. She tried to push into his thoughts to discern the truth of why he'd sought her out, but he carefully blocked her probing. Samuel shared blood from the line of those who'd brought her into the life yet he was as different from those she counted as family as night was from day.

"For some reason, Samuel, you've always felt I cheated you. It's as if I was the favored child and you were somehow left out. I don't know why you've fixed this sentiment on me, nor do I care."

"You will care, Gilda my girl."

"I only care that you stop leaping into my life as if I owed you some form of retribution."

Samuel's bellowing laugh was riddled with strands of his hatred. Two men lingering in front of the metal-shuttered doorway of a bodega glanced in their direction nervously then ambled up the street to another spot. Gilda recalled the way he'd always clung to the idea that he was the victim, even when he was inflicting pain.

When they'd first met, Gilda was new to their life and still learning the mores and responsibilities of her power. But she understood immediately that Samuel was one who believed in nothing but his own gain, his own life. And wherever he'd fallen into error, he found someone else to blame. They were connected by blood that had turned sour, and Gilda was weary of trying to clean Samuel's wounds.

"The follies of your life are your own. Leave me out of them," Gilda said. The chill of her disaffection made her voice flat.

"Fine. If you insist. I'd always thought there was fairness about you, Gilda. I'm sure I'm not mistaken."

Samuel had turned on his heel and disappeared into the darkness, leaving Gilda to continue on her way home with a rising sense of ill-defined dread. Samuel had drawn her into battle twice in the past century. She had no doubt he intended to do the same again, sometime soon.

She veered off of Broadway down to West End Avenue where grass sloped gently downward from the city street to the brackish river. The soft flowing of the water played in her ears, obscuring the city sound to her left and stirring her already bubbling uneasiness. She focused her attention to steel herself against the discomfort of the running water of the Hudson River so she could enjoy the textured darkness of the tree-lined avenue and try to rid herself of the image of Samuel.

Ahead of her, hidden from the streetlight by the shadows of a thick maple tree, Gilda saw a man leaning against the park fence. Her body tensed, but she felt no fear. It wasn't Samuel. This was a mortal, in his twenties, strongly built and obviously up to no good. He wore a sweat suit several sizes too large, but that did not conceal his muscled arms from her. A knit cap was pulled down over his brow to hide his dark features; it only exposed his vulnerability to Gilda. Gilda slowed her steps momentarily, and then thought: *he's just a man.*

A surprise flood of anger washed over her—first Samuel and now this one! She'd only recently understood such anger could be hers. Her mother, Fulani features hemmed into a placid gaze, had not been

Saint Louis 1990

allowed that luxury. She'd been a slave, admonished to be grateful. As a child Gilda had not understood: the master, who owned all and was responsible for everyone, never showed anger; his wife, whom he pampered and worshipped oppressively, was angry all the time. So too the overseer who regularly vented his anger on black flesh. But blacks were not thought to have anger any more than a mule or a tree cut down for kindling.

Gilda looked quickly behind her and saw several apartment dwellers moving casually past their windows, and a couple approaching a little more than a block behind her. No sign of Samuel, but the young man stood ahead of her under the maple, his intentions leering out from behind an empty grin.

Gilda's step was firm. She wondered what drove men—black, white, rich, poor, alive or otherwise—to need to leap out at women from the darkness. As she walked past she noted the sallow quality of his brown skin. He spoke low, almost directly in her ear, "Hey, Mama, don't walk so fast."

Gilda continued on, hoping he would take his loss and shut up.

He didn't. "Aw, Mama, come on. Be nice to me."

The wheedling in his voice scraped and scratched at her. That sound had been the undercurrent of every encounter she'd had with Samuel over the past century. His demands for her help, his threats to harm her, his pleas for her sympathy were all delivered in the same calculated, pitiful pitch; devised to take advantage of their blood relationship.

We're connected by blood, too, Gilda thought, as she felt the young black man waiting. She understood that the poverty she saw around her ground people into hopelessness. She, herself, fought each day to resist the predatory impulse which promised to ease her feelings of desperation. In the man before her she recognized his surrender to that impulse. Like Samuel, he reeked of his enjoyment of power over someone else he considered weaker, unworthy. His assault in the dark was the substitution for truly taking power.

Anger speared her, leaving a metallic taste in her mouth. Where were the words for what she felt?

Gilda stopped and turned to him smiling as she remembered the words of an irate Chicago waitress she'd overheard decades before: "I am not your mama. If I were, I would have drowned you at birth."

She walked on. He caught up. "Why you bitches so hard. Come on, sistuh, give me a break!"

Gilda continued walking. She had no desire to let her anxiety about Samuel push her to end the night with angry blood.

"Come on, sistuh, let me see that smile again." With that he seized her arm. His grip would have bruised another but Gilda shook free easily, leaving him off balance. In a smooth reach he snatched at her close-cropped hair, hoping to pull her into the darkness.

The image of Effie, waiting in their rooms, her sinewy form concealed in shadow, flashed through Gilda's mind. A low moan sounded in the back of her throat. She could almost feel her slim fingers clenched around his neck, snapping the connection to the spine. She replaced that sensation with the memory of a hot night thirty years before—Florida in 1950. She'd been sitting in an after-hours club watching the fighter show how he'd whipped a Tampa boy who said boxing was just a "coon show." His precision was awe-inspiring. As was the care he showed the young boys who clustered around him outside the club, waiting in the wee hours for a glimpse at their hero. More than his fists he had craft and commitment that seemed saintly when he looked down at the boys who worshiped him.

Gilda smiled again as she raised her left fist in perfect form and smashed it into the man's jaw. He fell unconscious to the cracked pavement, half-sprawled on the thin city grass.

Gilda lifted him from the street and held him to her as the couple she'd seen earlier passed by. Once they were several paces away she lowered the man to the ground so he sat against the maple tree. She knelt low, hiding him from the street, and smoothly sliced the flesh behind his ear with her fingernail. His eyes opened in shock, and Gilda held him in the grip of her hands and her mind. He was pinned against the tree, its rough bark biting into his shirt as Gilda rummaged amongst his thoughts. Confusion replaced shock, then rage followed. Unable to move, the young man bellowed internally.

Saint Louis 1990

His ideas were petty, self-centered; ignorant of any world except the small circle in which he traveled. Gilda knew the history, the triumphs she'd seen all meant nothing to him. He was so tainted by the hatred and fear others had of him he left no room inside for anything but that. Gilda had not felt so unrelated to a mortal since she'd taken on this life. In his eyes she observed the same deadness she often saw in Samuel's: they always looked inward, were always scavenging. They never really saw.

Gilda pressed her lips to the cut. Blood had begun to seep out onto his sweat shirt. The flesh was soft, and smelled of sweet soap. Gilda could imagine the boy he'd been, when he was still able to picture himself a part of the larger world. She drew her share of the blood from him swiftly, barely enjoying the warmth as it washed over her. His anger began to swell inside of her, wiping away the sensation of his youth. She was engorged yet continued taking the blood, unable to stop, feeling no need to leave something for him.

At the final moment she pulled back from the wound in his neck and looked into his almost dead eyes. She touched his nearly empty mind searching for a tiny space where there was no anger or hatred. She found too many places seared white with disappointment turned into rage. And then, a small moment where a treasured memory was hidden opened up. There she planted the understanding of what it could mean to really feel love toward a sister, and from that love find a connection to the rest of the world. In the shallow cavern of his thoughts she left him that one sensation to live for, to strive for as she held her hand to seal the wound. His pulse was faint but soon became steady. She lifted him gently and rested him on the park bench, placing his arms casually behind his head, as if he were only napping. She drew the cap back so it rested on the crown of his head but left his dark face open and smooth in the dim light. His lips were no longer curled in a smirk but rested partly open, ready to finally speak. She could see the young man he'd been, the young man he might still be.

As she rose to leave, Gilda was glad she had such a good memory. "Yeah, Joe Louis was a heck of a fighter," she said aloud.

She knew it would not be so simple with Samuel. A century of bitterness and jealousy, left over from times even Gilda couldn't remember, festering fuel. She looked down at the young man and hoped his bitterness would end here.

Gilda continued downtown, her sense of dread building. Samuel's words were like a prickly burr against her skin. Turning them over, back and forth Gilda searched for reasons Samuel would return at this particular time. The young man she'd left on the bench had probably lived all of his life under the sour message implying his worthlessness. He made victims of others out of ignorance. *Not just ignorance. Vanity!* Gilda thought. She probed the air around her looking for Samuel's thoughts, trying to discern his presence. She perceived only apartment dwellers and the homeless who slept in the park. It was a kind of vanity that drove both Samuel and the young man. They could not stand to be one of many, but only one— always alone, always outlawed. And that fooled them into thinking they were on top.

Her recollection of the last time Samuel had burst into her life did not comfort Gilda. For a moment it had seemed as if he'd forgotten their past, had learned to appreciate his special place in the world. He'd appeared in much the same way as he'd done this evening, with no warning, on a public street. Then he'd been more devious, trying to lull Gilda into a sense of goodwill. Her wariness had lingered and was proven justified. The battle between them had gone on for several hours, leaving both with gruesome injuries. Gilda had not wanted to fight him, or to kill him. It had been a draw and Samuel had retreated when he understood that Gilda could not be easily destroyed. Gilda shuddered. *There can be no fairness in a fight between us*, she thought.

Fair. The word resonated in Gilda's mind; there was something about the way he'd said the word several times. She felt the skin of her entire body become an antenna tingling with input. And then she understood. Samuel had said she was not fair—not light-skinned. Then he'd said there was "fairness about you." He was talking about Effie. In some cultures, the name Effie meant "fair." Effie herself had

Saint Louis 1990

told Gilda that when they first met. Samuel had come to hurt Gilda, just as she suspected, but he'd do that by hurting Effie.

A flame of terror shot through Gilda's body dispelling the chill that had settled on her. She now knew why the image of Effie had shown her in shadow. Anger pulsed through Gilda leaving no room for caution. She knew Effie had powers at least as strong as her own, yet fear for Effie's safety seared her heart. She pushed a warning through the air toward their home as she turned swiftly southward, then disappeared inside the wind blowing off the river.

Manhattan lay glittering like a sequined scarf, floating on the coastal waters of the Atlantic. Lights from the street, apartments and office buildings flickered in the darkness, multiplied by their reflections off the glass of windows, storefronts and shiny cars. Yet night was wrapped tightly around the city and its chill penetrated Gilda. She moved so quickly she was invisible to anyone looking down from one of the windows of the towering apartment buildings of Riverside Drive. The rustle of leaves was the only sign that she passed through the night air. A pedestrian, out for an evening stroll by the river would feel only the brush of an unexpectedly warm breeze. But Gilda was a whirlwind of emotion as she sped downtown to the danger she knew was also hurtling through the night toward her home.

Gilda's thoughts were a kaleidoscoping blur. She glimpsed the calm and elegant face of Effie, her brow furrowed with concern, then an image of the home they shared in lower Manhattan, with its startling murals of foreign cities created by her dear brother Julius. The almond shaped eyes of her tenant, Marci de Justo, who'd become almost as close a friend as those of her blood. Vivid sounds of Celia Cruz and Ismael Miranda wafting down from Marci's audio speakers out over her back yard garden like a warm mist usually welcomed her home. The faces of Sorel, Anthony, Julius and Marci—the men in her life—floated through her mind. Gilda often laughed at the image of the incongruous quartet. Her fear that a fifth, Samuel, was about to destroy all she held so precious swelled in her throat, almost choking off the air to her lungs. Even as she pushed herself to

Gilda wondered if she were imagining the menace she
when Samuel had spoken her name.

"The not-so-fair Gilda lives, I see." Samuel had said casually, as if he were simply observing the movements of a bug beneath his feet. Samuel continued to be the threat he'd always been. In less time than it took to think Samuel's name, Gilda had traversed the four miles downtown and was standing outside the door of her garden apartment. Located in a renovated brick building she'd owned for twenty years, the rooms provided both the privacy Gilda required and a natural place in the rhythm of the neighborhood that nourished her as much as the blood that maintained her long life.

She listened and was startled to hear such quiet enveloping the building. Peering at the two tall windows that faced the street and then through the intricate paintings Julius had applied to each pane, she saw the warm amber glow which bathed the front rooms. She unlocked the wrought iron gate that shielded her door and entered the spacious parlor.

As she'd come to spend more time with Gilda, Effie had added her own influences to the sparely decorated room. Fresh flowers sat on the low, cherry wood table in the center. A piece of Kente clothe was draped over the back of the overstuffed sofa and a small painting by Julius now hung between the tall windows. Gilda looked around, satisfied with her home which seemed the same as usual.

She drew in her breath and listened more closely: around her she heard the muted noises of her tenants and directly above, it sounded as if Marci were enjoying a romantic evening with soft music. But in her own flat she sensed no one. As she reached for the key to unlock the sleeping room her hands trembled with anxiety: "no one" could mean "no one alive." She flung open the heavy metal door which was paneled to look like oak and was relieved when it crashed against the wall and revealed an uninhabited room. The thick silk of the oriental carpet glistened in soft light, the yellow satin comforter rested on the sleeping platform where the soil of Gilda's home state was mixed with that of others of her family. Her eyes burned with the memory of the ritual blending—dark earth sprinkled together and sown into

Saint Louis 1990

layered pallets that allowed any of her family to rest in this place in safety. The wave of emotions was for those whose earth blended here with hers and for the many whose did not.

Gilda closed and locked the door, puzzled. Earlier she'd been certain she'd sensed that Effie was in danger. Samuel's fearsome cruelty had shone in his eyes, brighter than sunlight; and Effie had seemed to be his focus. She opened the door to the garden, clinging to the hope that it, too, would be unchanged. She rushed out to the small patch of roses, rhododendron and the queenly evergreen. Turning in circles, relieved and frustrated, Gilda saw nothing to either support or alleviate her fear. Danger was still near; Gilda knew it with all the molecules of her blood, but where?

She looked up at Marci's open windows. The shades were pulled down. A pale red glow emanated from inside, where music played softly. The red light was a sign that Marci was entertaining. Gilda watched the shadows on the window for a minute listening, but despite the music the room was cloaked in intimacy. Then Marci appeared at the window, snapping the shade up and lifting the window.

"*Hermana*, what are you doing down there? Is there something?" Marci leaned low out of the window, his shoulders swathed in a pale yellow silk blouse.

"I was just wondering where Effie might be." Gilda held her voice steady, letting it float on the air, falsely casual.

"Sister, she don't come up here with no red light, you know that." Marci laughed as the picture tickled him. "She was there, then she went out, downtown, I think."

Gilda marveled at how Marci could tell which direction people walked when they left the building, even though his apartment faced the back. He had a preternatural connection with all the tenants, listening to them, their needs, and their troubles. The mother hen of the building, he offered his vibrant wisdom spun from the practical Puerto Rican reality of his childhood and grounded in the ancient Taino spirits. It amazed Gilda how each of the tenants accommodated their own reluctant reliance on a Puerto Rican drag queen who'd made them his family when his own had rejected him. As the men around him succumbed in greater numbers to the unnamed disease Marci traveled across town, to the Bronx or Queens to help out bar acquaintances and old friends indiscriminately. He dispensed *mafongo* and advice liberally to everyone as if his thick stew and experiences were a universal resource.

In the years since she'd acquired the building, Marci had become her guide to the mortal world around their home. His music, the smell of his food, the love he showed for her and their building had made it a place of easy rest.

"Gotta go." Marci's voice sparkled in the night air.

"Hey I thought you were single as of last month?"

"Not tonight."

"Marci…are you being careful?"

He looked down at Gilda, affecting the face of a wounded child.

"Manuel de Justo," Gilda said solemnly. She knew how much he hated anyone to use his given name. "*Ten cuidado!*"

"Of course, I am the soul of careful." Marci's long lashes lowered modestly as his lips curled in a brilliant smile and he withdrew inside.

What a strange existence, Gilda thought. She warned her friend to be cautious of blood that had become dangerous in this decade. Around them young men had begun to sicken and die so quickly Gilda was uncertain how severely even she might be weakened by the infection. But her heightened senses enabled her to easily detect any illness and sidestep its perils. She'd helped tend many and still the affliction, just like her own nature, remained a mystery to her. She looked up at the window but saw no more movement in the ruby light. Quiet blanketed the building and Gilda felt afraid again.

She returned to her living room, beginning to trace the energy of Effie's route in the air, then noticed the slip of paper sticking out from beneath the vase of yellow roses:

Sorel and Anthony are back. Cocktails. E.

Saint Louis 1990

Excitement flooded Gilda, pushing thoughts of Samuel from her mind. Sorel and Anthony, who'd helped her learn her way through the world of their kind, were her blood family, bound to her as surely as her mother who'd died in slavery on a Mississippi plantation. Effie, who was newer in Gilda's life, was also part of this family, now linked with dozens of others around the world. She again raced through New York's city streets, this time her fear mixed with anticipation. The one gift from the confrontation with Samuel is that it had evoked the memory of Joe Louis. Gilda had always savored that brief time when she'd known him. She visualized his power and sense of community sometimes just to keep his face in her memory. The kids who admired him thought he *was* a saint. But he'd been better than that.

When Gilda stood on the corner of the Lower Manhattan street where Sorel and Anthony maintained their establishment she slowed to savor the feel of cobblestones beneath her feet. She could sense the three of them inside together, safe.

It had been almost a decade since Sorel and Anthony had made the difficult journey across the Atlantic to visit old friends and places they'd not seen for over a century. The moments Gilda spent apart from her family always seemed to fly by, yet they weighed on her heavily. She'd not yet learned how to let the years pass and trust in the future. In that way she felt too much like Samuel who also clung to the past. His rage at Gilda from almost a century before was as fresh for him as a new wound. The woman who'd betrayed him for Gilda had been dead longer now than she'd been alive. Gilda pushed the memory away from her, just as she wished she could do with Samuel.

The door of Sorel and Anthony's small bar was set right on the street, the ground level of an ancient factory which they owned. On the outside the door was covered by a modest sheet of metal, like many which lined the block. The seventeenth-century carved wood from Spain which was attached to the interior side of the door made it hang heavily in the frame. Once inside Gilda leaned back on the intricate, hard forms which pressed into her back as she breathed in deeply.

Sorel, in evening wear accentuated by a gold embroidered vest, sat in his booth holding Effie's hand. The bar was appointed like an elegant pub: wood paneling, coats of arms, gleaming crystal. The bar had deeply padded stools with backs; two were now occupied by people familiar to Gilda. The four booths, other than Sorel's, were empty.

Anthony, not wearing his usual apron but a blue silk suit, poured the wine expertly. Champagne for Sorel, a deep red for Effie. Gilda nodded a greeting at the thin, dark man behind the bar who'd worked with Anthony and Sorel since they'd opened the establishment long ago. He proffered her a champagne flute in a fluid movement. Gilda didn't break her stride as she took the glass and continued toward the dark green leather upholstered booth at the back.

"Ah, at last." Sorel rose from his seat, his rotund body moving lithely. His pale, delicate fingers encircled her large brown hand. "My daughter. I've missed you like sweet air."

Gilda never knew how to bridge these chasms. So much time seemed like only moments, yet their emotions were full. If tears had been possible for them their eyes would have been brimming. Instead they squeezed each other's hands, letting the magnitude of their happiness pulse between them.

When Gilda sat next to Effie her body completely relaxed. She looked up into Anthony's sardonic gaze.

"So you are still drinking this poor excuse for wine?" He asked nodding at the champagne flute.

"Anthony, you know I take after Sorel in that regard. The champagne grape has captured my soul almost as assuredly as Effie."

"Effie at least does not leave the blood sluggish."

"Thank you, Anthony." Effie's light voice carried a music of its own, distilled from hundreds of years of travel. She sipped the red wine through smiling lips. Gilda brushed her finger across Effie's mouth enjoying the warm fullness, savoring her relief at seeing her safe. Her round dark face was just as it had been for more than three hundred years. Her tightly braided hair curved across the crown of her head like a dark halo. She was petite and seemed to be swallowed up by

Saint Louis 1990

the deep leather banquet. As their skin touched Gilda sensed, not for the first time, Effie holding something hidden inside her. She pushed the sensation away and enjoyed her relief.

Sorel watched Gilda recognize a secret place inside Effie, and wondered how they would weather the coming years. He and Anthony had spent almost two centuries of living together, striking a balance between the separations they both appreciated and their desire to experience life side by side. The separations, sometimes weeks sometimes years, were part of the growing process for them. Living on one's own developed survival skills and helped each one of their family to stay connected to the world and not withdraw into safely guarded enclaves. It was within those isolated clans that the deadly patronizing attitude toward mortals was cultivated. Those like Samuel, who took no responsibility for his existence, thrived among those isolated circles. Within them they reinforced each others weaknesses and fed on dreams of power. Each decade he grew thick with paranoia and the blood of terrified victims slaughtered like deer in season.

Sorel understood how difficult the separations were for Gilda and had tried to help her see how important they were. Their life needed air as much as it needed blood. As he held her hand he could feel both her joy at his return and the edge of anxiety that anticipated his next trip. More than a hundred years had passed since Gilda's enslavement and the death of her mother under its brutality, yet she could still barely withstand separations. Every journey away from her was a move toward abandonment. This was another lesson Sorel was confidant Gilda would learn in time. As he'd held Effie's hand, he sensed her compelling need to move back out into the world. The lesson would be brought home to Gilda soon.

"We have so much to tell you about the land we left behind. It has changed, as you can imagine."

Laughter burst from Gilda and Effie, knowing that the last time Anthony and Sorel had seen France, Marie Antoinette was about to be led to the guillotine.

"But you have things to discuss with us, I believe." Sorel took a sip from his glass then sat back in the booth. Effie turned to Gilda, seeing the thoughts behind her eyes for the first time. Effie's blue black skin glistened in the soft light that bathed the room.

"What is it?" Effie's voice was low and even as the muscles in her body became alert. Her tiny figure became a tight coil of energy as she took in Gilda's concern.

"I don't want to spoil your homecoming," Gilda said looking up at Anthony. She could feel him not waiting for her to speak but probing her mind.

"Samuel." Anthony spit the name out.

"Yes."

"Samuel? I'd hoped we were done with him," Effie said, her voice as hard and sharp as a steel dagger.

"He came to me tonight. On the street. Again! Full of syrup overlaying the vinegar."

Anthony drank from his glass, set it down firmly on the table and walked away. The set of his back told them how angry he was.

"Did he make threats?" Effie asked.

"Not directly. He said something about seeing in the turn of the century together as we had in the past."

"He is a bit early," Sorel said, trying to mask his anxiety. "Off schedule as is his usual."

"But he made several references that worried me. He kept using the word 'fair' in odd ways. Not so odd really, just repeatedly. I didn't think anything of it at first. Then he disappeared with such a sense of bemusement I was…" Gilda stopped, unsure what to say. She looked to Effie whose brow was wrinkled in thought; then at Sorel, who looked alarmed. He'd known Samuel longer than any of them and understood that Gilda's concern was not misplaced.

"Why does he continue this? Eleanor used him and tried to use Gilda. She's been dead for almost one hundred years!" Effie spoke her anger aloud before she thought.

Sadness settled on Sorel's face like a carnival mask. In her mortal life Eleanor had been like a daughter to him. The sunny face of curiosity and hopefulness all of them struggled to hold on to. Her spirit

Saint Louis 1990

was as golden as the hills of Yerba Buena where miners dug for precious ore. Her selfishness was so strong it had infected Samuel.

"He's always blamed Gilda. Even Eleanor's death can't release him." Sorel's voice deepened with sorrow. Everyone was silent as he closed his eyes. His beautiful hands rested lightly on the table as the image of Eleanor sprang to life in his mind. The way she tossed her auburn hair had remained unchanged from the time she was five until the day she died—haughty and vulnerable at the same time. Sorel could almost feel the brush of it against his hand. But the picture he examined behind his eyes also revealed the glint of petulance in hers. Many of their blood acted deliberately cruel or brutal and Eleanor had done both. Yet there'd been no meanness in her. She'd cared deeply about everything, in the moment. Samuel and Gilda had both entranced her. But her most enduring care was for herself and her whims.

He'd brought Eleanor into their family impulsively. She had repeated that same mistake with Samuel then abandoned him in pursuit of others. It didn't matter to Samuel that Gilda was only one of many lovers she preferred to him.

Sorel opened his eyes, no longer able to bear the shining clarity of his memory. "I'll call him to me, make him see some sense."

"Sorel, this isn't your responsibility," Gilda said. She too remembered the feel of Eleanor; as well as all she might have done to keep Eleanor by her side. But she'd refused to accommodate Eleanor's profoundest desire—Samuel's death. "He was Eleanor's error in judgment, not yours."

"If we follow lineage, he is my mistake too."

"Don't blame yourself." Effie spoke from many more years of experience than even Sorel. "At some point, troublesome people have to take responsibility for their own actions."

"Samuel is not someone we can assume will recognize good sense, even if it's pointed out to him," Gilda said. "This time there'll be no avoiding him."

"I'm afraid you're wholly correct, Gilda." Anthony had returned to the table carrying a small wood box. Gilda was startled by the way the hardness in Anthony's voice mirrored Effie's. It was as if they knew a secret no one else could comprehend and they meant her to follow their lead without thought or sentiment.

The box sat ominously on the table. It was rough hewn but had three finely made bronze clasps. Anthony sat down beside Sorel, whose usually jovial expression was unreadable.

Gilda stared at the box unwilling to focus on what lie inside it.

"I think we can manage Samuel," Effie said.

"I'm sure you can," Anthony said, "but with this you both can avoid undue…"

"Please stop talking as if Samuel were a cockroach I'm going to squash under my boot. That's just how Samuel thinks!" Gilda's voice rose with emotion. "We spend so much of our time learning to respect life, to live beside mortals and share the world in a responsible way. Don't talk about disposing of Samuel as if he'd never been human, or one of us."

"Samuel listens to no one," Effie said, her anger tightening her throat. She pushed her glass away from her and locked Gilda in her gaze. "Everywhere we turn there are the angry ones, full of rage with no idea how they got that way. They have some vague idea of injustice and a hunger for redress. And nothing else."

"Not all of us can cast off our sorrow easily," Sorel said.

"Samuel's life is a poison to all of us, whatever his sorrows. And we are the ones who hold the responsibility for him, no one else." She finally looked away toward Anthony. "All of you know his hatred for Gilda."

They were silent in their assent. She went on, unable to let her feelings remain unspoken: "If it means not having to weep dry tears while I scatter the ashes of any of you…I will incinerate Samuel."

Effie's anger was a wave of fiery air in the room. Gilda had never seen her so implacable.

"But how can we say he's irredeemable? Eleanor may have made a poor decision, but we can't compound it." Gilda's voice was tight with pleading. "She cared enough to bring him into our family. We have to give him some chance."

Saint Louis 1990

They could feel the others in the room straining not to appear to hear their conversation, but the words would be as clear to the other patrons and the bartender as if whispered next to their ears. The clink of ice in glasses and the movement of the air around the room punctuated the rising emotion.

"Samuel was a choice she regretted almost immediately," Anthony stated. "He's tried to harm you more than once. Don't sentimentalize."

Gilda inhaled deeply, not willing to embrace the idea of destruction. "Tonight coming home, I encountered a young black man much like Samuel. Bitter, disappointed. He assumed by attacking me, maybe raping me he'd make himself a man. Have something to share with his brothers. Something the white man couldn't take away from him." Gilda hurried as she felt them resist her story. "I know many men who look at women like they watch sports. I'm not sentimentalizing anything. When he touched me I could have killed him, tossed his body in the river and few would have noticed his absence. But inside him was a boy who'd been hurt. When I was able to find that clear space I could help him. I know we can't always help. But when do we stop trying?"

It was at these moments that Sorel felt most weary and at the same time most proud. "If you want to handle Samuel on your own," he spoke softly, "I won't interfere. Not yet." He pushed the box across the table back toward Anthony. "But I assure you neither Anthony nor I will hesitate to protect you."

Gilda sat back in the booth and said: "Let's not talk about this any more then. I think Samuel is simply succeeding in making us give him attention. I imagine he's repaired to one of those establishments in this town where blood is spilled and mortals are tortured, braying with smugness that's he's frightened me."

Gilda didn't believe the words even as she spoke them. Nor did anyone else at the table, but they let the conversation turn to Sorel and Anthony's trip to Europe. The anxiety remained at the table, seated silently with them.

Effie and Gilda walked northward toward home slowly, enjoying the sporadic lights of lower Broadway and the people who moved around them. As they got closer to Chelsea Gilda felt her muscles tense, anticipating the danger awaiting her. She saw that Effie, too, was listening with her body.

"I don't think I've ever known such fear. Not since I escaped the plantation as a child," Gilda said almost in a whisper.

"Yes. There is something about being hunted silently that never leaves the blood."

"I can't deliberately kill him. I made the choice to let go of my mortality, but not humanity."

"I understand that, Gilda. But you need to understand Samuel has given away his humanity."

"I don't believe that."

"Then why did you rush home in terror?"

Gilda's hand went, automatically to her throat but she could not answer Effie. She did still fell him clawing at her; and could, if she let herself, still sense his murderous lust pouring through his hands into her as he tried to rip her life from her. Yet Gilda clung to the possibility of his goodness as desperately as he'd gripped her throat.

"He let go finally, and so must you," Effie said, expressing no regret for listening to Gilda's thoughts. The remaining blocks to their home were traversed in silence, neither Effie nor Gilda speaking or thinking.

The glow of their windows was a lighthouse, guiding them to a comfortable berth after turbulent emotions, many still unspoken. Once inside they shed their clothes and with it the scent of fear. They both listened to the building as always, assuring themselves that each of the tenants was safe. The apartments were wrapped in sleep except Marci's, where the stereo still played softly over the energy of desire.

"He must be in love!" Gilda said with laughter.

"This is news." Effie unlocked the door to the sleeping room and pulled the comforter back. The soft sheen of the black satin sheet which covered their pallets was inviting in the light of the candle Effie lit.

Saint Louis 1990

"He was wearing that yellow blouse that looks so beautiful on his skin when I saw him earlier this evening." Gilda followed her. "And grinning like a Mardi Gras mask."

"That sounds like love," Effie said and reached out to pull Gilda down to her.

"Your affection for Eleanor, your feelings of guilt for not staying with her, has made Samuel a cause you cannot win. I don't want to leave here worried that you'll end your life in a foolish battle with him."

Gilda stiffened in Effie's arms but Effie held on to her. The truth of the moment raced between them like an electrical current. Gilda had known even without the words. Sorel and Anthony spent most of their days and nights together. But often they separated for months and sometimes years. Bird, who'd helped bring her into this life, who'd known her even before they did, had traveled unceasingly, stopping only occasionally to look into the face of her daughter, Gilda. Each of them had told her this was their way to maintain the sense of anticipation and wonder at life. To keep returning to the world alone, seeking to learn from mortals, alone gave them a connection they'd never get keeping themselves secluded and apart. The natural pattern of eternal life frightened Gilda, it felt too much like an abyss. Gilda still didn't know how to manage the long days when she had no one to lie with and feared she never would.

When she was child she'd watched the overseer carrying her mother's body from their room. She understood it was no longer her mother, but now simply a "thing" just as the slave master had always insisted. At that moment she'd been consumed by knowing she'd never see her birth mother again. A huge vacuum had opened in front of her, sucking her into a breathless, infinite hole that she'd spent her subsequent years running from.

"It is our rhythm of living, my love. We are always together, even when we part. You've seen that with Bird, Anthony, Sorel. Good heavens, even with Samuel!" The sinewy muscle of Effie's arm held tight. The years Effie had spent wandering the world far outnumbered those of Anthony and Sorel. She enjoyed the many lives she'd touch as time passed and knew that Gilda would never be at ease until she too fully accepted the change in perspective that was necessary to them.

Gilda rested her head in the soft part of Effie's neck at her shoulder. She couldn't deny what she knew was true. When she'd raced home in fear for Effie she'd known then that the time was near for Effie to return to her travels.

"When?" Gilda asked.

"Let's not talk with our voices now," Effie said and covered Gilda's mouth with hers. At first Gilda could not respond, the ashes that would have been tears filled her mouth and eyes. Then the heat of Effie's lips drew her. Effie leaned backward onto the bed, her small breasts appealing in the dark. She pulled Gilda down to her. The moist earth shifted gently beneath them as Gilda let her weight press into Effie.

The desire they held for each other was heightened by the imminent separation and for the first time Gilda could let herself feel anticipation of that moment when they'd see each other again. Gilda stopped resisting and her desire pinned Effie to their bed. She thrust down feeling Effie's body meet hers. This was the first woman she'd ever made love to with the fullness of desire. She remembered so many fleeting touches, moments when desire floated around her like bright bubbles until she wiped them away into the air. Now she wanted to breath them in as she did when drinking Sorel's beloved champagne. With Effie she'd learned to open, to meet the needs of her body that ran just as deep as blood.

Pushing her knee between Effie's legs, Gilda straddled her tight thigh muscle and set a rhythmic pace that kept time with their breathing. Each inhalation drove them deeper into their hunger for each other. When Gilda felt they were both ready she slipped inside Effie, gently letting the tide of their desire guide her. The muscles in Gilda's arm tightened to solid cords as her thrusts grew more insistent and Effie's embrace tightened. Their bodies pulsated on the firm pallet in a rhythm both old and new. The sound of their breathing and the wetness of Effie's body rocking on Gilda's hand filled

Saint Louis 1990

the locked room. Everything around them was forgotten until Effie exploded into Gilda's hand. Gilda's body stiffened as she continued pushing harder. She thrust against Effie feeling every texture of her skin and feeling nothing at all except the wave crashing inside her. She muffled her final scream in the pillow at Effie's head.

The room vibrated with the passion that they'd released into the air. A damp mist floated above them as they both lay still until their breathing steadied.

Effie touched the softness of Gilda's close cut hair and was pleased to sense the change in Gilda's understanding. The worry had sat uneasily on her for weeks. She'd used all her energy to shield Gilda from the conflict she felt. Now she was able to open.

Gilda pulled the comforter up around them and they drifted into the rest that usually claimed all of them in the pre-dawn hours. After only moments of listening to Effie's breathing slow to almost nothing, Gilda, too, was no longer awake. Their room was steeped in darkness maintained by the painted windows and heavy drapes that hung in front of them. Their rest was not governed by a diurnal clock, but ebbed and flowed with their energy. Night was their natural milieu and daylight could drain their energy, but no hours were unavailable to them.

Just before the sun pushed against the covered window Gilda's eyes opened. She stared into the inky air, uncertain why she was suddenly alert at that moment. The house remained quiet all around her. Too quiet. Gilda reached out for Effie, who pulled herself back from sleep.

"He's here," Gilda said in a low hiss.

Effie was awake and reaching for her clothes within the moment. They both stepped into pants and sweaters as they listened to the air around them.

"The music." Effie said as she realized she could still hear a soft guitar from Marci's apartment above them. Without speaking Gilda and Effie bolted through the doors and out into the hall. The silence was thick, as they pushed their way through it. They moved swiftly up the stairs afraid of what they'd find. Samuel was there. Using his powers he'd shrouded Marci's room so nothing could be perceived except the record on the stereo. They stood outside the door for only a second then Effie twisted the knob off silently, the brass wrinkling between her fingers like paper, before she dropped it to the floor. Gilda pushed the door open to Marci's living room which glowed in red.

At first Gilda thought the walls were awash in blood but realized it was the lamplight that usually shone down into their yard. The shade moved against the open window where a figure stood. Samuel stepped forward, his face twisted in hatred. The torn yellow silk of Marci's blouse lay at his feet. Gilda looked quickly around the room. On the far side, across the plush couch he'd been so proud of, Marci lay sprawled, blood still draining onto the floor from his wound.

Gilda ran to Marci and knelt on the floor. Around his head, blood had soaked into the cushions of the couch and then pooled on the floor beside him. His eyes fluttered behind his lids. Gilda's anger rose through her throat.

"You didn't even take his blood. You spilled it like sewage!" Gilda pressed her hand to the wound in Marci's neck hoping to stem the flow before it was too late. Effie took a step closer and looked over at Marci, "I don't know Gilda."

"Forget about him," said Samuel the satisfaction clear in his voice.

"You were here with him, weren't you? When I was in the yard?"

Samuel's laughter was not mirthful. "Of course. The little slut was wiggling with glee. I could have slaughtered him right then. But I wanted you to see."

"No, Samuel, I think you wanted to be punished," Effie said, her voice unnaturally even, as if she were in a trance.

Samuel was startled as if he'd not noticed her before. He tried to move but found his limbs were sluggish.

"Marci...de Justo!" That's who you meant when you said "fair." Gilda spoke her realization aloud as if it might reel the hours back in and she could save her friend.

"My fight is with Gilda." Samuel almost shouted at Effie.

"And what is that quarrel?"

Saint Louis 1990

"She knows."

"An unarticulated complaint is an answer withheld. Speak!"

"Gilda knows."

"An answer withheld is an embrace of ignorance."

Samuel's face was filled with as much puzzlement as fear each time Effie spoke.

"He's barely breathing!" Gilda spoke as she clenched her hand tightly around Marci's neck.

"Careful. Press your lips to the wound."

"No! This isn't Marci's choice, I..."

"Do it, gently let your fluids mix. But take nothing from him, listen inside."

Samuel watched Gilda bend toward the small body. He doubted Marci could be revived without an infusion of blood and he believed Gilda too timid to give Marci life that way. He smirked in satisfaction that finally he'd found his revenge.

"Ignorance is a dull knife." Effie moved closer to Samuel, her muscles rippling like electricity under her clothes. Samuel thought he heard a noise in the yard below but was afraid to turn his eyes from Effie.

"All I wanted was peace," Samuel said, his voice a narrow whine that grated in the air.

"You wanted Eleanor to love you. She didn't! Can't you understand that? She didn't love anyone but herself," Effie said. She could feel Gilda's energy flowing through the room and sense Marci regaining consciousness. "Pull back!" she shouted.

Gilda raised her head and wiped Marci's blood from her mouth. The tiny portion of her blood she'd shared would give him the strength he needed. She would nurse him through the moment when he might have hunger without drawing him into their family against his wishes.

She stood, placing Marci tenderly back onto the couch with his legs raised on pillows. "*Mi hermano,*" she murmured to him softly to quiet the terror which returned with his consciousness. The wound had closed and she could feel fresh blood, enlivened by hers, coursing through his veins. His skin took on a more natural color as he struggled to open his eyes. Gilda rested her hands on his forehead willing him into sleep.

"She wouldn't leave us in peace," Samuel said to Effie as if that explained their friend bleeding on the couch.

"Peace is most difficult to endure, one of my teachers was fond of saying." Effie spoke as she moved closer to Samuel. His eyes hardened; he was unable to understand why he couldn't move. Effie held him in her gaze, not letting her anger or disgust distract her.

"You will now have peace," she said as she clasped her two hands together as if to pray. Her swing curved smoothly up through the air, her blow knocked Samuel back against the window frame, cracking the wood. She hit him again as he bounced forward, and the glass shattered. He struggled back toward Effie.

"No!" Gilda said, her voice rising out of the deep place she'd always run from. The thick, guttural tone was like broken ice showering around them. Gilda's stride carried her across the room before either Effie or Samuel saw her move. Samuel reached out with both hands for her throat as if he could silence her voice. Gilda dropped to her knees, eluding his grasp and yanked Marci's ruined blouse from beneath his feet. The tearing cloth reverberated in the room. With the shredded material gripped between her clenched fists Gilda rose, swinging upward. Her blow caught Samuel under his chin and she could hear his teeth clamp shut through the flesh of his tongue. This time he fell back through the window as the shade snapped open.

In the few seconds of his fall Samuel still smiled, the blood of his severed tongue creasing his face. He was certain he could not be hurt by a two story fall onto a garden. In his years he'd survived much worse.

At that moment Anthony took a step away from the artfully carved box on the ground, off of the carefully laid flagstones and into the path of Samuel's descent. He raised a broad silver dagger in his gloved hands. His pale skin glistened in the darkness of the yard. The shining metal and colorful gems which adorned the handle caught the hint of morning light which peeked over the horizon. The muscles

Saint Louis 1990

of Anthony's arm were taut, holding the silver dagger before him. He admired its beauty just as Samuel's spine made contact with the tip. Anthony released his hold as Samuel's body swallowed the blade and crashed to the ground. He lay on the grass, the hilt driven into the ground, the bloody blade gleaming from his chest. Samuel's eyes opened in disbelief, and then were empty.

Anthony looked up at the windows that surrounded the yard. All were dark and unoccupied except for Marci's, where Gilda and Effie looked down at him. "You will have peace now," he said. He ripped the blade of the knife and wrenched it downward, opening Samuel's chest. He then pushed the hilt deeper into the ground. Blood flowed like a stream into the roots of the evergreen. Anthony ripped at Samuel's clothes, removing them and his shoes which held his protective soil. He then stepped back into the shadow of Gilda's garden door and watched morning break over the city.

Gilda and Effie locked Marci's door, leaving him cocooned in sleep until they woke him later in the day. When they stood beside Anthony at the garden door they clasped each other's hands which were slick with blood.

"His life was much too long, Gilda. He didn't have the spirit for it," Effie said.

"I'm sorry it ended here," Anthony spoke softly.

"We saved Marci, that's a balance, I think," Gilda answered.

"More than a balance," Effie added.

"Do you remember Joe Louis?" Gilda asked Effie.

"Of course. His power was amazing!"

"He'd have loved your swing," Gilda laughed.

"I think you might make the college team, yourself," Effie said.

They retreated into the house as the sun took over the sky. Before anyone could look from their windows it had turned Samuel's body into ash leaving only the dagger in the soil. From above, its silver gleam looked like the tilted arm of a sundial greeting the day. Although windows were painted and the curtains were already drawn Effie tugged at their hems as if to fasten them more tightly.

"Come," Gilda said as she removed her clothes. After washing off the blood of their enemy and of their friend, the three climbed into the wide bed were the two women had made love only moments before. Pulling the gold comforter up, Effie, Gilda and Anthony turned to fit into the curves of each other's bodies. Each left the other to personal thoughts: Anthony remembered a time over a hundred years earlier when he'd helped the young Gilda wash away the filth of the road in a deep copper tub. At this cleansing tonight, he saw that naiveté was no longer a veil between her and the real world. Effie's mind drifted over the roads she might follow now that Gilda had her own path.

Gilda was at first startled that Samuel's death was a relief more than a burden. She'd watched the muscles of his face soften and his eyes lose their hardness, finally understanding he'd locked himself inside a torment that had only this release. She fell into sleep planning to clean Marci's rooms before awakening him, wondering where she'd find him a new silk blouse. They were all at rest before the sun's rays tapped at the shuttered windows.

Elm

Jamie Killen

Alice was seven when she met Elm for the first time. She had wandered into the woods where her house's back yard ended; her mother always told her not to go too far, but she had never said exactly what that meant and Alice had never asked. Today she went all the way to the little gully with the stream running along the bottom, well beyond the view of the house. She found a puddle and squatted down to watch tadpoles swarming through the murky water. Scooping some of it up in her hands, she closed her eyes and tried to hold perfectly still as the tadpoles' soft bodies brushed against her palms. When her eyes opened again, she saw the woman.

She stood across the stream, calmly watching Alice. Her hair hung long and dark down her back. She was naked, but seemed unaware of it, slim body held tall and poised. Alice stared, fascinated, at the woman's skin; at first glance it was a light brown, but there was also a green tinge to it. It was hairless, and slightly shiny, and covered with pale lines like the veins of leaves. That's what it looked like, Alice realized. Leaves.

"Why aren't you wearing clothes?" Alice asked.

The woman glanced down at herself before returning her gaze to Alice. "Because I don't need them."

Alice let the water and the tadpoles trickle through her fingers. "What about when it snows? Don't you get cold?"

She shook her head. "I sleep when it snows."

Alice stood and wiped her wet hands on her dress, remembering too late that her mother would be angry when she returned with muddy clothes. "My name's Alice."

"I know," the woman replied.

Alice waited. "Well," she said at last, "what's your name?"

The woman smiled for the first time. "We don't have names people can say. They're more like…smells, and tastes."

Alice studied her for a moment. "Are you a fairy?"

"No."

"Then what are you?"

"We live in the trees." The woman frowned and shook her head, as if that wasn't quite right.

"Is that why your skin looks like that?"

"Yes." The woman stepped across the stream and held out a hand to Alice. "Go on."

Alice reached out timidly and stroked the woman's palm. It felt smooth like a leaf, but stronger and warmer. Now that she was closer, Alice could smell sap and earth. "What kind of tree do you live in?"

The woman turned and pointed to the tall, stately tree across the stream. "That's it. You'd call it an elm."

"Elm." Alice tasted the word. "Okay, that's what I'll call you. Elm."

Elm's smile broadened. "That's fine."

Elm

Alice looked back toward the house. "I have to go, or Mama's gonna yell. But I can come back and play some more tomorrow."

"I'd like that."

Alice set off for the house. "Bye, Elm," she called over her shoulder.

"Goodbye, Alice."

∽

Alice returned the next day. She stood in the same spot next to the stream and turned a complete circle. "Elm?" she called.

"I'm here." The voice drifted down from above.

Alice looked up and smiled with relief. "Hi." Elm sat on one of her tree's wide branches, feet dangling in the air. "I didn't tell Mama you were here. I thought maybe…"

Elm cocked her head. "Maybe I wasn't really here? Maybe you're a little girl with a big imagination?"

Alice felt her cheeks redden. "I guess."

Elm dropped from the branch; she seemed to fall slower than she should have, landing easily on her feet. "Well, I am here. Still, it's wise not to mention me. They wouldn't believe you, and even if you brought them here I wouldn't show myself."

"Why not?"

Elm lifted one shoulder in a tiny shrug. "I choose my friends carefully. Come." She held out a hand to Alice.

"Where are we going?" Alice asked, taking Elm's hand.

"To meet someone."

Elm led her through the trees. They didn't follow the little trail next to the stream, moving instead through the dense brush. Elm found small gaps in the branches just big enough for Alice to pass through. As they moved farther from the stream, the shadows became darker and cooler. Alice smelled moss and blackberry bushes, and underneath that the clear green scent of Elm's skin. Around her she heard quick movements in the brush, birds and squirrels darting into hiding.

They stopped next to a fallen tree. The bark was silver with age and half-covered with creeping vines. Elm knelt and held a hand out to a hollow under the log. Alice crouched beside her. "Be still," Elm murmured.

As Alice watched, a sharp nose poked out of the hollow, sniffing Elm's hand. It was followed by a fox. He emerged cautiously from his burrow, freezing and baring his teeth when he saw Alice. She held her breath, willing herself into complete stillness. Elm let out a little hiss and ran her fingertips over the fox's head; his body relaxed and he came farther into the light.

"This is another of my friends," Elm said.

"Can he talk, too?"

"Of course. But you wouldn't be able to understand him, nor he you. Here," she took Alice's hand in her own and ran it gently down the fox's spine. Alice let out a little gasp as the fox arched his back into her palm like a cat.

After a few minutes the fox turned and scurried back into his burrow. "Come," Elm said again. "I have other friends for you to meet."

༄

"Careful, now. Show her you're not to be feared."

Alice took a deep breath and slowly extended her hand to the little cardinal perched on the branch before her. A small pile of seeds rested on her palm; wild seeds, gathered with Elm, not the uniform little ones her mother bought for their bird feeders. In the year since she had befriended Elm, Alice had learned to call some animals. Foxes and badgers were simple enough, but birds remained skittish. This one cocked his head and watched her, but didn't fly away. She got close enough that her fingertips just grazed his chest feathers. He hesitated for a moment, finally stepping onto her hand and pecking at the seed.

"Good." Elm swung onto a higher branch and stretched out on her side.

"Elm, did you ever have parents?" Alice asked, still watching the bird.

Elm's lips curved up in a little smile. "Of course. Why wouldn't I?"

Alice shrugged. "Well.... You're a tree. You're from a tree."

"I wasn't always." The smile remained, but her eyes turned distant.

Elm

The cardinal took one last bite of seed and flew away. Alice turned and looked up at Elm. "So what happened?"

Elm stared at her for a long time. Just as Alice was beginning to wonder if she'd made her angry, Elm spoke. "My family came from somewhere else. I remember being in a ship. Not much about it, just the smell. My father brought us into the forest, saying we'd make a living out of the land, but then he and my mother died of some sickness. I ran into the woods, and my tree…." Elm frowned, her arm reaching out as though to pluck the right words from the air. "*Recognized* me. Opened for me. It changed me into what I am now."

"So people can turn into one of you?"

"Some people."

Alice tipped her head back and watched the patches of blue sky visible through the tree's leaves. She thought about what it would be like if Mama and Daddy died and left her alone in the forest. "So there's more like you?" she asked after a while.

"Yes," Elm replied. "I've met some. But they aren't near here and we don't like to be away from our trees for long."

Alice nodded, realizing she had somehow already known this. "Do you miss your Mama and Daddy?"

Elm hooked one knee over a branch and slid off the side, letting herself dangle upside down. "Not anymore. I don't remember them well enough. My father was a big man, strong. He always sang while he worked."

Alice laughed. "That's weird."

"Why?"

"My daddy never sings while he's working."

Elm flipped backwards and landed softly on Alice's branch, as always not fully subject to gravity. She crouched and took one of Alice's hands in her own. "Is he happy?"

"Who?" Alice frowned.

"Your father. Is he happy?"

Alice started to answer, but something in Elm's eyes stopped her, something sad.

"He doesn't sing," Alice began carefully, "and sometimes he and Mama don't talk to each other. They don't yell or anything, but I can tell they're mad. They think I don't know, but I do."

"Do you know what they're angry about?"

"No." Alice thought about her parents' downcast eyes at the dinner table. She thought about the times she heard their low voices in the kitchen, and then the back door closing just a little too loud, the clatter of pots on the stove a bit too heavy. She wondered why she hadn't stopped to think about these things before, why it worried her now.

Elm's hands stayed wrapped around Alice's, but her gaze turned away. "So is he never happy?"

"He is! He's happy lots of times. Like whenever he's working on machines in the garage, and I go to keep him company. He always wants to hear about my day. He smiles a lot then."

Elm stayed silent for a moment. "Well, there's that at least." She stood and quickly turned away. "I think I'll rest now."

"Oh. Okay. Um.... Bye."

"Goodbye, Alice."

Alice walked home slowly, running through the conversation in her head. Something had been revealed, something she'd never been quite aware of even while seeing it every day, and even now couldn't quite articulate.

She didn't want to go home.

Alice kicked her shoes off next to the stream and began climbing Elm's tree. She was eleven now, so adept at climbing that it took no conscious effort. She swung her legs over a low branch, arranging herself with her back to the trunk. Elm dropped from nowhere to a nearby bough; it was a trick that had startled Alice the first few times but now didn't even make her blink. "I came to see you yesterday, but you weren't here."

Elm sat on her perch. "I was. But you were followed, so I hid myself."

"Followed?" Alice frowned.

"A boy. One about your age."

Alice kicked at the air and scowled. "That must have been Davey Jensen. He's always following me around."

Elm smiled. "He's smitten with you."

"*Ewww.* No. I don't like Davey."

"Why not?"

Alice shrugged. "I don't know. He's nice, I guess. I just don't like how he's always staring at me."

"You might, one day."

"No," Alice replied with careless certainty. "He doesn't like the woods. I mean, he's *scared* of them. How could I like a boy who's scared of the woods?"

Elm's laughter rang out through the trees; when Alice asked why, she only grinned and ran into a stand of birches, daring Alice to chase her.

 ∽

Alice wrapped her coat more tightly around herself and shivered as she made her way through the trees. The moon hung bright and full in the sky, but the blue light only seemed to intensify the cold. There was no snow yet, just a layer of frost crunching under Alice's boots. It would come soon, though. Alice never bothered with weather reports; she had learned to taste the air, to smell the first snow coming a week or more before it arrived. That taste was there now, and she felt a little pang at the thought of Elm disappearing into her tree until the snow melted. Each winter seemed longer than the last, and Alice knew this one would seem longest of all.

She found Elm by the stream, now just a trickle of icy slush. "You've come to say goodbye for the winter," she said with a sad smile.

Alice swallowed. "Yeah." She busied herself with unpacking the small bag she had snuck out of the house, willing herself not to remember last night's dream.

It hadn't been the first time she'd dreamt about Elm, but it was the most vivid. The first had been two or three months earlier, just days before her fourteenth birthday. That one had been just indistinct images, impressions: Elm's breath on her face, leaflike skin under her hands, the weight of her body. Alice had woken flushed and shaken, but had managed to quickly push the memory aside. She had been able to avoid thinking of it too much. But last night's...

She cleared her throat. "I brought that chocolate you like. Oh, and I stole some gin from my folks' liquor cabinet," she said.

Elm snatched up the chocolate and climbed her tree. "They won't notice it's gone? The gin?"

Alice shrugged. "My parents both drink it, but not together. I think each one will think the other finished it off." She followed Elm up the tree, gin bottle tucked into her coat pocket. "Does alcohol even work on trees?"

"Yes. It came as quite a shock when I found out. Come, there's enough room in the nest for us both."

Where the trunk of the tree split into two large boughs, smaller branches had grown together to form a spherical shelter like a woven basket. Alice settled next to Elm, leaning back slowly and listening for the sound of breaking branches. "You sure it can hold us both? I'm bigger than I used to be."

"Of course."

"How do you make this thing?" Alice tried to find a place where branches had been broken and woven together, but could find none.

"I don't. I just tell my tree winter's coming, and it knows what needs to be done. Now," she said with a grin, "let's have some of this chocolate."

Alice uncapped the gin. She felt the pressure of Elm's body along her left side, the tickle of her hair where it brushed the back of Alice's hand. Her immediate impulse was to pull away, put some distance between them, but she stopped herself. *Be normal,* she thought. *Be like you've always been.* Tipping back the bottle, she took a long swig.

"Here," she said with a grimace, passing the bottle to Elm. "Ugh, tastes awful."

"But it's not about the taste, is it?" Elm took a sip of her own, not showing the slightest distaste at the flavor. Alice felt a flash of envy as she thought about how graceful the other woman was even when guzzling gin, how graceful she *always* was. She silently watched Elm's body and pictured her own, comparing the two. They were both tall and thin, true, but she was all stretched out, bony angles where Elm had subtle curves. Like Elm, she had hair hanging to her waist, but hers was an unruly straw-colored mane next to the other woman's black silk. She wondered why she suddenly felt so inadequate, and if Elm noticed these flaws as well.

"What's wrong?" Elm asked.

"Nothing," Alice said, looking hastily away. "Just…winter, you know."

"Yes."

They talked about the forest, the animals, Alice's school. These were the things they had always talked about, but there seemed now to Alice to be a level of artifice to her words. Like she was holding herself back from something, not sure of what.

She willed herself to relax. "What's it like? Sleeping all winter?"

Elm reached for the gin. "It's not really sleep. I'm aware, but not truly conscious." She turned and stared silently at Alice for a moment. "I just…melt into the land. I feel what the trees feel. It's what I always do when I communicate with the ground and the plants, but more. There's no time, there's no thought. In a way, there's no *me*. There's just existence."

Alice kissed her. It was clumsy and unplanned, a rush of need become motion. Their lips pressed together, and Alice tasted sap and earth. Elm stayed still, neither reciprocating nor pushing her away.

Alice pulled back, pulse hammering in her throat. She tried to read Elm's expression and couldn't. "I'm sorry."

"You're still a child, Alice."

Even spoken in a calm murmur, the words felt like a slap. "I am *not*."

Elm turned to gaze out over the forest. "Yes, you are. You haven't the faintest idea of what it would mean to love me."

"I'm sorry," Alice said again.

"I'm not angry. But you need to go now."

Alice tried to think of something else to say, but couldn't. Elm didn't move as she climbed past her out of the nest. When she reached the ground, Alice turned back and watched Elm's nest slowly close and disappear within the tree's tangle of branches. She waited, hoping Elm would reemerge and tell her she had changed her mind, knowing she wouldn't. Then she walked home with the numb shock of an injury that has not yet begun to hurt.

Alice knew the moment she woke that winter had ended. For months, it had been one achingly cold day after another. At times it had seemed as though the winter was punishing her transgression, deliberately delaying the day she would see Elm again. But now she could taste the thaw in the air. She flung aside the covers and scrambled to find her clothes.

As Alice came down the stairs, her mother looked up from the newspaper spread out over the kitchen table. "What are you doing up so early?"

"Going for a walk."

"In the woods? Thought you'd grown out of that."

Alice said nothing in reply, just retrieved the bread and peanut butter from the pantry. She wondered if she should bring a better peace offering than a peanut butter sandwich, but could think of nothing that would be appropriate.

Her father opened the back door, stamping the slush off his boots as he came inside. "What's going on?" he asked.

"She's in a mood. Like always, these days."

Alice bit back a retort and settled for a glare. Most days she would have taken the bait without hesitation, but didn't want to risk being sent to her room. Not today.

"See ya, Dad," she said, smiling pointedly in her father's direction. He said nothing, just gave her the same weary expression he always wore when she and her mother were arguing. Lately, it was present whenever all three of them shared the same room.

Elm's nest was still closed when Alice reached the tree. She thought about coming back later, but no. All of her senses told her that Elm would awaken today, soon.

Elm

She sat on a fallen log to wait, trying to ignore the cold seeping through her jeans. At first she fidgeted and tapped, but it occurred to her that Elm would disapprove if she had been watching. *Stillness, Alice. Most people don't have the stillness to understand this place.*

Closing her eyes, Alice reached out a hand and began to hum, even and quiet like Elm had taught her. She kept her volume low, but projected the sound out into the woods until she could feel what she was looking for.

A twig cracked as the fox slid into the clearing. Alice kept her eyes closed as he circled her, waited for him to drop his guard. She could hear the little sounds of his movements, picture exactly where he was. A puff of breeze brought the musky scent of his pelt, strong enough that she knew he must be nearly within reach. Finally, she felt hot breath and fur nudging against her open palm.

She stopped humming and opened her eyes. The fox sat on his haunches, face turned up toward hers. She quietly stroked his back and scratched behind his ears. When he stood and ran off, Alice saw Elm watching her from the tree's upper bough.

They said nothing for a minute, just watching each other. Then Elm jumped to the ground. "Come. I want to see the river."

Alice swallowed the lump in her throat and forced herself to smile. "Okay."

It wasn't the resolution she wanted, but at least it was a kind of truce. At least she hadn't lost her.

⁂

"Just be patient. Figure out what's wrong with them."

Alice rubbed a leaf from the blackberry bush between her fingers. She smelled the berries, dug her fingers into the ground. "There's something in the soil, something they don't have enough of." She felt the roots straining, driven by need.

"Yes," Elm said. "Now, what is it?"

Alice closed her eyes and tried to be still. "Iron," she said at last.

Elm nodded. "Good. We'll fix it tomorrow." She picked up a wide patch of fallen tree bark and began piling it with plucked berries. "Would you like to come to the nest?"

"Sure." Alice followed her back to the tree and watched her climb, balancing the berries on one hand like a waiter with a dinner plate. She followed Elm, settling against the wall of the nest. For a fleeting moment, Alice was reminded of that night over three years ago, that night they had never discussed. Then, as always, she shoved the memory aside.

They ate in silence. "I'll be done with high school soon," Alice said when she was done. "Just one more year."

"What does that mean?" Elm asked, licking blackberry juice from her fingers.

"I don't know. College, I guess."

"You don't sound like you want to." Elm's skin was translucent in the moonlight, dark veins spidering up her arms. She sat in the nest's opening, face hidden by shadow.

Alice let out a hollow laugh. "No. But, then, I don't want any of the things I'm supposed to want. You know Davey Jensen asked me to the junior prom?"

"No."

"Well, he did." Alice leaned back against the wall of the nest and swigged from the bottle of cheap wine she had talked an older cousin into buying for her. "I told him I wasn't going to the prom. Why the fuck would I? My friend Sarah said I was nuts, most girls at that school would kill to go with Davey Jensen. Oh, sorry, it's supposed to be *Dave* Jensen now. Well, far as I'm concerned, they can have at him. God knows I'm not interested. In him or any other guy at that school." Her blood thrummed with the warmth of the wine, letting her hint at things she never quite spoke aloud.

"What are you interested in?" Elm's voice was a quiet whisper from behind her curtain of hair.

God, are you really going to make me say it? "This," Alice said after a moment. "Honestly, there's nothing I like more than this. Just…being part of this, being in the forest. Calling the animals. Listening. Out there nothing feels as, as real. It doesn't feel as alive." She laughed softly. "I think I was supposed to grow out of this, but I'm starting to think I won't."

Elm

Elm turned and looked at her for a long time, expression unreadable. She climbed from her perch and crossed to where Alice sat, deep in the nest. In one smooth motion, she straddled Alice's lap and took her face in her hands.

Alice's breath quickened. She let her hands rest against the cool, alien skin of Elm's thighs. "Does this mean I'm not still a child?"

"No," Elm murmured. "You're not a child anymore." And she kissed her.

When Alice woke, the sky had lightened to lavender. Elm's hair trailed along Alice's side as she kissed her neck, the base of her throat, her breasts. *I have to go soon,* Alice knew she should say. *I have to be back before Mom and Dad find out I was out all night.* Instead, she arched her back and wrapped her arms around Elm's waist.

The night before had been a frenzy, each of them touching and moving too eagerly to find the right rhythm. This morning they took their time, exploring each other with care. Alice lost herself in Elm's smell and taste and the coolness of her body, lost track of all time until Elm came, shuddering and gasping under her.

They lay tangled in the nest, unable to do anything more than breathe. Alice saw sunlight creeping through the leaves and knew that there would be trouble later. There would be shrill questions and lies and punishment, but that could wait. All of it could wait until she'd had a little more time here.

"Why'd you change your mind?" Alice whispered.

Elm stroked her cheek. "You know yourself now."

Alice was quiet for a time. "Maybe you did the right thing, back then," she said, running her fingertips along Elm's side, "but I'm so happy the wait's over."

Alice went to the woods nearly every night now. Sometimes she and Elm would walk the forest, tending to the trees, calling the animals, as they always had. Sometimes Elm ripped her clothes off the moment she reached the clearing and had her on the open ground. Always, though, they ended the night wrapped around each other in

Elm's nest. Each morning, Alice woke before sunrise and was back to the house before her parents were out of bed.

One lazy Sunday, they lay intertwined in a heap of auburn leaves beneath an ancient oak. Alice kissed Elm's neck, trying not to think of the long winter that was fast approaching. "I got a job at the nursery. Plants, not babies," she said after a comfortable lull in the conversation. "It's just a few hours each day after school."

"Oh?" Elm murmured, running her hand slowly up Alice's thigh.

Alice tried to keep her voice casual. "And the guy who owns it, Donald, he said I could start working full time in May, after I graduate."

Elm's gaze flicked toward her. "I thought you said after graduation was college."

"Yeah, well…. Maybe I'm taking a year off first. That's what I'm telling my folks, anyway. Really I just don't want to go. I'd miss this. And…I realized, it's not just you. I mean it is you, I love you, but it's also this place. I don't think I can leave it." She sighed. "It's scary, knowing that."

Elm looked away. "I've been dreading the day you'd leave," she said, almost too quiet for Alice to hear. "I'm glad you're not."

Alice watched her. It occurred to her that she had never seen Elm show need before. She said nothing, afraid of breaking something fragile. Instead she just stroked Elm's hair and held her close.

Alice was pulling on her left boot when her father walked into the kitchen. "Where you off to?" he asked.

"Just a walk. In the woods," Alice replied, concealing her eagerness under a tone of boredom. Winter had ended only weeks before, and she and Elm hadn't been able to get enough of each other.

"What is it you're always doing there? Always in those damn woods…" There was that look in his eye, that odd squint Alice had seen once or twice when he mentioned her frequent trips to the forest. Nervousness, maybe. A hint of suspicion.

"Oh, nothing." Alice grinned as she stood. "I just have a friend who's a tree spirit."

She was expecting an eye roll, a laugh, a little thrill from having casually spilled the truth without him even knowing. Instead his features froze in naked shock and pain. "You…" The word seemed to squeeze its way through his lips. Then, for the first time, Alice's father slapped her. The impact rocked her head to one side, made her stagger. She clutched her cheek and gasped.

They stared at each other in silence, mute and pale with the knowledge they shared. He opened his mouth as if to say something, but at that moment they heard the sound of the truck's tires on the gravel of the drive. Both of them glanced at the door, then at each other.

"Mom's gonna need help with the groceries," Alice muttered, astonished at the calm in her own voice.

"Alice…" He reached for her, but she pulled back.

"*Don't.* Just go help Mom," she said, shouldering past him and moving for the back door. The tears began as she stumbled down the porch steps. Her feet carried her onto the forest path and toward Elm's tree.

She spotted Elm by the stream, standing with her back to the path. She turned and Alice saw that smile she so loved before it was replaced by worry. "Alice?" Elm whispered, moving toward her, "What happened?"

Alice pushed her, clumsily, and Elm took a step back. "Why didn't you tell me?" she cried.

Elm's eyes closed and she took a slow, deep breath. "About your father."

"What the hell did you *do* to him?"

Elm flinched. "I didn't do anything to him. I loved him and he loved me. When he was young, before you were born."

Alice felt something in her chest crumple. "You lied to me," she whispered.

"No, I didn't." A spark of anger flashed in Elm's eyes. "I never said I didn't know him. I never said you were the first. I've been alive for over a century, Alice. 'Elm' isn't the first human name I've had, and you weren't the first I made love to. And you knew that, even if you never asked."

Alice turned away, unable to stop the sobs now. Elm moved up behind her, and she felt those slender hands touch her shoulders. "Alice. You need to listen to me."

"What?" She didn't turn around.

"It was when he was a young man, just a little older than you are now. I chose to show myself to him, and we grew close. We loved each other, for a time.

"But he wasn't like you. He wanted me to leave the forest. He wanted me to be a human woman, and that was something I could never be. Not the way he wanted me to. And he wasn't…he wasn't *right*, he wasn't a fit to become one of my kind. The forest wouldn't have taken him. When he met your mother, he made a choice. He wanted children, and a family, and that's what he chose."

"He…he did that?" Alice asked, turning to face Elm. Her eyes held pain Alice had never seen there.

"Yes. He left the forest and he came back just once. He came back with you, when you were a baby. Just days old. He said your name was Alice, and he wanted me to meet you. He was so proud."

"That's how you knew who I was," Alice breathed. "The day we met."

"Yes." Elm reached tentatively for Alice's cheekbone, already beginning to bruise where her father's ring had struck. "I didn't tell you because I could see from the first day that you were someone new, someone different. You weren't just his daughter."

Elm kissed her then; Alice stayed still for a moment before returning the kiss. Pulling back slightly, Elm asked, "Will you come with me?"

"Yes," Alice whispered.

Much later, they lay together in Elm's nest, catching their breath. Alice rested her head against Elm's shoulder and closed her eyes, inhaling the otherworldly scent of her lover's skin. She could feel Elm's fingers slowly stroking through her hair. "You said the forest wouldn't have taken him," she said.

"Yes," Elm replied, kissing the top of her head.

Alice took a deep breath. "What about me? Would it take me?"

Elm was silent for a long time. "Yes. It would."

Alice's pulse quickened. "I could be like you?" She felt Elm nod.

She pushed herself up so she could see Elm's face. "Is...is that something you would want?"

Time stopped as she waited for an answer. Elm stared back, sadness in her eyes. "Of course," she sighed. "But it's not something I'd ever ask of you. You'd be giving up so much, Alice."

"I never thought I could," Alice murmured. "I never thought I could be like you. But if I can—"

Elm covered her lips with cool fingers. "Don't choose now. Think. Be sure."

Alice froze mid-step. Down the path to Elm's tree, she heard voices. Shouting. She broke into a run, slowing only when she came in sight of the clearing.

Elm stood in the center. Alice's father paced along the edge, right arm cutting through the air as he shouted. His face was flecked with salt-and-pepper stubble, his hair greasy and uncombed. Alice recognized the bloodshot squint he got when he'd been at the whiskey. He'd been drinking more and more since the day he had slapped her, since their conversations had been replaced by thick, toxic silence.

"You had no right, no right—"

Elm's reply was level and calm. "You don't own her, Douglas."

"I'm her father, goddammit. How could you, you...*slept* with her? *How could you?*" His voice broke on the last word.

"That's enough, Dad." Alice moved to stand next to Elm.

"Go back to the house, Alice. I don't want you coming out here anymore." But there was defeat in his voice, and none of them pretended he could enforce the edict.

"Dad, why are you angry, huh?" Alice demanded.

"Don't play dumb, Alice."

She stepped forward until they stood eye to eye. "No, really I want to know. Is it because she's a woman? Because she's also not *human*, so the fact that she's a woman should be the least of your problems."

He winced and looked away.

"Or is it because she used to be yours? Is that really what this is about?" Alice spat the words out, some corner of her mind recoiling from the scorn in her own voice; it was like a boil had been lanced, poison pouring out of her.

Rage flared in her father's eyes. "Shut up," he growled.

"Alice…" Elm cautioned.

Alice ignored her. "Well, I'm sorry, Dad, I really am, but you gave her up. You made that choice."

"Shut your fucking mouth."

"And maybe marrying Mom and having me was a big fucking mistake, but it's not my fault, or hers."

"*I said be quiet!*" His arm pulled back, fist closed this time, and Alice braced herself to be hit again. Then Elm was there, holding back his arm with one slender hand.

"No." Her voice stayed tranquil, but her eyes shone with danger. None of them moved for a few seconds; even the birds had gone silent. Then Alice's father let out a shuddering sigh and fell to his knees, sobbing.

Elm knelt and wrapped her arms around him, murmuring something too soft for Alice to hear. Alice started toward them, but Elm shook her head once. "It's okay, Alice. Give us some time."

Alice's mother was at the table when she came inside. She gazed out the kitchen window, absently tapping her fingers in a dull rhythm against the wood. A half empty glass, vodka tonic, Alice thought, sweated beads of moisture onto one of the frayed place mats. "He's out there again, isn't he?" she asked without looking at Alice.

Alice froze. "What?"

"He's out there. With her."

Almost against her will, Alice sank into a chair across from where her mother sat. "Yeah."

Her mother nodded and sipped her drink. "He doesn't know I know."

Alice stared down at her folded hands, red and callused as any workman's, crescents of black potting soil under ragged nails. "How did you find out?"

Her mother lifted her left shoulder in a careless shrug. "Followed him, simple as that. It was back before we were married. He was always taking these walks in the woods, and I started to wonder what he could be doing out here. So one day I visited and pretended to leave, and then I followed him to see where he went.

"I only saw her for a few seconds, just a little peek, before she spooked and disappeared. I don't think she realized I got a look at her. I did, though. Not much, but it was enough. That's the clearest memory of my whole life, seeing that thing out in the woods."

"Why didn't you ever say anything?"

She let out a tired sigh and shook her head. "I don't know, Alice. Didn't know how, I guess. After a while it felt like too much time had gone by to talk about it. Then he asked me to marry him, and I thought, well, maybe that doesn't matter anymore. Or maybe it didn't really happen. It's the kind of thing crazy people see, right? So I tried to forget it, but your grandparents left us this damned house and your father made us stay. Never went into the woods again, not once past the yard, but he had to stay right on the edge of it. Like he was just torturing himself. I never could decide if it was because he couldn't stand to go too far away or if it was to prove to himself that he could do it."

Alice followed her mother's gaze out the window, to that little patch of clipped grass leading up to the trees. "Did you know I was going to see her, too?"

"Yeah, I knew," she snapped. "I'm not stupid, Alice. But how was I gonna stop you? Your father kept us here right near her, like he fucking *meant* for it to happen."

"I love her, Mom."

Alice's mother turned away from the window for the first time since they began to speak. She studied her daughter's face in silence. "Of course," she snorted after a moment. "Jesus, that figures."

There was movement on the path leading out of the woods. Alice caught a glimpse of her father's red flannel shirt between the trees. He made his way into the yard slowly, almost dazed, stopping to stare at the flower beds as though he had never seen them before.

Alice's mother stood and watched him through the window. Picking up her drink, she moved around the table. "Alice, go spend the night in the woods. Your father and I need to talk." As she went to the kitchen door, she stopped to squeeze Alice's shoulder. Alice covered her mother's hand with her own for a few seconds; then the older woman swept out of the room and was gone.

"Hey, Alice."

She set down the potted grape vine she had been carrying and brushed the soil off her hands. "Hi, Davey."

His eyes scanned the nursery. "This is a good job for you. Working with the plants." He had grown into a tall, broad shouldered young man with only traces of baby fat remaining in his cheeks. Alice remembered sophomore year, when many of the other girls at the school had started paying attention to him. She had thought then that he would forget about her. But, while she knew he had dated some of the other girls, she still caught him staring. He still had that nervous grin when they spoke.

"Ah, well, you know me," Alice said, keeping her voice light. "Ain't happy unless my hands are dirty."

Davey laughed a little too hard. "Yeah, I guess. Um, it's my mom's birthday, and my sister thought she'd like something for her garden, so…"

"Gotcha. Right this way."

After taking Alice's suggestion of a snapdragon and paying at the register, Davey lingered near the front counter. "So I was thinking," he began, "you want to go get some pizza later? For old times sake? Cause I'm going off to college soon, and I—"

"Sure, Davey," she interrupted, seeing that he would continue to ramble if she didn't stop him. "That'll be fun."

He gave her a relieved smile. "Great."

Elm

"I'll see you after work."

～

"So, if you don't mind me asking, why'd you take a year off before college?"

Alice chewed slowly, setting aside the remains of her pizza crust. "I guess I needed more time to figure out how my life is going to go."

"Isn't that what college is for?" Davey asked, just a hint of teasing in his voice.

"Maybe." She cleared her throat. "So, do you know what you'll major in?"

"I don't know. I was thinking engineering at first, and then maybe chemistry. My folks want me to go premed, but I don't know…"

As Davy spoke, Alice saw the choices before her. She saw the way the next few minutes, days, years could go if she wanted it. If she acted.

She could leave the pizza parlor with Davey, walk to his car, catch his eye, give him a kiss. Tell him she had always wanted him. She could go to college, to State with Davey; maybe start a semester behind, they'd graduate practically the same time. They'd stay close, and he'd finally be able to love her. And she might love him, in a way. Everything else would follow from there. Marriage, children, friends she'd yet to meet. She could travel, see the world. At the end of her life, she would look back and know she had seen more good than bad.

But always, she knew, there would be that hunger, that yearning to return to the forest. There would always be the danger that she would walk into the trees and never come back. She would, like her father, have to make that vow never to step into the woods again. She might have to go farther, move away, into the desert, some place like Arizona or New Mexico where she wouldn't be reminded of it every waking moment. And still, no matter where she went or how much time passed, her dreams would be full of Elm.

Sitting in the pizza parlor, a calm came over Alice. She smiled and nodded at something Davey had said, not knowing what it was. She knew that she had made her decision, but was in no hurry to put it in motion. Instead, she savored the details of her surroundings. The taste of red pepper. The slick linoleum under her fingertips. Davey's laugh.

Later, as they walked to his car, she said, "I had fun with you tonight, Davey. It was a good sendoff."

"Yeah, I thought so, too." He turned to face her, features alight with uncertain happiness.

Stepping forward, Alice took his face in her hands. "You're a good person, Davey. You're gonna have a good life. And I'm glad I knew you."

Standing up on tiptoes, she kissed his forehead. "Bye, Davey."

His brow furrowed in confusion, but she just turned and walked toward the edge of town.

"Wait, Alice, where are you going?" he called out as she moved away.

"Into the woods."

∽

The moon was full and clearly illuminated the path to Elm's tree. Alice didn't need it, of course, could navigate these woods in a thunderstorm at midnight. *Still,* she thought. *It's nice to have.*

She had brought nothing with her. Her only stop after leaving Davey had been to the house. She had thought to leave a note, something brief, but her father had been awake and sitting in the living room. They had stared at each other, not knowing what to say.

"I'm going to the woods. I won't be back," Alice had said at last.

"I know." Her father had gathered her in his arms then, holding her like he had when she was a child. "Be happy, Alice."

And, with that blessing, she left the house for the last time.

Elm stood and watched her approach from the center of the clearing. When she reached her lover, Alice stopped and undressed. Not brazenly, as she did for sex, but with slow and deliberate care. She folded her clothes, knelt, and dug a hole in the loamy soil. Even as Alice buried her clothes and shoes, Elm watched without a word.

When Alice stood, she saw tears in Elm's eyes.

Elm

Elm took Alice's hand and led her to a tree on the other side of the clearing, in sight of her own nest. "I'm going to leave you here now," Elm murmured. "But you won't be alone. I'll be here, I'll be with you."

Alice kissed her lightly on the lips. "I know. I'm ready."

She watched Elm make her way back to her own tree, climb, and vanish into the nest. Then Alice turned to face her own.

It was smaller than Elm's tree, but of the same species. The branches were broad and strong, the leaves lush. It would make a good home. Alice stepped forward and rested her palms against the bark.

For a moment, the tree remained motionless. Alice made herself still, willed her heartbeat to slow. There was a cracking sound, and the tree began to open. The opening wasn't ugly and splintered, like a wound; it looked like a natural hollow, worn by time. Alice knew it was supposed to be there, and that it was for her. Taking one last human breath, she stepped inside and let it close around her.

Winter Scheming

Brit Mandelo

On her way out of the coffee shop, Harvey flashed a last flirtatious grin at the blonde barista behind the counter. The girl lifted her hand in a wave, smiling, before the door shut between them. A surge of warmth rolled down to Harvey's toes. Being out of her apartment made such a difference; it was as if she'd come back to life. She trotted down the steps into the sunny winter's day, and as she lifted the cup to her mouth, she noticed a scrap of paper tucked into its cardboard sleeve.

She plucked free the wrinkled bit of receipt tape. The word *Lucinda* stared up at her in smudged blue ink, followed by a phone number. Harvey glanced up through the window and caught another glance of the barista's lustrous hair.

"Lucinda," she murmured. The syllables were sweet and slippery on her tongue.

The warmth returned, and it had nothing to do with the sip of rich coffee she took to soothe her prickling nerves. She hadn't gone out with the intention of finding a date but she couldn't ignore such a pretty girl. It had been months since—the summer. She tucked the paper into her back pocket with sweat-damp fingers. The daytime crowd milled by unaware.

They moved around and without her, like a stream around a boulder, rushing and noisy, a sudden immense pressure on every side. A sick chill washed over her; the ground tilted. She'd spent too long cooped up alone to deal with so many people all at once. She pressed her back against the wall of the building and lifted her gaze from the street. The sky was crisp, bright blue with wispy clouds, soothing and simple. The vertigo faded by degrees, but then a flash of color, gold-brown like wet blonde hair, swirled at the corner of her eye. Her breath hurtled to a stop in her chest. She turned sharply, slopping hot coffee over her sleeve.

It was a tawny owl, balanced on a street lamp down the block. The bird shifted, piercing gold eyes catching hers, and with one great flap took to the air.

Harvey found herself gasping, doubled over with a hand to her throat. The puckered ridge of a small, fresh scar under her fingers was a visceral reminder. Those cuts had hurt, had taken a long time to heal. *Wet hair like tearing silk, the taste of copper, a skull-thumping pulse, the burn of nails scoring down her cheek and neck as she shrugged away fighting hands.*

After another moment spent breathing while the attack ebbed, she forced her spine straight and shook herself. The owl was gone. The other people on the sidewalk were giving her a wider berth, glancing at her from the corners of their eyes. Her face burned. Clearly, she needed to fill her head with someone new, someone beautiful, and stop letting something as simple as a bird raise memories better left

Winter Scheming

buried. She needed—no, she deserved—a fresh start. She would be better.

∽

Harvey nuzzled at the pale, soft skin of Lucinda's lower stomach. Her hands mapped the other woman's legs from muscled calf to rounded hip, thumbs tracing the edge of lacey underwear. Her pulse thundered in her ears. Thrills hot and sharp bolted through her each time Lucinda allowed herself be maneuvered, pulled into position, tugged and scratched. The blonde met each rough-tender touch with a gasp of something like surprise. Leah had been that way, tractable and sweet, but she had also known how to push the wrong buttons at exactly the wrong time. Harvey stripped the red panties off and bent to her task, delighting in the way Lucinda's fingers combed through her short hair. It had been too long. She should have gone out before, once the scratches had healed, instead of waiting. She *deserved* to try again.

"Oh, *Harvey*," Lucinda said, which was flattering. Then, she tugged on Harvey's hair. "Look!"

She glanced up and froze. The tawny owl sat preening itself in the winter-bare tree outside her window, gold eyes watching them.

"Isn't it majestic?" Lucinda murmured.

"Right, majestic," Harvey said.

The owl's stare bored into her. It rustled its wings and made a soft hooting call. The discordant sound scraped up her nerves like cold, serrated claws. Once was a coincidence. Twice, like this, twice—

She took the bottom of the curtain in her fist and jerked it closed so hard that the bar rattled in protest. Lucinda raised a curious eyebrow but made no comment. She reclined on her back, hands out to gather Harvey to her body, and didn't protest the sting of Harvey's nails if her hands were rougher.

Afterwards, her pale skin mottled with marks, Lucinda rose and dressed. Her expression was tight around the edges, but when Harvey moved to climb off the bed, she pressed her down again with a soft kiss. Her lips were like silk. Harvey brushed a hand over her clothed hip, smiling. The tension left Lucinda's face.

"I'll let myself out. I promise I'll call," she said.

Harvey watched her go with held breath. The moment Lucinda's heel disappeared past the doorframe, she let out a sigh. A moment later, the front door creaked open—its hinges needed to be taken care of—and then closed with a sharp click. Harvey lay alone in her bed. Her skin crawled. She wasn't satisfied, though by all rights, she should have been. She unclenched fists she'd made without realizing it and slid off the bed, heading for the shower. Standing under the spray and feeling the water on her fingers, it was hard not to remember. Damp hair wrapped hard in her fist, tender flesh under her fingers. The way it had *felt*.

"I'm not a violent person," she whispered to herself, bracing palms on the cool damp tile. "I'm not."

∽

"I can't believe you did this to your beautiful hair," Harvey said, plucking hard at one of Lucinda's dreadlocks. The other woman flinched and leaned away from her on the couch. "What was wrong with it before? I liked it."

"I'm sorry," she said. "I didn't think to ask."

"It's fine," Harvey made herself say.

A couple of weeks wasn't such a long time, she thought. People didn't adapt to a partner so quickly, didn't think to ask a new girlfriend's opinions. It wasn't something to get mad about.

Except, she was. The anger settled on her like a heavy blanket, charged and electric. She plucked at one of the thick, waxy dreadlocks again. They were leaving marks on her couch. She bit her tongue.

"So," Lucinda said. "Have you seen that owl again? I thought I caught a glimpse of it the other day."

"Yes," she said.

The sound of her own voice, low and threatening, startled her a bit.

"Oh," Lucinda said. A brief silence settled.

Harvey had seen the owl more than once. At work, out doing her shopping, at the bar, at home, it appeared everywhere, watching her with glinting eyes and flexing its talons. That wasn't *natural*. For one

Winter Scheming

thing, she'd looked them up, and owls were nocturnal. It sure as shit shouldn't have been following her during the day.

And its color, the weight of its stare, the knowledge it seemed to have—

"Maybe it's your spirit-guide," Lucinda said.

"My *what*?"

Lucinda leaned away from her. "Why are you acting so weird? I went to this woman last summer, Anne. She runs a bird rehab a few hours out of the city. She told me all about them."

"Your new-age bullshit isn't going to help me with this goddamn bird," Harvey said. "It's bad luck, and it's not normal."

"I was just trying to help," Lucinda said. She rose from the couch. Her muscles were taut, shoulder lifted. She sucked her bottom lip under, looking down at Harvey. "I don't know what's wrong with you lately. You're being so harsh."

"Harsh?" Harvey echoed. The anger tilted into rage, filled with flecks of something like desire. She stood without intending to, loomed over the other woman. Her heart raced. "You want harsh, I can give you harsh."

She struck with her open palm, catching Lucinda across the face. The blow knocked her off balance; she stumbled against the coffee table with a cry, going down in a mess of limbs. Harvey tasted blood—she'd bitten her own lip. Her body trembled with pent-up need. Lucinda scrambled to her knees. Harvey grabbed a handful of her waxy, ugly hair and jerked. The dreadlocks slid through her fingers too easily. Lucinda screamed, a frightened bark of sound.

From outside, the shriek of an owl wailed like a siren, carrying under it something like an answering girl's shout. Harvey stopped in her tracks, chest heaving, and her nerveless fingers lost their grip. The fever of the moment went cold, doused.

Lucinda was crying.

Harvey collapsed onto her ass on the floor.

"I'm sorry," she said. "I didn't mean to. I didn't."

Lucinda stared at her, red-eyed, blood streaking her chin from a split lip. "I need to go," she whispered.

Harvey sat catching her breath as the other woman gingerly stood and wobbled out the door. The silence after it closed behind her was sharp and accusatory.

Her knuckles ached. She was shaking, her muscles liquid and weak. She covered her face. Now that the anger had abandoned her, nausea took its place. Lucinda hadn't been trying to push her buttons; she was no Leah. An apology was due, and she had to make it stick. She sat for a long time without moving, empty-headed, unable to force herself to stand.

After some while, she dragged herself to the bathroom and turned on the taps, eyes on the rippling, steaming water as the tub filled. Stripping was like undressing a doll's body, not her own. She choked back a sob, her eyes burning. The water stung when she lowered herself into it. Her toes turned bright red. She flipped the taps off and settled in. The hot water loosened her body, soothed her throbbing knuckles. She closed her eyes and floated. No ideas for how to make it right came to her, though she thought desperately. Instead, behind her eyelids, she saw the bright red blood on Lucinda's chin.

The problem was that she couldn't wash away how much she had *enjoyed* it, underneath the guilt, the sharp smack of skin under her hand both gratifying and fulfilling. That, if she was being truthful, frightened her, but she would just have to control herself better. Other people managed it every day.

༄

The next morning, after leaving a third profusely apologetic message on Lucinda's phone, she walked downstairs to find that the hood of her car was covered in deep gouges. Something had scratched away the paint viciously, leaving furrows that wouldn't be cheap to fix. A shiver worked its way down her spine and she glanced to the trees, but the owl wasn't there.

༄

"I don't want to see you anymore," Lucinda said. She stood with her hands on her hips, chin up, in the middle of Harvey's living room. "You scare me."

"But I thought you said you forgave me," Harvey said.

Winter Scheming

The other woman sighed and ran a hand over her dreadlocks. Her split lip was swollen. Harvey imagined the way it had felt when her knuckle struck just that spot.

"I forgive you, but that doesn't mean I'm going to date you," she said. "I came over to talk it out. I think you should get some help, Harvey. You're not—well."

"I bet you're already fucking somebody else," she spat. She could just picture Lucinda and those flirty glances she always seemed to give, handing out her number to another woman. "My last girlfriend thought that was the way to go. You're just like her."

"Harvey, seriously," Lucinda said.

She picked up the paperweight from her coffee table and hurled it overhand. Lucinda ducked and the glass shattered against the far wall, but Harvey was already striding toward her before she could straighten. This time, her fist was closed. She landed an awkward blow on the side of Lucinda's head.

"Stop!" the blonde shouted, her hands out to ward off another punch.

Harvey tackled her to the floor and planted a knee on her stomach. Her breath was coming in gasps. Blonde dreads tangled in front of Lucinda's face, her blue eyes wild and wide. Harvey wrapped her hands around the pale column of her throat, the rush coming again, promising it would all be better if she just took care of the problem.

A heavy thud and a shrieking that stabbed at her ears like needles startled her so badly that her grip slipped. Lucinda jammed an arm between them to protect her face. Harvey cursed. Outside the porch door, the owl flapped madly about, clawing at the glass. She yowled back at it and flung herself off Lucinda, scrambling to the door. When she got her hands on that fucking bird…

"Jesus Christ," Lucinda gasped behind her while fumbling at the front door.

"No—" Harvey said, but she was already running, the door hanging open in her wake.

Harvey glared at the owl, torn briefly between who to chase, then turned to pursue Lucinda. She didn't know what she was going to do, but it had to be something, because she couldn't let Lucinda get away. Not with this. She bounded out the door. Her feet slipped on the deck, sliding on a patch of iced-over slush, and she grabbed for the railing to right herself.

"Bitch!" she yelled, taking the steps two at a time.

Lucinda ran at full speed across the parking lot. Her arms pinwheeled as she fought to keep her balance on the snow and ice that no one had bothered to salt, but she didn't fall.

Harvey might have caught up to her, but after barely a stride, fire ripped through her scalp. She yelped, frozen by the pain, her hands flying up to touch the source. Blood slicked her fingers. She whirled and dove to the ground to avoid the owl's talons as it swooped at her, beak open, eyes ablaze with gold light. The cold concrete stung her hands and forearms. She scrambled to regain her footing, looking over her shoulder as the owl circled above her. Caught between letting Lucinda get away and the blades of those talons, Harvey retreated. The owl caught her once more on the steps as she fled, its claws sinking into the meat of her shoulder. She flung her arm back, battering at the soft, feathered body. With the contact came a flash of its hunger, alien and huge. The talons tore free with a rip of fabric and flesh. The owl tumbled onto the steps behind her, disoriented.

"Leah," she gasped.

The bird was beginning to right itself from her blow when she slammed the door between it and her. Blood spattered the floor. The pain was overwhelming, but worse was her failure. How had she thought she could handle a new start? She hadn't taken care of the fallout from her last girlfriend. Outside the glass balcony door, the owl was preening in the tree again, its feathers red with Harvey's blood. She fled into the bathroom where it couldn't see her.

Lucinda had said the woman's name was Anne, and she ran a bird rehab. She couldn't be hard to find. Then, it would all be over.

Wind chimes strung out of bones and thick grey twine clattered together as the wind rose in a sharp gust. The cold stung Harvey's chapped ears and the back of her neck around the high woolen collar

Winter Scheming

of her coat. She stood at the bottom of a porch between two snowdrifts that had blown up against the concrete steps. The hand-painted sign tacked onto the railing read "Wild Bird Rehabilitation." She spied the skull of some small animal, a rat or a vole, woven into the weather-bleached bones twisting above her head. The night Lucinda had run away, a storm had blown into the city and dumped slushy, freezing snow everywhere. The roads hadn't been cleared for two nerve-wracking days, and she'd spent them waiting for the police to come knocking on her door or for the owl to find its way inside, somehow. The snow had started again halfway through her drive, but she didn't turn back.

In the pockets of her greatcoat, her fingers clenched spasmodically—one hand around a leather-backed notebook, the other, her car keys. The metal edges dug in hard, chasing away the shudder threatening at the base of her spine. It was the wind that drove her up the steps more than courage. The razor edges of each gust felt paradoxically like boiling water dumped over her cold-scored bare skin. Her hand shook and fought her attempt to make a fist when she drew it out of her pocket to knock on the wooden door. The sound was anemic, fluttery. Waiting on the porch with only the dead-animal wind chimes for company made each moment stretch. Harvey stared down the winding country driveway. Her car was a green speck on the side of the route that had been plowed just enough for her to rumble down it. All the way up to the steps, her footprints punched through the pristine half a foot of snow.

It was solitary. The expanse of ice-crystallized woods and bare fields spurred an instinct in her to draw her shoulders up around her ears and hide. Anything could see her here, dark coat a smudge against blinding snow, especially if it were flying overhead with a hunting eye turned to the ground. She huddled close to the door to wait.

The door opened with a crack of breaking ice. She jumped, boots slipping on the slick porch, caught her balance and gasped. The woman in the doorway raised an eyebrow. Her hair was red-gold streaked with grey, bound in a ponytail that left her face stark and plain. She was in her late forties. Harvey cleared her throat.

"Hello," she said. It sounded awkward. She clenched her jaw against an oncoming shiver, cold to her bones. "I'm—"

"Why don't you come inside," the woman said, glancing down the drive to her car. "That's a long walk, and you're not dressed for it."

When the woman stepped to the side, she shook her boots free of snow and walked into the house. The foyer wasn't much warmer than the outside, but as she unbuttoned her coat and looked around, she saw the promising glow of a fire to the right of the entryway. She snagged her notebook out of the coat pocket before hanging it on one of the empty pegs running along the small hallway.

"I'm Anne," the woman said. She offered her hand. Harvey shook it, her stiff fingers clumsy. "What made you think today was a great day to visit the bird rehab?"

"There's only an inch or two of snow in the city," she answered. "It started coming down again while I drove. I didn't expect it to get so bad, and I was already an hour out, so I kept going."

Anne frowned, the smallest wrinkle appearing by her mouth. Harvey read disapproval in it. They stood in the space between the house and the outside, hovering, as if the other woman couldn't quite decide what to do with her. She looked around. The living room had couches with fuzzy throws spread over them, a low fire and scattered books. To the left was a dining area and heavy oak table scattered with papers.

"Tea, coffee?" Anne offered, taking one step away and turning on her heel. "You can have a seat on the couch and warm up."

"Tea, thank you," Harvey murmured.

The couch was deliciously warm and she closed her eyes for a moment, letting the heat soak through her thin sweater and jeans. She really had dressed wrong—city girl at heart, city girl in practice. Her fingers were so pale they seemed to be turning a little blue. She dropped her notebook on her lap and rubbed them together. The friction stung in the best way. As she sat alone in the living room, she noticed piece by piece that despite its inhabited appearance it was impersonal. The books were all on birds or nature, the throws were clean and artfully placed, not so much for personal use. Of course, it was a sort of business here, not just a woman's house. The owl on the cover of one of the magazines on the end-table had the same ear-tufts as the one she'd come to think of as the Omen Owl, the Bad Luck Owl. She swallowed. The picture didn't capture the rest of her bird, though—it didn't have those piercing, intent eyes. In it, she could see the majesty Lucinda had so insisted on. The thought of the other woman made her flinch.

"So, what brings you here without a bird?" Anne asked from behind her.

Harvey turned on the couch, one arm slung over the back, and saw her approaching with two steaming mugs of tea. She sat a careful distance away from Harvey and put their mugs on the coffee table. Her posture was a slouch, legs slightly apart, flannel shirt bunched up around her elbows and hanging low on her thighs. She was a broad person, taking up space with personality and body alike. Harvey reached out for the mug to warm her hands further and fumbled for her planned introduction, her ticket to speak, though now it seemed flimsy.

"I'm a journalist," she said. "I've heard about you from friends and I thought it would make a good piece for the human interest section."

"And you drove out from the city then hiked through a football field of snow, for that?"

Harvey glanced sidelong at her. "You're one of the only wild bird rehabs in the area."

"You don't seem like a birding type," Anne said.

"I'm not," she admitted. "But I needed the story."

"Why'd you come out here?" she repeated.

"I told you," she said.

"You lied," she countered.

The silence was as frosty as the weather outside. A gust rattled the windows. Harvey sipped the hot tea. Its bitter, astringent taste made her mouth pucker. No sugar, no honey, just sharp herbal flavor.

"Who told you to come?" Anne asked.

She wondered if she was imagining the softening in tone.

"A friend," she said finally.

"A friend who told you to go to the back-country wise woman," she murmured. "Not a friend who told you to write a story about the fucking bird rehab."

The profanity drew a surprised twitch from her. She put the tea down. Her hands were too warm now; they still shook, but she had no excuse.

"Okay," she said. "All right, yes."

"What was the friend's name?"

"Lucy," she said. "Lucinda. She said you do—traditional things."

"Probably one of the ten or twenty fresh young things I see every year that want a spirit journey or a self-help guru," Anne said. She leaned toward Harvey on the couch, spreading an arm across the back. Her forearms were thick with muscle. "I walk them out to the woods and give them some things to think about. They coo over the birds, think they see an omen, and I get a hundred bucks to run my rehab."

"So I'm an idiot," Harvey said.

"I didn't say I couldn't help."

Harvey weighed her with a stare, the strong hands and easy posture, wearing her body like a comfortable glove. She had a good jaw. She found not a trace of mockery in the woman's face, though she'd expected it.

"I have a problem with an owl," she said.

"I don't do extermination," Anne replied.

"Not that kind of problem. Not that kind of owl," she corrected with a choking laugh. She knew she sounded like a lunatic, out of control of herself with fear and suspicion. "It won't leave me alone."

"An owl," the older woman annunciated carefully. "Won't leave you alone?"

"I'm sure it's here somewhere," she said. "It's been following me for a month. Same bird, day and night, when I'm at work or home or the grocery—"

Winter Scheming

Her own escalating voice stopped her, halfway to a shriek, and she gripped the knobs of her knees hard enough to bruise. Her breath was suddenly stuttering and heavy. She swallowed, reached for her tea and took one more bitter sip.

"What do you think it is?" Anne asked.

"I don't care," she said.

"You don't believe in any of what I'm about to say, I'm assuming," the older woman said.

"I want it gone, and I'm out of explanations," she replied.

Anne stood and walked to the windows. The wind rocketed against the glass, trails of white drifting down from the sky. The clouds were black and blue. Harvey's car would be buried again, soon, judging by the weight of the falling flakes and their speed. She fought the urge to flee; she needed to know what was happening. It was unnatural. It made no sense. If she wanted it fixed, she had to stand her ground, and she held onto that thought.

"It's starting to really come down," Anne said. "You'll be stuck here."

"I can go now," she said quietly.

"I have a guest room by the aviary," the other woman said.

"Aviary?"

"Not all of the birds I take in can be released again. I keep the ones that survive," she said. "I'll show you."

Harvey wanted to protest—she'd had enough of birds for an entire damned lifetime—but there was a coolness in the older woman's eyes. If she were too irritated, she could throw her out into the approaching blizzard, Bad Luck Owl still trailing her with its accusing yellow stare. Harvey stood, knees creaking, and followed Anne down the hall of the sprawling ranch-style house. She glimpsed a kitchen as they passed it and then she heard the first soft rustles of sound.

Dread crept up her spine like a spider with blade-tipped legs. A strange woman's house, a blizzard, a room full of birds, her owl out there somewhere hunting her—unease was a gentle word for what she was starting to feel. Anne opened one door and Harvey was surprised to see a screen door on the inside of the house, leading to a huge room that must have once been divided by a wall. It had small trees, perches, nesting materials, toys, everything she'd ever seen in a bird cage but quadrupled.

Inside there were owls hidden in trees, a leg pulled up here and there in their rest. Their sleepy stares made her skin itch. Anne slipped in, closing the screen door firmly between them, and the nearest bird, a crow, let out a welcoming caw.

Harvey shook her head. Crows, owls, a pigeon in the corner—these were not animals who coexisted. They couldn't. She knew that. So how were they, here? Anne murmured to the crow, her red-and-grey hair glinting under the domed safe-lights. Her voice sounded like nothing Harvey had ever heard before.

The woman looked up and caught her staring. The return glance was more of a glare. After a moment, Anne slipped back into the hall and closed the door. The bedroom on the other side of the hall was empty and pristine except for a daybed and a desk. She gestured to it.

"That'll be yours. Don't touch the door to the aviary. They aren't fond of strangers," she said.

"All right," Harvey agreed.

"I want to talk to you about your owl," she said.

The tone was less than welcoming. Harvey wondered why anyone would ever come to this woman for advice. She was too sharp, too rude, too unreadable. Maybe her usual "students" liked the mysterious and aloof bullshit, but Harvey was losing her sanity by inches, and she needed real concrete help. The seething frustration that sprung up in her chest soothed her with its familiar tension.

"I can go," she said. "I'll find someone else."

"That owl isn't a bird," Anne said. She gestured for Harvey to sit on the couch again. She did, mollified. "Real birds can't do what you're saying it's done. They don't care. They want to eat, mate, and have comfortable places to rest. They don't follow people. Not even pet birds do that."

"So am I hallucinating?" she asked.

"Has anyone else seen it?" Anne countered.

Winter Scheming

"Yes," she said.

"Then no," she answered with an edge. "Who did you piss off recently? Who passed on still angry at you?"

The question stopped her breath in her throat like a stone. She coughed, again and again, then cleared her throat with a rasping noise.

"You're saying it's a ghost?"

"You don't believe in the spirit, do you," Anne said.

"No," she answered. "Electrical impulses, yes. Souls, no."

"Then explain your owl," she said.

Harvey wound her fingers together and squeezed until her knuckles turned white and sparked pain up her arms. She knew the brown of its feathers, the dappled golden brown of honey, of a girl's hair wrapped in her fists and streaked with bright, wet color.

"What does it want?" she asked.

"To hazard a guess—you," Anne said.

Harvey jerked, looking up. Anne was already turning away to clear the mugs from the table. She bit back the urge to say *no shit* and took a calming breath. The blizzard outside was howling now, sheets of snow pounding down onto the ground. It wasn't letting up, and she was trapped.

"I knew that," she said. "What can I do to make it go away?"

"Remember what you did to make it angry, and make up for that."

She snapped her mouth shut and ground her teeth. "I can't talk to a bird."

"Have you tried?" she asked.

The conversation ended there because the older woman left the room, wandering down the hall. Harvey heard a door open and close. She wondered if Anne had gone to her aviary to be with her impossible menagerie. She clenched and unclenched her fists.

The house creaked with the pressure of the storm. Harvey sat on the couch until the fire went out, fiddling with her cell phone and drawing in her notebook, nonsense swirls. Anne Caulfield was a liar and a terrible hostess. She hadn't come back to talk, hadn't offered any food or even shown her where the bathroom was, though she'd found it on her own. She heard a door slam once, maybe to the yard and woods out back.

The dread-spiders had come back with relatives and associates. Her whole body was one knot, waiting for something to happen, but nothing quite did. The stone in her throat had migrated to her belly. *Someone you've wronged,* her mind kept repeating sibilantly. Then came the flash of memory, the brown and gold and red, a wet nasal cry echoing in her ears and chaotic struggling flesh under her fingers, curved to grip and squeeze.

The house was wrong. It was all wrong. The isolation, the storm, the birds cooing and rustling down the hall as if gossiping; all of the pressures lumped into one thing: trap. She had been trapped. The certainty of it locked her to the couch, her eyes longingly tracing the vague shapes of the outside in the dark. There must be a foot of snow. She would die of hypothermia out there.

True dark came like a blanket draped over the world. The door in the kitchen banged again. Harvey twisted to see Anne come inside, brushing snow from her clothes and thumping around in huge rubber snow boots.

The woman's face was closed off, her red hair a frizzy damp halo. There was something fearsome in her eyes. Harvey reigned in her legs' urge to make for the front door and run until she couldn't run anymore. Her instincts would not stop shrieking at her to leave, to run, to hide. There would be no help from this quarter.

"It's late," Anne said. "I'm going to bed. They should plow the road in the morning and you'll be able to leave."

Harvey only nodded. The woman walked down the hall into the dark.

After a long, silent moment, Harvey made her way stiffly to the guest bedroom and closed the door, locking it for good measure. The sheets she slid between fully clothed were cold as ice and just as crisp, starched to sharpness. She kept her eyes open. The aviary across the hall made a thousand tiny inescapable sounds that grated on her ears. A sort of madness settled on her. Anne was up to something.

Winter Scheming

She knew it. The nature-loving bitch was plotting, scheming. But sitting up in bed, her hands fisted in the covers, the notion seemed insane. She lay back down and tried to settle. She was just stressed and angry and ready to lash out—those were not new things. Would she really attack a woman in her own home, her own bed, for a bad attitude? She buried her face in the cover and sighed.

There were footsteps in the hallway. She froze. They meandered past her door without stopping and her muscles slowly unkinked. She heard other sounds, scuffling and clinking like a refrigerator raid, late-night. That relaxed her. A door closed.

Against the odds, she had begun to drift to sleep when a strange noise pulled her up from her half-dreams. The lock to her door clicked open visibly in the twilight of the moon streaming through the windows and she sat up in a rush. The door swung open. The hall was dark but she saw the yellow eyes and let out a low moan, scrabbling off the bed and pressing her back to the wall.

The owl hooted at her and ruffled its wings from its perch on Anne Caulfield's arm. Her up-tilted face was that of a vengeful deity. Harvey fumbled for anything she could throw on the desk and came up empty, her hands bare and useless. Her heart raced to a thundering beat. An icy sweat prickled down her back.

"I suspected as much," the woman said.

The owl on her arm hooted again, blinking. Its heart-shaped face wasn't able to smile, but Harvey knew it was mocking her. It had to be. It shifted its monstrous talons carefully on Anne's arm.

"I wonder—" Anne said. "Did you come here because you knew it was time to pay the piper, or because you honestly didn't believe I would be able to talk to this beautiful girl and know what you did?"

"What?" Harvey sputtered through her fear.

"I didn't think you were that good a person," Anne sneered.

Words were shriveled hard things in Harvey's mouth, ashen in flavor. She had no excuses because there was a terrible knowledge in her captors' eyes, yellow and human brown.

"Leah," she pleaded.

The owl flew at her, talons first; she raised her hands in front of her face and screamed. The knife-edged claws ripped along her forearms, biting easily through cloth and flesh. Heavy wings buffeted her head as the owl screeched, its talons losing purchase as she collapsed to the floor. The sound of it rang in her ears. The owl landed next to her with a heavy thud, its head bobbing in anger, a low hiss coming from its break. It blinked rapidly. Harvey rolled onto her stomach and moved to stagger to her feet, panting, but her blood-wet hands slipped on the floor and she landed in a heap.

"Fair trade," Anne said.

Harvey caught a last glimpse of her lounging in the doorway with a smile on her face. Then, the owl was her whole vision, and the girl that was the owl with her bruised throat and the water of the lake still streaming from her hair. Harvey didn't say she was sorry. Feathers slid through her fingers like liquid as she pushed against the owl that was everywhere, the owl that was the world, the owl that was sinking now inside her chest like a second heart.

The morning was bright and shatteringly white with its coating of snow. Anne walked the bandaged, wobbly young woman to the door. Her eyes were golden-brown where they had been hazel. Her mouth formed soft cooing answers as easily as it did words. The owl-girl who had once been Harvey smiled beatifically at her and flung herself into a clumsy hug.

"You'll learn to wear the body soon," Anne murmured into the shell of her ear.

"Fair's fair," the owl-girl who was Leah murmured back. "How did you learn to speak to birds?"

"I know how to listen," she answered.

"Harvey was a bad listener," she said.

"I noticed."

"Did you know when she came, what she'd done to me?" the owl-girl asked.

"No," she said. "But I knew when I saw you in the trees. You're not my first hungry ghost."

Winter Scheming

"You're a nice woman," the new Leah said.

She fidgeted, smoothing fingers down her aching arms and playing with the thick bandages. This bare-fleshed body and its attendant pains—it had been so long it was nearly a new sensation. A thick silence settled between them. She looked up from under her eyelids, head bobbing low and birdlike for a brief moment.

"You can stay awhile if you need to adjust," Anne offered.

"All right," she said. Her smile was tentative and fresh. "Until we can clear her car—my car—out."

"I'll make tea."

The owl-girl tested her human hands by taking Anne's arm and drawing her into another embrace. The flannel was luxuriously soft under fingertips that felt as sensitive as a baby's. She let out a humming sound and the older woman hugged her back, the press of a hand on the back of her neck a warm caress. Her found-life was full to bursting with possibilities.

Reality Girl

RICHARD BOWES

1.

You want to know who I am and how I got here?

∽

Reality Girl is the name my mother gave me but Real's what I'm called. I'm fourteen and until one day a week or so back my ambition was making it to fifteen. What I want to tell starts that day.

Me and Dare—my girlfriend and partner—led our boys, Nice and Not, Hassid and Rock down to the river for this appointment I'd set up.

It could have been any October afternoon: hot orange light and the sun hanging over the smashed towers on the Jersey Shore. Like always, rumors ran of everything from a new plague to war between the Northeast Command and the Liberty Land militia.

But I could see planes coming in and taking off from Liberty Land Stronghold in Jersey like always. And along the waterfront little ferry boats took people on, unloaded freight.

The world that day was the way I was used to: broken cement under bare feet, bad sunlight that'd take off your skin if you let it, the smell of rot and acid on the water. Mostly I was trying to get control of this thing inside me. I wasn't sure I owned it or it owned me.

Dare looked all ways, kept her hands inside her robes so no one knew what weapon she was holding, ignored the boy babble.

Hassid told Rock, "You look too much at who's watching you dive instead of on the gold."

"I gotta take this from a loser midget?"

"Listen to the lovers," Nice said.

Dare stood tall with that crest of hair like a web singer or some photo you see and know is of a hero. "Look tough," she told them and they formed a front as we moved down to the waterline.

Me, I just stared around, looked downtown where black Hudson tide water was over the banks and in the street. Anyone looking maybe would guess I was Dare's useless little girl trick. In truth I was seeing through her eyes which was part of the thing inside me.

When I was a little kid I had flashes where I was inside someone else's head for a second. It began to happen more often once my monthlies started. It scared me till I saw it as a weapon and tried to take control.

This summer was me and Dare's second together and we fit like a knife in a fist. At first she hated it when I began slipping into her brain and we fought. Then she saw what we could do with it and went along.

That day I saw what Dare could see: used-up diving boys with the skin coming off them in clumps and scavenger ladies with bags of garbage all turned towards us snarling. But Dare saw fear in their eyes, knew they were looking for ways to back off and gave them the chance.

Reality Girl

For what was left of the afternoon we owned that stretch of the shore. But even here some water spilled over the walls onto the walkway. And barefoot kids don't ever want to touch river water unless there's gold in the air.

Then Dare and me caught sight of a long ground car with tinted windows and double treads coming down the highway, dodging the holes, bouncing over the rubble. According to the deal I set up with Depose this was a party of tourists who wanted to see New York diving boys.

The car stopped, the doors opened and Depose's people jumped out of it holding their AK474s ready. One kept an eye on Dare and the rest of us—cradled the rapid-fire in her arms. Two covered the other directions, on the alert but not tense. One stayed at the wheel.

When Depose runs things there's no reason to worry. You don't cross her and you're okay unless she's been given the contract on you or she sees some reason her life would get better without you. In those cases you're dead. Simple, the way not much else is in this world.

Next the tourists in their protective suits and helmets got out of the car. A pile of wreckage juts out from the walkway and into the water. Security escorted them up there so they could see the show, then stood guard.

Dare and the boys looked up at them. Not said, "Aliens," and spat into the water but Dare signaled him to cool it. Not and Nice became partners that summer and Nice rubbed his back and whispered, something. They and Hassid, who's single and older than any of us—eighteen—stepped out of their shorts and moved right to the edge of the cement. Rock, our fourth boy, was new with us and not easy but he did the same.

Tourists get off on American kids staring up like starving dogs. Tourists want to see us bare ass and risking our lives. Dare and me hated them as much as Not did, but this was the cleanest way we'd come up with to get money out of them.

At first this bunch seemed the usual: half a dozen figures with white insulated helmets to keep the sun off their faces, conditioned coveralls to make them comfortable, shields to protect their eyes and masks so they breathed clean air.

Under all that protection you can't even tell what sex they are. They could be alien conquerors built like insects, soft and lovely ladies in silk from China where everyone is rich, kings and queens from Fairyland. You hear stories of creatures like those coming to see how New York got laid low. I maybe could have gone into their brains but I didn't want to give away that secret until I really knew what I was doing.

Then the tourists shifted and one who'd been hidden by the others stepped out front and showed me something very different.

This one didn't wear coveralls, helmet or mask and was female with copper skin and hair not far from mine. She wore goggles and took breaths out of a tube she carried while someone held a metal shade above her.

She looked familiar as I saw her through Dare's eyes and I felt my partner's surprise at how much the tourist girl looked like me.

This one was the center of the group's attention and concern. They clustered around like they'd stop bullets for her. Because of the goggles I couldn't see her eyes but I could tell she was staring my way.

Looking back, maybe I kept my talent too much a secret. If I'd gone inside a couple more heads we'd have been spared a lot of grief. As it was when Rock turned to look my way Dare said, "Eyes front," under her breath because we didn't want me drawing attention.

Dare checked the boys one last time, made sure their skin was intact and that they had the safety lenses in their eyes before they hit the water. She took some extra care with Rock. Dare was a diver herself before she hooked up with me. She got out of it in time but she remembers.

If no one managed divers, Tourists would make them compete so they drove each other to death. With murder and the diseases they get and being drafted to serve in the militias, boys are scarce and talented ones like ours are rare. Dare and I kept the ones we had healthy.

Reality Girl

Then sunlight flashed as a tourist's hand came out of a pouch. Dare, calm and steady, nodded to the boys to stand right on the edge of the busted pavement in the spaces where there are no rails.

The hand went up, snapped the gold coin into the air where it turned over as it fell toward the water a bit too far away for a boy to make an easy catch.

Dare had tapped Nice and he dived forward in an arc, snapped it up as he hit the water. Nice flipped over and swam back and the tourists applauded, laughed. Nice was back up on the pavement with Dare taking the gold out of his mouth as the next coin sailed up in the air.

This was further away and thrown harder but Hassid kept his eyes on it as he dived and was a yard away from where it went into the water. He came up with the coin and headed back as the next coin went further out and Not showing his skill and class went under and grabbed it.

The tourists applauded but this is how they always do it, throwing each one a little further away, watching kids risk skin and eyes in water full of everything from turds to nuclear waste, seeing if their nerve will fail, hoping for the thrill of seeing one go under and not come up. The girl on the block pile watched it all intently. It didn't seem possible anyone from my world could have the wealth and power she did.

Jackie Boy is the legend they've heard about. Jackie skimmed over the surface of the water and no matter how far or hard it got thrown, could catch tourist money in his teeth before either he or the gold hit the river. Maybe he wasn't human. I'd started wondering if I was.

The tourists that day didn't work the boys as hard as lots of them do. We got all the coins except for one that Rock missed. But it turned out all this was just a test.

One time that afternoon a plane, a fighter, flew low over the city and we flinched but the tourists paid no attention. This meant that it was nothing important.

Then maybe they got bored and started climbing down the rock pile. Right that second a chimera, the one called Silky who's half seal,

103

half woman and old like they all are, came out of the water a bit further upstream and caught their attention. Her skin is tough and she doesn't stay in long and maybe that or luck lets her survive.

Chimeras come from when things were falling apart but some people in the city still had money and tech and a big need to keep amused. There aren't any new chimeras; probably no one knows how to make them any more.

Tourist helmets flashed as they took pictures of Silky. I saw the girl look my way again and say something to one of the guys in protective gear who took a few pictures of me.

When tourists lose interest and city smells and poisons start getting in their masks they go back to the expensive air at hotels in the Security Zone. Seeing the lights from the Zone way uptown always twisted my stomach, made me want to do a lot more than spit in their direction.

We got the boys cleaned off. There's stuff the U.N. clinic in Times Square gives to people exposed to the river or harbor and we rubbed them down. We used expensive pure water to clean out their eyes and mouths.

All of a sudden Depose drove up. The girl said something to her before the tourist party got in the big ground car and took off. Depose, wide and mean, and her bodyguard stayed behind. Through Dare's eyes I saw her stride towards us. But I didn't look up until Depose went right past Dare without even nodding to her.

"Real," her voice is this low growl and she motioned for me to step away from the others, stood over me bearing down, sticking her face close to mine. "My clients are in the city to shoot a Net episode. I brought you out today so they could look at you and your fags. Mai Kin wants to use you!"

She watched through those heavy lids for a reaction. Depose went through girl and boyfriends like they were toilet paper but liked them a little older than me. Otherwise I'd want to stay away from her. I nodded that I understood, shrugged like it was no great matter.

But that was why the tourist girl looked familiar. Mai Kin was a rising star right then playing *Astasia X99*, a girl super heroine who's supposed to be around sixteen and who goes from place to place having adventures, fighting crime and vampires and it's so dumb that you can laugh at it.

Astasia has the power of disguise. She's totally different in each episode. The last time I saw her she was in a big city in Africa and she was dark with wild black hair, infiltrating a revolutionary group.

What I just saw I guessed, was the way she'd look here in New York. Pictures of Mai Kin before *Astasia X99* show an okay-looking Asian girl who's maybe twenty.

"The one called Caravaggio is going to direct this thing," Depose told me. "He'll get in touch. I trust you not to screw this up. Remember, Real, you owe me. You're smart. You don't need these dumb kids," she indicated Dare and the boys.

And I nodded, kept my face straight, my eyes right on hers.

Depose was a power—when the militia at Liberty Land needed something done in the city she was the one they hired. Somewhere down the line she'd want me working for her but I didn't want to get close and didn't want to have to find out what was inside her brain.

2.

In October the sun starts going down fast. We bought food and water at the Red Crescent kitchen before we headed back to our place, made a tight group with the boys on the outside and Dare and me and the gold in the center.

I told Dare what Depose told me and she said, "If that's Mai Kin, she tried to make herself look like you. Why did that happen?"

I shook my head because I didn't know. "If what Depose told me means anything there'll be money."

Dare said. "I don't want that bull to think she owns us."

Old people who remember twenty-five years back talk about how hot it is now but winter when it comes still kills if you can't stay warm. "We both felt cold a couple of nights ago," I said. "It's still okay in the days but that's what's coming. Things are jumpy lately and we may need lots of gold to survive."

Dare listened and said, "Okay, you're right," and I reached up and kissed her. Dumb girls have boyfriends smart girls have other girls. And smart girls and gay boys are natural allies.

The street we were walking on had a lot of burned houses and an old railroad overhead that had mostly fallen down. Eighth Avenue when we crossed it had people. An open market about ten blocks uptown was breaking up; people loaded carts and trucks. Downtown, a U.N. Peacekeepers armored car was crossing the avenue.

On the next block a bicycle boy whizzed past turned a hundred feet away and looked us over. Another bike boy was on the other side of the busted street, then a third and a fourth. All of them thin with faces like the vultures you see sometimes near the river. They knew us and that we were coming back with gold, they called us faggots and dykes.

But the Peacekeepers shoot people like them if they see they have guns and we'd handled these guys before. Our boys had their knives out, Dare had her hand on the jump pistol under her caftan, Not and Hassid yelled that the bike boys would starve soon. We never stopped moving and they kept circling but never closed.

Then because it felt like the right time, I looked one in the face and caught sight of us in his eyes, caught the way he saw us: we were gold, we were sex. Then he knew something was inside him and freaked, almost fell off his bike before he and the rest of them faded away.

My mother knew some stuff. When there were still parties, when there was the thought of getting close to the ones running things and running with them, my mother was on the job. But wherever I got this skill I didn't get it from her.

I never met my father but she told me he was someone who traveled in important circles. He must have been some kind of prospect because I think the reason she had me was to try and make him marry her.

People my mother's age were big on names. When there's no money people do things like that. Dare's mother named her only daughter Virginia Dare after the first European baby born in the U.S.A.. The

Reality Girl

Virginia part got discarded since anything you hear about Washington and Virginia sounds worse than here.

But she kept the Dare. It's an old word meaning tough which is what she is: tough and beautiful. "Real!" she said and I looked where she was looking. We were almost at our place. But on the next corner a building had fallen down last winter and blocked most of the street and on the wreckage were Regalia and her crew.

Regalia was a six-foot-tall queen with paint on her face and an ax in her hand. A couple of years ago she had this giant boy Call who followed her like a stray dog and her crew was it.

But Call was dead white and got too much sun which did him in. They say his face is partly gone and he's a skeleton. I haven't heard he's dead but I haven't seen him either.

In the last few weeks the city seemed to go desperate. For the second time in two blocks a gang wanted to take us off for a few gold coins. Again Dare took the lead and we came on like they weren't even there. Her blade was in her right hand and her left was under her robe. Two steps more and she'd have drawn the jump gun and put a slug in Regalia's stomach. I was reaching for Regalia's brain.

It would have been better if things had played out and we'd gone in and snuffed Regalia right then. Instead a truck with guys standing on the back and packing rifles came out of the twilight.

Regalia's people saw this and a couple started to back away. Then out of the cab jumped this bear-looking mean and huge in that light. One of Regalia's crew yelled and started to run, another followed him and Regalia went back howling at all of them.

Dare turned to face the bear but I already knew what this was about. Caravaggio always had chimeras around him. The bear pulled himself up and said, "I am Ursus. I have a message for Real." The voice was mostly human and hoarse and old. When I nodded he said, "Caravaggio wishes that you come with us."

Dare didn't take her eyes off the bear and the guards on the back of the truck. "It's okay," I said, "This is what Depose talked about."

Dare said, "I need to come with you."

"I'd like that too. But we need you to guard the money. To make sure our place is defended. To come get me if something goes wrong." I reached inside and showed her what we'd do together when I came back.

Finally she nodded and I climbed into the truck and headed downtown to Studio Caravaggio. I know about the studio and about him.

That name is some artist hero in the past. Lots of old people took big artist names. We still got Mozart in the streets playing the same tune every day on a busted clarinet.

The quarter moon was up so there was some light, people slipping through the shadows where there were buildings standing. We passed a convoy of cars full of tourists and guards. The driver moved the truck around the holes and piles of rubbish in the street. He slowed when a religious crowd from the projects carrying torches and saints' pictures and chanting crossed town on Fourteenth.

I saw Caravaggio when I was small and he drove by in a big car, had a grey beard and hair and dark eyes that stared out like a hunter's and someone told me he was looking for kids and if he liked you and brought you home you never worked or went hungry. Someone else said he took your soul first.

Years after that, they had this film festival and he showed a movie against the wall of a building at night. It was pieces of old past century movies with people crashing cars and blowing up buildings, making jokes as they broke glass, gunned down people and wrecked New York and dozens of other places just for their own amusement.

All the kids watching it screamed and threw things at the stupid grinning twelve foot tall guys and women, the destroyers who used up our city and our world. Caravaggio was there nodding approval at our anger.

3.

Studio Caravaggio is downtown on some blocks of old buildings still in good shape with generators and lights. Neighborhood guards with rifles stood on roofs and watched us come down the street. Their guns meant the Peacekeepers respected them like they did Depose.

Reality Girl

Ursus went to a big metal gate, reached through that to a brass knocker on an iron door. He slammed the knocker a few times and a spy slot opened. "I brought the Reality Girl."

The spy slot closed, the iron door opened, dim light spilled out and a feathered chimera in slippers appeared, unlocked the metal gate and stood aside. We entered this huge space like a warehouse with old, historic furniture, gold Chinese screens, long tables covered with lenses and tools. One wall was painted to look like a faraway city with tall buildings.

The chimera took me past rooms with lights from screens where people watched and worked. Others were dark with humans and chimeras lying on mattresses. Some watched us pass. At a work table a fox, a cat and a lizard chimera showed some human kids how to polish models of the old empire building and the statue of the lady that was in the harbor and stuff.

Those get sold to tourists and the metal they're made of is supposed to be from the original buildings and statues. And I guessed this studio was where they got made.

A guy was cleaning the floors and I smelled food cooking. From right then I wanted some of this for me and Dare and our crew.

From somewhere deep in Studio Caravaggio a voice, hoarse and kind of shaky said, "Visitors from the Orient encounter visitors from the future and fight it out in the ruins of New York while the natives dive for tourist gold is what it's about. Where did I get the story? My dear sir it's my life. I look out my window and it's what I see."

Ursus turned a corner and down a short hall bright light shone out a doorway. The bear stopped at the door and we both looked at Caravaggio.

Before when I saw him, he was old but strong and dangerous and needing to be respected.

Now he was in a white robe with stains on the front, holding a long glass of wine in a shaky hand. His face was thin and he slumped in a big, soft chair with a fan playing on him. What I thought was a boy in silk shorts held a bowl of something and a spoon like he'd been feeding him.

Caravaggio's eyes moved, focused on me and he said into a tiny disc in his open hand, "That's the scenario, Assad. As always I'm interested in financial backing. My health? I'm not going to die before I complete this, I promise you. But now I've got to talk to someone."

When the boy put down the bowl and took a plug-in from behind Caravaggio's ear, I saw he was maybe pushing thirty and I recognized him as Tagalong, who was on the street with a gang when I was small. He nodded to me.

"I've brought Reality Girl," said the chimera.

"Depose says you wanted to see me," I said.

Caravaggio said nothing, just stared at me through eyes that looked like he was crying but his face didn't move. Tagalong tried to feed him from the bowl. Caravaggio brushed it away. He drained the glass, picked up a bottle with both hands and drank out of it. Wine dribbled out the side of his mouth.

"My scouts talked about you," he said.

"You want to use my boys diving for the tourists?"

"The boys sure, but mostly it's you I'm interested in." He moved his hand over a glass surface then pointed at something behind me, wanting me to turn and look. I wasn't doing that, but I stepped back, kept him and Tagalong in my sight. Tagalong shook his head like he couldn't believe me.

What I saw was a flat screen. It took a second to know I was watching myself. First I was on the riverfront that summer with Dare and the boys. Then Dare and I walked through the early morning streets before the sun got bad and we kissed. Next we were at the U.N. clinic in Times Square getting ointments and medicine.

Don't get scared, get mad was Dare's motto and mine. "You and your freaks followed me!"

"If we meant you harm we could have done it many times," Caravaggio said. "I've been thinking of you, imagining you in a film. The tourists you saw today were impressed by these pictures and were impressed by you." Mai Kin's face popped up on the screen. "At my suggestion Mai Kin has been redone in your image." Seeing her again, she didn't look that much like me.

Reality Girl

Next I saw myself in the evening walking all alone down an empty Fifth Avenue. This was fake; none of us ever went anywhere alone. Caravaggio talked on the soundtrack.

"Once this was the most famous city in the most powerful nation in the world," he said. "Then the bombs fell, the earth quaked, the waters rose, the government collapsed. Around the world cities and nations fell but none fell further. Mighty Gotham is a ruin at a crossroads with local warlords like Liberty Land and the Northeast Command fighting for possession."

He touched the surface again and I disappeared. Color and faces exploded on the screen. A girl in leather smashed mirrors in some huge bathroom. Maybe it was a party, maybe it was a riot, but the camera spun around in an enormous space. A mob dressed better than anyone in the city is now poured fuel on chairs and set them on fire, smashed glass doors, shot out the lights high overhead.

"A fiesta of destruction made a ruin of Madison Square Garden," Caravaggio told me, "Caught for my first full length film. But places remain on this planet where people are still rich and bored. The films I've made have kept the eyes of that world on us and that's what I'm still doing."

The city opened before me. Buildings were down but ones I'd never seen before stood. The streets were full of people. Cars went by; I saw a bus! It was New York after the bombs but before the quakes. A girl in a silk dress walked arm in arm with a chimera gorilla.

"What did you bring me here for?" I asked.

"I want you in a film. I'll use you as Mai Kin's body double. She's more a prop than an actor. You'll stand in for her in certain scenes. But it will be more than that. They think to use me to film the New York sequences for an episode of that idiotic series.

"But I'm going to use *them* to tell the story of kids on the waterline. I want you and your crew. Anything can be faked but what's true will always stand revealed."

"I want a hundred gold pieces a day," I said because that's as much money as I've ever seen at once and because gold is the only thing everyone trusts. "I want the first day's pay up front," I said because that's what I know about doing business.

"I created the legend of Jackie the angel of divers." he said like he hadn't heard me. "Now I want to give the tourists a taste of the desperation of diver kids' lives."

I said, "What about the money."

"Once I dreamed of showing Jackie returning to the city like an avenging angel come to save the place," he said, "My new vision of the city will be you and your friends." Again his hand moved over a glass surface in front of him.

A boy in long hair and shorts stood on a pier in the full light of day. Big crowds of people watched as a coin was flung and the boy leaped, seemed to flicker like silver light in the gold sun. He skimmed over the water and caught the coin in his hand. It looked fake.

What got to me was how the riverfront wasn't all smashed up. The water was lower than the walks. New Jersey was wrecked but not totally. Boats sailed and people didn't look scared. I remembered some of that from when I was real little and got angry it was gone.

I wanted to see more but the screen went blank. I got careless and reached for Caravaggio wanting to see what he remembered. I touched his brain and saw a jumble of faces, heard a tourist talking about a hundred million yen deal, tasted the wine he had just drunk, caught the smell of Silken Night, a perfume he remembered.

Caravaggio looked startled and confused. He tried to stand and knocked over the wine bottle. Tag caught it, stared at me wide eyed like he had a hint of what just happened.

It was stupid to give myself away. But I just shrugged. Then I remembered what we'd been talking about before Caravaggio started showing me pictures.

"A hundred gold pieces, right now," I said. "And I'm not going in the water." I didn't say that even if I got as dumb as a boy, I couldn't swim.

"We'll talk about that," he said. "Fifty. Any more will get you and your friends killed." He was suspicious, maybe frightened after what he felt me do.

Reality Girl

We settled on seventy-five and he said shooting began in a few days. Tag counted the coins out for me in a little room near the front door of the Studio. He whispered, "I followed you around and took those shots of you and your crew. I got him interested." He looked at me curious and scared like he guessed my secret. I nodded and said nothing but now I knew Depose had nothing to do with my getting hired.

In that huge front room, an owl showed humans how to make posters of Jackie look old and how to tell tourists they had found them in old trunks. I knew that even the ones who said there had really been a Jackie Boy said Caravaggio kept him chained like a dog and only let him out to make movies until he escaped.

The bear and the truck waited for me outside. As we drove away I looked back: the lights, the guards, the street with people standing outside their buildings talking, little kids playing after dark, was magic and I wanted all of it.

Riding home I was cold and the only light ahead of us was the glow from the Tourist Zone way uptown, I thought about the city Caravaggio showed me and remembered how my Mom died when the superflu was killing everyone. The U.N. medics couldn't stop it. Some of them died. They told me I must have good genes and wanted to know who my father was but I couldn't help them.

It was then that I met Dare. Her mother was dead too so we had that in common and she was tough, took me under her wing, protected me until I got able to take care of myself. She had done gold diving but gave it up when she saw what happened to older kids. Together we worked out the deal with the boys.

The truck stopped in Madison Square which is semi-wrecked buildings around a park that's a jungle nobody wants to go near. We have a lair in the cellar of a building that still stands on the west side of the Square and has water and we've got the entrances booby trapped.

Lott, who's too sick to dive, guards the place night and day. We brought in Rock as his replacement. Ursus made the truck wait while

I rattled the gates and said the password and Lott let me in before they drove away.

The Indians at the clinic say Lott's got a few things wrong but it's lung cancer that's going to kill him. Dare thinks it's because we got him too late and if we'd been looking out for him sooner he'd be okay.

The boys were behind the curtains at the back of our place laughing about the way we'd stood down the bike boys and Regalia. I could hear Lott's heavy breathing.

Dare said, "I don't much trust this deal you have." I didn't either but it was the best deal we'd ever had. I wanted to show her the Studio but when I tried what I found in her was fear that she was going to lose me.

So instead I told her about Caravaggio and Tagalong and the studio, made it funny and had her laughing.

4.

Once we started shooting I spent more time any day in the deadly sun with less protection than I had all that summer. One morning I stood on a rusty fire escape ladder just above a flooded street with the tide coming in and waited for Caravaggio's signal. He and the camera crew were on the roof of the next building.

Three times I'd climbed four stories to the roof of this burned out factory building where *Astasia X99*'s boyfriend was being held by alien pirates. Each time something went wrong and I had to do it again.

Dare was angry at what I was doing but she tested the ladder herself and cleaned every rung before she'd let me go near it. After each take I got dowsed in purified water. The long T-shirt and shorts clung to me; my hair was wet and flat on my head.

All my life pimps, militias and gangs were on the prowl. A lot of any kid's life in this city is not getting noticed. Now I'd given that up to bring in money.

Reality Girl

Early that morning before the shoot we went up to the U.N. clinic in the big temporary building that's been standing ever since I can remember in the empty space people call Times Square.

Everyone in line was tense but nobody knew anything. Dare told the medicos what we needed. The Indian guy at the counter gave us double orders of salves, lotions, water purifier pills. "Just in case," he said but didn't know much either.

I was thinking about that when someone said, "Action!" Just like before I grabbed the handrails, held my breath, shut my eyes, ducked under the water, jumped out like I'd just swum there and ran up the ladder to the roof.

Caravaggio was slumped in a chair but he raised his head and said, "Great!" I knew what was great was me coming out of the poison muck. For my crew I was doing stuff I didn't know I could do. Up on the roof Dare led me behind a blanket in the shade, got my clothes off, doused me in clean water and oil and put me in a robe.

Mai Kin stood maybe thirty feet away under a metal awning surrounded by guys in protective gear. Her character, *Astasia X99*, gets made over and re-arranged in every installment. We watched a bunch of episodes. She has a boyfriend Anselm that she always has to rescue.

The actor who plays Anselm spent most of his time coming on to Rock. The other boys were jealous.

The episodes always take place in danger spots like New York. Mai Kin and company go in and shoot for a few days when it's quiet then get out and finish the thing somewhere safe. There's always some other guy Astasia gets involved with before going back to Anselm. But that would get shot somewhere else.

Fighter planes streaked over the city. Mai Kin glanced up then looked at one of her handlers. His head shake was so slight as to be invisible. Looking away, I went inside him; found he was getting news every couple of minutes. The U.N. had Liberty Land and Northeast Command negotiating. *Touch and go* was the thought on his mind. I got out before he noticed.

Mai Kin wore a silk robe decorated with pictures of the planets. Dare said that up close she looked old and mean and way over twenty. Mai Kin was wired like most tourists, spoke into an implant in her left hand, and shook her head at something she heard. She never spoke to me or smiled but never took her eyes off me.

I didn't have to get in her head to know that she hated me for looking like I did, for being alive in the same world she was. She slipped out of her robe and, wearing clothes identical to mine, walked to the spot where I'd come off the ladder onto the roof. Shooting her, Tagalong said, was like filming a robot.

When the light was gone and shooting stopped we headed home, moved fast in the moonlight. Rock had disappeared.

"Making it with that actor tourist—that whore," Not said. Dare was pissed but sorry to lose him.

Not far from our place there was on explosion up ahead. We'd heard enough of them to know this was small, a grenade, not a bomb. We sped up and I tried to scan, to find Lott and see through his eyes but I couldn't.

Turning the corner we saw our lair with the door and bars and locks all blown off. Smoke drifted out. "Lott!" Dare yelled.

Regalia came out the door with a couple of her crew. She had an AK474 knock-off. The Peacekeepers would have shot her for carrying it which meant they weren't around. She leveled it at us and said, "Drop whatever you got—weapons, money—and you won't get hurt."

Dare held our gold. She stared back at Regalia and didn't move. I went into Regalia's head. The first thing I saw was all of us standing, eyes wide staring at her. She thought that was funny because she was about to shoot us down one by one. For her the sight of Lott's bloody corpse was funny.

Her trigger finger twitched. I found her right arm and jerked the AK474 up. A burst went into the air.

She tried to get control of her hands. I yanked her to the side, fired a burst at her crew. One went down screaming; the other backed off. A couple more came out the door of our lair. I turned her their way, fired again, caught one in the face. Then the gun jammed.

Reality Girl

I found Regalia's heart and lungs, tried to tear them out of her body. Her eyes bulged. I moved her legs, ran her to the side of the building and made her smash her head against the wall until the brains came out. All the time she made strangled noises and danced like a headless bird. When life went out of her, I couldn't make the body move and she fell to the ground.

The rest of her crew had come out the door. Dare had her gun out, threatened to kill them. Hassid and Not slammed them around, took back the stuff they'd stolen. One that had been shot half crawled away. Another was dead. The boys stared at the bodies. Only Dare knew what I'd done. She made Regalia's crew drag their dead away with them.

We found Lott inside where the blast had killed him, wrapped his body in blankets and carried him into the park. We had a shovel and took turns digging it deep so the rats couldn't get him. We buried the AK474 in another place.

Dare talked a little about how much we loved him. All I could think was I didn't want to die like that. Even Dare was kind of afraid of me.

We huddled together in the lair, knowing we'd never stay there again. No one slept much but I sat awake on guard. Almost at dawn I started crying and Dare held me, whispering, "You saved all of us. You're a hero."

5.

The next morning Caravaggio was shooting on the waterfront. The crew and I were there because we had nowhere else to go. I looked for a chance to beg him for a place to stay. Our lair was gone. I felt older than Caravaggio, older than anyone. Rock had left us, Lott was dead and after what I saw and did the night before I half wished I was dead too.

Nice, Not and Hassid dived for fake coins tossed by actors dressed in protective gear. The boys' hearts weren't in it. We were zombies. They missed the coins and Caravaggio screamed at them, screamed at Dare and me.

Mai Kin and her handlers hadn't shown up. Caravaggio yelled at Tagalong who couldn't contact them. Everyone said the Peacekeepers weren't around. On the water, scared passengers were cramming onto the ferries. Copters and planes took off from Liberty Land.

This world of mine was tougher now than it ever had been. Tagalong got definite word that the U.N. had been withdrawn from the city. I said we had nowhere to live and asked him if we could stay at the Studio until we found a place. He just sighed and looked at Caravaggio who was yelling about traitors and ingrates.

I stood out on the seawall and Nice stood with me, rubbed my neck. I had my arm around him for comfort. We heard jets but didn't see them. Then over in New Jersey lights flashed like the sun on a knife blade. Next came explosions, big muffled ones. Caravaggio suddenly shut up. A moment later there was smoke over Liberty Land Stronghold, more flashes.

"Seems like Northeast Command took them out," someone said softly.

We should have been looking closer to us. I saw the ferries moving fast on the river, trying to scatter before I heard the copters. Rockets exploded. The seawall slid out from under my feet. Nice got torn away from me. I flew toward a huge wave and hit the water face first.

It was in my eyes and nose, drowning me. I reached out for Dare, caught other minds. I felt Nice get cut in two. Someone's legs were crushed. Water was in my mouth and nose. I sank into the filth of the river bottom. I wanted Dare to have her arms around me. Then I was rising, pulled by my hair.

My head broke the surface. Not far away flames floated on the water. People screamed. Dare hauled me up onto solid ground, pulled the clothes off me. Hassid was there. He washed me off and I let him. They put lotion on me.

Dare held me. She was crying. Nice was gone. They couldn't find his body. Only when I sat up did I see the gash on Dare's leg and knew what she risked to save me. She didn't make a sound when Hassid cleaned and bandaged her wound.

Reality Girl

As if he was far away I heard Caravaggio crying, "When I first came to the city, it was half wrecked but vibrant in its death dance." I caught images in his brain of destroyed streets with kids in costume dancing through them. A flickering figure flew into the air, caught a coin in his mouth, bounced off the water. Then there was nothing and I knew Caravaggio was dead.

We went to Tagalong who stood in tears as Caravaggio got lifted onto the truck. Dare and Not and Hassid were with me. Through his eyes, I saw how sad and ragged we were. Then I showed him what had happened to us and to Regalia and asked if we could stay at the Studio. Scared but impressed, he nodded.

6.

"He loved the chimeras," Tagalong said a little later when we brought Caravaggio's body home. More of them than I thought were still alive waited outside the Studio. Ursus was there and the bird woman who was in charge of the door, a pony and the cat and the man who was part fox, a cat woman, Silky the Seal, big dogs, a goat and the owl. I didn't even know what some of the others were. They howled and moaned when they saw the corpse.

They laid Caravaggio out in the big front room and dressed him like a king in silks and furs. Flowers appeared and candles lighted the place. A hundred and more people came from the neighborhood; a few even came from further away, risking the streets to see him one last time.

Some brought food. The people in the kitchen cooked more.

Tagalong gave the four of us a large enough room with futons on the floor. We piled them together lay on them, held each other and cried. Dare made plans to go next day and find Nice's body. I didn't want to think.

The chimeras were chanting when I heard engines outside. Tagalong appeared and told me Depose was there with cars full of her people and wanted to come in. I understood that he wanted me to do something and this was why I was here.

So I stood at a peep hole beside the door, watched Depose without her seeing me. "We need to confirm that Caravaggio is dead," she told the doorkeeper bird who looked scared. "Various of his associates and backers need to know. And we need to find that film he was making. I don't want to use force."

I didn't need to go inside her to know that she was going to use force and when she got in here this place would be looted. I looked back at Caravaggio laid out and the candles and the chimeras.

At the same time I found Depose and showed her what I was seeing. For a second she didn't understand what had happened. Then Depose realized who was doing this and remembered what she heard that morning about me and Regalia.

Still she hesitated so I showed her a moment of Regalia and the wall. Depose headed for her car fast and I let her know that if she wanted the film, she'd need to come alone and bring a lot of gold.

I felt shaky when it was over but I waited for the engine sounds to fade. As I went back to our room everyone in the Studio stood and applauded and I figured we'd won our place here.

We sat on a mattress and leaned against pillows. "Maybe you should have done her like Regalia," Dare whispered.

"Maybe," I told her. "But I didn't have all the anger and fear like I did with Regalia. And I can't kill everyone and Depose can be bought."

Dare understood and put one arm around me. She cuddled Not and I held Hassid.

That's how we were when Tagalong came in with a camera and two women who did stuff with lights. He said he wanted to film me talking about what happened. "We need a hero," he said. "We'll call this *real*. We need to advertise you." And I thought about Caravaggio and Jackie Boy.

Dare told him, "Her name's Reality Girl.

"Great!" Tagalong said and with the camera running he asked, "Reality Girl, can you tell us how you came to be here?"

What I remembered first was me and the crew walking down to the Waterline a week or maybe ten days ago.

Oracle Gretel

Julia Rios

Teeth:

Gretel was in love with her boss. Ms. L. Thorne spoke in short, clipped sentences, and when she smiled, which was rare, it looked like the curved edge of a wicked blade.

At night, at home, while she attempted yet again to bind her flyaway curls into something more elegant, Gretel told Hansel all about what Ms. L. Thorne had done that day, and what she had worn. Hansel twitched his ginger tail, insouciant as only siblings and house cats could be. "Oh not Missilethorn again," he said. "I hope you didn't let that creature distract you so much that you forgot my food."

"As if you need fattening," Gretel said. "A witch will eat you if you don't watch out."

"You're the only witch I know," was Hansel's rumbling reply.

"I am no witch," Gretel said, but she was too much in the dreamy stage to be properly annoyed. She scratched him under his chin, and opened the tab on the Fancy Feast. Hansel listened while he ate, or at least, if he wasn't listening, his mouth was too full to talk about other things.

Ms. L. Thorne was cool and smooth. She always wore business suits, and kept her hair coiled neatly instead of loose and free. She did not play by anyone's rules, but made her own and allowed others to obey them. She'd hired Gretel because in the interview Gretel had said she didn't like sweets.

"Good," said Ms. L. Thorne. "I don't want any of this office cupcake nonsense. I'm very particular about what I put in my mouth. Can you respect that?"

"Of course," said Gretel. She scribbled it in her dayplanner: "New job. No cupcakes." Ms. L. Thorne regarded this with a tilted head, haughty and swanlike, but not disapproving.

"You'll do," she said. Then she flashed one of those scimitar smiles, and in it Gretel saw the whole hopeless arc of her future with the company.

Rider-Waite:

When they were still children, such a long time ago, everything was supersaturated, thickly outlined, clear. The world was ruled by men, and women were cunning, relied on their charms. The infant mortality rate was high, and infancy lasted until puberty, usually eleven or twelve. Gretel was nine when the business with the witch happened. And with the stepmother. She ought to hate the stepmother, according to the dictates of the world, but she understood too well for hate. Children must do what they could to survive, and adults were just children in bigger skin.

Gretel had tried and tried to be good, scrubbing, fetching, carrying, eating only the barest of the bare. The burnt ends of the bread, and a few spoons of porridge. It didn't matter, though. It never matters when there is meat and bread enough for only two, and you are four, when your brother eats enough for three all on his own.

"Temperance," she cautioned, filling water jugs from the well, but Hansel didn't heed it. He chewed the flesh of a late autumn apple and dropped the core in the dirt, so Gretel couldn't even suck the last of the juice. He believed he'd grow into Strength, like their father, a lion of a woodcutter if ever there was one. But of course that lion was bested by a woman, harnessed with a chain of flowers. They never had a chance.

It was a relief when she sent them away. Gretel had wasted to nearly nothing by then, and she was emotionally wasted, too, from the knowing. Every night in the fire (there was never a lack of heat in the woodcutter's cottage), she saw the laughter of the gods, and the promise of danger and hard times to come. Harder even than the ones at hand.

To prove their use, the stepmother said, they must go forth and bring down a hart. Never mind the king, for how could he know? He never came this way. And if not a hart, a doe. Even a fawn would do. But food they must have, and they weren't to return without meat enough to equal their combined weight.

"We haven't arrows, Mother," said Hansel, and Gretel could hear by his wheedling tone that he actually thought it would sway her.

"Art not the son of a woodsman?" the stepmother asked. "Canst thou not *make* them with twigs all 'round?"

Hansel was not quick-witted enough to form a retort, and Gretel was too quick-witted by half, and so it was that they went out into the wild with naught but a loaf of bread. Easy enough for the stepmother to part with that when she knew they'd not trouble her more.

FAERIES:

The Faeries will tell you what they think you need to hear. Sometimes this is the truth. Sometimes it is what you want to hear. Sometimes it is a blatant lie. You will not know the difference until later, but then you will agree that what counsel they gave was the only thing you could have borne.

Gretel consulted the Faeries whenever she felt like consulting something. It was folly for an oracle to consult anything, of course. She couldn't help seeing, hearing, knowing things, whatever she did. But sometimes she could almost believe the lies.

"Will Ms. L. Thorne love me?" she asked the night after her first day of work.

Yes, the Faeries said. Ecstasy, marriage, warmth and sun. Go to work joyfully, for you will not be disappointed.

Gretel had seen already the knife-edged smile, but she paid it no mind. That night she gave herself over to fancy, as she knew she would for at least two weeks.

On the armrest next to Gretel, Hansel sighed contentedly. Food and love were bountiful when Gretel fell for someone. His cat brain could remember the shape of her buoyancy, and the association with treats. It did not yet connect them with the crash of withdrawal that lay over the curve of the scimitar blade.

Silver Shoes:

The one thing she'd kept as long as Hansel was a pair of silver shoes left to her by the true mother. They were chased filigree, and they never looked quite the same from one wear to the next. When she wore them, the road ahead was a thin gold line, pulling her where she needed to go. They never tarnished.

The true mother had been an oracle, too. Perhaps that was why she had left. Their father said she had died, and she may have died, or she may have gone over to wandering. If there was one thing Gretel understood, it was that oracles didn't stay in one place comfortably. Not for long.

In the forest, Gretel had carried the shoes in her kerchief, carefully bundled to look careless and messy so the stepmother wouldn't remark upon it. She didn't put them on until the bread was gone, half eaten by Hansel, and half by the birds. When it was cold, and dark, and they had no shelter, when Hansel's whining had passed over annoyance and into fear, then Gretel slipped them onto her small, dirty feet. They fit perfectly. They always fit perfectly. They never pinched or gave a blister, and they never fell off, either.

Gretel's stomach complained from the lack of food, and her head swam with dizziness, but the shoes pulled her forward, tripping through the darkness along that golden line. She held fast to Hansel's hand, refusing to lose him in the night. When the witch's house appeared, it was nearly dawn, and Gretel was too near the point of death to question such a miracle. She ate and ate from the shingled sides, until her tongue and gums bled from the roughness of sugary bread. When she retched, it smelled like Christmas.

She was too weak to protest when the witch came out and tucked them into the cage, but not too weak to notice that the witch couldn't loose the shoes from her feet.

Computer Games:
At work, Ms. L. Thorne gave her assignments over social networking games.

First it was Sim Farm. "Ms. L. Thorne has offered you a dozen eggs in exchange for a day of plowing," the notification said. "Personal message: I don't like eggs. Run the Cranville reports and settle the discrepancies with accounting."

Gretel did as she was told, efficiently, quickly, determined to show that she was also cool and smooth, and worthy of being loved. When her farm threatened to become more productive than Ms. L. Thorne's, the game changed.

Gemsplosion came next. "Ms. L. Thorne challenges you to beat her high score: three ruby explosions in one minute. Personal message: Arrange the quarterly meeting. No fattening food. Buy a better suit."

Gretel ordered sushi for the meeting's lunch, and personally oversaw the cleaning and setup of the conference space. At home she tore through her wardrobe, trying on every skirt and blazer and pair of slacks before she settled on going shopping after all.

Hansel watched this from the bed, wary of the giddy desperation that left pink spots in Gretel's cheeks. It reminded him of other times, of distraction and neglect, of being forced to sustain himself on dry food.

When Gretel achieved a diamond explosion, the game switched to Word Cross. "Ms. L. Thorne has played 'thistle' for 100 points." Gretel's available letters left her with only one viable option: "norns" for twenty-eight points. Missiles, thorns, thistles, norns. She did not wish to consider what this could mean. She was losing quite badly, but that was probably for the best. Ms. L. Thorne did not like to be beaten.

Once Gretel had had an Italian lover who was also no good at being beaten. In cards, in fights, in anything. He would roar like a bear, and send thugs to kill his opponents. Gretel always let him win. When the whole affair fell apart, when Gretel fled in the night in the silver shoes, with Hansel in her kerchief, she swore she would never do that again.

But, she told herself, Ms. L. Thorne was different. Of course she would be sensitive about winning. She was a woman in a world which was still tough on women, no matter how much times had changed.

The meeting went smoothly, though Ms. L. Thorne did not notice the new suit, which Gretel had spent a full paycheck to buy. Gretel resolved to try harder.

Eggs:

In the witch time, after Gretel had been let out of the cage, but before she had worked out how to escape, Gretel had learned about eggs. The witch showed her how to reach under a brooding hen without disturbing her, and how to tell what the day would bring based on the number inside each nest. One for sorrow, two for work, three for a decent breakfast.

The witch would let her eat as much as she wanted, but Gretel was careful not to overdo. One egg a day left her strong enough to work, but skinny enough not to get eaten. Hansel stayed in the cage, eating six or seven in a sitting, ignoring his sister's entreaties to abstain. Gretel had seen her escape in the clouds, and she knew when it came,

Oracle Gretel

there would be no boy at her side, but she tried to reason with him all the same.

There were a number of ways to prepare eggs, and each had its own divination method. "With hard-boiled eggs, it matters how they peel," said the witch. "You can learn everything in the world from cracked shells." She said the same thing about the color of raw yolks, and the curves of scrambles.

Gretel was beating whites for meringue one afternoon, content in the way that complacency can make one be. She had food, measurable tasks, and as much security as she had ever enjoyed, so she had not tried too hard to fight her circumstances. In fact, she had turned to dreaming of other things entirely.

"Will I find true love?" she asked the whites. If they stiffened before she counted to ten, she would. If they didn't, she wouldn't. She had reached five when the witch came in and placed her gnarled hand over Gretel's, stilling the whisk.

"You should never fall in love," the witch said. "Loving people never does anyone any good. You should do better to ask if you will always have food enough to eat."

Gretel thought that was stupid. In her short life to date, she had already seen that food was unreliable. Even having it didn't mean safety. Hansel was destined for the soup pot, after all.

Songs:

One thing Gretel had always loved was music: folk ballads and operas, waltzes and rock. So long as it had a melody, it made Gretel's heart swell. These days she didn't have to wait for concerts and dances, or carry the tunes in her head. Music was portable now. There were benefits to living in this modern age.

The problem with being an oracle, though, was that she couldn't escape the knowing. All Gretel wanted was a good thumping dance beat to propel her from her apartment to the bus stop, and on to her office. Unfortunately, her MP3 player refused to play anything but "Love Will Tear Us Apart."

The year was winding down. Word Cross had been the game of choice for three full weeks, because Gretel never won. She didn't even have to try to throw the games. The letters distributed themselves in the right patterns to make Gretel unlucky and Ms. L. Thorne very lucky indeed. On the morning of the holiday party, Gretel played "wife" for fourteen points, and Ms. L. Thorne played "never" for fifty-six.

That night Gretel wore a new dress, one that would sparkle under the lights on the dance floor. Hansel yawned when Gretel asked how she looked. "It won't work," he said. "She doesn't love you. Don't forget to feed me before you go."

Gretel gave him the shrimp flavored can of food because she knew he liked it least.

At the party, everyone got drunk. The company was paying for taxis to take them home. Gretel found herself leaning hazily against Ms. L. Thorne's bony shoulder. It was sharp enough almost to cut if her skin hadn't been in the way, but Gretel didn't mind. She thought it was sexy.

"Dear little Gretel. It's cute that you want me," said Ms. L. Thorne, "but I'm never going to be into you. I have all the power in this relationship. People fall for others with more perceived power, not less."

It was the most Ms. L. Thorne had ever said to Gretel at one time, and it rang horribly of truth. The song changed from "All I Want For Christmas Is You" to "Closing Time."

The party was over.

OUIJA:

A century earlier, Gretel had made her living as a medium. Sometimes when people knocked on wood for luck, she would remember the nights of table tapping, and producing lengths of silk "ectoplasm" from her mouth. It was a profitable trend, but she'd hated it. Her tongue had always been dry, and the only spirits who would talk to her were ones she'd rather have avoided.

"Is my dear Billy in Heaven?" a wartime mother asked one night. The planchette whooshed over the board.

Oracle Gretel

H.-V-N. S. L-V-N-G. Y.

"It says, 'Heaven is living, yes,'" said Gretel. But her voice trembled, because she knew it really meant *Heaven is loving you*, which was what her last admirer had said to win her affections. His abject adoration had rankled, and Gretel had been relieved when he'd succumbed to the Spanish influenza, though it made her a tiny bit guilty to admit it.

W-H-Y. D-N-T. Y. L-V. M.

"What does that mean?" asked the client.

Why don't you love me? Gretel thought, and it made her angry. She wasn't talking to him. He was gone, he should move on. This Billy obviously had. Why couldn't her ex-not-boyfriend do the same?

The client was staring expectantly. The room smelled too closely of incense and fevered hope. Gretel trained her eyes on the candle flame and willed herself to think fast.

"He says, 'Why don't you leave me?' He's moved on to better places. He wants you to be happy for him, and to move on also."

The client left happy, but the next night was more of the same, and the night after as well. Gretel grew ever more exasperated until one night, in the middle of a séance, she shouted, "Go beyond the veil, already!"

After that she stuck to secretarial work.

Sweets:

Gretel had learned to bake at the witch's house. She had learned how to make cakes come out just right to entice a young child. She had learned the secret to making gingerbread strong as wood, how to use sugar paste as glue, how to bind up a wish in the crust of a pie. She had learned all these things from the witch, and some other things too, from the stack of dusty books in the witch's pantry. The witch, it turned out, was not very good at aspects of witching that didn't revolve around food. As long as she was well fed, she didn't care, either.

Gretel studied the books whenever the witch was out. She paid special attention to the sections on transmogrification, learning how to change her brother into a cat so he could slip through the bars of his cage. The books didn't tell how to reverse the effect, but that turned out to be all right.

"What use is a cat to me?" the witch cried, upon finding Hansel sniffing about the kitchen. She didn't try anything violent, though, or even tell Hansel to leave. Rather, she seemed to like it when he curled up on her lap of an evening, for all she called him useless and lazy.

In the end, Gretel left with her blessing, which was nice of her to give, even if it wasn't worth as much as a fairy blessing would have been. "One day you'll make a fine witch," she told Gretel as she waved her goodbye. "If you ever stop worrying about this love nonsense, that is."

"I am no witch," Gretel said.

Lately, though, she tired of the roller coaster ups and downs of love affairs. She wearied of always losing at Word Cross, and of showing up to work with a horrible hope that would rise only to be dashed again. Ms. L. Thorne began flirting with Amanda in accounting. She was in line to become a senior VP, while Gretel was still an admin ass. As Gretel's hope faded, her bitterness grew, and she found herself craving sweets.

"This job isn't good for you," Hansel said. He was huffy because Gretel had been to the store for cookies, and forgotten to pick up canned food. "I thought you didn't like sweets." He glared at her as she chewed.

"I didn't before. I do now. A woman can change her mind."

"Any decent woman would remember to buy her poor brother a meal while she was at it," said Hansel. "It's not like I have thumbs, you know. You always forget me when you fall out of love."

Gretel stopped mid-bite. "You're right," she said. She left the half-eaten cookie for Hansel, and started emptying the kitchen cupboards.

"Cats aren't supposed to eat chocolate," called Hansel. "I could die."

"Then don't eat it," Gretel said.

But he did, and he didn't die, just sicked up on the bedroom floor. Gretel was too busy baking to notice.

Oracle Gretel

The next morning she packed everything into suitcases, Hansel included, and donned the silver shoes. She followed the golden line to Ms. L. Thorne's desk, and left a cake atop it, beautifully iced in calligraphy letters that spelled, "I QUIT!"

Ms. L. Thorne would not eat the cake, Gretel knew. It would annoy her, though, which was somewhat satisfying.

The shoes pulled her into another city, and stopped at an abandoned tearoom with a flat above it.

"What are we doing here?" Hansel asked.

"*I* am opening a bake shop," said Gretel. "*You* will stay out of the way."

It was a life of hard toil, but Gretel enjoyed it. She grew slightly plump, and her hair began to grey. She stopped worrying that anyone would try to eat her, or what they thought of her at all. She allowed the fishmonger (a boisterous woman whose laugh was as open as her heart) to court her with scraps for Hansel, surprising herself by developing a sincere and comfortable attachment. She was, for the first time in her very long life, happy.

When the girl showed up, she was skinny and sad, with large, imploring eyes. She came to the shop every afternoon in her school uniform to stare longingly at the cakes.

Gretel let it go on for a couple of weeks before she gave in. One afternoon she placed two jagged halves of a heart cookie on the counter. "Here. This one's broken anyway," she said.

The girl ate it hungrily, but Gretel could see remorse in the splay of her maidenly eyelashes. She feared eating a broken heart would doom her to having one.

"You should never worry about love," Gretel said, thinking of herself, and of Ms. L. Thorne, whose sharpness she still glimpsed from time to time in mirrors and razors. "That never does anyone any good."

The girl's eyes widened, impossibly becoming more round.

"Oh for pity's sake, you look like a cartoon," Gretel said. "Stay here a minute and watch the shop. I have to go get something."

When she came back, the girl was fidgeting, and shifting her slight weight from one foot to the other. Had Gretel ever looked so pathetic? She held out the silver shoes.

"Take these. They'll fit you. I don't need them anymore. They'll show you where to go."

"Oh, but I couldn't," the girl said. "They must be very expensive."

"I paid nothing for them," said Gretel.

The girl clasped her hands behind her back. "Aunt says never to take gifts from strangers."

Gretel sighed. "You took the cookie."

"That was different," said the girl, but the splay of her eyelashes said she was lying, and that she wouldn't be satisfied until she felt her debt was repaid.

"Fine," said Gretel. "You can work for them if you must. Come here after school tomorrow, and I'll have something for you to do."

That evening, upstairs, Hansel purred by the hearth, his belly full of fish.

"She thinks you might eat her," he said, smug as house cats and siblings are wont to be.

"She's a fool," said Gretel. "I don't eat children."

"She doesn't know that," said Hansel. "She only knows you're a witch."

Gretel pressed her lips together, but said nothing, for she knew he was right.

Otherwise

Nisi Shawl

"Let's cross it while it's still floating." Aim was always in a hurry these days. Nineteen, and she didn't figure she had a whole lot of time left before she'd go Otherwise.

"Hold up," I told her, and she listened. I listened, too, and I heard that weird noise again above the soft wind: an engine running. That was what cars sounded like; they used to fill the roads, back when I was only thirteen. Some of the older models still worked—the ones built without no chips.

A steady purr, like a big, fat cat—and there, I saw a glint moving far out on the bridge: sun on a hood or windshield. I raised my binoculars and confirmed it: a pickup truck, headed our way, east, coming towards us out of Seattle.

"What, Lo?" Aim asked.

If I could see them, maybe they could see us. "Come on. Bring the rolly; I'll help." We lifted our rolling suitcase together and I led us into the bushes crowding over the road's edge. Leaves and thorns slashed at our pant legs and sleeves and faces—I beat them away and found a kind of clear area in their middle. Maybe there used to be something, a concrete pad for trash cans or something there. Moss, black and dry from the summer, crunched as we walked over it. We lowered the suitcase, heavy with Aim's tools, and I was about to explain to her why we were hiding but by now that truck was loud and I could tell she heard it, too. All she said was, "What are they gonna think if they see our tracks disappear?"

I had a knife, and I kept it sharp. I pulled it out of the leather sheath I'd made. That was answer enough for Aim. She smiled—a nasty smile, but I loved it the way I loved everything about her: her smell; her long braids; her grimy, stubby nails.

I thought we'd lucked out when the truck barreled by fast—must have been going thirty miles an hour—but then it screeched to a stop. Two doors creaked open. Boot heels clopped on the asphalt. Getting louder. Pausing about even with where I'd ducked us off into the brush.

"Hey!" A dude. "You can come out—we ain't gonna do ya no harm."

Neither one of us moved a hair. Swearing, then thrashing noises, more swearing, louder as Truckdude crashed through the blackberries. He'll never find us, I thought, and I was right. It was his partner who snuck up on our other side, silent as a tick.

"Got 'em, Claude," he yelled, standing up from the weeds with a gun in his hand. He waved it at me and Aim and spoke in a normal tone. "You two can get up if you want. But do it slow."

He raised his voice again. "Chicas. One of 'em's kinda pretty but the other's fat," he told Claude. "You wanna arm wrestle?"

Claude stopped swearing but kept breaking branches and tearing his clothes as he whacked his way over to us. I stayed hunkered down so they'd underestimate me, and so my knife wouldn't fall out from where I had it clamped between my thighs. I felt Aim's arm tremble against mine as Claude emerged from the shadows. She'd be fine, though. Exactly like on a salvage run. I leaned against her a second to let her know that.

The dude with the gun looked a little older than us. Not much older, of course, or he'd have already gone Otherwise, found his own pocket universe, like nearly everyone else whose brain had reached "maturity"—at least that's how the rumors went.

Claude looked my age, or a year or two younger: fifteen, sixteen. He and his partner had the same brown hair and squinty eyes; brothers, then. Probably.

I leered up at Guntoter. "You wanna watch me and her do it first?"

He spat on my upturned face. "Freak! You keep quiet till I tell you talk." The spit tickled as it ran down my cheek.

I didn't hate him. Didn't have the time; I was too busy planning my next move.

"Hey, Dwight, what you think they got in here?" Claude had found our suitcase and given me a name for Guntoter.

"Open 'er up and find out, dickhead."

I couldn't turn around to see the rolly without looking away from Dwight, which didn't seem like a good idea. I heard its zipper and the clink of steel on steel: chisels, hammers, wrenches, clamps, banging against each other as they spilled out on the ground.

"Whoa! Looky at these, Claude. You think that ugly one knows how to use this stuff?" Dwight took his eyes off us and lowered the gun like I'd been waiting for him to do. I launched myself at his legs, a two-hundred-twenty-pound dodgeball. Heard a crack as his left knee bent backwards. Then a loud shot from his gun—but only one before I had my knife at his throat.

"Eennngh!" he whined. Knee must have hurt, but my blade poking against the underside of his chin kept his mouth shut.

I nodded at Aim and she relieved him of his gun. Claude had run off—I heard him thrashing through the bushes in the direction of the road. "Be right back, Lo." Aim was fine, as I'd predicted, thinking straight and acting cool. She stalked after her prey calm and careful, gun at the ready.

I rocked back on my haunches, easing off Dwight's ribs a bit. That leg had to be fractured, Problema; how was I supposed to deal with him, wounded like this? Maybe I shouldn't have hit him so hard. Not as if I could take him to a hospital. I felt him sucking in his breath, winding up for a scream, and sank my full weight on his chest again.

"Lo! You gotta come here!" Aim yelled from the road.

Come there? What? "Why? You can't handle—You didn't let him get his truck back, did—"

"Just come!" She sounded pissed.

Dwight wasn't going anywhere on his own any time soon, but just in case I tugged off his belt and boots and pants and took away the rest of his weapons: a razor poking through a piece of wood, a folding knife with half the blade of mine, and a long leather bag filled with something heavier than sand. I only hurt him a little stripping off the pants.

I got to my feet and looked down a second, wondering if I should shoot the man and get his misery over with. Even after years of leading salvage runs I didn't have it in me, though.

I loaded dude's junk and Aim's spilled-out tools in the rolly and dragged it along behind me into the bushes. When he saw I was leaving him he started hollering for help like it might come. That worried me. I hurried out to Aim. Had Claude somehow armed himself?

Claude was nowhere in sight. Aim stood by the truck—our truck, now. She had the door open, staring inside. The gun—our gun, now—hung loose in one hand and the other stretched inside. "Come on," she said, not to me. "It's okay." She hauled her hand back with a kid attached: white with brown hair, like his brothers. They must have been his brothers—I got closer and saw he had that same squintiness going on.

"Look," I said, "leave him here and climb in. If they got any backup—" Boom! Shotguns make a hecka loud noise. Pellets and gravel went pinging off the road. Scared me so much I swung the rolly up into the truck bed by myself. Then I shoved Aim through the door and jumped in after her. Turned the ignition—they had left the key in it—and backed out of there fast as I could rev. Maybe forty feet along, I swung around and switched to second gear. I hit third by the time we made the bridge, jouncing over pits in the asphalt. Some sections were awful low—leaky pontoons. Next storm would sink the whole thing, Aim had said. I told myself if the thing held up on the dudes' ride over here it was gonna be fine for us heading back.

I looked to my right. Aim had pushed the kid ahead of her so he was huddled against the far door. I braked. "Okay, here you go." But he made no move to leave. "What's the matter, you think I'll shoot? Go on, we won't hurt you."

"He's shaking," Aim reported. "Bad. I think he's freaking out."

"Well that's great. Open the door for him yourself then, and let's go."

"No."

I sighed. Aim had this stubbornness no one would suspect unless they spent a long time with her. "Listen, Aim, it was genius to keep him till I drove out of shooting range, but—"

"We can't just dump him off alone."

"He's not alone; his brothers are right behind us!"

"One of 'em with a broken leg."

"Knee." But I took her point. "So, yeah, they're not gonna be much use for making this little guy feel all better again real soon. C'est la flippin vie." I reached past her to the door handle. She looked at me and I dropped my hand in my lap. "Aw, Aim...."

Aim missed her family. I knew all about how they'd gone on vacation to Disney World without her when she insisted she was too old for that stuff. Their flights back got canceled, first one, then the next, and the next, till no one pretended anymore there might be another, and the cells stopped working and the last bus into Pasco unloaded and they weren't on it.

"Hector—" She couldn't say more than his name.

"Aim, he's twelve now. He's fine. Even if your—" Even if her mom and dad had deserted him like so many other parents, leaving our world to live Otherwise, where they had anything, everything, whatever they wanted, same as when they drank the drug, but now for always. Or so the rumors said. Perfect homes. Perfect jobs. Perfect daughters. Perfect sons.

"All right. Kid, you wanna come with us or stay here with—um, Claude and Dwight?"

Nothing.

I tried again. "Kid, we gotta leave. We're meeting a friend in—" In the rearview I saw five dudes on foot racing up the road. One waved a long, thin black thing over his head. That shotgun? I slammed the truck out of neutral and tore off. They dwindled in the dust.

Aim punched my shoulder and grinned at me. "You done good," she said. I looked and she had one arm around the little kid, holding him steady, so I concentrated on finding a path for the truck that included mostly even pavement.

Here came the tunnel under Mercer Island. Scary, and not only because its lights were bound to be out—I turned the trucks' on and they made bright spots on the ivy hanging over the tunnel's mouth. That took care of that. Better than if we'd been on foot, even.

But richies…more of them had stayed around than went Otherwise. Which made sense; they had their own drugs they used instead of Likewise, and everything already perfect anyways. Or everything used to be perfect for them till too many ordinary people left and they couldn't find no one to scrub their toilets or take out their garbage. Only us.

When things got bad and the governments broke down, richies were the law, all the law around. What they wanted they got, in this world as much as any Otherwise. And what they wanted was slaves. Servants, they called us, but slaves is what it really was; who'd want to spend whatever time they had before they went Otherwise on doing stupid jobs for somebody else? Nobody who wasn't forced to.

We drove through the ivy curtain. I jabbed on the high beams and slowed to watch for nets or other signs of ambush. Which of course there were gonna be none, because hadn't this very truck come through here less than half an hour ago? But.

"Can't be too careful." Aim always knew what I was thinking.

The headlights caught on a heap of something brown and gray spread over most of the road and I had two sets of choices: speed up, or slow down more; drive right over it, or swerve around. I picked A and A: stomped the gas pedal and held the steering wheel tight. Suddenly closer I saw legs, arms, bloated faces, smelled the stink of death. I felt the awful give beneath our tires. It was a roadblock of bodies—broken glass glittered where we would have gone if I'd tried to avoid them, and two fresh corpses splayed on the concrete, blood still wet and red. A trap, but a sprung one. Thanks, Claude. Thanks, Dwight.

The pile of rotting dead people fell behind us mercifully fast. I risked a glance at the kid. He stared straight forward like we were bringing him home from seeing a movie he had put on mental replay. Like there was nothing to see outside the truck and never had been and never would be.

"Maybe this was what freaked him out in the first place?" asked Aim. "You know, before he even got to us?" It was a theory.

We came out into the glorious light again. One more short tunnel as the road entered the city was how I remembered the route. I stopped the truck to think. When my fingers started aching I let go of the wheel.

A bird landed on a loose section of the other bridge that used to run parallel. Fall before last it had been the widest of its kind in the world, according to Aim.

She cared about those kinds of things.

The sun was fairly high yet. We'd left our camp in the mountains early this morning and come twelve mostly downhill miles before meeting up with the kid's brothers. The plan had been to cross the bridge inconspicuously, on foot, hole up in Seward Park with the Rattlers and wait for Rob to show. Well, we'd blown the inconspicuous part.

"Sure you don't wanna go back?" I asked Aim. "They'll be glad to see us. And the truck'll make it a short trip, and it's awesome salvage, too…." I trailed off.

"You can if you rather." But she knew the answer. I didn't have to say it. Aim was why I'd stayed in Pasco instead of claiming a place on the res, which even a mix had a right to do. Now I had come with her this far for love. And I'd go further. To the edge of the continent. All the way.

Rob had better be worth it, though. With his red hair and freckles and singing and guitar-playing Aim couldn't shut up about since we got his message. And that secret fire she said was burning inside him like a cigarette, back when they were at their arts camp. He better be worthy of *her*.

"Stop pouting." She puckered her face and crossed her eyes. "Your face will get stuck like that. Let me drive. Chevies are sweet." She handed me the gun, our only distance weapon—and I hadn't even gotten Dwight's cartridges, but too late to think of that—then slid so her warm hip pressed against mine for a moment. "Go on. Get out."

The kid didn't move when I opened the passenger door so I crawled in over him.

Aim drove like there was traffic: careful, using signals. Guess she learned it from watching her folks. The tunnel turned out clear except for a couple of crappy modern RVs no one had bothered torching yet. One still had curtains in its smashed windows, fluttering when we went by. We exited onto the main drag—Rainier Avenue, I recalled. Aim braked at the end of the ramp. "Which way?"

"South." I pointed left.

Rainier had seen some action. Weed-covered concrete rubble lined the road's edges, narrowing it to one lane. A half-burned restaurant sign advertised hotcakes. A sandbag bunker, evidently empty, guarded an intersection filled with a downed walkway. A shred of tattered camo clung to a wrecked lamppost. Must be relics of the early days; soldiers had been some of the first outside jail to head Otherwise, deserting in larger and larger numbers as real life got lousier and lousier.

"Wow. What a mess." Aim eased over a spill of bricks and stayed in low gear to rubberneck. "How're we gonna get off of this and find the park?"

Otherwise

"Uhhh." Would we have to dig ourselves a turnoff? No—"Here!" More sandbags, but some had tumbled down from their makeshift walls, and we only had to shove a few aside to reach a four-lane street straight to the lakeshore. We followed that around to where the first of the Rattlers' lookouts towered up like a giant birdhouse for ostriches with fifty-foot legs. A chica had already sighted us and trained her slingshot on the truck's windshield. Her companion called out and we identified ourselves enough that they let us through to the gate in their chain-link fence. Another building, this one more like the bunker on Rainier, blocked the way inside. Four Rattlers were stationed here, looking like paintball geeks gone to heaven. We satisfied them of our bona fides, too, using the sheet of crypto and half a rubber snake their runner had turned over with Rob's message. They took my knife. I didn't blame 'em. They let us keep our gun, but minus the bullets.

"What's in the back?"

I hadn't even looked after tossing up the rolly. Dumb. When the sentries opened the big metal drums, though, they found nothing but fuel in them, no one hiding till they could bust out and slit our throats.

Four of those, and the rest of the bed was filled with covered five-gallon tubs: white plastic, the high grade kind you use to ferment beer in. And that's what was in the ten they checked.

"Welcome home," one chica maybe my age said. Grudgingly, but she said it. She walked ahead to guide us into their main camp.

Didn't take her long. A few minutes and I saw firepits, and picnic tables set together in parts of circles, tarps strung between trees over platforms, a handful of big tents. We pulled up next to their playground as the sun was barely beginning to wonder was it time to set. The chica banged on our hood twice, then nodded and scowled at us. Aim nodded too and shut off the ignition.

The kid opened the truck's passenger door. Aim and I looked at each other in silence. Then she grinned. "I guess we're there yet!"

Maybe it was the other littles on the swings and jungle gyms that got through to him. He slid to the ground and walked a few steps toward them, then stopped. I got out too and slammed the door. Didn't faze him. He was focused on the fun and games.

"What have we here?" A longhaired dude wearing a mustache and a skirt came over from watching the littles play.

Aim opened her door and got out too. "We're a day or so early I guess—Amy Niehauser and Dolores Grant." I always tease Aim about how she ended up with such a non-Hispanic name, and she gives me grief right back about not having something made-up, like "Shaniqua" or "Running Fawn." "We're from Kiona. In Pasco?"

Dude nodded. "Sure. Since Britney was bringing you in I figured that was who you must be. I'm Curtis. We weren't expecting a vehicle, though." He waved a hand at the truck.

Britney had hopped up on the bed again while we talked, lifting the lids off the rest of the plastic tubs. "Likewise!" she shouted. "Look at this!"

Aim and I leaned up over the side to see. Britney was tearing off cover after cover. Sure enough, the five tubs furthest in were all at least three-quarters full of thick, indigo blue liquid with specks of pale purple foam. I had never seen so much Likewise in one place.

Curtis lost his cool. "What the hell! We told you we don't allow that—that—" He didn't have the vocabulary to call the drug a bad enough name.

"No, it's not ours—we stole this truck and we didn't know—" Aim tried to calm him down. She tugged at the tub nearest the end. "Here, we'll help you pour 'em in the lake."

"You seriously think we wanna pollute our water like that?"

"Look, I'm just saying we'll get rid of it. We didn't know, we just took this truck from some dudes acting like cowboys on the other side of the bridge, the little dude's big brothers, and they had a few friends—"

That got Britney's attention. "They follow you?"

"Not real far," I said, breaking in. "Since when we took this we left 'em on foot." And they hadn't shot at us more than once—the fuel explained why. "They ain't the only trouble you got for neighbors, either—I'd be more worried about Mercer Island if I were you than

Otherwise

them bridge dudes—or a load of Likewise we can dump anywhere you want."

"Right." Curtis seemed to quiet down and consider this. "Yeah, we'll dig a hole or something...."

No one had proved a connection between Likewise and all the adults talking about living Otherwise, then disappearing. No one had proved anything in a long time that I'd heard of. But the prisons where it first got made were the same ones so many "escaped" from early on, which is the only reason anyone even noticed a bunch of poor people had gone missing, IMO. News reports began about the time it was getting so popular outside, here and in a few more countries.

Some of us still cooked it up. Some of us still drank it. How long did the side-effects last? If you indulged at the age of sixteen would you vanish years later, as soon as your brain was ready? Could you even tell whether you went or not?

The ones who knew were in no position to tell us. They were Otherwise.

Britney went to report us to the committee, she said. A pair of twelve-year-olds came and showed us where to unload the fuel drums. I helped Aim lower the rolly from the bed—how had I got it up there on my own? My arms were gonna hurt bad when the adrenaline wore off—and she handed them the keys. They drove to the bunker with the Likewise for the sentries to watch over.

Aim had to head back to the playground after that. The little dude seemed thoroughly recovered: he'd thrown off his jacket and was running wild and yelling with the other kids like he belonged there.

The Rattlers' committee met with us over dinner in this ridiculous tipi they'd rigged up down by the swimming beach. Buffaloes and lightning painted on the sides. I mean, even I knew tipis were plains technology and had nothing to do with tribes in these parts. But, well, the Rattlers acted proud and solemn bringing us inside, telling us to take off our shoes and which way to circle around the fire, and damn if they didn't actually pass a real, live pipe after feeding us salads plus some beige glop that looked a lot worse than it tasted. And tortillas, which they insisted on calling frybread.

Tina, their eldest, sat on a sofa cushion; she looked maybe Aim's age, but probably she was older. Trying to show the rest of the committee how to run things when she was gone Otherwise, she asked about folks at Kiona: who had hooked up with who, how many pregnant, any cool salvage we'd come across, any adults we'd noticed still sticking around. Aim answered her. There were two dudes, one on either side of Tina—husbands, maybe?—Rattlers were known for doing that kinda thing—and a couple younger chicas chiming in with compliments about how well we were doing for ourselves. I waited politely for them to raise the subject they wanted to talk about. Which was, as I'd figured, the five tubs of Likewise.

They decided to forgive us and opted to pour 'em in a hole like Aim suggested.

Tina had brains. "What's interesting is that they were bringing this shipment *out* of Seattle." She stretched her legs straight, pointed her toes up and pushed toward the fire with her wool-socked heels. August, and the evenings were on the verge of chilly.

"Not like the whole city's sworn off," one of the chicas ventured to say.

"Yeah." I had the dude that agreed pegged for a husband because he wore a ring matching the one on Tina's left hand. "That crew up in Gas Works? They could be brewing big old vats of Likewise and how would we know?"

The second dude chimed in. "They sure wouldn't expect us to barter for any." He wore a ring that matched the one on Tina's right.

The young chica who'd already spoken wondered if it was their responsibility to keep the whole of Seattle clean, suburbs too. Husband One opined that they'd better think a while about that.

"Next question." That was Tina again. "What are those bridge boys gonna do to get their shipment back?" She looked at me, though it was Aim who started talking.

We hadn't told Claude or Dwight where we were going, or made a map for 'em or anything, so I thought the Rattlers were pretty safe.

Plus I had hurt Dwight, broken at least one bone. But the committee decided the truck was a liability even if they painted it, and told us we better take it with us when we departed their territory. Which would have to be soon—"Tomorrow?" asked Husband Two.

Aim folded her lips between her front teeth a few seconds in that worried way she had. We'd expected more of a welcome, considering her skills. Kinda hoped she'd be able to set up a forge here for at least a week. Were the Rattlers gonna make us miss her date with Rob? But according to the committee's spies he was close, already landed on this side of the Sound and heading south. He'd arrive any minute now. So we could keep our rendezvous.

Dammit.

Then I finally got to find out more on where all those corpses in the tunnel came from: richies, as I'd suspected. Didn't seem like the committee wanted to go further into it, though. The dead people were who? People the richies had killed. How? Didn't know. Didn't think it mattered; dead was dead. And why were they stacked up on the road all unhygienic-like instead of properly buried? Have to send a detail to take care of that. And the two fresh ones? Tina said she figured the way I did that they were fallout from Claude and Dwayne's trip through the blockade.

So why? Well, that was obvious, too: use the dead ones to catch us, alive, to work for 'em.

It became more obvious when Curtis took us to where we were supposed to sleep: a tree house far up the central hill of the park's peninsula. He climbed the rope ladder ahead of us and showed us the pisspot, the water bucket and dipper, the bell to ring if one of us suddenly took violently ill in the night. Then he wanted to know if we'd seen his little sister's body in the pile.

"Uh, no, we kinda—we had to go fast, didn't see much. Really." Aim could tell a great lie.

"She had nice hair, in ponytails. And big, light green eyes."

Anybody's eyes that had been open in that pile, they weren't a color you'd recognize anymore. Mostly they were gone. Along with big chunks of face. "No, we, uh, we had to get out of there too fast. Really didn't see. Sorry."

He left us alone at last.

Alone as we were going to get—there was a lot of other tree houses nearby; dusk was settling in fast but we could see people moving up their own ladders, hear 'em talking soft and quiet.

"Lie down." I patted the floor mat. She came into my arms. I had her body, no problema. I did hurt from heaving the rolly around, but that didn't matter much. I stroked her bangs back from her pretty face that I knew even in the dark.

"What'd they do with Dwayne?"

"Who?"

"Dwayne, you know, the little dude?"

Right: Claude and Dwight's kid brother. "That what you wanna call him?"

Aim snorted. "It's his *name*. He told Curtis. I heard him."

My fingers wandered down to the arches of her eyebrows, smoothing them flat. "You worried about him? He looked happy on the playground. They must have places for kids to sleep here. We seen plenty of 'em."

"Yeah. You're right." The skin above her nose crinkled. I traced her profile, trying to give her something else to think of. It sort of worked.

"Why don't the committee care more about the Mercer Island richies? That was—horrible. In the tunnel."

I laughed, though it wasn't the littlest bit funny. "Fail. Mega Fail—they were supposed to be protecting these people here and the richies raided 'em. I wouldn't wanna talk about it either."

I felt her forehead relax. "Yeah." She reached up and tugged my scarf free so she could run her hands over my close-clipped scalp. That was more like it. I snuggled my head against the denim of her coat.

That was our last night together as a couple.

She only mentioned Rob once.

Otherwise

Next morning my arm felt even sorer. And my shoulder had turned stiff. And my wrist. Was getting old like this? No wonder people went Otherwise.

Aim and I woke up at the same time, same as at home and on salvage runs. "Good dreams?" I asked. She nodded and gave me a sheepish half-smile, so I didn't have to ask who she'd dreamed about. It wasn't me.

What kind of universe would Aim make if she went Otherwise? It wouldn't be the same as mine.

Curtis had pointed out a latrine on the way to our treehouse. We dumped the pisspot there and took care of our other morning needs. It was a nice latrine, with soap and a bowl of water.

Down we went, following the trail to the main camp. Aim held my hand when we could walk side by side. Sweet moments. I knew I better treasure 'em.

I helped set out breakfast, which was berries and bars of what appeared to be last night's beige glop, fossilized. Aim retrieved the rolly from where we'd left it under a supply tarp. She cleaned the gun, which she called Walter, and shined up her tools. Soon enough she attracted a clientele.

First come a dude could have been fourteen or fifteen; he wanted her to help him fix up an underwater trap for turtles and crayfish. Then he had a friend a little older who asked her to help him take apart a motor to power his boat. Actually, he had taken it apart already, and wanted her to put it together again with him.

Aim called a break for herself after a couple hours of this so she could go check out how Dwayne was doing. And she wanted to bring him a plum from the ones I collected for snacks. I waited by the tools for her to come back. A shadow cut the warm sun and I looked up from the dropcloth.

"Hey." A dude's voice. All I could see was a silhouette. Like an eclipse—a gold rim around darkness.

"Hey back."

"You're not Amy."

"Nope."

He sat down fast, folding his legs. "Must be Dolores, then? I'm Rob." He held out a hand to shake, so I took it.

Now I could see him, dude was every bit as pretty as Aim had said. Dammit. Hair like new copper, tied back smooth and bright and loose below a wide-brimmed straw fedora. Eyes large, a strange, pale blue. Freckles like cinnamon all over his snub-nosed face and his long arms where they poked out of the black-and-white print shirt he wore. But not on his throat, which was smooth as vanilla ice cream and made me want to—no. This was Aim's crush.

His hand was a little damp around the palm. Fingers long and strong. I let it go. "Aim's around here somewhere; she'll be back in a minute, I think, if you wanna wait."

"Sure." He had a tiny little stick, a twig, in the corner of his mouth. His lips were pink, not real thin for a white boy. Dammit.

"Where's your guitar?" I asked.

"Left it back home, at the bunkers. The Herons'll take care of it for me; too much to travel with. But I packed my pennywhistle." He swapped the stick for something longer, shiny black and silver. He played a sad-sounding song, mostly slow, with some fast parts where one line ended and the next began. Then he speeded up, did a new, sort of jazzy tune. Then another, and I recognized it: "Firework."

Aim recognized it, too. Or him, anyway—she came running up behind me shouting his name: "Rob! Rob!" She hauled him up with a hug. "I'm so glad! So glad!" He hugged her back. They both laughed and leaned away enough to look each other in the eyes.

"Oh, wow—" "Did you—" They started and stopped talking at the same time. Cute.

Dwayne had showed up in Aim's wake. He stood to one side, hands in his front pockets, about as awkward as I felt.

Rob and Aim let go of each others' arms. "Who's this?" he asked her, bending his knees to put his face on the kid's level.

"I'm Dwayne. I come all the way from Issaquah." Which was nine times more words than I'd ever heard him use before. Maybe he liked white dudes.

"That's pretty far. But I met somebody came even further."

Otherwise

"Who're you?"

"I'm Rob. I live in Fort Worden, other side of the Sound."

"Issaquah is twenty-two miles from Seattle."

"Well, this chica I'm talking about sailed to Fort Worden over the ocean from Liloan. That's in the Philippines. Six thousand miles."

"She did not!"

"I'm telling you."

Here came Curtis over from the playground. He said hey and dragged Dwayne back with him with the promise of a swim, "—so you can get packed quick."

The Rattlers wanted us gone yesterday. While Rob met with their committee to tell them the news out of Liloan—how the Philippines had been mostly missed by the EMPs and other tech-killers thrown around in the first mass panic—Aim loaded her tools in the rolly, and I went to find the truck. At the fuel shed they directed me up the remains of a service road. The twelve-year-olds had parked at the end of it; they were just through filling in the hole they'd dug, tamping down dirt with a couple of shovels. The empty Likewise tubs lay on their sides in the dead pine needles.

"Thanks," I said. "We were gonna do that."

"'Sall right," the bigger one said. "Didn't take long."

"Yes it did." Her friend wasn't about to lie. "But we're done, now, and nobody drunk it.

"Have you ever—" The smaller girl smacked the bigger one on her head. "Stop! I was only asking!" She turned to me again. "You ever taken any Likewise yourself?"

Once. A single dose was low risk—I'd heard of adults with the same history as me, twenty-four, twenty-five, and still not Otherwise.

"Tastes like dog slobber," I told her. "Like spit bugs crapped in a bottle of glue."

"Eeuuw!" They made faces and giggled. I thought about the questions they didn't ask as they brought me back down in the truck. About how Likewise felt, what happened when I had it in me.

You could call it a dream. In it, my mom had never hit me and my dad had never got stoned. I was living in a house with Aim. The drug was specific: a yellow house with white trim, a picket fence. We had a dog named Quincy Jones and a parakeet named Sam. The governments were still running everything. We had a kid and jobs we went to. I remember falling asleep and waking up and getting maybe a little bored at work, but basically being happy. So happy.

Seemed like it went on for years. I was out for eight hours.

∽

We could have driven all the way to Fort Worden, only Aim wanted to see the Space Needle. "C'mon, when are we gonna have another chance?"

I rolled my eyes. "You can *see* it from freakin *anywhere*, Aim. Ask *them* if *they* see it." I pointed up at the chicas in the fifty-foot-high lookout.

"Okay. Touch it then. I mean touch it."

Our first fight.

Of course Rob took her side. "Yeah, the truck; tough to let it go, but there's no connections for us in Tacoma. Olympia either; can't say who or what we might run into going south. I told the captain up at Edmonds I'd be back in a week. Maybe he can stow it for us? And even if we're early that's our best bet. North. So the Space Needle's not much of a detour."

Aim looked at me. "*All flippin right,*" I said.

I drove again. Aim took the middle seat, but it wasn't me she pressed up against.

Rattlers had told us where to avoid, and I did my best. From Rainier I had to guess the route, and sometimes I guessed wrong. And sometimes my guesses would have been good if the roads didn't have huge holes in 'em or obstacles too hard to move out of our way. We didn't see anyone else, only signs they'd been around: coiled up wires, stacks of wood—not a surprise, since anyone on a scavenge run would have lookouts. Groups had mainly settled in parks where you could grow crops, and we weren't trying to cross those.

We reached Seattle Center late. No time to find anywhere else to spend the night.

Otherwise

There had been action here, too. I remembered the news stories, though they hadn't made any sense. Not then, and not now—why would anyone fight over such a place, so far off from any water? But tanks had crawled their way onto the grounds, smashing trees and sculptures, shooting fire and smoke back and forth. They left scars we could still see: burned-out buildings, craters, bullet holes.

The Space Needle stood in the middle of about an acre of blackberries covering torn-up concrete—what used to be a plaza. Old black soot and orange rust marked its once-white legs. I tooled us under a pair of concrete pillars for the dead Monorail and backed in as close as I could get without slicing open a tire. "There you go," I said. "Touch it." Which was a little mean, I admit.

Rob climbed out the window without opening the door and got up on the truck cab's roof. He stuck his arm in and hauled Aim after him. I heard the two of 'em talking about chopping a path through the thorns if they'd had swords, and how to forge them, and a trick Aim knew called damascening. Aim recited her facts about how high the thing was, how long it took to erect, et cetera.

Then I didn't hear anything for a while. Then her breath. I turned on the radio, like there'd be something more than static to cover up the sounds they were going to make.

One of them shifted and the metal above my head popped in and out. That gave me courage to hit the horn—a short blast like it was an accident—and open the door. Very, very slowly.

Shin deep in brambles I unhooked from my pants one by one, I took a blanket from the boxes of supplies the Rattlers sent us off with. Then I couldn't help myself; I looked. They both had all their clothes on and were sitting up. For the moment. Aim waved. Rob pretended to stroke a beard he didn't have and smiled.

"In a minute," I said, meaning I'd come back. Eventually. Give me strength, I thought, and I smiled, too, and waded carefully along the trail the truck had smashed.

She wanted to be with him. I loved her anyhow. To the edge of the continent. All the way.

I would follow her.

But tonight I would sleep alone.

∾

At least that was the plan. When it came down to it, though, I didn't dare rest my eyes. Dark was falling. The place was too open—bad juju. I had a feeling, once I got out from under my jealousy. So I found a trash barrel, rolled it up a ramp in the side of some place looked like a giant scorched wad of metal gum. I set the barrel upright, climbed and balanced on its rim, and scrabbled from there to lie on my stomach on a low roof—must have been the only flat surface to the whole building, even before the howitzers and grenade-launchers and whatever else attacked it.

Me and Walter settled in to keep watch. The Rattlers had returned his magazine when they gave me back my knife, and there were seven rounds left.

Aim and Rob were maybe fifty feet south. I still heard 'em clear enough to keep me awake till Claude and his friends showed up.

Trying to be smart, the bridge dudes turned off whatever vehicle they drove blocks away. The engine's noise was a clue, and its silence was another. Insects went quiet to my east in case I needed a third.

Starlight's not the best to see by. I couldn't really count 'em—four or five dudes it must be, I figured, same as yesterday. They zeroed in on Aim and Rob, who were talking again.

"Hands up!" a dude commanded. How were they gonna tell, I wondered, but one of 'em opened the truck door and the courtesy light came on. There was Aim and Rob, a bit tousled up. Too bad I didn't want to shoot *them*. Couldn't get a line on anyone else.

"Get your sorry asses outta me and Dwight's—outta my truck." That would be Claude.

"Daddy? Where's Daddy?" And that would be that kid Dwayne? His age was all wrong for Dwight to be his dad, but who else was it rising out of that supply box, pale-faced in the yellow courtesy light?

The kid must have stowed away. He held out his arms and kicked free of something and Claude stepped up to grab and lift him and now I had a great shot. Couldn't have been better. But I didn't take it.

Otherwise

Next minute I wished I had when dudes on either side yanked Aim and Rob out of opposite doors. I heard her yell at them and get slapped.

Someone else was yelling, too—not me, I was busy shimmying off the roof while there was cover for my noise. "No! Don't hit her! No! Put me down!" Little Dwayne was on our side?

Brightness. Someone had switched on the truck's headlamps. I ducked down. Aim was crying hard. They shoved her to the pavement. I hadn't heard a peep outta Rob. When they marched him into the light I saw one dude's hand over his mouth and a shiny piece of metal right below his ear. Knife or a gun—didn't matter which. Woulda kept me quiet, too.

Only four of 'em. Plus Dwayne. Seven bullets seemed plenty—if I didn't mind losing Rob.

I didn't. But Aim would.

Bang! Bang! Walter wasn't quite loud as a shotgun. Glass and metal pinged off the pavement, flew away into the sudden dark. Only one round each for the truck's headlamps. I was proud of myself.

Light still came out of the cab from the overhead courtesy. Not much. I couldn't see anybody.

But I could hear 'em shouting to each other to find the chica, and shooting. Randomly, I hoped. No screams, so Rob had probably got away all right.

I shifted position, which made the next part trickier, but would keep the dudes guessing where to kill me. I went round to one side, with the frame of the open driver's door blocking my vision. Walter stayed steady—I gripped him with both hands and squeezed. Got it in one. I was good. Total night, now. I squirmed off on my belly for a ways to be sure no one had a flashlight, then crawled, then stumbled to my feet and walked. Headed north by the stars, with nothing on me but Walter, my knife, my binoculars. A blanket. Not even a bottle for water.

It was a shame to leave all the provisions the Rattlers had given us. And too bad I had to damage a high-functioning machine like that truck. Aim would cuss me out for it when we caught up with one another at Edmonds.

Aim would be fine. She always was. Rob, too, most likely.

∽

I took the rest of that night and part of a day to walk there. It was easy: 99 most of the way. The stars were enough to see that by, and the Aurora Bridge was practically intact. I wondered what facts Aim would have told me about it if we were going over it together. All I knew was people used to kill themselves here by jumping off. Kids? Didn't we used to have the highest rates of suicide?

If Aim didn't show up at Edmonds in a few days maybe I'd come back. Or find some Likewise.

I snuck in the dark past where they used to have a zoo, worried I might run into some weird predator. I didn't; when the animals got out they must've headed for the lake on the road's other side. The sky got lighter and I began to look for pursuit as well as listening for it. Nobody came. The stores and restaurants lining the highway would have been scavenged out long ago. I was alone.

No Aim in sight.

Rain started to fall. I hung the blanket over my head like the Virgin Mary. Because of the clouds it was hard to tell time, but I figured I turned on to 104 a couple of hours after sunrise.

I went down a long slope to the water. Rob had said if we got split up to meet by a statue of sea lions on the beach.

This was my first time to be at the ocean. It was big, but I could see land out in its middle. Looked like I could just swim there.

Route 104 continued right on into the water. The statue was supposed to be to its south. The sand moved, soft and tiresome under my wet chucks. I spotted a clump of kids digging for something further towards the water, five or six of 'em. They didn't try to stop me and I kept on without asking directions. A couple of 'em had slings out, but I must not have seemed too threatening; neither chica pointed 'em my way.

A metal seal humped up some stairs to a patch of green. Was this the place? I climbed up beside it. At the top, a garden. I could tell it was a garden since it wasn't blackberries, though I had no idea what these plants were. But they grew in circles and lines, real patterns. And more metal seal sculptures—okay, sea lions—stuck out from between them.

Definitely. I was here. I curled up in the statue's shelter and the rain stopped. I fell asleep.

A whisper woke me. "Lo!" My heart revved. Aim? Eyes open, all I saw was Rob.

"You can't call me that."

"Sorry. Didn't want you to shoot me."

I sat up straight and realized I had Walter in my hand. Falling asleep hadn't been so stupid after all.

Rob's ice cream throat had a red inch-long slice on one side, so it had been a knife the bridge dude held there. He seemed fine besides that. "Is she around?" he asked. "She and you came together?" I shook my head and he folded up his legs and sat down beside me. Too close. I scooted over.

We didn't say anything for a long time. Could have been an hour. I was thirsty. And hungry. I wondered if maybe I ought to eat from the garden.

Rob held out his water bottle for me and I took it and drank. When I gave it back he didn't even wipe the mouth off.

The clouds pulled themselves apart and let this beautiful golden orange light streak through. The sun was going down. I'd slept the whole afternoon.

"Look," said Rob. "Look. I know you and Aim—"

"You can't call her that."

"Yes I can! Listen. Look. You were with her before me and I don't want to—to mess with that."

As if he hadn't. "And?"

"And—and we were talking." Among other things. "And she was saying if we got married—if she got married she would want to marry *both* of us."

I stared at him hard to make sure he was serious. Me and Aim had teased each other about being married ever since we met in gym class. Even before people over twenty began going Otherwise.

Apparently I wasn't the only one it was more than a joke for.

"So would you?"

"Would I what?" But I knew.

"Would you freakin marry me! Would you—"

"But I'm a lesbian! You're a dude!"

"Well, duh."

"And only because you wanna hook up with *my* chica? Unh-unh."

"Well, it's not only that."

"Really?" I stood up. He did too. "What, you're in love with me? I'm fat, I'm a big mouth, a smartass—"

"You're plain old smart! And brave, and Aim thinks you're the closest thing to a goddess who ever walked the earth."

"What if I am?" I wanted to leave. But this was where she would come. I had to be here. I wrapped the blanket around me and tucked my arms tight.

"Yeah. What if you are? What if she's right? I kinda think—" He quit talking a minute and looked over his shoulder at the beach. "I kinda think she is. You are."

If he had tried to touch me then I would have knocked the fool unconscious.

Instead, he turned around and looked at the beach again. "That's him," he said. "Captain Lee." He pointed and I saw a bright yellow triangle sailing toward us out of the west. "Our ride's here ahead of time. I have to go meet him and tell him we need to wait for Aim." He left me alone with my wet blanket.

It was almost dark by the time he came back, carrying a bucket. "Here you go. Supper." I was ready to eat, no doubt. Inside was a hot baked yam and some greens with greasy pink fish mixed in. I washed it all down with more of Rob's water.

We took turns hanging out at the statue. Rob had connections with the locals, the Hammerheads and this other group, the Twisters. He stayed with them, and I bunked on Lee's boat.

Otherwise

Three days dragged past. I got used to a certain idea. I let him put his arm around me once when we met on the stairs. And another time when he introduced me to a dude he brought to pick some herbs in the garden—they were for medicines, not that nice to eat.

And another time. We were there together, but with my binoculars I saw her first. I shouted and he hugged me. Both arms. I broke away and ran and ran and yes, it was Aim! And Dwayne, which explained a lot when I thought about it afterwards, but I didn't care right then.

"Aim! Aim!" I lifted her in the air and whirled us around and we kissed each other long and hard. I was with her and it was this reality, hers and mine and everybody else's, not one I created just for me. I cried and laughed and yelled at the blue sky, so glad. Oh so freakin' glad.

Of course I had known all along she'd make it.

And then Rob caught up with me and he kissed her too. She held my hand the whole time. So how could I feel jealous and left out?

Well, I could. But that might change, someday. Someday, it might be otherwise.

Harrowing Emily

Megan Arkenberg

"It's like no matter how much I shower," Emily says, "I can't get the smell of grave dust out of my hair." She stands in the bedroom door, wrapped in a burgundy bath towel, and all I can smell is her soap and banana-scented shampoo.

"I wonder if Persephone feels like this after she claws her way out of Hell." She towels her hair brutally and leaves it as it falls, small blonde spikes sticking up at her temples and behind her ears, a crown of colorless thorns. With one hand pinning her wrap across her breasts, she rummages through the closet, settles on a sweatshirt and a pair of jeans, and slips back into the bathroom to change.

She never used to be shy about changing in front of me. And she never used to talk about gods.

༄

The therapist told me to stop listing the things that are different about her. Of course, the therapist doesn't believe that Emily died in February—died and came back. And I have no proof. I didn't call an ambulance, or the neighbors; I spent that hellish night curled around her cold body on our bed, too numb to move. Then, in the morning, she was here again.

Except it wasn't quite her.

(She never used to eat rare meat. She never used to lie on the couch in her pajamas, watching daytime television. She never used to cover her face when she passed the hall mirror, as though afraid of her reflection.)

"You had a very frightening experience, Zoe," the therapist says. She has settled on "experience" as the proper word for my girlfriend's death, damnation, and resurrection. "It's changed the way you view Emily. But you've told me yourself that this list, this catalog, isn't helping you heal. It's not helping you confront the reality of your fear for Emily."

(She never used to wear long sleeves in summer. She never used to hate the smell of lilacs. She never used to go days without sleeping, standing at the kitchen window, watching the moon climb over our neighbor's trees.)

"Perhaps we should have Emily join us for a session," the therapist says. I tell her I don't think that's a good idea.

༄

Emily's brother has visited once since his sister died. We ate grilled cheese sandwiches at the kitchen counter. Kevin and I sat on the bar stools and Emily stood by the sink, nibbling at her sandwich as though she didn't quite know what it was.

"Our family has...that is, there's a history..." Kevin began, haltingly, and I was tempted to finish his sentence. *Of coming back from the dead? Of going to Hell?* He bit into his sandwich, chewed and swallowed slowly. "Our maternal grandmother used to see things. After

Harrowing Emily

Aunt Alice died. Grandma thought she saw Alice sitting at the piano in the living room."

"Are you saying I only think I see Emily?"

"No, no...this isn't about *you*, Zoe. All I'm saying is, people in our family have a habit of changing. And they don't need to go through Hell to do it."

(She never used to sleep fully clothed, on top of the bedspread. She never used to pull flowers out of the vase on the dresser, swearing she could hear them die.)

༄

"What did Emily do that would have gotten her sent to Hell?" my mother asks. She is infinitely practical.

She sits back on her heels, drags off her ladybug-patterned gardening gloves, and frowns at the twig of a rosebush she's just finished potting. It has a charred look to it, like something rescued from a burning house.

"I don't know," I say. "Maybe God hates lesbians."

Mother snorts. I remember that she hated most of my girlfriends when I was growing up—thought they were sloppy, uncouth. Emily changed all that—Emily, who was nothing like my usual type, who had asked me out six or seven times before I finally gave her a chance. She took me *dancing*. Mother loved Emily long before I did.

"What did she die of?" Mother waves an empty hand at me, her sign for me to pass the water bottle, which is full of vodka and lemonade.

"I don't know. Nothing obvious." Like a gunshot, I mean. Or suicide. "She's had hypertension for years, so I thought maybe a stroke or an aneurism."

"Aneurism. Uncle Pavlos died of that." She nods her head, as though she approves, as though that were an acceptable thing from which to die.

(The hypertension is gone now. Emily told me after her last physical. And that scar behind her knee, from the motorcycle accident her sophomore year of college—gone, like chalk wiped from a slate.)

"Can you be damned preemptively?" Mother asks. "For driving your girlfriend to drink?"

I lift my mouth guiltily from her bottle, wiping spiked lemonade from my chin.

∽

I went through her internet history. Link after link for recipe exchange forums, the Facebook pages of her friends from graduate school. Tons of local classifieds, a few not-so-local. (She never told me she'd considered moving to Oregon to find work—even when she knew it would mean leaving me behind, knew I'd never lived a week of my life outside of an hour's drive from Chicago.) She'd bookmarked a blog post with a picture of a kitten in a kiddy pool, above a caption that I didn't get.

I closed the browser window with more questions than answers.

She hasn't touched me since she came back from Hell. Nothing more involved than a cold peck on the cheek. If she nudges me accidentally while we're making the bed or while I'm pouring a bowl of cereal, she quickly apologizes and skitters out of the way.

(She never used to apologize. She used to go out of the way to jostle me, saying things like *Hey, gorgeous* and *You should get in my way more often.*)

She's stopped looking for work, too. Well-meaning friends still leave classified pages in the mail slot, or drop them off at my office, with some ad highlighted or outlined in thick marker. Emily crumples them up and throws them away without reading.

(She never used to put newspaper in the garbage. She used to recycle.)

"Zoe, what are you afraid of?" the therapist asks. I'm curled up on her ugly couch, a ring of damp tissues around the wastebasket below me—I've never had good aim.

"Her," I say, which isn't entirely true. Or it is true, but grossly oversimplified. The truth is, I'm afraid I've lost her for good. Afraid that she's gone, and I'll never have the courage to admit it.

∽

Harrowing Emily

At four in the morning, I come downstairs to refill the glass of water from my bedside table and find her standing over the sink. Her hands are folded, fingertips neatly up-pointed, like a first communicant or a statue of an angel. The sky above the treetops is already purple, working its way toward dawn.

"So what was it like?" I ask.

She doesn't turn. (She never used to speak to me without looking me in the eye.) "It was like stepping outside on the hottest day in August and getting slapped in the face by the humidity." She looks down, inspecting her fingertips, as though they belong to a stranger. "It smelled…dead. And floral. Damp, in a way, but also like dust. I can't get the smell out of my hair."

"What did they do to you?"

"They fixed me," she says. "They made it so I wouldn't be sad anymore."

(She never used to complain of sadness.)

"So you're happy now?" I ask. I try not to make it sound like an accusation.

"No." She shakes her head. "But I'm not sad."

⁓

I never used to pray. I started by accident. I was walking around our yard, noting which bushes needed trimming, which beds would need fresh mulch when the weather dried out, when I saw a strange flower poking its head out of the yew hedge. It was a crocus. The flower that distracted Persephone so that Hades could drag her down into the underworld. And suddenly I was angry, deeply angry, and all my wrath was directed at that tiny purple hell-opening flower.

I knelt to tear it up.

And I began to pray instead.

Dear God, I've learned my lesson. Please give me back the woman I love. I promise she will never be sad again. I promise to do better, this time.

His answer came in the smell of the crocus.

Dear child, what makes you think this has anything to do with you?

⁓

"Zoe," she says. She's opened my door without knocking, and she's standing there in her bath towel, her hair dripping down her back. "Are you awake?"

I put down my book, set my reading glasses by the ceramic coaster beneath my glass of water. It's a few minutes past midnight. "What's happening, Emily?"

Without taking a step, she is standing at my bedside, and her icy hand cups my cheek.

"I'm dying. And this time they won't send me back."

I cover her hand with mine. Her calluses are harder than I remember. "I think this was a test," she says. "To prove to me that I wouldn't want things different from the way they were. That I wouldn't choose to live without sorrow."

"I never even knew you were sad."

"But Zoe, don't you see? The sadness didn't matter. Not for me, anyway. Maybe that's what they sent me back to learn. That feeling sadness was better than feeling nothing."

"That's what I felt, before you died. Nothing."

"That's what Hell is." She strokes my cheek, her rough fingers moving beneath mine like muscle sliding beneath skin. "I'm not going back there, now. I'm going to be happy, Zoe, happy like I've never been."

"I'm sorry," I say, but she covers my lips.

"Hush. This was never about you."

(She never used to push me away.)

She crawls into bed beside me. I wrap her damp body in my arms and hold her until she stops breathing.

"I suppose it hurts," Mother says, "that she didn't let you play a part in that story."

We are sitting on a flannel blanket in my back yard, watching the moon bleach the colors out of the roses on the patio. From tonight until the winter solstice, the days will get shorter. I will spend more time in a colorless garden, with only the moon for company.

Harrowing Emily

Mother refills my glass. Vodka and orange juice—fortifying, she said, as she said of the sturdy black suit I wore to Emily's funeral. Makes you stand up straight. Makes you pay attention.

I find myself thinking, again, that I never paid enough attention to Emily when she was alive. I never *felt* for her. And now the crocus is there, smiling out of the yew. *Dear child, this has nothing to do with you.*

"Yeah," I say. "Yeah, it hurts like hell."

"You never used to cry," Mother says.

It's true. I wipe the sticky tears from my cheeks, touching them lightly, with wonder, as if I've never touched tears before. Mother watches me for a moment, then folds me in her arms, rocking me back and forth.

"Oh, honey, it's okay. My honey, my *korë*, it's okay. *You* came back, honey. You came back."

The Witch Sea

Sarah Diemer

I knew what she was. When she came up the path, feet upon the stone steps, quiet, deliberate, I knew it from the way she moved, the web between her fine toes, how she faltered when she reached the lighthouse landing, like she had never seen things like stairs before. I knew, and I said nothing, because we were all, in our own way, monsters.

"Nor," she said, sticking out her hand as if she expected me to shake it.

"That's what he named you?" I asked, arms folded before me.

"That's what my mother named me," she said, the first of a thousand lies.

I did not touch her then.

She had come by boat. They all did. They could not touch the saltwater. He wouldn't let them, anyway, and they must obey him, but if they touched the water, if they could, the spray made them scream, cry out, mouths wide, tongues distended. A wave made them crumple, skin sagging and bloated, until it fell apart, obliterated by the blue, leaving a clean, new creature beneath. Sometimes, a seal, wet coat slick, brown eyes still human. Sometimes, a walrus broke through the man's pelt, growing until it burst apart, revealing tusk and tooth. Sometimes, it was a small, silver fish that would flop helplessly until it reached the water, or did not, lying, rotting, in the sunshine.

She wasn't human, Nor. But neither was I.

"They call you a witch," she said, smiling, moving facial muscles into a ferocious grin, like a kind of growl. "Are any of the stories true? Do you keep the fish from the bay, so that the people starve? Do you dance in the moonlight? Did you sell your soul?"

She had not yet asked my name.

"I am not what you think I am," I said, and let her into my house, with her wet brown eyes and hands she kept clasped in front of her, skin over knuckles so white, like waves. If I had shut the door, if I had kept her out, she would have remained on my island anyway. He had sent her. We both knew he had sent her. He was dauntless.

"They call you Meriel," she said, then, sitting down at the table stiffly. "Is that your name?"

"It is the name I use, yes."

"You hate us."

"I do not."

"You hate me?"

A seal's eyes are innocent, contain no malice, no human anger or rage, and though she showed a human shape now, she was still seal. Her eyes were limpid, wide, when she looked up at me, hands on the table, widespread. They were webbed, too, but only a little. He was getting better.

"I do not hate you," I told her. It was not a lie.

"He hopes that you will reconsider his offer, you know. He is not a bad man. He never was a bad man."

"No," I said.

I should not have let her in. It was the first of my mistakes.

"I will come again tomorrow," she said, and she stood, too sudden, jerky. "I hope that you will reconsider, too, Meriel." Her voice was soft and lovely, skin smooth, brown, beautiful.

She held out her hand again, when she departed. I did not take it.

I watched her as she walked away and down the dirt path. Her hips swung softly, from side to side, the shape of the skirt lying along the curves.

He had tried everything else, and this was a last resort, we all knew it. Again, he would fail, she would fail.

But I thought of her that night, hand over my own breast, listening to the crash of the waves against the rock outside my window, seeing the faint flash of silver upon the ceiling, reflection of my finely woven net of spells that kept the fish out of the bay.

In the morning, I checked the line, standing on the shore, hands extended, feeling the push and pull of the tide and waves as I crawled over every inch of the silver net with my head and heart, testing it and pulling it and mending it where mends were needed, shaping the magic in long lines, crisscrossed, always crisscrossed. The bright sunshine reflected off the water, blinding me, and I did not see her approach in the little boat, did not see her get out and climb the path to me. I felt her, though, felt her when she stepped off the coracle and upon the sand. I rose from my work, and I went to meet her, bright spots along my vision like flashes, outlining her in a riot of color.

"Good morning, Meriel," she said, and she curtsied. She moved smoother than the day before, graceful. It did not take them long to get used to the land, to how their new limbs and muscles worked. She seemed almost human now.

"Good morning, Nor," I told her.

"He wishes to ask if you will reconsider today, Meriel. He has said that he will double his offer, if you will cease."

"I will not," I said, and it seemed so laughable, the formalities, how pretty he'd dressed her, how he'd double or triple his offer of gold, of house and land and a hundred thousand things he thought might seduce me. It did not, it would not. I wondered when he would tire.

The sea was patient. He was patient. But patience could wear thin.

"Oh," was what she said, and it was obvious she thought today would be the day when I would smile, nod, agree to his demands. She opened her mouth and shut it, so like a fish, they were always like fish.

"Go back," I said, not unkindly. "Tell him 'never.'"

"He will not accept that, you know," she lowered her voice, looked over her shoulder, stepped closer. She smelled of salt. "He will send me, every day, Meriel."

"As you will," I said.

She left.

∽

I was born on Bound Island. My mother pushed me out, and—that same night—had to tend to the nets. Back then, it was roughly every seven days that breaks would occur, that magic would have to be woven back into the silver strands. Now, it was every day.

Nothing living could slip through the net and enter the bay. If it did, it would…change. And become his—Galo's.

So I tended the nets.

One night, my mother told me the story of Galo. She banked the fire, drew me close, traced a protective circle in the dirt about our forms. She whispered it.

Long ago, before man or woman or stories, there was the sea. It crashed and roared and boiled, churning life into being. At the center of the sea swam Galo. He was larger than the island, larger than the bay, with four fins that turned into tentacles that turned into legs, and a long, equine nose with teeth as long as oars and sharp as stars. He had been in the sea from the beginning, rising from the muck and mud at the bottom of the world, fully formed. He was the oldest sea god, and the most powerful. Storms came from him, whirlpools followed his hooves that sometimes changed to fins. His heart was black, and he knew only chaos, and everything in the sea feared him mightily.

Land came, then. And some things from the sea ventured upon it, exchanging their fins for legs, their gills for lungs. Man came into the world and the sea was forsaken. They forgot their origins, forgot their

The Witch Sea

fathers who had crept from the salt, and shook their fists at the water. They built boats and crossed the seas and believed they had conquered the waves.

Forgotten, Galo slept at the bottom of the world. One day, he awoke and saw how much had changed, saw how man defiled his mother, the sea, saw how there was no reverence in man's heart for the ocean that had given him life. Galo's black heart grew even blacker, and he thought and he thought, and he formed a plan.

He changed his equine form, shed his fins and sharp teeth, and crawled upon the land, now a man with a blacker heart. He shaped a town from mud, and he turned back to the waters and gave a great cry. And out of the ocean crept all manner of creatures: the whales and the fish and the octopus and the shark, and they began to shed their animal forms and become people, too.

"We will make a great army," he said to them, "and when we have enough, we will punish the humans for their sacrilege. We will destroy them on land, we will devour them upon the sea, and man will cease to be. The ocean will reign again."

The sea people, as one, gave a great shout, and said, "We will obey you, Galo, for you are mighty and strong." And more creatures began to come from the sea, and more and more, until the beach teemed with people who had shark eyes and whale hearts and dripping hair and tusk teeth.

But then, the parade of animals stopped. For, at the mouth of the bay, upon our own Bound Island—though it was not known as such, back then—stepped a witch. Your great grandmother, Meriel, for whom you are named. She drew down a star, and from its shimmering bulk, she fashioned something so large, so ludicrous, it stretched across the entire mouth of the bay, both ways.

She said, "While those of my blood live, Galo, you will never get your creatures. I curse you to remain in the town you have built, trapped and unable to summon the sea to your aid."

And, because Galo was small and human and no longer mighty, the curse stuck.

I sometimes wondered at the audacity of grandmother. The oldest god of the sea took the form of a mortal man, and—in that moment—she wove a net and curse so tightly that he was spellbound by it. Did she ever fear retribution? Did she ever look through the curtains of the tiny cottage at night and watch the people come to the edge of the water, all along the beach of the bay? Did she watch them stand, silent, looking out to the sea they could no longer touch, would never touch again, as long as the curse remained? Galo was cruel. While he must remain in the town he had fashioned, he demanded that all of his creations did, too. The people would stand, at night, along the shore and look out to the sea and mourn its loss. And curse my grandmother.

And my mother.

And now me.

I used to think this was bigger than all of us. My mother would tell me the story of Galo and of my grandmother, and how we must remain, for all time, upon the island. We were the axis for the world, she'd told me, dusting my nose with flour or tossing me into the air. We were important. Though I never believed I was.

My mother told me, before she died, how she'd seduced my father to the island. How I, too, would have to seduce a man here to keep the lineage going. If the lineage did not continue, the curse would not remain, and the world would end. I must seduce a man. She'd said it so matter-of-factly, hands upon the washboard, drawing the tea towels over the ridges again and again, scrubbing the stains out. I watched her hands go up and down, and felt a remorse like fire rake through my stomach, my heart. I would not seduce a man, and there was no good way to tell my mother this. So I never did.

The year she died, I brought a woman to the island.

Marguerite had traveled from a far town by the name of Celena, and she came because I summoned her. I used the same spell that my mother had taught me to bring flour, vegetables, bits of meat to our pantry. We could not leave the island, so we could enchant small things we needed to us. "Never use it for any other reason," my mother had admonished me. But my mother was dead.

The Witch Sea

Marguerite was witty and charming and beautiful—everything I had spun into the spell. When she kissed me, she tasted of strawberries, and when we were together, I saw stars. I thought I loved her. Magic should not be used on mortals, as the old laws went, and though I loved her, and she thought she loved me, it was the threads of the spell and nothing more. She left in a storm and did not look back as she paddled for shore, and I felt the small newness of my heart break that day and never mend.

My mother had left me the island and a legacy and a stone. The first two were a burden, the last was my saving grace in those first lonely days. It was a plain stone, the size of my palm, and clear. When I stared down and within, it would show me what I wished to see. Not fantasies, but facts, as they happened—real, true life.

I watched the townsfolk, and I watched Galo in the stone's depths. If they ever thought an outsider could see them, watched them, they made no movement to indicate it. They moved within the stone like little pictures, stories, lives I could not touch.

Sometimes, when I was little, I had whisked away my mother's stone (it did not have a name, nothing in our tiny span of existence of the island had a name. I had a theory that my mother had only named me because it was after my grandmother, her mother, her entire world). I would peer into its depths, and I would ask it for friends. It would show me some of the inhabitants of the bay town, then, would show me the women with hair like tentacles, the men with shark eyes and sharp teeth, and I would wonder why it would show me something so contrary to what I asked it for.

Over time, over the years, they did become my friends. In a way.

When Nor left me for the second time, I dusted my hands along my apron pockets, and climbed up and into the lighthouse. The shack along the lighthouse proper, where a lighthouse tender should have lived, had long since disintegrated, crumbling to the ground like any man made thing left too long near the unforgiving kiss of the sea. I had to live in the lighthouse itself now, a solid stone structure that towered up towards the heavens, and wouldn't disintegrate for as long as I was alive, anyway. That's all that mattered, then.

I tugged up the corner of my mattress and took out the comforting stone, shaped like a tiny pillow, able and capable of filling my entire palm with a sense of peace. I pressed its worn curves to my hand and closed my eyes, cleared my mind.

"Show me Galo," I whispered to it, and as light spiraled out from the center of the stone, it began to comply with my wish.

At first, there was always dark shadows spinning out over the stone, and then it focused, as if waters parted.

Galo had never been a handsome man, not even when I was little, and stole the stone to frighten myself with his visage. He sat at a small table, now, and had his head in his hands. His long, tangled hair—white as the crests of foam—curled around his ears and down and over his back and chest.

Sometimes, I pitied him.

There was no sound to accompany these pictures, so when the cottage door opened, when Nor entered to stand behind Galo, I started. Almost tenderly, she stepped forward and touched his shoulder with one fin-long hand.

He shrugged her off, quickly, said something, pointed. She drew away from him, mouth downturned, and left the room.

I put the stone away.

That night, I gathered my cloak about me, my grandmother's cloak, much patched and mended, and wandered out of the lighthouse into the star soaked night. I went down to my own, small shore, and stood up on the trunk of a tree that the last storm had washed onto my island. I shielded my eyes against the grinning moon and watched the procession of the townspeople.

They came from their houses, from their shacks, from their mansions. Sometimes, when my mother told the story of how Galo had made the town, forming it from mud, she would smirk beneath her hand, would say: "He didn't know what a town was made of, so he shaped the houses to what he'd seen from the water. He didn't know how they functioned, how they worked, what walls and windows were, and what the sea people were left with was empty hovels and doors that did not open." But I'd seen the inside of those houses, knew that this part of my mother's story wasn't quite right. Perhaps they'd gotten what they needed from other towns, trading fish or stories for chairs and bowls.

The people came, now, trails of people, men and women, walking stately, jerky, graceless and graceful in turns, down to the edge of the sea in the harbor, a spit of beach as smiling as the moon.

They gathered in a long line, one after the other, all turned toward me, but not really me. They were looking out to the sea, the ocean that could not embrace or touch them, the water closed off to them.

They stood, on the sand of the beach, and they did not move. They did not speak. The splash of the waves was silent upon my own little shore, and I watched them, as I did every night. And they watched me.

The moon shifted overhead, slowly, silently, and I grew tired as a sentinel, and stepped down from the tree trunk. I went back inside, shut and locked the door as I had done a hundred times before, a thousand times, and I went to bed while the sea people stood along the shoreline and stared, unmoving, at an untouchable sea.

I felt her before she stepped upon my sands this time. It was morning, again I checked the nets, mended the breaks, spun the magic to replace the strings that were too faded, did it all from the edge of the water, eyes closed, hands extended. Her little coracle bumped upon the edge of the sands, and I paused, opened my eyes, turned to take in her small shape as she dragged the boat up onto the beach. She moved like a girl, now, all trace of animal gone. You'd have to know what to look for to see it. I saw it.

"Hello," said Nor, coming to greet me, smiling shyly, hand extended. Today, I took it, felt the smooth, perfumed skin brush against my calluses and too-rough fingers. She held my hand a bit too long, and dropped it awkwardly. Still not human enough.

"Today..." she began, but I shook my head.

"No," I told her, as I would always tell her.

She nodded, still smiling, as if she'd expected my answer. "Is it all right if I sup with you? I brought lunch…"

I opened and shut my mouth and nodded. What could I say? It was an almost free island.

It was a quiche, with bits of seaweed sprinkled throughout, giving it a delicious, albeit fishy, aftertaste. I wrinkled my nose from time to time, but ate my portion without saying anything, staring down at my hands and small, china plate, and not up and across at my visitor who ate her quiche with a knife and fork and had folded her napkin upon her lap.

"Are you ever lonely?" she asked. I shook my head.

"You're brave," she said. "I would be."

I shook my head again. I wasn't brave.

She leaned back in her chair, took in the roundness of the lighthouse, the scrubbed cupboards, the neatly made husk bed at the furthest swell, opposite the table. She got up, ran her fingers along the wood and stone, circled the room as I watched her from hooded eyes, nervous. Would her touch leave a linger of her perfume? It was not unpleasant, but it was different, and I did not like different things.

"You live here, all alone?" she asked.

I nodded.

"Did you grow up alone?"

I sighed. "I grew up with my mother. She died when I was fifteen."

"Was that hard?" She sat across from me with her wide, brown eyes, and I knew it was not a joke of a question, but a genuine one. She was genuinely curious.

I cleared my throat. "In some ways. In others, no."

This seemed to satisfy her, for she stood and gathered her things in her small, plain basket, brushing her fingers over mine when she reached to take my plate. I shuddered, but she seemed not to notice, and she smiled at me when I rose.

"It was lovely to talk to you. You are not a bad witch. I have decided it."

The Witch Sea

I was too stunned to say a reply until after she had left, withdrawing out of my old, worn door, the memory of her scent remaining in the small space. It was not too different.

What I said after her was: "Thank you."

∽

"Show me Nor," I whispered to the stone, pressing my hands together. When I looked down at the stone, held between them, it showed a muddy, distorted image and then there she was.

She was laughing, throwing back her head and laughing at something a tall, thin man said, bending down almost double at the waist to whisper a word in her tiny, shell-shaped ear.

She was surrounded by people, and they stood in Galo's house, the largest of them all in the town. There were tapestries along the wall, and thick carpets along the floor, and I had never once felt sorry for him in all that finery.

He came striding down the staircase now. He was dressed in too loose pants, and a dirty white shirt. His hair rose up and about his head like a creature, in and of itself, and he said something to Nor, who sighed and shook her head, but did not look the least bit afraid. I wondered if I would be afraid, confronted by that angry of an elder, with hair that moved as if alive, with teeth sharper than the shark men. He said something else, and the people backed away from Nor, but she shook her head again, folded her arms.

He turned and stood along the far wall, looking through a window. I could see the view through that window, knew it looked out upon the bay, and, past that, to my own island.

I covered the stone with my hands and put it away.

I drew water from the magicked well and washed my face in it. It was so cold, I shuddered, put my hands upon the well rim, stood for a long moment, letting the waves of chill pass through and away from me. The salt breeze was blowing from the north today, and my mother had often told omens by the wind's direction. North was ill tidings, always ill tidings, she'd whispered to me so many times, spinning the circle about herself as if it could protect her.

Nor came a second time that day, so my mother might have been right.

"I brought you dinner," she explained, not even greeting me, but brushing past me where I stood on the hillock before the shore, staring at her, open mouthed. "Do you like biscuits? I brought you biscuits, and a good, fish gravy."

"My answer is still 'no,'" I told her, following after her, pressing my hands together to keep my fingers from shaking. "I will not ever answer his demands with a 'yes.'"

"And I did not ask you, did I?" She looked up from setting my tiny, meager table, and her eyes were flashing, and her wide smile turned her lips up at the corners, almost teasing.

"Why else would you have come?" I asked her, voice quiet.

"To keep you company," she replied, and spread a bright red and white checked cloth over the table. It hid the cracks and the well scrubbed surface, and made it almost cheerful.

"Come, sup with me," she said, then.

And I did.

That night, when I walked out to the shore, and my tree trunk, and my vigil, thoughts chased each other in my head, and I almost tripped, climbing up the bark to stand at my usual, well-worn place.

The dinner had been very good.

I shielded my eyes against the almost new moon, even though it shed too little light to really obscure my vision. I watched the processional of the sea peoples out of their houses and hovels, making their own well-worn ways down to the shore of the sea. They stood, one beside the other, stretching all the way around the bay, and they raised up their faces to the scent of the surf, and the stars, and they trained their eyes to the deep blue waters, and they did not move, they did not speak, they did nothing but stare with a longing I could almost understand.

This was the first night I saw Nor among them.

I looked for her tonight, doing my best to see far away shapes—I was too far for faces. I felt Galo's presence to the center of the line, and there was Nor, beside him on the right. I don't know how I knew her, but I did, and she stood, just as still and silent as her brothers and sisters, which surprised me, and I didn't really know why. I supposed I had expected her to be different from the others, for she was already different to me than all the others.

I dreaded the new moon. Tomorrow.

I did not sleep that night. I tossed and I turned, and—once or twice—I rose to peek out of my curtained window. The threadbare cloth did little to block the light during the day, or even during the night if the moon was bright, but it made me feel secure in the fact that—no matter what—the lighthouse was secure to the nighttime attentions and gazes of the sea people. I didn't know what I was afraid of, or why my skin crawled sometimes, and not others, when they made their nightly line and watched the ocean. My mother's stories were loud in my head that night, though, and I remembered how she said they waited and watched for weakness, waiting to destroy me so that they could be free.

I was exhausted by morning.

"You do not look well," said Nor when she arrived, when she dragged her coracle up on the shore, met me at the edge of the grass and the sand. I sat, tiredly, my head in my hands, and when she bent down beside, I did not even move farther away from her, though she sat much too close, the warmth of her body hot against my leg.

I did not answer her, and when I gave no answer, she handed me an apple, sun ripe and hard, and a piece of thick, crumbly bread.

"Breakfast," she said, and did not look at me, but rather, back the way she had come, toward the town. I ate in silence.

With her hands clasped in her lap, her hair disheveled and tossed in whichever direction the wind teased it, she looked calm and content, though wild. I envied the townspeople sometimes, and felt shame for that envy. She was prisoner to an old, forgotten god, kept from her home, probably never to see it again, and yet—the way she sat, poised, calm, clear like a full moon night, she looked much happier than I, the witch who contained them all, the jailer with the key.

I could not finish my breakfast, dropped the half eaten piece of bread to the ground as I rose. An angry gull swooped in, audacious enough to land beside Nor, and scooped it up and down into his gullet before either of us could protest. He took off with great sweeps of his wings, and flew out to sea.

"They are despicable, vermin," I spat out, realizing from some far, removed place, that my mother had said the exact same thing, in the exact same voice, once.

"He was only hungry," said Nor, upturning her eyes to me, face drawn.

She left without asking the question.

Even though the moon was new, I could sense where it hung in the sky, suspended and ponderous, out of reach and dark to us. I shivered within my cloak, even though the breeze was warm, and drew it closer about myself, as if I could bind safety to me with its worn, patched fabric. It smelled of seaweed and salt, fish and sweat, and it smelled like my grandmother and my mother, and I suppose that, now, it smelled of me. In that line, there was nothing that differentiated my scent from that of my mother's or my grandmother's, and that—for some reason—filled my heart with alarm. I was already nervous from the moon's dark ascension in the sky, and when I climbed the tree trunk, waiting for the procession, my heart beat a rhythm that the waves could not drown.

The moon affected my powers, but never so strongly than the new and full nights. On the full moon, I was drunk from the energies. The shining nets, suspended underwater, glowed so brightly that the entire bay shone from it. But on the new…

No living creature got past the nets. Save for on a new moon night.

Nor had come on the last new moon.

I rubbed my eyes tiredly, remembered the night, a month past, clear as glass, like a moment ago. I slept badly on the nights leading up to the new moon, tossing and turning as I thought how best to keep my lineage's oath, how best to thwart Galo's plans. But the

The Witch Sea

more I thought, the more I worried—the more I worried, the worse I slept. And then, the night came, and I was exhausted and nervous and shaky, and absolutely terrified that I would be the disappointment of a line of women who had given their lives to a curse.

I didn't want to be a disappointment. I did my best. Sometimes, I failed in that. Like last month.

It had been such a cold, black night. A storm had kicked up during the afternoon, and when I came out to keep my vigil, the driving rain lanced down slantwise, and I could not see, save for the breaking waves, and a slowly creeping mist that hung suspended over the water.

The seal bolted through the net. I know that much, but not how. She might have gotten spooked in the water—maybe a shark chased her. But, however she did it, she came through, slicing through the silver strands of the net, and I crumpled when she did, for the net was tied to me like all other parts of the island. When she broke it, I cried out from the pain, hand over my heart, falling to my knees in the roar and rush of the gale. I could feel her, the seal, darting through the bay toward the shore, and I knew that Galo called her. I did my best, in that biting rain, to repair the break, and I mourned the fact that yet another sea creature had lost its freedom.

My mother had told me that Galo called to the sea always, and that all of its creatures wanted nothing more than to please him and answer that call. That's why it was so important to maintain vigilance, to never falter, to repair the nets whenever there was the slightest break. Every new creature that rose from the seas to be transformed by Galo was another nail in the coffin of humanity—a fact my mother told me, day in and day out. What she didn't say, but what was understood, was that every creature that got through the net was our failing.

Now, it was another new moon. I had never let a creature through, had never faltered enough to truly fail, until Nor, but it had been a great failing. Galo was using her to get to me. I knew it. I scrubbed at my face, tried to peer through the mist.

Sometimes, I dreamed of what Galo must have been like before he assumed his human shape. The stories my mother had told me to frighten me were always fresh in my mind, dripping with dark water, clouding the bright days. I scrubbed at my eyes again and climbed the tree trunk. My skin rose in pimples, and I was chilled, strung taut, like a bow, and twice as tight.

Galo called the sea creatures—he always called to the sea creatures. I glanced uneasily over my shoulder at the dark night, and the ever present shush of the waves on the side of the island that looked out to the sea. They battered the rocks there, day and night, the rocks that held up my lighthouse.

What if…what if Galo ever called up a monster? What if Galo called up something so gargantuan, so sinister, that no amount of magic could combat him, no net could keep him out? What if the lighthouse, a massive structure, was dwarfed by his great bulk…what if he blocked out the stars…

I started so violently that I almost fell off of the tree when a loud splash sounded ahead of me in the mist. Fish often leapt up, sometimes dolphins came nosing around the bay, but my imagination traced dark grooves back to my worries and fears, and the hair along my neck rose, and I felt myself quake.

I had been alone for so long that I never thought about what it was to be with someone, that solidity of companionship that I would have, in that moment, given my heart for.

That's when I heard it.

Soft, small splashes came across the water, sounding loud and echoed in the misty stillness. Oars. A boat. Someone came from the town, at night, on a boat. This had never happened before.

The sea peoples, since the curse began, came together, at night, along the beach. They formed a silent line, and—together—they watched the ocean. All night. Every night. This had never changed, had never wavered, was as dependable as the seasons spinning on or the moon waxing and waning. I climbed down from the tree, filled with dread. My mother had taught me that changes were never good. I had always believed her.

The Witch Sea

The coracle was small and shadowed in the wake of the mist, and when it nosed up and onto my shore, I stared. Nor, small and sleek, leapt out of the boat, careful to keep her feet from the lapping waves, and dragged her small craft up further onto the sands.

"Hello," she said, quietly, staring up at me, eyes unblinking. "Good evening."

"What…" I said, and licked my lips, cleared my throat. I carefully folded my arms over my chest. "What are you doing here?"

She shrugged her shoulders, and—in the darkness—I could not see her expression. "I have been here a month."

I watched her.

"Don't you ever want this to stop?" she whispered.

I was so surprised by the question. I stood, and I opened and closed my mouth, and knew that there was no good answer to give her. Yes, I wanted it to stop. Every day, I wanted it to stop, I wanted it to be over. Sometimes, I thought about what it might be like if I'd been born to another mother, if I had not been raised on an island to nurse a curse that was not my own. Sometimes, I watched the seagulls and felt a welling of desire in me so fierce that it burned through me like a fire, a tongue of flame that licked my skin and spoke a single, sibilant word in my ear, over and over and over again:

Freedom.

She had not moved, but simply watched me, standing, hands clasped and folded before her, on the sands of my small, lonely spit of beach.

"What are you doing to me," I asked her. My voice cracked.

"Nothing," she said, tiredly. I believed her.

I felt paralyzed. Should I invite her in? It was so cold, so wet out here in the dark and the mist. She had come all this way, and she hadn't said why, but there she stood, on my beach, hands clasped, small mouth closed, wide eyes searching mine. I stepped aside, held out one hand, pointing to my lighthouse.

"Come," I told her, and ushered us both inside.

The night held a new tone, a new sensation as she hung up her cloak over my cloak upon the peg, drawing out the chair she usually sat in, taking off her wet gloves. There was no fire in the grate because I had already banked it, but I set about asking it to wake up with a few bits of sea grass, and a liberal push of magic.

"Do you use magic for everything?" she asked me, voice soft in the quiet of the lighthouse. I nodded, didn't look at her.

"I use it a lot." I fed the fire another handful of grass.

"You are what keeps the nets going." It was not a question.

"Yes."

"Why?"

I sat down upon the ground, turning a twig over and over in my hands. I had never touched a tree, often felt base wonder when I brought a load of wood to my island. I liked to feel the bark, tracing my fingers along the branches, the knots and whorls of the wood that would feed my fire. I could feel how it had been alive, if children had played beneath it, if it had been too small, when cut, if it had cried out on a level no human could hear. A witch wasn't human. I felt certain, every time I touched a twig, that I would have heard the tree scream, if I had felled it.

I didn't know how to answer her question, felt broken as I tried to think of an answer, of any response. I didn't know why I kept up the curse that had been my grandmother's business, why I had listened to my mother's stories with anything other than a healthy dose of skepticism. But I had listened to them. I had believed her, that we were the last wall of goodness between a monster and the annihilation of the human race.

Sometimes, when I saw Galo in my stone, I laughed, put my hand over my mouth, held back a sob. He looked old, worn, tired—as far from a monster as I could have imagined.

This is what I kept as prisoner. This is how I lived my life.

I could not tell Nor these things, these crumpled feelings of rage and despair and pain that ate up my heart from the inside, tiny jaws with sharp teeth eating up all those things that made me Meriel, spitting out replications of my mother instead.

So I sat on the floor, and I twisted the branch in my fingers, and I did not respond. I said not a word.

The Witch Sea

I heard a scrape of wood against wood, and looked up, just as Nor rose from her chair, sunk down on the floor beside me.

She was too close. She smelled of salt, always soft. She reached across the small divide between us and took up my hand, touched my rough skin with her smooth fingers, held my hand in her own as she drew it close, into her lap.

I stared, unable to move, as she held it tight and close, face hidden by a wave of long, brown hair that swept down and in front of it, concealing her from me as she turned away her face. She was so small, so fragile, as she held my hand in her lap, and the fire crackled, far, far away, as I took in the sea girl's slight form, the wave of her hair, the arch of her shoulder under the poorly spun gray cloth.

"I have decided," she said, words so low, I could almost not hear them, "that we are both prisoners, you and I."

"I'm not…" I said, and stopped myself. Anything I said after that would be a lie. I did many things. But I did not lie.

"Don't you ever wish…" she whispered, and I could not see her face until she looked up, glanced up at me quickly, wildly, and I saw the tears tracing down her cheeks, leaving a groove of soft, warm silver over her skin. "Don't you ever wish that it was all over. That things were the way they might have been…if this had never happened?"

I did.

I closed my hand, in her lap, to a fist. She dropped her fingers away from me, I drew back my limb, cradled it close to my chest as if it had been poisoned. I could not look at her. If I looked at her, I would lose my nerve, and I could not lose my nerve.

"You're trying to get me to say 'yes.' It won't work."

"That's not—"

"You're all alike," I said, surprised at the words that came tumbling out of my mouth. My mouth, but my mother's words. "Deceitful. Treacherous. You're all alike, and I will not yield to you."

A small part of myself, a lost, lone part, cried out from the dark within me as she rose, quick, jerky, always jerky. I would always be able to tell she'd been an animal. She wasn't human. She'd never be human.

"What part of you thinks this is right?" she asked me, then, and I could hear the tears in her voice, but dared not look up at her. If I saw them, if I saw her, I would lose my nerve. I could not lose it. "What part of you, Meriel?"

I pointed toward the door, terrified that, if I spoke, I would say the truth.

The old, worn thing crashed against the side of the lighthouse when she slammed it behind her. I waited until I felt her presence leave, entering the coracle and the cold and lonely bay. Then, when I knew she had gone, when there was no trace of her that had possibly remained to be a betrayer of the truth, I whispered it into the air, because I could not keep it inside any longer.

"None of me," I told the ghost of the sea girl, and sat, hollow, beside the dying fire.

∽

That had been too close. I needed to strengthen my resolve, my spells, my promise to my mother.

I had no choice. I must do a Calling.

The amount of energy necessary to do a Calling, the amount of magic I would need to spin, was gargantuan, all gargantuan. And it was the night after the new moon. But I couldn't think about that. I had no choice. I must.

I gathered bits of dried sea grass along the edge of the beach, the next morning, and I waited for Nor to come. But she did not. I sat along the beginning of the sand, and I twisted the grasses together nervously, and waited and was disappointed when she did not show. Which was sick, a sick reaction, and I knew that. When the sea grasses had been braided together, when I rose and made my way back to the lighthouse without any trace of Nor, I felt relief and pain wash over me in equal waves. It was good that she had not come. And, despite my best intentions, I was sad that she hadn't.

I built up the fire, laying my braided grasses in a special pattern in the flames. When all was ready, I built the circle about myself with chanted words and gestures, and, when it came, fully formed, I sat in the center of it and waited.

"Grandmother," I said into the cool calm within the lighthouse. "Come to me."

She did.

I had only ever spoken to my grandmother once, when my own mother had done a Calling when I was small, for the nets had broken almost beyond her repair, and she had needed counsel. What I remembered from that exchange, from my first time of seeing the woman who was the cause of all of this, was that she was smaller than I had thought she might be. She had been so strong, shouldn't she have been tall? But no—she was worn, and stooped, and her eyes were rheumy, even in death, like she couldn't see before her well, or even at all.

She came now, and she had not changed from my memory. She stood, stooped, leaning on the ghost of a cane. I could see through her, see the crackling flames behind her. She cast about, took in the state of the lighthouse, that I was performing the spell here, rather than the nonexistence cottage, and shook her head.

"Why have you summoned me, girl?" My grandmother, always to the point.

"I needed counsel," I said guardedly, and realized when I spoke those words, that I had absolutely nothing to say to my grandmother. What could I speak? What could I tell her? That my resolve was weakening for this curse because of a beautiful girl?

That was it, wasn't it? When I closed my eyes, I saw Nor's face. When I dreamed, I dreamed of her, and when she had not come that morning, I felt a small part of myself shriveling up, growing weak…dying.

My grandmother watched me work my jaw with an impassive face. Perhaps she could not see me and pass her condemnations. I did not know much of the nature of ghosts, but I could only assume that my grandmother had mastered a ghostly existence, much as she had mastered this one.

"Well? Spit it out, girly," she said at last, not unkindly. I folded my hands in my lap and stared down at my fingers.

"A seal got through the net."

"It's bound to happen," she said wearily, closing her eyes. "Did you kill it?"

"Kill it?" I choked out. I shook my head. "No..." I couldn't even fathom such a thing. In that small moment, I could not fathom my existence without Nor.

"That's what you must do, when they enter the bay. Better to die, make a meal for you, then serve Galo, trapped forevermore...that's not an existence we would wish on our worst enemies." She spoke to me as she'd spoken to my mother—imperious, like a child sat before her, not a grown woman with her own wants and wishes.

I watched my grandmother hover, for a long moment, and felt nothing but disgust.

"Be gone," I whispered, and when she opened her mouth, outraged, she vanished. She'd been about to scold me, surely. Call me weak hearted, like she'd called my mother. I remembered that, now.

I put my head in my hands and breathed steadily for several long moments. I was so tired, so unspeakably tired.

A knock at the door.

I sat, frozen, fear moving through my blood like fire. It was impossible—no creature, living or dead, could come upon my island without my knowing of it. I reached out, questing with my head and heart. I felt nothing. But again, there it was—a knock at the door.

I rose, mouth open. I didn't know what to do.

Again, the knock.

I opened the door.

She stood there, eyes wide and brown and beautiful, staring up at me as if she had never left. Her mouth was in a firm, hard line, and she did not smile at me like before.

"He made me come," she said quietly, simply, "to ask the question. Will you take his offer, Meriel?"

"How are you here?" I whispered to her, stared past her to the meadow, to the beach, to her little, bobbing coracle on the sand.

"I..." she wrinkled her brow, did not understand the question. I took her by the wrist then, circled her fair, pale skin with my rough fingers, and drew her inside.

The Witch Sea

"How did you get here," I whispered, "without my sensing you?"

She shook her head, her eyes growing wider. "I just came."

We stared at one another for a long moment, and I knew I was much too close to her, could smell the salt of her, the warmth of her skin that made my belly turn, doing somersaults within me. She leaned against the door and looked up at me through long, thick lashes, pressing her fingers against the wood my grandmother had lashed together to form a gateway I could never escape from.

"You." I licked my lips, closed my eyes. "You're making me want you. With magic."

She sighed, then, breathed out, and I opened my eyes. Her own shone, and I knew there were tears there, watched them fall, tracing lines down her delicate, upturned nose.

"I am not bewitching you. How could I bewitch a witch?" she murmured back. "Maybe this has nothing to do with magic, Meriel."

"You're magic," I told her, and when the words had left my mouth, I knew how true they were, how deeply true. She was magic to me, a sort of beautiful spell that I could not make, could not understand.

She stepped forward. It was tentative, uncertain, when she put her hands up through the space between us, drew them about my neck as if I could be easily broken and she did not wish to break me. She leaned up and against me, and on her tiptoes, she pressed her mouth to mine.

Her lips were salty, her tongue hot and smooth and soft, and I realized my hands were tightly about her waist long after I had placed them there. Heat rushed through me, and I felt my toes upturn, and then I stepped forward, pressing her to me, wrapping my arms about her so tightly, her breath rushed out, and she laughed a little against my mouth, a laugh of delight, high and soft. I wrapped my arms about her, gentle, then, and I pressed my lips against hers, and my tongue against hers, and our teeth clicked against one another. I was graceless, desperate, and when I shoved her against the bulk of the door, picked up her leg, put my hand beneath her bottom, I heard a sound like a whine, a sad, pathetic thing that came from my own lungs. I was starved, and she knew it, and she loved it, for her lips raked my skin, and her tongue trailed down my neck, and her hands were suddenly sharp as her nails raked down my back when I pressed her harder against the wood, fumbling with my fingers, completely unsure of what to do with something so lovely.

"Here," she said, and she took my hand, closed her fingers around mine, and guided my palm up and along her thigh where her skin was hot and soft and wet. I closed my eyes, and I stopped, in that moment. Every thing I was strained against the pause, crying out, screaming and roaring within me. She stopped, and I heard our breath between us, sharp and short and hard.

"What is it," she whispered, haltingly, not a question. She knew. I knew.

"I can't do this," I told her, and I gritted my teeth, satisfied to feel the pain of it thunder up and through my skull, bringing a red clarity. But I did not move my hand.

"Why can't you?" she asked, panting against me. She moved her body, then, brought her hips down upon my fingers, brushed her lips against my jaw. "There is no law against this. This does not break the curse. Everything you do remains safe, Meriel. This will not damn you."

And then, she whispered, "Please."

When I closed my eyes, I saw my grandmother's disapproving face, my mother's weak one, the line of sea creatures along the shore, the way that Galo put his head in his hands every afternoon and remained for hours in despair. When I closed my eyes, I saw my long, lonely years of unchanging monotony, the times that I fell asleep listening to the roar of the sea and the wind and wishing for...I didn't even know what I wished for, sometimes. Others, I did, a drumming of blood within me that called for something I knew I could never attain. Freedom.

I closed my eyes, and when I did, this all flashed in an instant. And when I opened them, there she was, in front of me, in my arms, bare skin against my hand, eyes wide and beautiful and wild and not the least bit human. She was a monster, I was a monster, and when I bent my head and kissed her again, tasting the salt of an ocean that was prison and home to us both, I forgot everything else but that kiss, but Nor. It didn't matter, nothing mattered, and when we found the bed, when I pressed down on top of her and in her and for her, our blood rushed at the same pull of tide and shore, and when she cried out, I cried out, the wind that roared and whipped the sea up into a frenzy carried our voices away into the great nothingness of blue.

We were so small, but in that span of moments that turned into hours, I merged into something that did not have a name. I felt, for the first time, the only time, that I mattered.

At dark, she said my name, kissed my neck, bowed beneath me.

I did not know what love felt. I wondered if I knew it, then.

She left the bed that night. I woke with the shifting of the thin mattress, watched her in the dark as she gathered up her underthings, her skirt, her blouse, and put them on slowly, letting the fabric drape along her warm skin. She left the cottage without looking back at me, and slowly, stiffly, I followed her.

Nor went down to the edge of the sea, her small form bright beneath the tiniest fragment of moon that hung in the sky, suspended. She came to the shore, and she straightened herself, stood, tall and unbending. I watched the mass of sea creature peoples on the bay's edge, watched as she looked to them, as they looked to her, as the only sound that roared about us was the sing of water and wind and the howling of an approaching storm.

I walked across the meadows, drawing my nightgown up and over my head, shivering in the cold, but unstoppable. I came, and I stood beside her.

"Why do you do this?" I asked her, then. I didn't expect an answer. For my entire life, the peoples had stood in silence all night, every night. But she opened her mouth, and she said:

"Because we must."

I waited for her to continue, but she did not. She did not even look at me. She stared at the water, and she said no more words.

"Why must you, Nor?" I reached out and touched her arm. She did not move beneath my fingers.

"Because we miss it," she said, and she said it so quietly, I almost did not hear her. Together, we stared at the ocean. I felt myself unraveling.

"I don't know why I do this anymore," I said then, gulping down air, rubbing at my face. Now that it was out in the open, I couldn't take it back. She didn't move, didn't stop watching the water. But she sighed.

"We all do what we must," she said, after so many heartbeats, I had forgotten that there was anything left in the world but the water and the stars and the heartless moon overhead.

In the dark, she moved her hand until it was in mine, curling her fingers about my own.

The unraveling stopped.

༄

"It's been three days," she whispered, when she kissed me. "I can feel him. He's calling me back."

"Don't go," I whispered, swallowed, felt my heart breaking. "Please don't go."

"I must obey his summons," she said, and traced her fingers along my collarbones, down my ribs, over my hips. I shivered and moved closer to her, pillowing my head over her heart.

"When will you be back?" I asked her, curling my fingers about her waist, feeling her pulse beat beneath my skin.

"Soon." She kissed my eyes, my nose, my mouth, my heart. Nor rose then, dressed, left the cottage. I lay on the mattress, crippled, unable to breath. I had not felt her come upon the island because she was part of it, now. I knew that. But when she left, I felt myself leaving, felt some small piece of me remove itself, launching out upon the waters and away from my flesh and bones. I felt her go, and I felt myself breaking, and I did not know what to do for the longest moment of my life.

I had not tended the nets for three days. I remembered that, as I lay, breathing, and I rose, felt my bones creaking. I raked my fingers through my hair, put on a clean shift, climbed out of bed.

The nets had about twenty small breaks, but nothing substantial or terrible. I stared for a very long time, trying to wrap my head around what I was supposed to do. I remembered, but it took too long, and I was frustrated as I began to mend the nets. Angry. I did not want to do this thing, this chore. I hated it, I hated it passionately, deeply, and as the first mend began to repair, I broke away from the energies and spells, felt them ricochet about and finally lodge in a small boulder at the edge of the water.

Disgusted, I turned away and went back inside.

"Show me Nor," I whispered to the small stone. I knelt beside the bed, and I held it in my hands, and I waited.

She was in Galo's house, and she sat beside him. He lay on the thick carpet before the empty fireplace, and I stared in horror. The old man wept, wept piteously, burying his face in her lap as she stroked his hair and stared ahead, eyes and face completely blank.

She wept, too, silver tears tracing down a face that had been meant for them.

I threw the stone away from me, heard it breaking as it hit the lighthouse wall, shattering into tiny pieces that could never be patched back together. I breathed out and put my face in my hands, and I felt my body shaking.

"I don't know what to do," I wailed, and it came out broken, disjointed, taken up by the wind that whistled through the open door, and carried out and away from me, over the open sea. "I don't know what to do," I whispered, then, and I kept the words close to me, whirling about me as I stood, as I hugged myself, as I paced the floor of the lighthouse over and over and over again, feeling the familiar wood against my bare feet, feeling the grooves I knew by heart beneath my toes, and then my knees when I knelt down again beside my bed, pressed my fingers to the sheets, to the threadbare blanket that had covered us both.

If I left.

If I left...

If I...left.

I would never see Nor again.

Galo would shatter the curse, would call us his sea army, would destroy the world.

I would break my mother's heart. My grandmother's heart. *I* would destroy the world.

Wouldn't I?

I spread my fingers across the cream sheets, counted them like I had when I was a child. One, two, three, four…I swallowed and pressed them harder against the bed, so hard I felt it creak beneath me as I stood up, as I held my hands together then, as if in prayer.

I wasn't sorry, and I wouldn't say it. I turned, and I left the lighthouse, standing uncertain at the edge of the sand.

"First, he'll set fire to the world, burn the crops, bring diseases," my mother had said, and I heard her voice in the wind now, the condemnation and damnation and all the stories she'd spun for me when I was little, the nightmares I had had each night feeding off her words. "He will laugh as man dies. He has no pity."

I had seen him weep.

"They are monsters," she'd told me over and over and over again, making me repeat it until my tongue was tired.

Wasn't I a monster, too?

I rubbed my shoulders, and then I took a step forward. I felt the magic settle about me as I pulled, and then, before me, was Nor's coracle, summoned by my spell, bobbing up and down at the edge of the water.

I stood in the sand. I felt the tide come up and touch my bare feet, felt it run over my skin, so cold, I let out my breath in a hiss.

I closed my eyes, balled my hands into fists, and stumbled into the boat, feeling my feet leave land for the first time in my life.

I took the oar and clumsily pushed off from the sand, even as I began to hear the breaking behind me. I heard the scream of stone against stone and I did not look behind me, but saw the tall shadow of the lighthouse in the water as it began to sway, back and forth, back and forth, crumbling. The roar surrounded me as I began to paddle for shore, and the storm that had threatened for the night and morning began to hit as I felt the spell unravel, as the lighthouse fell down, as the net began to shatter.

I paddled as the rain hit, paddled hard as the swells began to grow, tossing the coracle back and forth, filling it with water, and then emptying it in the same heartbeat. I gritted my teeth, and I paddled against the sea as the last wisps of the net unwound themselves, as I felt the net disappear entirely. The roar of the wind, the howl of the sea, surrounded me, and I wept in the salt water, in the rain water, my tears mingling with all the water, water everywhere.

Somehow, eventually, I reached the shore. The sea creature peoples were gathered there, and they stared at me with open mouths as the boat pitched itself upon the sand. I fell as I climbed out, felt the solidity of sand and land beneath my hands and let out a great cry that was lost in the bellow of the people as they raised their heads up to the sky, to the great, gathered storm clouds, and let out a cry that dwarfed the music of the storm.

And then, Nor was there.

She came down the shore, her eyes wide, wild, and she helped me rise, her hands soft against my own. Tears streaked down her long nose, and when she kissed me, she tasted of salt. Galo came behind her. He was skeletal, almost unrecognizable, and he stared at me with haunted eyes.

One by one, the sea peoples began to walk into the water.

Galo was the first. He walked past me, limping, and when he entered the sea, the first bit of white foam touching his legs, he let out a cry, as if in pain. But then he sunk below the water, and was gone, something large and dark moving through the bay, just below the surface.

I took Nor's hand, and I kissed it. She stood, for a long moment, but it was not long enough, would never be long enough, when I remembered it, and she mouthed two words before she turned and entered the water with her brothers and sisters and an army of people who had never belonged here, going home.

What she said was: "Thank you."

Barn-stormers

Wendy N. Wagner

The last knot of people waved goodbye at the edge of the makeshift airfield, grinning and clutching their autographs tight. Casey waved back until they were too small to see. Then she patted the side of the trailer, smiling up at the stowed mechs. The smile changed to a frown. Jolene had landed her mech with its grasping units—which Casey would always think of as hands—framing its cockpit, the opposable flexors set in an unmistakable "thumbs up" pose. The glass bubble of the cockpit stared down at Casey in bland mockery.

A mech could take an artillery round to the chest, but if the hands were open, one rainstorm could should out the delicate joints of the grasping units. And since Casey had set the security features to maximum for the summer, the PEAV's neural interface would only recognize Jolene's brain patterns. If Jolene didn't climb up in the rig and stow the damn thing properly, the PEAV would thumbs-up the world all night long.

Casey spent several minutes cleaning up empty water bottles and popcorn boxes before fury ebbed enough to cross the field to the tent site. The glowing tip of Jolene's joint served as a beacon, calling Casey through the evening gloom.

Jolene lay on a sheet spread beside side of the tent, naked, smoking, staring up at the clouds sculling across the darkening sky. Casey threw herself down beside her. She knew this mood, an ugly hybrid of anger and depression. The moods had been infrequent when she and Jolie first started building the show, two chicks brought together by the VA Benefits Office waiting room and the same taste in beer. These days, the moods were as regular as popcorn sales.

Casey pushed herself up on one elbow. "You could help clean, you know. We want to be able to use this field next summer."

Jolene inhaled and held the smoke deep inside her. She was still beautiful to Casey, despite the long white scar running up her hip, her ribs, into her armpit. Despite the strange square shape of her reconstructed collarbone and the white plastic socket jutting out of her chest, which allowed easy recharge of her replacement heart. Even broken, Jolene was the perfect shape of woman.

Smoke trickled from her nose. "There won't be a next summer."

"Jolie—"

"No. I can't do it anymore. Every day on the road, nights in a tent—I can't take that anymore. I hurt. And watching all those assholes stare at me is like cutting out my heart all over again."

Meeting you every summer is like cutting out my heart again, Casey thought. But she didn't say it. It wasn't anything Jolene could understand. She fucked men, and women were invisible to her. Friendship sometimes seemed like a strong word for what she and Casey had; they were business partners, plain and simple. Co-workers.

But she was going to have to convince Jolene to stick out the last of the season. Just for business. There was money to recoup, fields and big air shows already confirmed. Casey put on her sweetest expression.

"It's hard, I know. You're a combat veteran with multiple decorations, not a vaudeville actress. But just think about all the joy you're bringing these people. They're tied to their farms, they can't travel. Our show is the best thing they've seen since the Reconstruction began." She sat up, smiling benignly. "You're making a difference, Jolie."

Jolene sucked back half an inch of joint in one sharp inhalation. She shook her head while the smoke seared into her lungs. The combat docs on Mars had done the best they could, but even five follow-up surgeries had done nothing for Jolie's chronic pain. She woke up screaming sometimes. Casey had rocked her to sleep more than she could count.

Casey pressed on. Jolene's face was hard and cold now, but tomorrow she'd feel different. She always did. "Just stay till Wichita. We've got a recruiter coming to the show. He's got the first half of our summer paycheck."

"Recruiters. I can't believe we're helping the Air Force hire more grunts. These farm kids look up at our fancy machines and they think PEAVs are all pink smoke and synchronized dance. They forget the damn things aren't toys. They're Power-Enhanced Armor-Vehicles. *Armor*, Casey."

Casey knew that if she didn't stop Jolene now, she'd work herself up into a full-on screaming rage. The Air Force took her collarbone. The Air Force took her heart. The Air Force took her mother-fucking husband and she didn't even get to bury his body. Casey had heard it a lot the last few weeks. She suspected something had happened to Jolene this winter, because for the first time, the bad shit could no longer be contained by medical marijuana and two hours a day in the cockpit, flying free.

So she stole the joint from Jolene's fingers and sucked down a long drag of it, letting the grin spread wide and crooked across her face. "Fuck that shit. Let's go get drunk."

It was the right thing to say. The vitriol hung in Jolene's eyes a second and then a smile appeared on her own face, growing dimples. "If they've got more than near-beer in this shit-hole town."

Casey pushed herself to her feet and offered Jolene her hand. "Only one way to find out."

～

They walked into town. It would have taken too much effort to unhitch the mechs' trailer from the truck, and with any luck they'd be in no shape to drive after a couple of hours. Town lay about a mile and a half down the gravel road. Once there'd been pavement, but there wasn't enough oil left in the world to justify asphalt these days.

Casey kept her arm around Jolene's waist as they walked, but they didn't talk. Casey let her mind play over the time before Reconstruction. She couldn't remember it too well, she'd been so young. There was oil, and then there wasn't. There were suburbs, and then there weren't. As a kid, her parents had lived in a west coast city with a symphony and a dozen libraries and jobs that ran off computers. Her memories of her childhood were scattered and few, rattling around in a mental box that kept them smelling like Christmas and her mother's perfume. They'd gone to the Nutcracker every year. She'd never forget the stiff velvet of the dresses her mother bought her to wear at the performances.

But then, the Reconstruction. They'd been relocated to a government farm not that different from these ones. Casey wanted to pause and lean on a fence post beside the road, take a moment and study the crops. She'd learned how to test soil by placing it on her tongue, learning the mineral contents by their flavors. The neighbor had taught her how to fix tractors at the same time he taught her father.

It was Jolene who stopped, staring at a red rag fluttering on the strand of barbed wire. "That's where they'll start tomorrow morning," she murmured. "When they come out to finish checking the fence line."

She started walking again, faster, and Casey had to jog a step to catch up with her.

"I spent a summer fixing fences," Jolene muttered.

"I thought you grew up in Chicago."

"They sent kids out to the farms every summer. 'Everybody has to pitch in for the agricultural effort!'" She kicked a stone and they both watched it soar ahead of them. "Fucking hated that farm shit."

Casey would have answered, but a pickup truck roared past, the teenagers in the back whooping and catcalling as they shot by. Casey thought she recognized them from the air show, a knot of sullen kids who'd passed a joint in the back of the field. But that was what teenagers did out here, she knew—there was nothing else for them. Drugs, and fucking, and getting dirt under their nails. Less than one percent had a chance at college under Reconstructionist policy.

She felt lucky then. She smiled at Jolene. "Aren't you glad the GI Bill pays for school? I sure as hell wasn't cut out to work on a farm."

Jolene gave her a sideways look. She was in her second year of graduate school, gearing up to write a thesis on particle physics. Casey knew Jolene looked down on Casey's job teaching welding at a community college. She tried not to give a shit.

They passed into the center of town. Neon lights called them from the end of the block: Coors. Budweiser. Miller. Casey hoped there was tequila. They passed a grocery store on their right and an electrical recharge shop on the left, the shop advertising automotive repair and the cheapest battery jumps in a two hundred mile radius. Casey made a note—the truck could use a charge if they were going to make it to the next town south. If she could convince Jolene they should go to the next town.

The teenagers had parked their truck in front of the automotive shop, and their laughter sounded hard and bright as the two vets passed the place. A girl came out of the shop, so blond and tall that Casey caught herself looking back over her shoulder as she walked past. She was as pretty as Jolene, and that was saying something.

Jolene tugged on Casey's arm. "I see an Absolut sign in the window."

The prospect of hard liquor drove the girl out of Casey's mind. She broke into a little jog and tugged open the door. She held it for Jolene, waving her in.

Country music billowed out on a wash of warm air ripe with the funk of spilled beer. Casey hesitated, but Jolene was already inside, headed straight for the dimly lit bar. A couple of flickering fluorescent tubes lit up the taps and single shelf of hard liquor. The rest of the place hid itself in darkness.

Jolene leaned over the bar to deliver her order. She'd worn her costume into town, the black shorts and white tanktop, revealing muscles still sculpted and strong. For a second Casey could imagine her on a Martian base, playing cards with the other aces in their wife-beaters, all ease and grins until their radio implants called them out to the flight deck. It hadn't been like that on Luna. The Chinese had mostly given up on the moon by the time Casey signed up. The good stuff, the rare earth elements and metal ores, were all bound up on Mars and in the asteroid belt. Earth's dirt was mostly played out, worth more for crops than minerals.

She shook off the stupor of memory and surmise, hurrying to join Jolene while there was still a second shot glass on the table. She gave it a sniff. "What the hell is this shit?"

Jolene grinned. "Grain liquor. Half the price of vodka and cut with ascorbic acid and salt. The bartender swears it tastes just like tequila with lime."

Casey knocked it back. Who was she to argue? She hadn't seen a lime since she was ten years old.

A man in a ball cap made his way out of the darkness. "Next round is on me. You ladies sure know how to put on a show." Beside him, his buddy in a cowboy hat bobbed his head in agreement.

"Thanks." Casey knew it was her job to talk to him, to put on a smile.

The bartender appeared with two more shot glasses, and Ball Cap slid one down to Jolene. He offered the second to Casey, his fingers touching hers. "And you're a real nice-looking lady." He leaned in a little closer. "At least when you've got that skull jack covered up. A man don't like to be reminded his lady fought the Chinks."

Jolene knocked back her shot. "Thanks for the drinks. You gents play pool?" She caught the bartender's eye. "Keep the shots coming to the pool table."

She looked back over her shoulder at Casey and the men, her pupils huge from dim light and THC. "Any of you got any change?"

Casey rolled her eyes and hurried to catch up with Jolene, catching her elbow and pulling her ear into whispering distance. "Really? Pool? These guys are walking sacks of manure."

"Just trying to have fun," Jolene cooed. She slipped her fingers into Casey's hip pocket and worked free a quarter. "Look what I found!"

"Just one game," Casey warned. She didn't like it when Jolene let her hormones think for her. Didn't trust things to stay safe in this dirty corner of nowhere. She snatched the coin out of Jolene's fingers and made her way to the pool table. It was dark enough in this corner of the room that Casey had to feel her way down the side of the table, fumbling her quarter into the slot. The single fluorescent bulb strung above the table flickered on, and the balls rattled down the chute.

"Who's ready to have their ass handed to them?" Jolene put on hand on her hip and studied the farm boys. "I've never lost a game…on this planet anyway."

"Sounds like quite the claim." Cowboy Hat leaned across her to reach the pool cues, but Jolene's smile was fixed on Ball Cap.

Casey thought of the way he'd pushed his fingers against hers when he passed her the shot glass, and she knew exactly what Jolene was doing. Every show, she said she hated to be watched, but out of the cockpit, Jolene hated it when anyone else got the attention. Casey shook her head as she racked up the balls.

Ball Cap and Cowboy Hat exchanged glances.

"May the best man win!" Ball Cap announced.

The door to the bar slammed open and the kids from the red pickup truck piled inside. Their leader, a good-looking boy with his arm slung around the beautiful blond from the automotive station, muscled his way to the bar. Casey was disappointed to see the bartender pass them three cases of beer. But that was life in a small town, she remembered. It was easier to take the money and look the other way than deal with troubles that would you couldn't walk away from.

Or maybe it was just sympathy. Since the oil ran dry and the power got rationed, there wasn't nearly enough for kids to do, and with the agricultural workers' quotas, it wasn't like these kids had futures to look forward to. Just dust, and wheat, and nights in a bar like this for the rest of their lives. A beer and a blond was the best that good-looking boy could expect from the world.

When the bartender laid a row of shot glasses down on the pool table, Casey was the first to reach for one.

Casey and Jolie had a rule on the road: don't fuck the rubes. Jolene had slipped up in four other towns, and every time she'd come out of it with bruises and cops breathing down their neck. One of those towns, C & J Air Show was still banned from performing. So when Jolene put Ball Cap's hands on her hips and wiggled her ass against his thighs as she lined up her shot, Casey knew it was time to get out. They'd played three games of pool and the table was lined with shot glasses.

"Soon as you finish this game, Jolie, we should wrap it up. Long drive tomorrow, remember?" Casey said it with a smile, but Jolene just shot her a glare.

"I'm not going anywhere tomorrow, remember Casey? Because I quit your stupid show. Remember?"

Ball Cap laughed. He'd introduced himself some time, but Casey'd forgotten it four or five drinks ago. She could feel a burning in her belly, and was glad she'd stopped putting back the rotgut. A hangover was worse after a night sleeping on the ground.

She slipped her cue back into the rack. Now Jolene was whispering something in Cowboy Hat's ear, pressing his hand against her tit. Casey shook her head in disgust.

"Hey, you been flirting with me all night. What the shit's going on?" Ball Cap's face was red and twisted ugly.

Jolie giggled. He put his hand out to grab her shirt, but misjudged and closed his fist on air.

Casey stepped between the two. "She's drunk. She gets real dumb when she's drunk." She dug her fingers in Jolie's biceps. "Come on, Jolie, we've done enough damage here."

"But I feel terrific." Jolene wobbled a second and then settled her head on Casey's shoulder.

Ball Cap pulled back his fist. "You two dykes? Think it's funny coming on to men and leaving them worked up?"

Casey felt ice knot around the booze in her gut. She had a knife in her boot, but she wanted a gun. Hell, she wanted her mech.

Cowboy Hat snorted. "Aww, shit, Bruce. She wasn't into you. I was the one gonna take her home."

Then Jolene's legs went out from under her, and Casey just managed to catch her by the elbows, and she wished like hell she'd already paid the bar tab and could run out of this dark and muggy place before something horrible happened.

"Ain't worth wasting your time now," Cowboy Hat laughed. "That girl's passed out."

Casey didn't say a word as she started backing out of the bar, Jolie's heels bouncing on the bumps and cracks in the worn floor. She slipped her arm around Jolie's middle so she had a free hand to find the last of their money in her pocket. She dropped a hundred dollar bill on the counter and didn't bother waiting for her change.

Her stomach loosened a little as the door closed behind them.

Out on the front step, a little breeze ruffled the strands that had come loose of Casey's braid. She closed her eyes to work up the energy to drag Jolie onto her feet. The breeze felt cool and sweet after the bar's closeness, and her head felt pleasantly light. It could have been a good night if Jolene hadn't fucked up back there.

"I think I'm going to be sick."

Casey pivoted Jolene with reflexes sharp despite the alcohol. She hadn't dealt with a puker since her first tour of duty, but some skills are never lost. She breathed shallowly through her mouth while Jolene emptied a pint or two of pseudo-tequila all over the bar's siding.

Jolene coughed and retched again. She gave a whimper and took a few steps away from the mess, wobbling a little before thumping down on her ass in the thick dust. Her shoulders shook, and it took Casey a second to realize she was crying.

She squatted beside Jolene, rubbing her back.

"I'm sorry." Jolie heaved between her knees, but there was nothing left to come up. "That was stupid."

"S'okay."

"Oh fuck, Casey, I don't know what to do." She spat over her shoulder and wiped her face on her arm. "The VA says they're canceling my funds. They say the national allotment of graduate students has been exceeded, and they're cutting money devoted to the theoretical programs."

Casey sank onto her butt. "Shit."

"They say I can reapply next year. But I'll have to take a year off from school while I wait for the bullshit paperwork to clear. What the hell am I going to do for a year, Casey? I can't stay at the university without money!"

Casey pressed her cheek against Jolene's shoulder. She didn't have an answer. But Jolene's moods this summer finally made sense.

"They say they're upping the agricultural workers quota. Gonna make me work on a farm." She leaned her head against Casey's and choked off a sob.

And then they heard it. Maybe there'd been other sounds when they'd stumbled out of the bar, but the sound of a girl shrieking "Leave me alone!" finally penetrated the haze of booze and unhappiness.

Jolene went stiff. Casey found herself reaching for the sidearm she no longer carried. Adrenaline replaced alcohol, and they jumped to their feet, running toward the sound.

It had come from the automotive shop. Casey thought of the pickup truck full of teenagers, stupid and now drunk and probably stoned out of their brains, and her heart raced even as her training kicked in. She ran to the left, Jolene to the right, their boots quiet on the gravel road. Running lightly. Taking their weapons from their boot tops. Civilians might be forbidden firearms, but that didn't mean they were stupid enough to travel without weaponry.

Casey shifted her switchblade to her left hand and her brass knuckles to her right. The red pickup still sat at the charging station, and bent over its hood she could see the beautiful blond, pinned down by the good-looking boy with his hand wriggling beneath her t-shirt. The girl wriggled, and the boy slapped her with his free hand.

"Stop being such a bitch, Mel."

There were other sounds, giggles from the back of the red pickup, crickets in the distant fields, her own breathing, but they disappeared in the tidal surge of Casey's rage.

He turned around at the sound of her snarl.

She reached the boy at the same time as Jolene. Their fists took parallel paths into his face, side-by-side explosions of teeth and spit and blood. They didn't bother with the switchblades. He wasn't that much bigger than either of them.

Jolene lashed out with her boot, toppling him. There were no sounds from the pickup truck anymore. The sound of his whimpers were that much louder.

Jolene stepped down onto his gut, pinning him in place. She held the blond girl's gaze. "You want a shot at him?" They were surrounded by a knot of staring teenagers, but Jolene didn't spare them a glance.

The girl stared down at him. He clutched his face, already puffy even in the faint phosphor glow of the station's nighttime lighting. Her lips twisted. "Hell yeah."

She kicked him in the ribs, twice. "I told you leave me alone!" She kicked him again. When she looked up, her eyes were bright and her nose ran snot down her lip. She wasn't crying. She was keeping it in. "How many times did I have to ask him to just leave me alone?"

The girl swiped at the snot and left streaks of grease across her face. It hit Casey then: the grease-black hands, the stained rag stuffed in her back pocket, the faded and holey clothes. She *worked* at the automotive shop. She was the girl Casey had been at eighteen, but thin and beautiful, not awkward and stocky.

Casey's heart twisted for the girl. She stretched out a hand to her, squeezed her shoulder. "You going to be okay?"

The girl nodded. "I think so." She wiped her nose on the back of her hand again. "At least he'll have some tender targets for me to aim at the next time."

She sounded resigned to the idea of a next time. And in a place like this, flat and boring and short on anything beautiful, it was probably only a matter of time until there was. Casey thought of Ball Cap, back in the bar, and felt lucky that kind of next time hadn't happened to her or Jolie.

She reached for some kind of advice, something she could tell the girl that would protect her or help her in any way. "Be careful," she finally said. She wanted to say *come with us*. She wanted to say *I'll save you*. But there was no way to say it.

Jolene kicked the boy in the ass as she turned away, and Casey knew it was time to get out of town. The kids were starting to whisper now, and two of the boys were kneeling next to their buddy. Casey gave the girl an awkward wave and followed Jolene back to the main road. The dust seemed drier and thicker than it had when they'd first come into town.

They made it almost a hundred yards before the girl shouted at them. They stopped and let her catch up. She panted a little, her cheeks gloriously flushed as she tried to catch her breath.

"You're the ladies with the flying show. The mech pilots."

Casey nodded.

"Did you fly in the Air Force? Is that where you learned it?"

"Yeah. I served two tours of duty on Luna, and Jolene served two and a half tours in the asteroid belt and the Martian combat zone. Protecting our mining bases."

The girl's eyes looked huge in the moonlight. She hesitated, looking from Casey to Jolene. "Did you like the Air Force? Was it okay?"

Jolene opened her mouth, and for a second, Casey thought that she would spill it all out, the dead husband, the chronic pain, the artificial heart, the grad school fuck-over. But instead, Jolene said: "It's pretty good."

Casey just stared at her.

"Yeah, the service can really take you places if you let it. It paid for me to go to college. I'm in grad school now."

"College? It'll pay for college?"

Both Casey and Jolene nodded.

The girl launched herself at Jolene, giving her an awkward hug. "Thanks." She hugged Casey, too. "Thanks," she repeated.

"Good luck," Casey said. And then Jolene was tugging her back down the road, Casey walking backward as she waved at the girl, who beamed and waved back until she was just a speck in the distance.

The shoulders of the mechs gleamed white in the moonlight, their cockpits sparkling under the twinkle of the stars. It was a clear night, the sky stretching wide without cloud cover or light pollution. At home, back in Seattle, it was never like this. Casey let her head fall back, cricking her neck to take in the glimmering expanse.

"Ahh shit. I gotta go stow my mech's graspers."

Casey couldn't take her eyes off the stars. Ursa Major looked ready to tumble down out of the sky. "It's not gonna rain. Don't worry about it." Her earlier anger at Jolene's silly thumbs-up stunt had disappeared in the booze and the fight.

"Might as well do it now, so I don't have to get up and do it in the morning."

Casey heard the grass swishing around Jolene's legs, the hiss of the cockpit opening, the grumble of her PEAV firing up.

"Hey!"

She finally dropped her gaze back to earth. "Hey, what?"

"Let's fly. Just for fun. Just to remember how good it is."

Jolene smiled down at her, a tiny figure in the giant suit of armor. Casey smiled back. In a minute, she was jacking in, the comforting presence of the PEAV operating system appearing in her mind.

They didn't even need radio: they just launched in synchronicity, shooting up toward the stars, moving so fast it felt for a second like they might catch themselves on the Big Dipper, lift it back up into the top of the sky where it belonged. Without an audience, they didn't bother with the colored steam or music cues. They just flew. For themselves. And as the mechs twisted and leaped, flight became dance.

A barn rose up ahead, and they pulled the mechs up sharp, just clearing the roofline. Casey stretched her grasping unit out to the Jolene's mech, letting momentum spin the big machine back to her like a ballroom dancer spinning his partner. They whirled a second above the barn.

This, night flight in a million-dollar killing machine turned to entertainment, this dance above a barn and not inside one—that was what the Air Force had given Casey. And right now, it was enough. Tomorrow there'd be dirt and the long drive to Wichita. She'd be a dyke and Jolene would be a cripple. Tomorrow they'd smile nice for the Air Force recruiter and pray that the check didn't bounce.

Tonight they danced.

Nightfall in the Scent Garden

Claire Humphrey

If you read this, you'll tell me what grew over the arbor was ivy, not wisteria. If you are in a forgiving mood, you'll open the envelope, and you'll remind me how your father's van broke down and we were late back. How we sat drinking iced tea while the radiator steamed.

You might dig out that picture, the one with the two of us sitting on the willow stump, and point out how small we were, how pudgy, how like any other pair of schoolgirls. How our ill-cut hair straggled over the shoulders of our flannel shirts.

You'll remind me of the stories we used to tell each other. We spent hours embroidering them, improving on each other's inventions. We built palaces and peopled them with dynasties, you'll say, and we made ourselves emperors in every one, and every one was false.

If you read this, you'll call your mother, or mine. They'll confirm what you recall.

By then, though, you will begin to disbelieve it yourself.

If you think on it long enough, you'll recall the kiss. I left it there untouched, the single thread you could pull to unravel this whole tapestry.

You'll start to understand none of these things happened the way you remember. If you read this, you'll learn how I betrayed you.

We gave ourselves names of power. We signed them in the guest book at the gallery. I called myself Faustine Fiamma, after a dream. And you: Rosa Mundi. Rose of the world, rose of alchemy. Flame and flower, two girls in flannel and training bras. We made up addresses in Paris, Ontario, because we could not speak enough French to have come from the other Paris.

Your father carried his sculpture, wrapped in brown burlap. One of the ones he'd done of you, as a smaller child, dancing. You whispered to me that now every art-lover in Ontario would know you had an outie.

We slipped away, outdoors: this much, I left you. In the garden was the sundial. A great barbed face streaked with verdigris. It told no time just then; the sun too low behind the curtain of purple blossom, the light pearly. Herbs grew in beds around the plinth. Thyme and rosemary both, probably, and a dozen other things; I don't remember them all. Only the warmed scents of them on the air. We walked counterclockwise about the beds, touching all of the brass plaques, which bore the names of the herbs in Roman capitals and in Braille.

You shut your eyes, and I wrapped my scarf about your head and tied it behind, and led you by both hands.

Here's where I stopped. To be safe. Here's where your father came outside and told us it was time to go. I think I made him realistic, don't you? Fox-bright eyes and hair, and a dozen pockets on his jacket; I think he really had a jacket like that.

Nightfall in the Scent Garden

You're thinking right now that you don't want to hear what comes next. Stop reading, then. I can make my choice without you, if I must.

Your father didn't enter the garden. He didn't take us out to the van or back to Toronto, not then. He didn't finish up with his friends in the gallery until after midnight.

No. You and I circuited the garden. After a while the sun went down, but the light in the sky lingered, grainy and soft like an old photograph. Bats darted overhead.

"It's nearly time," you said.

"Time?" I plucked a sprig of rosemary; I bit down on one of the leaves, and I placed another at the entrance to your mouth. You opened, tasted it; your breath warm on my fingertips.

"I've had enough of being blind," you said.

I untied my scarf from your eyes.

I saw your pupils blown open. Like those wells the glaciers grind in rock, deep and wide, breathing cold air.

You looked past me.

"Can you hear that?" you said. "A horse. Someone's coming."

And you fell down at my feet.

Grass crushed beneath you. I felt the tender shoots of it smear my hands when I reached under you. I lifted you, by your shoulders; I dragged you against my body but I could not raise you up.

You were awake, though. Your eyes huge and swimming dark, your lips parted, smiling.

"She comes for me," you said.

She came, indeed. I heard her horse stamp and breathe. I heard her stirrup chime. I felt her step on the earth. I kept my face turned down.

"Rosa Mundi," she said.

༄

You always told me such vivid stories. I countered with stories of my own. We pirouetted through hours of fascinating lies. If we'd been a bit younger, or a bit more innocent, it would have been a game of let's-pretend.

Instead it was let's-become. We spun ourselves costumes to wear into the world. Our stories were about ourselves, the people we might be someday, the people we might love. Play was turning into practice.

I gave myself a dozen different fathers better than my own, who was no more than a cigar box full of yellowed Polaroids. You gave yourself a wise-woman to replace your mother, who was often drunk in those days. You related how she taught you to weave a chain of clover for luck in your dance recital, to burn an owl-feather to keep away nightmares. It was too bad she was a fiction.

Or so I thought, until she came for you.

"Queen of Air," you said, which was a phrase you had said before, amidst your tales. Your voice strained, winter-husky.

She laughed, and answered to it. "Rosa," she said. "My Rosa. You are mine, are you not?"

"Yes," you whispered. I pinched your arm, where it was palest and softest, but you twitched away. "Yes," you said again, nearly soundless.

"Not your father's muse. Not your mother's helper."

"No," your mouth shaped. Your lips began to darken.

"Not the one to warm your brother's milk."

"No."

"Not the one to pour your stepfather's wine."

"No." You arched your back. Your arm fell free of my embrace.

"Not your teacher's pet. Not the one to…. What is it that you are to this one, Rosa Mundi?"

You tried to answer. Froth burst on your lower lip.

"She's my friend," I said to the ground.

Her laughter withered the grass around her feet. I saw it shrivel, spreading out from the toe of her slim brown boot.

I still had not looked at her face.

"What are the rights of a friend, Rosa Mundi?"

You were past answering by then. I could feel you shivering in long wracking waves.

Nightfall in the Scent Garden

All the stories you'd told me were true. Wonders and horrors.

I knew the shape stories took. I was a studious child.

"She's my love," I said.

By claiming it, did I make it true?

The Queen of Air heard me and stood still. No noise of boot on grass, no ring of horse-gear.

Only a moth in the thyme, a bat in the dusk, a gnat caught in the long strands of my hair.

"Faustine," she said.

I still wonder what would have happened if we had named ourselves different names that day.

"Faustine, maker of bargains. Bargain with me. Of what worth is your love?"

༶

My first kiss: Dane Ellison, behind the portable, during the sixth grade Hallowe'en dance.

My second: Dane again, under the willow by the creek behind his subdivision.

My third kiss: you know my third. I left it in your memory just as it was. I know you have not forgotten, although you will never speak of it.

Those earlier kisses were to this one as ice cubes in a glass of tap water are to an iceberg, looming above and beneath the sea.

༶

The Queen of Air, for I still have no other name for her, bargained with me. Even before she finished speaking, I felt the breath shock back into your body, the rigidity leave your spine. You turned against me, coughing and heaving. I found later a spot of blood upon the leg of my jeans.

Maybe we all get such offers, once or twice or thrice in our little lives. Maybe someone takes every one of us up on the mountain, shows us the breadth of the world, and tells us it could be ours.

Maybe, in our wisdom, most of us turn it down.

I took it. The breadth of the world was held in the span of my hands, spitting blood onto my pants.

I took the bargain. I took the choice from you.

∽

The kiss: my grass-stained hands cradling your face, knotting in the wealth of your hair. You tasted of blood and rosemary.

Your lips shut for a moment against mine but your breath still came hard. You pulled away to pant through your mouth.

I watched your pupils narrow down, and the sinews in your wrist draw tight as your hand closed.

It closed on nothing. The Queen had turned away. The fur at the edge of her mantle brushed my elbow; I still have the scar, a pale frost burn.

You gulped air, wiped your mouth on your sleeve. You shook your head dizzily.

When I saw your eyes meet mine again—proper blue now, tear-wet—I touched your hair and smoothed it down and freed a broken stem from the strands.

You slapped my hand away.

"What will I do now?" you said, your voice still scraped raw. "Where else can I go?"

∽

By the time your father had done selling his sculpture, the one of you as a little girl dancing, I had cleaned up everything. You, your mind, your face, my hands. All except for the spot of blood on my jeans, which no one noticed.

Some of the richness went: the royal purple wisteria dulled down to plain greenery, the sunset smeared and pale. Some of it stayed: the taste of herbs, and the brightness of your hair.

∽

I left you the kiss, but you never let me repeat it. You met Jason Krantz not long after that, and you dated him most of the way through high school. I never saw you with another girl.

Jason Krantz used to corner you in the stairwell and rope your hair around his fist and pull your head close to his, seizing the tip of your ear between his teeth. He used to make you sit on his lap in the coffee shop, and he'd pinch your thigh if you moved too much.

Nightfall in the Scent Garden

I asked the Queen if I could do something about Jason Krantz. She reminded me of the terms of my bargain. I asked her about the clover-chains, the owl-feathers, the little protections she had given you once upon a time. She told me they had not been protections.

You went through a plump phase, and then through a phase where you were thin as a grass-stem, bent under the weight of your sweaters. You and I took to hanging out in one of the restaurants on Spadina where no one asked for ID. You would order Tsingtao while I ate chicken fried rice. If you stumbled on the way out, I would walk you home.

All of this happened just as you recall, and I am to blame.

I said you were my love. I made you stay.

I get to know, each morning, that I'm waking into the same world in which you live. I get to see you, every few months when you're back in the province. Sometimes I even get a stiff little hug, and my hand touches the paintbrush edge of your hair before you pull away.

(Not lately. Not since those things I said after your wedding. I wrote to apologize. You didn't write back.)

I get to hear, from my own mother, that you and your husband are in town over the holidays. I get to imagine you in your old house, sitting on the window seat. For a few days you and I get to share the same weather. I get to leave messages at your mother's house, and wait for your call, which does not come.

For this, I'm promised to a hundred years beneath the hill.

The winter before our graduation, you held the hand of your stepfather as he lingered in a morphine dream. You told me you'd forgiven him, and I watched your fingers go tight and bloodless on his. When he was gone you stopped wearing the gold cross he'd given you for your First Communion.

You said you'd go to prom with me. I bought a suit in the boys' department at Eaton's. A week before the night, you said you were going to get back together with Jason Krantz instead, and wasn't it great that you had found a real date. I went home silently and cancelled the order for your corsage.

You dropped out of Art, and passed History, and aced Chem. On the edges of your notes, you wrote your first name, and a blank line for your last, with hearts and question marks about it. Never Rosa Mundi, nor any other such name. You had stopped telling stories by then.

Sometimes I'd catch that wide dark look in your eyes. In the cafeteria, while you picked the chocolate chips out of your muffin. Outside the locker room, while you waited for Jason Krantz to pack up his football gear. Or in the Annex, as we walked past the dance studio, where you were no longer enrolled.

You still wanted to leave. You couldn't remember how.

༄

I caught the bouquet at your wedding. It crumbled to dust in my hands, not right then, but later, in the hospitality suite, at the end of the night. The Queen and I agree on this: you are my love, and I will have no other.

You, however, have always been free to love as you will. I did not have the foresight to arrange it any other way, and for this I am grateful; I was not a cruel child, but I was a child. I could have made things so much worse.

There is a Faustine in a poem, you see, who I did not know when I chose the name. To love her is to court death.

You seem happy with your love, truly. Eric Farrar: a real person, a person you chose for yourself. He has given you a son. He likes trading stocks and baking cakes, he dislikes motorcycles and fitness enthusiasts, and he does not remind me of either your stepfather or your father. On your wedding day, Eric Farrar wore a lake-blue pocket square to match your eyes. You took his name.

I haven't seen the dark look on you in some years, now that I think of it.

The Queen comes, now and again, to watch you when you are near me. She breathes over my neck, leaving blisters. She reminds me that

Nightfall in the Scent Garden

if I break my bargain, you must go with her. She tells me all I need to do is ask.

If I break my bargain, I will not spend a hundred years under the hill, and I will not have an icy Queen stirring the curtains of my bedroom, driving away any lover who might spend the night. I will not have to pant over the tiny scraps I have of you: a hair ribbon, a sport top you left at my house.

You will not have Eric Farrar. Your son will not have his mother. But you'll have what you wanted, all those years ago, in the garden.

If you read this, you can tell me: do you want it still? Does the Queen's voice ever call to you, out of my hearing, subtle and cold? Do you ever wake troubled, forgetting your dream, with a frost on your lips?

Are you opening my letters? Or will this one, like the last, be thrown away still sealed?

The Queen brought me that one to taunt me, I think; she left it on my bedside table, the envelope cold-parched and wrinkled by her fingertips. Your address was smudged a bit, as if by rain. Through the paper I saw the ghost of my own script, heavy and black.

This choice should not be all mine to make, but how can I compel you to answer me? Shall I stand beneath your sensible vinyl-framed bedroom window and cry out until you rise from your marriage bed?

Rosa Mundi, in which world will you bloom? In which world will I finally catch fire?

Beneath Impossible Circumstances

Andrea Kneeland

The sky is tender as a fitted leather glove lined with silk; firm but soft. Safe. The brightness of it, cap-like and rounded across the horizon, makes me feel tethered.

When the birds drop from the sky, I'm not sure where the fall begins, because I never see them in the cap of blue. The cap of blue today looks spotless, but the streets are lined with feathered carcasses. This is the kind of day that makes me feel more like a janitor than anything else.

My latex gloves are smeared with blood and yellowish fluid and stuck with feathers. I've already loaded five bags of the tiny bodies into my truck. By the time I'm done cleaning the street, I'll only have enough time to test ten of the corpses. There is no way I can convince myself that ten would be a representative sample. Ten will be statistically insignificant.

I go home and do it anyway, submit my report a little after eight p.m.

❧

Analise wants to have a baby. A real baby. I tell her that if we had a baby together, it would be a real baby. It would be a real baby and it would have parts from both of us, and it would be a real person made from both of our genes, and that I want parts of myself in a child just as much as she wants parts of herself in a child. When I tell her these things, she turns on the faucet or runs the vacuum or opens the refrigerator door wide and sticks her head in like she's looking for something so she can pretend not to hear me and I can pretend not to see how damp and salted her reddening cheeks are, and on days like these, when I tell her things like these, the bed sheets between us stay cool and dry and I remind myself of the virtue of silence and I bite my lip to draw blood so that in the morning, when I move my mouth, the pain will remind me not to say a thing.

❧

The sun is a white-haired girl, fever sleeping and swaddled in a blue blanket. The sun pretends not to notice that birds are shaking free from her blanket in alarming numbers, broken and useless. As the sungirl sleeps, she becomes hotter and hotter. One day we will die from her sickness. Our death will only be a symptom, not a final result.

Government work is not glamorous, but it's stable and pays relatively well. I have a pension, and the pension is guaranteed. The work, it's not going anywhere, no matter how much further the economy dives. Analise told me that when I say that phrase to her, that *the economy is diving*, she remembers photos she saw in a history class when she was a little girl, of a man named Jacques Cousteau and another named Émile Gagnan. Men in suits made for breathing beneath impossible circumstances, all rubber and harness and threatening tubes, explorers from a time when the sea was nothing but an expansive blue geometry of cold and mystique. Explorers from

Beneath Impossible Circumstances

before we knew what we know now. She imagines them combing the bottom like man lobsters, like simian bottom-feeders, fingering pockets into the smooth-soft ocean floor, searching for coins.

The slush of bird skin and gore lining the streets in the morning: that's my job security. I am only worried about what happens when we discover the cause of the mass avian deaths. The discovery of a cause is the true threat to my job. I tell myself that even if we do find the cause, another species will start dying, and my pension will be safe. Donkeys. Wasps. Rabbits.

And we are so far away. So far away from anything right now. It's been three years now, and we don't know if the problem is a short circuit in the battery of the caudal thoracic air sac or an organic de-evolution of the nidopallium. We can't replace the birds as quickly as they're disappearing, either. Birds are one of the most expensive animals to produce; even a dust-brown nothing of a finch costs more than pig or a horse. Especially with the Chinese economy also diving, and them pulling out of the bioelectrical species rehabilitation project.

My hair is clumped with sweat and sticking to my skin in spite of the low humidity in the air, the atmosphere dry as bleached bones. I slick my bangs back with my fingers, only to realize that I have not yet removed my gloves. I peel the latex off of my hands, a synthetic skin gummied with sweated powder, shed my clothing, step into the shower, and stand beneath the hot water, face up, rubbing the sticky blood from my forehead.

༄

Analise's preoccupation with our baby's source began after she made new friends. A group of Naturalists who had been frequenting her restaurant for the last year or so. At first suspicious, Analise began to hover by their table as they talked, motivated more by boredom than anything else. What began as entertainment gave way to something else that took hold of her like religion on a child. I can't say that I understand, no matter how many different ways she has tried to explain it to me, and if I do admit to myself that I understand, I am overcome with an overwhelming sadness that pitches me through the night like a dying gull.

"Because soon," she says, "nothing in the world will be real."

"But I'm real." I try to hold her in my arms, and she shrugs away. "The birds; they're real," I say. "I hold the corpses in my hands every day. Life; all of it is real. It doesn't matter what the specific components are or how the life is made." I pause, searching. "Wires don't unmake reality." I know this is the wrong thing to say to her.

Even in the dark, I can see her eyes shining with tears. I can barely remember anymore what she looks like when she's not crying.

The kitten is black, with one blue eye and one yellow eye. She says the imperfection of its face is what makes her love it. I ask her what makes her love me and she ignores my voice completely.

Geraldo, the Naturalist she talks about the most, gave her the cat. I am too worried to ask her how he got it. I am worried that we will be discovered and I will lose my job and we will be arrested. I am worried that she is moving farther and farther away from me in both her mind and her body. The second worry is greater than the first worry, so I don't mention what being charged with a felony for harboring an unlicensed naturally bred species will do to our family. I know I cannot say my worry out loud because she will contest whether two people constitutes a family, and that argument would be more than I could bear.

After she brings home the kitten, she allows me to make love to her for the first time in months. I am overcome with gratefulness and need, even as I realize that this moment is tinged with something terrible; the same terrible thing that has overshadowed every moment of our togetherness for longer than I can remember. That thing that moves her to tears at any moment of the day has taken hold even in this moment, and as I run my tongue inside the groove between her legs, I can feel her body trembling, choking back sobs.

I give up and hold her against me. She pushes her face between my breasts and covers my skin with sticky tears. I know she is think-

Beneath Impossible Circumstances

ing about what is beneath my flesh, and cataloging the difference between us.

I curl up on the couch and cuddle the kitten against my cheek and it purrs loudly. I keep the animal there, a warm radiant of blood-heat and quivering muscle, and I whisper in its ear, to show Analise what a nurturing person I am, to remind her that I want desperately to be a parent. I can see her body tense with jealousy that the kitten does not reserve its affection exclusively for her and I wonder what can happen to a person to change them so absolutely.

"Analise," I say, "It would not even be possible." The kitten climbs onto my shoulder and chews on my hair. "Between us, the way you want a baby, would not be possible, even if the internal differences did not exist. You know that." The kitten begins making hacking noises and I reach back to remove my hair from its teeth and its tongue. While I am engaged in this calming endeavor, studying the miniature teeth of its mouth carefully, unwinding the threads of thin brown protein, I finally ask what I have been asking with every unspoken word for over a year. "Do you want to have a baby with me or not?"

Seconds later, Analise is next to me on the couch, sobbing so loudly that the kitten runs, frightened, to hide behind the refrigerator. Analise is clutching at my arms and my legs and my breasts, words pouring out of her that I eventually recognize as repetitions, that I eventually am able to pair with meanings. "I want to raise the baby with *you*," she is saying, "not Geraldo. I want to raise the baby with *you*," and this is when I realize that it is not a theoretical baby she is speaking of; that she is speaking of a baby that is alive, a pod-like cluster of flesh that is blossoming in her abdomen; that she has gone out and created a new life form the way she wanted it, free of wires or hardware or synthetics or any of the miracles that will keep the planet running until a temperature change too fierce or a bomb too large makes scientific advancements inconsequential.

I feel my heart convulsing against my chest like a test rabbit in a cage, panicked and sick and wild, and I know that this is the same way Analise feels her insides and emotions, regardless of whether they are tinged with circuitry or not. She and I are exactly the same, except that she only has compassion for kittens and criminals.

I rise from the couch and coax the kitten out from behind the refrigerator; no small feat with Analise wailing on the sofa as if someone has died. I stand with the kitten clutched to my hip, manage to keep it there even while it squirms in a mixture of confusion and defiance. "We've had this kitten for a month and you've never even named it," I say. "You'll make a terrible mother."

I am so filled with hurt that I don't know what I believe about anything. And the issue of naming is, admittedly, a less serious offense than her selfish disregard for potential disease or immune deficiencies the kitten, to say nothing of the baby, may pose to the delicate circuitry of my nervous system, or to our ability to live within the confines of the law.

Even beneath this enormous emotional strain and shock, I am able to make it to my van without losing the kitten. I place it in one of the government issued canvas bags I use for my collections and draw the string at the top. I look away from its squirming and when I hear its mewls, I envision Geraldo and his body and his hands against and on top of and inside of my wife, and this quickens my hurt further and muffles every other sensation.

I pull to the curb down the street from the police station. A bird thuds against the windshield and sticks, and I trigger the wiper. The band of rubber grinds the bloody clump of feathers to the hood of my car. A smear of gore streaks the glass. The kitten screams.

"Evidence," I scream back at it. "You are evidence," I scream. "They will slice you open and your insides will be damning enough to issue a warrant to search Geraldo's house."

I pick the canvas sack up and press the heat of the kitten against my face for a long time, then pull away from the curb and drive back home. When I arrive, Analise is gone. I fall asleep beneath the evidence, its delicate, antiquated body rumbling like a dying motor.

Feed Me the Bones of Our Saints

Alex Dally MacFarlane

Jump up! Take arms! Bare teeth!
    We fight for these sands.
    Sink iron knives and white teeth into their scented flesh, their soft city flesh, those stealers of our homes. This is our city now, this desert with its winds that scour our cheeks, its dunes that join us in song, its rare springs that we lap at so gently. We once gulped rivers of rubies and pearls; now they do and we will never be able to claim them back. We will not let them take this final city of air and graveyards from us! Jump up!
    We fight for these sands with everything we have and sometimes we forget the feel of a sister's shoulder beneath our heads, we've been so long without sleep—but today will be remembered for more than this.

Today we retrieve the bodies of our Saints.

Nishir and Aree the Courageous, Nishir and Aree the Fierce, Nishir and Aree the Kind. We write their names on every rock we pass, because we fear that one day we will all be killed, and then who will tell their stories? We imagine a foxless woman hundreds of years from now deciphering the desert's rocks and holding them close to her heart like a new-born child and kit.

It pains us to imagine a future where the suns cross and no child and kit are born onto the hot sands. No other people are born like us.

We buried Nishir and Aree only fifty years ago, when we still numbered in the hundreds, when we still inhabited cities and slept under ceilings of scuffed gold.

Jump up!

We send our bravest, brightest daughters for this most sacred task. Jiresh and Iskree first perform the dawn mourning, barking ten times into the wind the names of our most recently lost sisters. We cook their breakfast. A feast: mice and snakes in neat rows, roasted cactus flesh, crushed agari petals and rare kurik stamens. They take small bites, and then Jiresh holds out the plates to the rest of us, smiling. "Eat, sisters. We must all be strong." Iskree licks her dye-whorled tail as we share the food. We help them prepare. Fifty years ago we still hung so much silver from our ears that the flesh stretched, hanging around our shoulders, and we still dusted our faces with the powder of sapphires. Going into battle, we used to gild our nails and claws, and fit ourselves with mail that shone like small suns, like our mothers. Now we anoint Jiresh and Iskree with shattered knives. We bind the triangles to their foreheads with leather, and the jagged edges draw small beads of red. For each drop of their blood, we think, may a thousand fall from our enemies.

One by one, we embrace them.

Feed Me the Bones of Our Saints

Dutash holds Jiresh last, and whispers, "Stay safe, stay safe. I will dream of you every night. Bring me back dates, if they still grow there."

"I will," Jiresh whispers against Dutash's lips, holding her lover close, "I will, I will."

Iskree and Tounee inhale each other's scents, snout to snout, to carry close to their hearts.

And then Jiresh and Iskree walk into the desert, woman and fox, towards bold Barsime, the city whose walls threw themselves to the ground when we were forced out.

⁂

Few of us remember our cities' glory.

Mere villages, our enemies say. But we were never so numerous, never capable of filling each city with thousands upon thousands. What need did we have of numbers when our cities were so beautiful?

We know Onashek: how could we not? We held onto it the longest, Onashek of cinnamon, carved into such beautiful houses. Even when crowded with refugees, it failed to lose all its lustre beneath their detritus. It made the sweetest fires; its smoke scented the tears that covered our faces as we fled.

We know Eriphos of our well-scribed stones. We launch rare raids into its remains, pillaging the stones that are covered in our stories, in the script our enemies call crude, simple. A child masters it so quickly, they say, surely it is only a plaything, like scribbles of the suns. We only want our human sisters to learn quickly. They need to fight—it is a remnant of our luxury that we also want them to write, just as we make dangerous journeys to the places where indigo grows, so that our fox sisters can harvest leaves and dye their tails with their traditional shapes, denoting histories.

We know Barsime of the green sarcophagus, where Nishir and Aree lie under a heavy lid. Our oldest sisters tell of the sarcophagus's unforgettable beauty.

⁂

The way to Barsime is long and dry, but Jiresh and Iskree are used to hardship. They walk together, barking and singing in poor harmony, chasing lizards, seizing animals that emerge at night. The stars point a path from oasis to oasis, so that they can fill their leather water-bags and with careful rationing keep their tongues wet.

They find rocks covered in our human script, and Jiresh stops to read out every story. Young as she is, she has heard only a few of them.

Once, we knew more stories than there were stars to follow and admire at night. We wrote them in the desert for fun. What we have lost since that time is immeasurable.

Jiresh and Iskree cross the desert, walking the dotted line on Jiresh's map, until they reach the triangle of Barsime.

They almost miss it.

The sands have swallowed the city's remains, so that Barsime is only a strange pattern of small rises in the ground. Jiresh, tired and thirsting, walks blindly among them, stepping on and off the fallen walls. It is only because of Iskree, who never tires of digging for lizards, that she doesn't walk on to the salt flats and die looking.

It is the first sun's dawn. As warmth covers Jiresh's body, she sighs in relief. The night is always so cold.

Iskree finds worked stone.

Her barks draw Jiresh back. "Barsime," Jiresh says. "Then there must be an oasis, or a well." But they cannot find water. The date palms are gone, torn down and burnt. The careful irrigation system is lost. The desert has claimed back the land once held by our city. There will be no dates for Dutash. "Maybe there's still water underground."

The oldest among us recall that the sarcophagus is buried, and told them so before they left.

In the early morning's shadows, Jiresh and Iskree decipher the pattern of Barsime's fallen walls and by the time sweat is soaking their bodies under two high suns, they stand in its centre. Iskree digs. Jiresh helps her, on hands and knees sweeping aside the sand until they reveal a door, leading down.

Feed Me the Bones of Our Saints

Its jewels and bronze decorations are gone.

Nauseated, Jiresh pushes the stone door completely off the hole. Iskree, who sees better in the dim, leads the way down the cool stone steps. The temperature is a relief. They smell damp, and feel renewed hope for a well—and there it is, in the middle of the subterranean road. There is no bucket. Jiresh unhooks the bucket she carries on her back and lowers it on some of her best rope until it strikes liquid.

The water is perfectly, beautifully pure. She sets the bucket on the floor so that she and Iskree can both drink.

When they and their leather bags are full, they walk on.

There is enough light for Jiresh to see that the walls' decorations are also gone, prised off.

Jiresh wants hope. She wants it like she wants fine food and perfume and a house with windows of stained glass: it is a thing she knows that others possess and think nothing of, while she only has an emptiness that wants to hold it.

At the end of a long corridor, she and Iskree step into a small chamber.

The pedestal is swirled with blue like a tail and engraved with lines of letters, declaring in both scripts: *Here is the final sleeping place of Nishir and Aree, who taught us all to be strong.*

That the pedestal is bare of its green sarcophagus and sacred bodies doesn't surprise her.

∽

Our enemies say that our stories are all lies, that we never were born each time the suns' paths crossed, we never were, that we were just women who went mad, who raped men to get their daughters, killed sons out of the womb, who tamed foxes with meat and bestial sex.

They say we never lived in those cities they filled with locks and guns and foxless people.

∽

Iskree whines as if wounded.

"Why have you taken them if you think we're worthless?" Jiresh shouts to the empty chamber. "Why can't you just leave us alone?"

She falls to her knees, sobbing. "You've won. You've already won. Why can't you stop stealing from us?"

⁓

When we later hear this tale, we will keen for their pain, and wish we were there to press against them and stroke their fur and hair.

⁓

"We only want to honour them," Jiresh cries. "We want to bury them in a place far from our enemies, where they'll be safe and we can always return to make offerings."

She lies on the floor, too tired to consider walking.

Iskree licks her cheeks and barks—it's not yet time to give up.

"We don't know where they've been taken," Jiresh says.

Iskree barks and barks, reminding Jiresh that yes, they do.

She and Jiresh are considered brave for more than their willingness to stand and fight while their maimed and younger and more fearful sisters flee an attack. They were once captured and taken to an enemy town, a place where our people die as easily as cacti under a blade. In their cell, as they planned an escape, they overheard the guards talking. One, a woman, said that she hadn't even believed the fox-fuckers to be real until she took her current job. She'd thought the exhibits in the Museum of Caa were hoaxes, like the skeletons of dog-headed men from the far North. Iskree and Jiresh happily killed all the guards several hours later.

Now they give thanks for being slowly, tediously taught the enemies' language as children.

"If they collect our artefacts in Caa," Jiresh says to Iskree, and the words taste foul as suns-turned meat, "then the bodies of Nishir and Aree will be the museum's finest display." Iskree barks agreement.

The concept of museums is strange to them, even after seeing one of the enemy's towns. A life under roofs, in a house that is safe, full of children, full of food and copper pots that bubble over with meat and spices—they dream of such things. They feasted on the bowls of plain rice in that cell, ignoring the guards when they laughed, when they asked if Jiresh would fuck her fox, and could they watch.

Feed Me the Bones of Our Saints

Caa is even further away than that town—but it was once one of our cities, so it is on Jiresh's map.

Iskree barks and Jiresh nods, determined. "We will not fail our mission. At dusk we'll begin walking west."

They sleep near the base of the steps to the subterranean part of the city, until they sense the darkening of the day, wake, drink further from the well, and depart.

⁓

They cross the western desert, and it tries like the drammik of legend to kill them. The land is truly plant-less, the water scarce, the sun unrelenting, though they find deep cracks in the ground and curl in them during the day, pressed to the earth in a desperate sleeping search for shadows. They sleep nose-to-nose; Jiresh has liked waking with hers wet since early childhood. They pine for Dutash and Tounee. Sometimes when they are tired, they lie under the stars, Iskree on Jiresh's chest, barking a rhythm in time to Jiresh's fingers drumming on the hard ground.

⁓

They sit on a stony ridge where agari flowers grow, and watch the city of Caa. Its old walls are tiled in emerald. Its old roofs gleam silver. Our walls. Most of the city is newly built of sand-brick, full of so many people. Iskree can already smell their food, and her gut cramps in longing.

Numerous times she and Jiresh have leaped into hiding as merchants leave the city, on their way to another of the enemy's cities. In this place, the fertile land is riddled with old rock formations that make easy hiding places.

"You have to hide," Jiresh says to Iskree.

Iskree growls.

"You have to. I can pretend to be one of them, poor and wild-haired, and they'll kick me a little but they'll let me in. I can steal their clothes, even, and find a stream to wash in, and bind up my hair, and they might let me right into the museum. If I walk in with a fox…"

Iskree snaps her teeth.

Jiresh buries her face in her hands, moaning softly. In truth she cannot bear the thought of separation from Iskree.

She remembers that she has seen women and men carrying large woven baskets of goods.

"I have a plan."

It is a long wait.

For this, Jiresh convinces Iskree to stay hidden. Jiresh too is out of sight, among rocks—among badly scratched, defaced stories of how we raise our suns-born young—until finally the wait is over. A woman approaches, with corn poking from the top of her basket. Looking at the quality of her jacket, its colours in patterns so fine that Jiresh thinks surely they're a figment of her imagination, Jiresh assumes that she traded cloth for food in the city. But how she got the food and basket matters little.

As she passes, Jiresh leaps out from her hiding place and strikes her on the head with a heavy stone. The woman crumples with a groan, and lies on the road, twitching. Only when Jiresh has dragged her into the rocks and stripped her of her fine clothes, untangled strings of beads from her beautifully combed hair and taken her basket, does she slit the woman's throat. The blood gathers in dips in the rock, like soup in bowls. Jiresh and Iskree feast on corn and small packets of raw meat from the basket.

Jiresh wants to wear the jacket, but fears someone will recognise it as belonging to the dead woman, so she only dons the dress underneath—and cannot resist the belt, on which bells jangle like a continuous song. There she hangs her knife. She reluctantly unbinds her feet from their worn, tattered dark cloth, and puts on the woman's boots. Her long wild hair she winds into a knot at the back of her head, fastened with silver pins taken from the woman's head. She removes the knife-shards from her forehead and hides their small cuts with beads.

She worries that she will be instantly recognised as an impostor.

She uses the jacket and remaining corn as a cushion and concealment for Iskree, who gives her a long look before curling inside.

"You know I wouldn't do this if there was another way."

Feed Me the Bones of Our Saints

Iskree licks her paws: she is unhappy, but she understands.

And so Jiresh, born under the crossed paths of two suns on a bed of hot sand, raised in the shells of old cities and under temporary canvas, walks into the thriving stolen city of Caa carrying Iskree on her back.

∽

It is unimaginably big. She must keep walking. It crowds her: the voices, so loud and numerous, speaking that language not so different to her own. The colours of the clothes. Oh—the fruits, the powdered spices in pyramids, the smell of cooking meat. She drools and has to wipe and wipe her chin. Iskree buries her snout in the jacket to muffle her whimpers. "I know, I know," she hears Jiresh whisper. "Shh." They want to leap on the vendors and steal their food. Jiresh tries not to stare at women with big breasts, at men, at people of all ages who don't show their bones on their skin. The buildings are so tall, several times her height. There are so many children. There are no foxes. There are men.

There are so many styles of clothing that her unfinished theft of an outfit is complete next to others. There are so many kinds of faces that her darker, wind-scoured one is not so unusual. People look at her, and her shoulders are torsion-tense, and the worst they do is eye her apparent poverty with disdain, concern, wariness.

She thinks: We are just a story to you, a folk tale or highly questioned part of history, and you might not believe me if I said I've walked weeks in the desert to reach here, and I'll steal our Saints' bones back or die trying.

Even though she has seen some of this before, in the enemies' town, it is too much, too different, and she is barely across the market at the gates when she wants to run back into the desert and sit under the sky's horizon-wide stretch, with the rocks and the agari flowers growing like little banquets.

She clenches her fists on the straps of her basket and walks on, up a major street, towards the distant roofs that sparkle in the suns' light.

When she walks in the remains of our old city, she must fight the urge to cry, to shout and rail against the theft of these walls. It's all so wrong! So full of intruders. Fists clenching ever tighter, Jiresh follows the winding pattern of the streets, but cannot find the museum. Increasingly uncomfortable under clothes and corn, Iskree turns and turns. She hears Jiresh begin talking in that ugly language. She imagines a whole city full of foxless people and nearly keens aloud for Tounee.

"I'm looking for the museum," Jiresh says to a vendor, who displays small, intricately detailed statues carved of bone on a bright red mat. It draws her attention even as she tries to carry out a conversation. Bone and blood, and under it dusty stones. Simultaneously familiar and wrong—a keen bundles in her throat like fabric.

Jiresh hopes the woman thinks her accent only distant-strange.

"Which one?"

"Um." Iskree circles again. Jiresh wishes that she could whisper apologies. What a fine city this is, with so many museums like gemstones on a necklace. "The one with the desert people in it? The women and foxes?" She doesn't know their non-derogatory terms for us.

"Sorry," the woman says, smiling, "but I don't actually know where that one is. You'll have to ask someone else."

"Oh. Thanks." Jiresh cannot smile back, and stalks off to find someone who cares enough about our people to know where our Saints are kept.

A man in a brilliant blue tunic overhears her question to another woman. "I know where it is," he says, with a smile as warm as tea. He has hair on his chin. He is tall and broad, like a wall, and his trousers subtly bulge. It's like talking to an inscription on Barsime's subterranean walls; even as more words pass between them, she can't imagine that she is doing this thing. "Do you want me to show you?"

"Yes."

Jiresh follows the man through the winding streets, with the walls only sporadically flashing green in the sunlight. They have faded in the seventy years since Caa was taken, and many of the tiles have been removed. She wonders how far away these people have taken our city. How many distant men and women admire their tile of green, perhaps scratched with a word or a cutter's careless tool, with no idea who gathered the emerald from the desert and turned it into a home?

"What's your interest in the fox-women?" her guide asks.

She glares at his back. "Their Saints are here. In a sarcophagus."

"Ah, the sarcophagus. It's the museum's greatest artefact, a perfect example of traditional burial practises and the veneration of important figures—"

"It's been stolen from its proper place," she says—the first thing that falls off her tongue—just to stop him from hearing Iskree's growls.

"There are some who argue that, but I believe this would have otherwise been lost. It's important to retain such artefacts. But I'm the curator's son, so of course I'm biased."

His smile is warm again. Jiresh imagines cutting off his lips and feeding them to him. Iskree thinks more simply of his throat.

They pass through an archway of tarnished silver, embossed with a story that Jiresh yearns to stop and read.

Inside the museum is cool, like the underground passages in Barsime. Barely anyone is visiting. "Do you want a tour," the man—Tulan—says.

"Yes. But I want to see the sarcophagus first. Please." She belatedly remembers being told that a brusque attitude is rude to these people, so richly burdened with the time to adorn their words as prettily as their clothes.

"All right." Yet again that smile.

So Tulan leads her past a collection of minor objects of our people—some that she doesn't even recognise—coins, cloth, crafts, knives, presented alongside paintings and sketches of our cities in their various states, occupied or ruined or remembered. There's a small story-stone. Jiresh runs her fingers over it, tracing words that don't belong in this cool, plain-walled room, with a smiling man in blue. There's a tail, and Jiresh retches at the thought of these people cutting apart a sister for their wall.

"And here it is," Tulan says, with a flourish, oblivious to her hatred. "I'm awed by it every time."

The sarcophagus stands on a pedestal in the middle of a wider room at the end of the corridor. Another man stands on guard, so large that Jiresh could fit herself three times into him. A woman and a child browse the items on the nearest wall.

It is beautiful. It catches Jiresh, so bright a green and covered in the tales of Nishir and Aree, carved in the shapes of stone-stories and tail-stories. Its lid is half off. She steps forward. Inside—she could reach out and touch them—lie the mummified remains of Nishir and Aree.

Jiresh turns and draws her knife, fast as a dust storm, and slashes Tulan so deep across his stomach that his guts fall over his tunic before he can move his hands to the wound. Jump up! Iskree struggles free of the basket's contents. The giant moves, quicker than Jiresh expected. The woman and child scream. Jiresh throws her knife and the giant falls, crashing, and she darts forward to retrieve her knife as Iskree leaps from the basket, growling, teeth bared. Jump up! The woman is sobbing, begging, "Please, please, don't hurt my boy, please."

"Don't stop me."

"I won't, we won't, oh…" Her next words are lost in her sobs. The boy hides his face in her clothes.

Jiresh holds her knife between her teeth and reaches into the sarcophagus. Our Saints are stiff, brittle. Shouts, heavy feet—more guards. Iskree waits for them at the room's entrance. Cursing, Jiresh puts the remains of Aree whole into her basket. She needs her hands to fight. She cannot carry Nishir. So she snaps Nishir into pieces. "I hate them, I hate them," she hisses, with tears gathering in her eyes like dew. Saints should not be treated this way.

Iskree barks at the six approaching men.

"Stop!"

"Stop!"

Voices like rocks falling.

The pieces of Nishir fit into her basket, and she gets the beautiful jacket over them, holding them in place, before the men are grabbing for her. She darts away, while Iskree leaps forward, tearing at their heels through their fine boots. One man cries out and goes down.

"Slow and stupid and *fucking thieves*!" Jiresh screams, knife back in her hand. Who to strike first? Soon they'll use their little guns. "We won't let you take them from us!"

The leader of the five remaining men raises his gun and Jiresh throws her knife. They both dodge the other's weapons. The bullet shatters something behind her.

"I hate you!"

Iskree is too quick to be kicked. Jiresh reaches over her shoulder and grabs corn, throws it, confusing them, and she runs to a wall where she pulls away a knife with small emeralds embedded in its blade. Another man screams as his heel is torn open. His blood runs over Iskree's teeth and she runs at the next. The little guns are making noise. Jiresh feels one, two, three bullets strike the basket as she leaps for cover behind the pedestal.

They are blocking the way into the corridor—until Iskree tears at shins, breaking their attention. Jiresh runs at them, slashing with the knife. One of the men grabs her arm and yanks away the knife, growls, "Hold still, little bitch."

"Never!"

She bites his hand and he cries out, lets go, and the others don't have time to stop her from running past.

More bullets strike the basket. Something fire-hot grazes her thigh, but she keeps going. Iskree follows, heart beating fast at the sight of blood on Jiresh's leg.

Jiresh shouts wordlessly with triumph, even though she knows there is a whole city to escape.

Another gunshot. Agony. Iskree screams.

No. And another. "No!"

Jiresh turns and the man fires again. A bullet slams into her shoulder. She sees Iskree lying on the floor, bleeding too fast, lying in a growing pool of red like that woman's bone-covered mat. "No, no, no…" She crumples to her knees, tears like a flash flood. Iskree is already dead. Not even a final bark.

The men are reloading their guns. Soon they will kill her, as they have killed Iskree.

"No." The basket is heavy on her shoulders, full of Saints. Either she can die avenging Iskree or she can take Nishir and Aree from this vile place, the task Iskree died trying to complete. She wants to do both. She wants to tear out every throat in this city. "I will avenge you."

She is quick enough to dart forward, grab Iskree's body—twitching, death's last movements—and clutch her sister to her chest, and then she runs from the museum, so full of hate.

∽

The sight of a woman bleeding, weeping, holding something small and furred and dead is so strange that it is watched by hundreds. A few reach forward, as if to grab, and Jiresh dodges them. She runs until she's back in the desert, back among the labyrinthine rocks outside the city, far from a path this time, and there she hides, weeping.

Even when her chest and throat hurt as much as the wound in her shoulder, she weeps.

∽

In Barsime, she leaves Iskree on the empty pedestal.

∽

In Barsime, almost blind with tears, unable to climb those stairs and leave Iskree, she is not quite blind enough to read a story inscribed on the wall of the Saints' chamber. It sets her jagged, broken thoughts ablaze.

∽

"Feed me the bones of our Saints."

We stare at Jiresh, our skinny, blood-stained, foxless sister with bones and flaps of skin in her arms.

"They will kill us like they killed Iskree. Every year their weapons are stronger, every year we are hungrier. They will kill us all, and we will be completely forgotten. Our rocks will be scoured by the sand-heavy winds until future historians can only sigh into their notes and say that some old culture lived here, but too much is lost now to say who we were. How brave and strong we were. Jump up." She speaks our battle cry, and it is raw as a wound. "Jump up. Let me tell you a story I found in Barsime. We have forgotten what we carved into stone only fifty years ago. Let me tell you about bones."

Some of us, old enough to remember the construction of that subterranean chamber, know this story, and begin to grieve, knowing that we cannot stop this; and some begin to imagine a victory.

Jiresh stands with those bones in her shaking arms and says, "Once, over five hundred years ago, when two more sisters were born *every* time the suns' paths crossed, there was fighting. We and another people competed for a great region of gold, where even the most pitiful bushes were said to shine with the brightness of it in the soil, and two of our sisters were especially honoured for their skill in combat, and were agreed to be Saints. Eventually they were killed, in one of the bloodiest battles of all. Their lovers feared that their bodies would fall into the hands of the enemies, and so consumed them entirely, hiding in a gully. When the lovers returned to the field, they felt the weight of the suns like a heavy knife in its sheath upon their backs. They wielded it, and that is how we won the fields of gold, to build the first of our cities that was stolen in this century."

We stare.

Some of us know that she did not finish the story. Did not say, *And the destruction so horrified them that it became one of the great sins of our history. No one has ever used this power since.*

Fifty years ago, we still thought we might survive. We carved our history into that burial chamber and imagined writing about our victory, or our remaining cities becoming more beautiful than ever, or our tentative peace with the enemies—something that was not hunger and death in the open desert.

"We can wield the suns," Jiresh says. "I don't know what it means, exactly, but it's a weapon. It's…I think it's an end."

"For whoever wields it, too," Dutash whispers.

"Yes."

Jiresh cannot quite look at Dutash.

The wind gusts between us all, mournfully.

"Will anyone come with me?" Jiresh says. "In case…"

In case anyone else wants to watch Caa consumed by fire. In case anyone wants to join this vengeance.

And, hidden in her words: Jiresh doesn't want to die alone.

One of our oldest sisters snarls her disagreement, and another takes up the sound—and another, womanless Koree, jumps at them with her teeth bared. Tounee and many others join her. Dutash looks away, less certain than Tounee. Foxless Lizir stands up and says, "I will come with you."

"And I."

"I want to."

Voices young and old, human and fox—but this is not a quick argument.

"It will be brutal," an old sister says. "You must know that."

She is laughed at. As if the war hasn't been brutal.

"This is not a battle," she persists, "where two sides are equal. I know that is how this entire war has been waged. I know. I understand. But you must know that are planning to join them in sin. It is not a decision to be made lightly."

"I'm going to do it," Jiresh says softly. "I crossed the desert alone. It took weeks. I carried these bones and I never stopped thinking about it."

"I know, sister." There is nothing more she can say.

We cook our dinner, comb the children's hair and fur, set up tents for the night, murmur lullabies to the single pair of babies—they are so fragile in their early months, so easily killed by the desert—and the argument goes on, too complex to be sewn into the finest enemy jacket.

We touch our Saints' bones, one by one, with snouts and lips.

We cannot all agree.

We decide to separate, permanently, and it pains us more than the fall of every city combined.

Jiresh consumes the bones, pounds them with one story-covered stone onto another, making a plate of a battle tale. "I will make a finer tale than this," she chants. "I will make a finer tale than this." She scoops handfuls of dust and pours it down her throat, and her lips are stained pale. Though she coughs and chokes, she keeps eating it, periodically licking under her fingernails and scraping the stone's incisions and scratches free of powder. She whispers, almost too quiet for anyone to hear, "I didn't think it would taste so horrid."

A whisper for a fox that no longer lives.

She stands, still coughing, and massages her neck with one hand. "We should go," she says. "Gather your weapons."

No tremendous change has overcome her.

"Have faith," she says, with a sly smile that curves her lips like the word for victory.

We make ready.

～

Jiresh gives the skulls of Nishir and Aree to those of us who will remain in the desert. "Bury them together," she says softly, "with every rite we still possess, with every song. Bury them touching, as if they are just sleeping side-by-side."

～

We who remain in the desert mourn as they leave.

～

We cross the desert without any song, with the suns hot on Jiresh's back. Dutash walks with us—the only sister to stop and score our story on rocks, lingering at each one as if she might not have to continue. Tounee's desire convinced her not to stay at the place where Jiresh consumed our Saints. Jiresh's determination drags her, hurts her.

"Jump up," Jiresh says as we grow nearer to the city. "Jump up. Jump up."

She rarely speaks without repeating. Only at night, as we curl together in a far smaller pile of skin and fur than we are used to, does she murmur single sentences, confused and painful, into Dutash's hair or Toree's flank or the sand, cooling against her cheek.

"Jump up."

Caa reveals itself, large in its gentle green valley.

We feel the suns, now.

"Jump up."

"Jiresh," Dutash says, reaching forward to touch her lover's arm—hotter than silver poured into its mould. Dutash yelps and snatches back her finger, and sucks on it. The suns' heat intensifies. "Jiresh," Dutash says again. "Jiresh."

"Jump up!"

Jiresh runs fox-fast along the road to the city and takes the suns with her.

Knives in hands, teeth bared, we yell. *Jump up! Jump up! You can't forget us! We'll burn you from your homes! We'll set you all ablaze! We'll slide teeth and silver into the last throats!* As we run towards the city it bursts into flames, swallowing Jiresh in a flare like a blink.

The fire spreads quicker than a dust storm, covering the entire city in minutes. The air is full of roaring and cracking and screams. People cannot move—they are burnt to their bones, their blackened, broken bones that crunch under our feet. The houses fall.

Jiresh's voice carries through the flames. *You took my sister! You! See how your arteries singe off my teeth like hair.* We hear her laughter. We hear her screams.

༶

We who remain in the desert hear her, whisper soft, unstoppable as the suns' light, which glows so bright in the Northwest.

༶

Her fire-body is pain, is power. Is everything she dreamed, in that long, lonely walk from Caa to Barsime with Iskree in her arms, to the camp where sisters lived in fear of more deaths to bark at dawn.

You will never forget us! she screams with every part of her body.

༶

We scream.

We don't die. The fire licks our bodies tenderly as tongues, so that Dutash, following Tounee into the emerald walled—black-walled, wall-less—city-heart thinks the fox could be caressing her.

"Jiresh!" Dutash cries into the fire.

Not every person in Caa is immediately consumed. In the minutes before the fire spread, some fled through the seven open gates. Some

Feed Me the Bones of Our Saints

of us chase them. We laugh as the fire leaps after them, thrown like knives—Jiresh roars triumph as each one falls—and we finish whoever we find beyond the fire's reach.

We jump back into the flames, cradled by our burning sister.

"Jiresh!"

Dutash's feet crunch over blackened bones, which crumble away like cheek-powder in the wind.

Another sister cries out, "Here, here, there are more of them!"

Our enemies hide in underground chambers and caves, in places where running water keeps them cool. Dutash sees them cowering and thinks: How many times have we done this, hiding in fear? Thinks: Some of them are too young to have ever attacked us. She doesn't want to make this decision. She cuts their throats. None of them survive. None of them will kill us.

She imagines those who lived in the fields, who fled or hid when they first saw women and foxes running along the wide road into Caa, finding these unburnt bodies amid the wreckage above and knowing how well we learnt not to show mercy.

You will never forget us! You will never look at a fire without remembering Caa! You will never look at emerald or silver without remembering how it all fell into dust and you will never, never take another of my sisters from me!

As blood soaks her feet, she staggers up the rocky steps.

She can't see walls through the flames. She can't see Tounee. She shuts her eyes and runs.

"Jiresh! Stop!"

Tounee climbs blackened steps into the streets, where the fire surrounds her like Dutash's arms. Where is her sister? The fight is over.

The suns are getting hotter.

Tounee runs and Dutash runs and there are no sounds of life, only fragmented city-pieces and bones under their feet.

You will remember us!

Jiresh's voice is fainter now. The suns are hurting Dutash, who stumbles. Sisters across the city fall. "Tounee!" Dutash gasps. "Tounee, where are you?" She weeps, and the fire burns away every drop. She longs for the desert and her sister and a time when—she cannot think of a time she wants. But each memory of Caa is an agony. Fire and bones and our enemies' blood running over her hands for the first time in her life.

She wishes she hadn't followed Jiresh. "Tounee." Like her sisters, she falls.

A murmur from the flames: *They'll never forget us. Never.*

"Never," sisters whisper and bark across the city, as the fire blisters their skin. Some still have the energy to run. Some almost make it to the gates.

Jiresh feels her sisters in the flames and presses against them, finally afraid of her death, seeking comfort.

Never.

Tounee, who turned away from the killing to follow her reluctant sister, reaches the place where a great arch once stood, and doors of wood and bronze. Through the flames she sees a horizon. She sees Dutash, fallen on the ground, too fire-blind to see the way out. She barks in joy. Nothing. She bites.

"Tou..."

Tounee grabs onto Dutash's elbow and begins dragging her, though the fire is burning her eyes and her body.

~

An hour after Tounee drags Dutash into one of the streams feebly running between burned, bone-covered fields, the fire dies down. Black dust remains. For months it blows through the desert, and there is no one who does not know its source.

~

Two sisters walk with the wind at their backs, blind, lost.

~

We find them. We who went to Caa to find the remains of our sisters bring them slowly back to the place where we have buried Nishir and Aree. As the wind speckles our skin with black, we wait—afraid and determined, angry and grieving.

~

Narrative Only

Kate Harrad

Today, as specified, my nose is like a gondola at twilight. Like the arch of a lover's back. Like the angled ruin of a Roman temple. I have a flair for describing noses, and the iTem has responded magnificently: I have been admiring it for some Ame. Today's nose chimes in perfectly with today's body; which, since you ask, is tall, olive-skinned and black-haired. I have hips you could stop a train with. Childbearing hips, if…

I can't change my eyes. The technology is there, and my descriptive powers are certainly up to it, but Jani asked me not to. I'm okay with it. I don't even wear coloured contact lenses, although the pale blue of my pupils is not in any way working with today's complexion. Never mind. I don't have to go anywhere today; not that anyone would comment if I did. The range of bodies out there, for those who still have bodies, is now limited only by the imagination of their owners.

I peer under my hair at my ears, just to check.

As I expected, my ears are mundane.

I never got the hang of ears, I don't have anything interesting to say about them.

Sometimes the iTem creates tiny pointy ears for me, or large floppy ones.

Or on one memorable occasion Mickey Mouse ears, which did not assist with the femme fatale look I'd been going for that day.

Now I ask for "normal-looking ears" every morning and it obliges.

If it gets bored, it doesn't say so.

"Nice nose," says Jani.

"The curviness is also appreciated. Yesterday you were a bit bony, I thought."

Why would you care, I think, but don't say.

What I say is: "I thought you'd like the nose. I think I'm going to save the specifications for this one."

"Save the body specs too," she says.

"Jθ"

"Smile," I respond, and the iTem transcribes it into a smiley face for me.

The more advanced ones add emoticons based on the tone of your voice, but we couldn't afford that for mine.

All the money went on Jani's equipment.

If I sound resentful, I'm not: not about the money.

I miss Jani's body, that's all there is to it.

I knew I would.

I don't know if she realizes how much I miss it.

Sometimes when she's asleep—insofar as she sleeps—I talk to my friend Rallen, who is also in what we refer to as a "mixed marriage."

He finds it hard too.

Narrative Only

He misses Fi's body, he says, but more than that he misses his voice.

Fi and Jani both incorporated their voices into their NO personas, but there's an overlay of metal there now. Not like a robot.

More like a background thrumming, the faraway noise of a train, echoing against their words. I'm not used to it yet. It's only been six months since Jani went NO.

Maybe I'll adjust. Oh well.

I glance at Jani. Her text says she's getting dressed.

Pictures flicker along the screen: different coloured jeans, boots, high-heeled sandals.

"I feel butch today," she says to herself/to me.

"Black corduroys, white tee shirt, no bra. Approve?"

"Sounds great," I say. "Very sexy."

The picture settles into Jani's image of herself for the day. She's given herself a buzzcut, I notice, to go with the outfit. Tomorrow she might have waist-length ringlets and a plunging red velvet dress: it's one of the advantages for her, of being NO.

"But I can do that too!" I shouted at her once, during an argument soon after the translation.

"If you just want to change your body, change it! Why do you have to go narrative-only?"

But I knew the answers.

She wants to be at the cutting edge. She wants to escape the limitations of physicality.

And she wants to live forever.

Which she will, provided there's someone around to keep her charged—me, or one of the robotboys you can hire for more—or—less eternity.

So I didn't finish the argument. No point: it was already too late. Instead I lay awake listening to the gentle chatter of her iTem, The words scrolling down the screen in curly night font:

"I dream of fish, of endless schools of silver minnows in a sea of ink.
I dream of ice trapped in fire.

I dream that I have to travel across the world but I only have a canoe made of fox skin.
I dream of Lanh."

At least I'm in her dreams.

The day, the day of my Roman gondola nose, passes quietly. We work. We have lunch together: I eat a sandwich, she produces a vivid and evocative paragraph about her smoked salmon and brie salad. That evening, while she goes to a NO e-party, I look for Rallen online. He's there, but something has changed. He doesn't need to tell me what it is.

"You did it."

"Yes."

We both fall silent for a moment.

"I had to," he types, eventually. "Living with Fi, my body started seeming so…physical, so cumbersome. He kept going on about how free he was."

I type quickly, overlapping with him: "But what's it like now? Is it worth it?"

The screen is quiet for a moment, then Rallen says: "Lanh, you have to do it.

If you love Jani. Trust me."

The next morning, I look in the mirror. I admire my height, my hips, my skin. I admire my nose. It will be my last nose. I'm glad it was so impressive.

"Jani," I say.

"Lanh?"

"It's Ame. I'm translating myself today."

She doesn't speak: instead she breaks out into a shower of glowing colours, a rainbow disco ball. Triumphant music plays as I programme the iTem to upgrade itself, to narrativise me. Jani and I will share our story from now on. It will be okay.

And—finally, wonderfully—we can have sequels.

Nine Days and Seven Tears

JL Merrow

"You don't get seals on the Isle of Wight, Briony Brain-dead. It was probably a rock. A big, fat, rock." Col punctuated his words with wide-armed gestures, and when he'd finally shut his stupid mouth, he blew out his cheeks.

I pretended to yawn. Maybe I wasn't a stick insect with a pair of melons for boobs, like all the girls in the porno mags he kept hidden in an old Airfix kit box under his bed, but so bloody what?

Maybe I'd skip pudding tonight, though. Well, depending on what it was. Mum did some great puddings.

"I know what I saw, all right? Anyway, they had a bloody whale in the Thames. Why can't we get a seal blown off course 'round here or something?" I didn't even realize I was standing there with my hands on my hips until he started mimicking me. I shoved my fists in my pockets and stomped along the sea wall away from him.

God, I hated this place. Nothing here but sand and sea, and people who remembered every daft thing you did when you were a kid.

All right. I didn't hate the place. Maybe I even loved it, with the fresh island breezes and the smell of the sea everywhere you went. But I didn't love the lack of opportunities and the narrow-mindedness. There's a reason the word "insular" comes from the word "island." I was stuck here, fresh out of uni with a degree no one wanted and no bloody job. Not likely to find one round here either, but I'd have to be mad to leave home without some money coming in, wouldn't I?

Col didn't care. He had it all planned out. He was going to finish at the tech college and get a job stacking shelves somewhere, and live at home so he could spend his pay out drinking with his mates every Friday night, with just enough left over to take his girlfriend out somewhere cheap on Saturday.

I hated her too. Sharp-faced little cow in skinny jeans, always offering to lend me her clothes, like she couldn't see there were three sizes between us—and that was on one of my good days.

If she'd been here she'd have been laughing at me too. But I knew what I'd seen. I'd seen a seal. Beautiful, it was, with eyes you could dive right into. It'd looked straight at me, head cocked like it was studying me, and then it ducked back under the waves. I'd looked for ages, trying to see it again, until Col came up and asked me why I was staring out to sea like a zombie had come up and eaten my brain. Not that it would have been more than a snack, according to my bloody brother.

I didn't hate Col. Not really. I just didn't like him very much, that's all.

༶

I came out again after tea. I'd had two helpings of jam roly-poly just to prove Col hadn't gotten to me, so I needed the walk. And I wanted to see if she was there again.

Nine Days and Seven Tears

I'd decided the seal must have been a she. Too graceful to be male, she was. Maybe I'd only seen a sleek head and the curve of her back as she dived, but I knew she was grace itself. I wanted to see her again. I wanted to watch the sunset gild her fur while I stood on the beach like a love-starved sailor of old, seeing mermaids in the gloaming.

I'd forgotten it would be high tide by then.

The wind was whipping up the waves to crash against the sea wall, sending up clouds of spray that spattered my face and left me tasting salt on my lips. There was no beach left at all, and the gulls were circling high above me, crying at its loss. I shivered, hoping my seal had found somewhere safe to rest for the night.

I turned to walk back home—and almost bumped right into her. Not my seal, of course. A girl. Well, a woman, really; just about my age, to look at her. She'd pulled down the top half of her wetsuit to show her black swimsuit underneath, swelling with the curve of her full breasts.

"Hello," she said, smiling at me. "I'm not quite sure where I am."

"Sandown," I said. "Well, Yaverland, really, this far down, but you won't have heard of the village." And I blushed, because there she was, a beautiful woman come out of nowhere, and there I was, getting pernickety about parish boundaries.

She cocked her head to one side, her dark, wet hair drifting in the wind like seaweed in the swell. "Yaverland? I like the name."

Her accent was strange—reminded me of all those Scandinavian crime shows on the telly, though my swimmer would fill out a Faroe sweater much better than what's-her-face in that Danish show.

"Where have you come from?" I blurted out.

"Oh, my boat's out there," she said, waving an arm vaguely out to sea. I looked, but I couldn't see a single light. "Like I said, I think I got lost."

"You swam in from a boat?" My heart felt cold as I looked at the waves thundering against the breakwaters, crushing driftwood to pieces. "You can't go back in this sea!"

"It's all right," she said, her hand soft on my arm. "I'm a very strong swimmer."

"Look, why don't you come back to my mum and dad's? They're out—it's ballroom dancing night. You can have a cup of coffee and—" *And I can try and stop you swimming to your death.*

She looked at me for a long, long moment. "You're sure? That's very kind of you. I'm Freyja."

"Briony," I said. "And, um, my brother Col's going to be home, but just ignore him, okay?"

"Ah. I know—I have lots of brothers." She slipped her hand into the crook of my arm and we set off back home, my skin tingling every time our hips brushed.

∽

Col didn't even look up from his Playstation when we walked in the door. I didn't want to talk to Freyja with guns blaring in the background, so I took her in the kitchen, ducking under Dad's freshly-ironed shirts hanging by the door. We sat at the little wooden table with the wonky chairs, breathing in the scents of fabric softener and the lasagna left over from tea.

"How long are you going to be here?" I asked, as I handed her a mug of coffee made with all hot milk to keep out the chill.

She smiled crookedly. "I can't stay. I need to get back to Hvammstangi—I really shouldn't be here at all. I don't know what drew me down here." As she spoke, she laid her hand, warm from the mug and from the heart of her, on my arm. I placed my own hand over it and twined my fingers into hers, my stomach feeling like it was full of little fishes darting joyfully in all directions. "But I'm glad I came," she whispered.

"Me too," I said, and I leaned over the table and dared to kiss her. She tasted of salt and fresh air and freedom, and I pulled her to me, not wanting to let her go.

Her breasts were warm and soft against mine, her skin like velvet. She clambered onto my lap, still half in her wetsuit like a butterfly coming out of its chrysalis, and we clung together, wordless, until she rested her forehead on mine. "I have to go. I'm sorry, Briony."

Nine Days and Seven Tears

I tried to stop her. "No, you can't go." I pulled at her wetsuit, but she looked so sad I dropped my hand. "I wish you'd stay," I whispered, defeated.

"Remember me," she said softly. "Remember me, and perhaps we'll meet again."

"When?"

"Nine days' time, if you still remember me. Nine days' time. I can stay that long."

"Then why not stay with me?" I begged.

"I can't," she said. "But I can come to you once more."

I walked her back to the seafront. The wind was quieter now, and the sea was soft and welcoming. Freyja put her hand to the zip of her wetsuit. "Don't watch me go," she said, so I turned and walked away, but the splash I listened for never came. For a moment I thought she'd changed her mind, but then I heard her voice on the wind, as if a gull had carried it to me.

"Nine days," she called. "Remember that, Briony. Nine days, and seven tears!"

There's a lot you can learn in nine days. You can learn all about the different types of seals, and where they live. You can learn that Freyja's an Icelandic name, and Hvammstangi's a small town in their north. You can learn that Iceland's a much more tolerant place than some islands you could think of.

You can realize that if you have to spend many more months here you'll go mad, and that while hope can inspire you, it can hurt you too.

It was a calm, clear night when I went back down to the sea, Mum's apple crumble and ice cream a cold comfort in my stomach. Nine days, she'd said, and here I was. Maybe I'd already gone mad. After all, who'd seen her, apart from me? Col hadn't even noticed her passing through.

It wasn't hard, keeping her second condition, as I sat on the sea wall with my legs dangling over the edge, hugging myself while I let my tears drop into the water. Harder to keep to seven, they flowed so fast, but I hoped she'd forgive me.

I thought I saw my seal, but she was gone before I could blink—and then Freyja was beside me, her wetsuit half undone once more.

"You didn't forget," she whispered, and she was crying too.

I pulled her close to me, the soft warmth of her flesh revitalizing me. "You're like a hot spring," I told her. "Warmed by the spirits of the earth."

Freyja cocked her head on one side, and smiled. "And you're a rock for basking on, heated by the sun."

"Come and bask with me," I said, and we stood and walked back to my parents' house.

I didn't disturb them, watching telly with Col. I took Freyja straight up to my room. I peeled off her wetsuit and her swimsuit too and left them on my bedroom floor. My breathing hitched as I kissed her full breasts and the curve of her stomach, her body all softness and warmth. I traced her contours with my tongue, which tingled from the sea-salt on her body, and I kissed her lower still, where the milky white of her skin gave way to darkness and musk. I found where the heat of her was centered, and as she opened for me like a sea anemone she arched her back and hummed with pleasure. The scent and the flavor of her almost overwhelming me, I tongued that hard, crimson bud again and again, until Freyja shuddered and came, crying out softly in an ancient language I longed to understand.

"You make me so hot," she whispered, but her white fingers felt cool on my heated skin, like the lap of the sea on a hot summer's day. They rippled over me, bringing life and yearning to every part they caressed, and then they dove inside me, darting in and out with a touch that both burned and soothed. I gasped as her mouth closed over my nipple, feeling the heat of it deep within me. Her tongue teased me without mercy, but I ached for my loss as it left me—only for my Freyja to murmur soothing sounds as her dark head dipped lower, her silky hair flowing like water over my body. I had to stifle my cries in case Col might hear as she found me again, this time right at my center. She suckled on my clitoris as her fingers moved within me,

Nine Days and Seven Tears

bringing me higher and higher on a wave of sensation, and I cried out aloud as I crested that wave and broke, tumbling down to float on smooth water, little ripples moving me still.

Afterward, I held her in my arms and we basked together in a tangle of cool sheets and warm bodies. "I'm going to see you again," I told her.

"I can't stay," she said sadly, her hair caressing my skin like warm, dry sand as she shook her head.

"I know," I said. "But I'm going to see you again."

∽

If I were a man, I might have stolen her wetsuit as she slept, and never let her swim away from me.

But I'm not a man, and despite my name I'm not one to cling onto what's not mine by right. So I kissed my love in the dawn's pink glow, and I walked her down to the beach before anyone was up. I turned my back once more as she swam away while the gulls mourned for the both of us.

But then again, what do gulls know? I booked a flight to Reykjavik with my credit card and started looking for a job there over the Internet.

"Why do you have to go to Iceland? There's nothing there!" Col grumbled as I packed my bags.

"Well, it's like you said. You don't get seals on the Isle of Wight." I shut my case with a snap, and Col sneered at me and twirled a finger round by the side of his head, muttering "Briony Basket-case."

And I smiled, and started counting the days until I'd see my selkie again.

∽

Chang'e Dashes from the Moon

Benjanun Sriduangkaew

1.

There's a lady on the moon and she has a rabbit; at mid-autumn we have mooncakes when her husband visits.

Long ago the moon grew a city on its skin like nacreous shell around a pearl, and in this barren city lives a goddess who was once a girl.

The goddess counts the years, at the beginning.

She folds gold paper and silver paper in the proper months, and burns them for her mother. She makes houses of glassy yellow windows and pale walls, double-storeyed, and burns those so that her mother will have a comfortable residence in her passage through death. She makes animals, companions, furniture.

When she begins counting in decades instead of years she starts burning offerings for her niece. It is the wrong way around; she is the elder, and she should be the one waiting beyond for her niece's sendings.

But she is immortal, and her family is not.

After the first century she burns offerings for her mother, her niece, and her niece's children. Who knows what descendants do now, whether they remember their duty? So she takes it upon herself, just to be safe. She watches the houses in the mortal realms change and lengthen, until they become towers which pierce the clouds, until their cities are thick and thronged and she can't imagine locating her kin anymore in the million-millions that overwhelm the streets.

Sometimes her name slips away from her. In defiance she etches into the soft stone of the lunar city, *I am Chang'e, and I have a wife whom every night I long to meet.* Her chiseling erases itself before an hour finishes.

The walls are high to fill her sight. The houses are huge to make her small.

In moments where she can rouse herself from lassitude, Chang'e indulges in fury. Though her mortal life she learned much, the knife and the bow. Cut though she might, the moon does not bleed. She loosens flaming arrows into the dark, but the moon does not burn. There are moments where, stepping through a garden gate or passing through a door, she glimpses a world under sunlight. It does not last.

Often she watches the rabbit toil at its mortar. It makes no mention of leaving; this it seems to consider its rightful place. But it is the closest she has to a friend.

"Does the moon think?" she asks, as though in idle wonderment.

The rabbit pauses its pounding. "What makes you think so, Lady Chang'e?"

"It is only a thought." She nods at its jars and pots. "What are you making?"

This medicine, it explains, reunites flesh and spirit: those chased out of their own skin by malicious devils, those who have spent too long in dreams, those sent to the underworld by an accounting error. Many ills require such a cure.

Chang'e peers into the mortar at the thick, glittering purple paste. "It'll work on any body?"

"Even ones not of flesh," the rabbit says with solemn pride. "My pharmacology is unrivaled, though many have tried to match it."

She smiles and strokes its long ears. "Perhaps one day you can make me a pill to make me heavy, so heavy that I will sink from the sky and return to the earth."

Its nose twitches and it looks at her with sad red eyes. "I wish you would be happy, Lady Chang'e."

"I'm happy, rabbit."

She does not say that happy does not come from wishing. Once she thought that was so, swept into the arms of the archer god who came into being full-grown and graceful as though born from a wish. Centuries later she has learned otherwise.

A ghost butterfly alights on her shoulder. There are many of those in the gardens of the moon, phantom swans and mute songbirds, wisps of feathers and beaks that come apart if she looks at them too hard. A menagerie on the verge of breaking down.

Chang'e will not break with them.

She inhales the scent of the rabbit's works, smells bitter and tart, fierce and demure. In the chambers of her heart she holds an idea, a solution. Clutching it behind her sternum—so the moon will not hear, so the moon will not see—she leaves the rabbit and, steps light as the passing of autumn, follows the ghosts.

Heroic Houyi shot down nine sun-crows to save humanity, and through schemes of the jealous came to his ruin; in death he rose to the tenth sun, where ever after he made his home.

For material Chang'e would have liked clay, soft and obedient to her hands, but the city is pavement end to end, and hard soil or harder rock where it is not. She settles with cherrywood, which is all they have to make anything from, there being an endless supply from the one tree. Over and over she's watched its leaves unfurl green and fresh and branches burst forth stronger and steelier than before. The faster Wu Gang hews, the faster it regrows. Like the rabbit he never mentions escape, content to suffer and wait out his sentence on the moon, but sometimes she thinks it is merely that he has no one to return to.

Appropriating chisel and saw from the woodsman's cache she learns the fundamentals of carving, and over the months comes to understand where to chip, where to cut, where to etch: the subtleties of grain and knots, the differences between sap- and heartwood. Though she isn't done when Houyi's visit nears, it is progress and it keeps her busy, elbow-deep in shavings and dust.

On this day mortals kindle lanterns for her and Houyi, she hears, and put on dragon dances. And marry: it's been absorbed into the matchmakers' calendars, one of the most favorable dates in the year and certainly the most in the season. Chang'e doesn't know how to feel about that. Perhaps mortals are different now, and marriages are happier things. Houyi has suggested they might be, but she finds that beyond the reach of imagination.

Zhongqiujie has become an annual celebration for the inhabitants of the moon—which is to say, all three of them—as though to make up for the lack of congratulations and liquor when Chang'e wedded Houyi. Wu Gang brings lanterns shaped as vast lotuses and serpents. The rabbit makes cakes, viscous lotus paste inside and the salted yolks of ghost birds: they were pale rather than orange, but they taste no less rich. She thanks them, heartfelt. "It means more than I can say, both to me and Houyi."

"It is good for husband and wife to unite, Lady Chang'e."

Her smile stiffens. With effort she keeps it from hardening into a rictus. Tact has become as necessary as the air they breathe, and so Chang'e has ever avoided the subject. "You have met Houyi."

His mouth sets. "I have had the honor of acquaintance with heaven's best archer, Lady Chang'e."

"I realize Houyi doesn't dress as most women do. It pleases her to dress as she does, and she requires no more reason than that."

Chang'e Dashes from the Moon

"Goddess, it's never been my place to criticize how the divine garb their sacred persons."

"Very good. So, Houyi is a woman. On this we can at least establish a common ground?"

The woodsman nods.

She wishes she could say this marks progress. Unfortunately Wu Gang has never mistaken Houyi's gender: he has always recognized that her wife is female, that Chang'e is monogamous. Yet he puts that side by side with the idea that Chang'e has a husband, and in a stunning blast of illogic reconciles the two. "Houyi is married to me. This makes her my wife, as I am hers. There is no one else."

He looks down at his feet. He looks up at the moon's roof. Delicately, he hedges, "Have you considered, Lady Chang'e, that the archer is in truth a lord, and when he comes to you puts on a woman's guise to please your tastes?"

Chang'e very much would like to remain poised, graceful, unassailable. Instead she wants to strike him. "I was there when she entered the court. She's always been as she is, and must've lost count of the times she is asked whether she would like to incarnate as a man."

The woodsman kneels by one of the lantern beasts and makes a pretense of patting the silk flat. "Husbands do not always tell their wives everything, goddess. On this I can attest. It's not maliciously meant; men cannot give themselves wholly to their spouses."

For a long time she looks at him. "Then it is quite fortunate I didn't marry a man, isn't it?"

"Lady Chang'e, I didn't mean to give offense. You know that."

"No," she says, "you didn't." It would profit neither of them to say that only makes it worse.

To his credit Wu Gang has done much to ensure their privacy, having built from nothing a pavilion large enough to contain a small court: embellishing and furnishing it with enough ornaments for the same. All colors, all light: the rabbit's wine steams amber, the wood shines defiant red.

She takes one of the lacquered chairs, sits, and counts. Cherrywood armrests dig into her palms.

She feels her wife's arrival on her eyelids, a finger of heat down her cheeks. When she looks again Houyi is there, warm and real, a little breathless.

The first moments are always difficult: they have gotten used to over three hundred days without the other. Absence has become more familiar than presence. Neither knows what to say, how to re-acquaint herself to the actuality of her wife.

Chang'e stands. They embrace and habit takes charge. Habit makes Chang'e take Houyi by the wrist, and lead her to the cushions, silk and satin the color of bridal drapes.

"There are no walls," Houyi murmurs.

"No one will watch," Chang'e says and discovers there is more than habit, that despite everything—the sheer stretch of the centuries—there is still desire. She draws her wife down with her, and for the next moments they do not speak at all.

Eventually they come to the wine, a single cup between the two of them. Chang'e straddles Houyi's lap, sipping amber heat that goes down scalding, tangerine-tart. Given their position, which they settle into as surely as key into lock, she feels awkward when she finally asks, "What have you been doing?"

"Bearing your absence without grace."

She traces a line down the archer's breast, doubling and circling back. Her palm pushes gently against Houyi's heart. "Do you still think of us as married? Or just—"

"Friends who become lovers, very briefly, once a year?" Houyi leans into her touch, eyelids fluttering against her cheek. "I have thought on it, though I feel the time differently."

"My kin are all dead."

"Yes," the archer says gently, "that's why the centuries pass unmarked for me, for I've nothing on the changing mortal earth, but for you…I've consulted many gods, many sages. Most continue to say that in a few centuries perhaps your sentence will lift, and you need only to wait it out. Obviously I disagree."

Chang'e presses her nails to the edge of her mouth. "I can't—not another century. Not another decade."

Chang'e Dashes from the Moon

"I know." Houyi exhales. "If there's a way we will find it; if there's anything I can do I will do it, and none will stand between me and your freedom. I swear this."

Chang'e makes herself smile. She might have made herself say that she is absolute, that she has no doubts, that what is between them is steadfast as the moorings of a continent. But it was Houyi's forthrightness that first made her say, *Oh, may we have a thing like marriage, might we become wife and wife?* It was that, and many things besides, which Chang'e loved. Between them there can be no lies, and few secrets. So she whispers, while they're still so close their teeth are on each other's lips, the fragment of a thought she's been hoarding close to her breast.

Long after the chariot has gone Chang'e remains to watch its trail, wisps of gold that too quickly dissipate, a thin memory of stars.

2.

On earth Houyi, too, dresses like a man. But in this place of chrome and skyscrapers it is less remarkable than it once was. Having let her hair down she becomes even more ordinary, for mortal men now keep theirs very short. Some are clean-shaven entirely, even though they aren't monks.

She comes at night, when her duty relents, and haunts the ocean's side. She watches the ferries crossing the gulf between city districts: strange to think that Hong Kong and Kowloon, once very much unlike, can now be counted two parts of the same whole. It's taken her several centuries, to track as she has never before, not prey of hooves and fangs and tiger-fur, but a thin faded line of blood. A long time ago she met the mother, brother and niece of her wife, and when she looked again they were all gone.

But the hunt is Houyi's domain and delight. Though there is nothing left she could recognize, no commonality of name—for people speak differently now, and name their children differently especially on this isle—and little to see in the cast of skull and shape of eyes, she's chased the tracks of genealogy to Hong Kong.

It is not that she keeps secrets from Chang'e. But she doesn't want to hold out a false hope, when it's taken her this long, when it's this thin and flimsy a thing.

In the Space Museum it is almost empty, climate-controlled air whispering against her skin, a quiet hum of electricity. She goes past the glass cases of spacesuits and shuttle models, the gravity well demonstration with its whirling metal spheres, the instrument panels that simulate a cockpit. But it is the photographs of lunar landings that snatch at her attention, make her linger.

"You've been showing up every other night."

She glances up, unsurprised. "You work here."

"Unfortunately." The young woman is in the process of locking down doors, dressed for the cold. Belatedly Houyi realizes she is not. "Well, we're closing soon."

They leave the museum separately, and board the same boat off Star Ferry to Wanchai. Houyi sits by the railing, where the winds buffet her hair and tear at her skin. When the young woman settles beside her, Houyi hears her frown before she even asks, "Aren't you even a little cold?"

"It doesn't bother me. You are Julienne, I think?"

Julienne's hand brushes the spot on her sweater that corresponds to where her employee's card has been. "People don't wear name tags in real life. It's awful."

"Hau Ngai."

The young woman blinks, but offers no commentary nor wonders aloud just why it is that she has a name so masculine.

Chang'e continues in testing and measuring her enemy.

With no drop of joy but plenty of grim clarity, she sets one of the houses on fire. No small feat, for the moon is cold and the building pure rock, but the rabbit keeps bottles of phoenix flame. Small collection—even in heaven the substance is rare—but she pinches one anyway, guilty but not guilty enough to seek another solution. After a stone house is reduced to blackened rubble, Chang'e finds herself unable to leave the pavilion Wu Gang built for days after. The surrounding courtyard turns in upon itself, and she can venture no further than the edges. Like an impertinent child in need of correction she has been punished.

The rabbit visits with sticky rice wrapped in ghostly lotus leaves. It plucks at its whiskers nervously. "Why did you do this?"

To that she only gives a serene smile. "What could be done to me?"

"If you wreak such ruin regularly? Banishment to earth as a mortal, or a demon. Or worse, Lady. You aren't beyond the wheel, and when it turns it can break you, pulping flesh and grinding bones. Immortal doesn't mean impervious."

Her expression tightens. "I'll keep that in mind. Thank you, rabbit."

Subsequent experimenting becomes subtler. She notes the times when she can glimpse the earth through windows, through archways. Then she might step through, and be on a mountain, in a temple, on the street of a city. She's never fast enough, but it is a close race.

So, then, what she wants to do might work. As long as the symbolism, the center of story, is satisfied.

The ghost animals have neither voices nor words of their own. A few eels and frogs can be coaxed to echo Chang'e, and that suits her purposes. The trouble lies in luring them. They do not behave much like their living counterparts, neither eating nor mating; owls and starlings sometimes swim languidly in the lakes, and twice she's seen carps up in the branches of a stone cypress. She's tried to tempt them with cakes, fruits, wine, dumplings. None avails. Tatters of fabric and melted candle wax do even less.

Finally she starts giving out pieces of herself.

Clipped locks of her hair attract middling interest. She turns to pain, a hairline thread open in her hand—and they come, attending her blood like courtiers around an empress, wet toothless mouths latching onto her skin. She whispers words at them in slow stressed syllables: her name, common phrases, the way she greets the rabbit and the woodsman. *Thank you* and *You didn't have to* and *The food you made is delicious*. It is like reciting poetry. Conversations so repetitive she can conduct them on her own, exhausted to banality and prescribed lines.

Chang'e melts the rabbit's remedy, the one that unites spirit to body, and blends it with her blood.

The mixture takes a long time to boil, blood and medicine far thicker than water, and when she pours it into sculpted mouths too quickly it splashes and scalds her. Her eyes water at the pain. She does not allow it to slow her down.

She finishes the statue in what she imagines is winter, where the moon's lapses are more frequent and she gets to see the earth almost every day; her prison's mind turns to deserts and brightness, while hers turn to sanding and polishing.

Her features are duplicated across the carved face. No amount of paint will make it seem flesh, but she has prepared a solution for that.

She waits as the ghost animals slip into the mannequin, drawn irresistibly to arterial sweetness. Perhaps they sip at this mixture, and are content; perhaps they struggle to escape. They can't. Having imbibed the medicine they will be bound.

Hands on the shoulders of the statue she concentrates. It isn't something she'd have been able to do mortal—martial practitioners may, and she was never that—but her ascendance has bought more than imprisonment. It will cost her, for she is guided by instinct, not discipline.

A brush of vitality she can scarcely afford to spare trickles through her fingertips. With it, a fraction of herself, that which makes her Chang'e and divine. It suckles at her as though a babe, and she nurses it into a facsimile of life. When she is done her knees are weak.

She clasps the wooden doll to her, mouth to wooden mouth, "You are Chang'e."

It is silent. Only wood, sanded and painted amateurishly.

"You are Chang'e," she repeats, "and you have a wife whom every night you long to meet. You met her in heaven. Under a golden tree and black petals she first kissed you. Her name is Houyi, and you are wedded wives."

Chang'e Dashes from the Moon

"I am," it repeats haltingly, in a voice not quite hers, "Chang'e."

Once the first word has been uttered color flourishes, wood limbs softening to skin, chiseled hair flowing into soft strands. In the best silks she has she dresses the statue, and on its head she puts pearls and ivory. When she is done she hides it deep among the ghosts, draping it in swans and lions winter-pale.

The second time Houyi sees Juliene the latter exclaims, "You can't find these things that interesting."

The archer smiles faintly. "Do you have mooncakes at Zungcauz-it?"

"Of course." Julienne glances sidelong at the moon-walk box. "What does that have to do with anything?"

This time they end up at a Maxim's outlet, which even at this time of the night is crowded, noisy, and not especially glamorous. They order and have indifferent honeyed pork, dim sum, and pearl tea. Julienne wrings her sleeves and bites her lip. "I do know nicer places."

"I don't mind," Houyi says. "There's something to be said for convenience."

"You're so unpicky. Where are you from?"

"The mainland."

A disbelieving laugh, as though she believes someone who dresses as elegantly as Houyi—and her choice of attire is that, by accident—couldn't possibly have so provincial an origin. "Shenzhen? Peking?"

"I'm not much for cities." She looks across the room, where one woman—catching Houyi's gaze—stops giggling with her friends and blanches. A spider demon. Her shadow briefly flares extra limbs as she scrambles, upsetting iced tea, and excuses herself from the table. "They are too easy to hide in. But I'd rather know about you."

Julienne sets down her chopsticks. "Are you flirting with me?"

This surprises a chuckle out of Houyi. "I'm much too advanced in age for that. Old aunts shouldn't flirt with young ladies."

"You can't be more than thirty-five."

"You shouldn't affront your elders by suggesting they're less than they seem. Regardless I have a wife."

The girl puts the tip of a chopstick back in her mouth and chews it with a peculiar fervor. "You got married abroad, I suppose. What's her name?"

"Seung Ngo."

"Oh come on."

"That's actually her name." Houyi signals a waitress—she has to call only once to gain attention, which seems to awe Julienne disproportionately—and despite the girl's protest she pays the entire bill. "I'm about to ask you something very odd and rather personal."

"How odd can it be?" Julienne gestures with her glass, whose bottom is black with ice-trapped tapioca beads.

"Do you visit a cemetery during Chingming?"

Julienne leans away from the table. "That is a bit personal. And you aren't even single."

"I'm not that bewitching, child."

"Well, fine. I don't go. I don't owe my parents anything, not even burning them bits of shiny paper."

"Ah," the archer murmurs. There's little family resemblance; marriages, migrations, and sheer eons have washed those out, sculpted quite something else in the place of features possessed by Chang'e. But there is, perhaps, something of the same sharpness. "I have a boon I would ask of you."

"You talk like you just stepped out of a mowhab set."

Houyi has seen her share of those films. They amuse, mostly because when gods do battle there is a great deal more fanfare than even the most ostentatious special effects. "It's hard to get out of character."

They step outside the Maxim's, into a night thick with neon signs and street vendors peddling counterfeit watches. Houyi thinks, and hopes, that Chang'e will like this place, this era. It will surely suit her curiosity.

She holds out a hand to Julienne, who frowns but takes it.

When they reappear in the silence of Che Kung the girl staggers, looks about wildly, and bites down on her knuckles. There isn't much light apart from the bulbs illuminating a shrine full of Guanyins in

Chang'e Dashes from the Moon

white and gold, clothes colorful and colorless. Houyi eases Julienne down to the lip of a blue pool, at whose center yet another Guanyin stands with child in hand.

"I'm not going," Julienne says, voice gone thin and breathy, "to scream. I'm not."

"I hoped you wouldn't."

When she has gotten herself under control Julienne demands, "What do you want from me?"

"To burn something." Houyi draws out what she's hidden by the shrine. It is caked in ashes, but undamaged: coils of silvered paper linked together, braided into a rope ladder. The length isn't anywhere near enough, objectively, but she's learned that such things are only symbols. "While thinking of a…great-aunt many times over."

Julienne takes the paper ladder in hand. "This isn't the right time, there isn't a picture, I have no incense, there isn't a grave. I don't even know her name."

"It is Seung Ngo."

"Oh," the girl says, giving a vindicated little clap, "of course. Of course your wife is the goddess on the moon and you're the archer who shot down nine suns. Does she have a pet rabbit too?"

"I wouldn't call it precisely a pet. There's also a woodsman on the moon, if you were curious."

Houyi describes Chang'e to Julienne quietly, quickly, as she makes a fire and wishes she had some skill at sketching. Julienne kneels dazed, but concentrates on Houyi's voice. She feeds the paper ladder to the flames all at once, as such things are meant to be consigned, and watches as it crumbles. That takes longer than most offerings; Houyi made the ladder strong and thick, just to be sure.

When all that remains is smoke—Julienne exclaiming how illegal it is to litter temple grounds as they have—Houyi feels as though she has emptied herself into that fire, into that rope ladder of paper, and now as the ashes drift skyward this has flitted beyond her grasp. There's nothing more she may do.

"Will I get to see whoever it is that I just burned that for? The great-aunt. Great-grandaunt."

Houyi touches the base of her throat, chasing the recall of her wife's touch. "We will see. I believe she will wish to meet you."

"She isn't a ghost?"

"Flesh and blood, and beautiful." The archer stands. "Shall I bring you somewhere else?"

"I'd hate having to explain myself to the police."

She takes the grand-niece of her wife near the Sha Tin station, in a spot quiet and empty enough that they were not seen except by a stray cat. It hisses at Houyi and turns tail, though not before she notes that its eyes are an unnatural, lambent blue.

Before she leaves Houyi allows her clothes to reweave themselves into the form she favors, a man's robe and trousers in pale blue. Bow and quiver at her back, reassuring solidity and weight against her spine.

Julienne stares at her, dumbfounded, as she presses her palm over her fist and bows to the girl in that old way mortals don't bother with anymore except at New Year. As Houyi departs she can still hear Julienne muttering something about mowhab sets.

3.

When the rope ladder appears Chang'e knows it is time.

It drapes halfway in, halfway out of her window. Touching it she knows at once whose hand wove it into shape, whose hand touched it and made the passing of it to her possible. It is still warm, as though hiding in its strands a secret heat. The length of it seems immeasurable. The strength of it feels muscular, the flexibility of it prehensile.

She sits, gripping the ladder tight, until she feels its gravity bleed into her bones.

The weight of earth. The weight, perhaps, of kinship.

Chang'e races over the roof with a lightness impossible anywhere else, toward the garden where she's hidden a part of herself. She peels away the swans and lions and tigers, the foliage and shrubs not quite real, the leaves and fruits that taste of honey and ice.

Chang'e Dashes from the Moon

The moon is greedy and will not let her go. And there must, always, be a woman on the moon. Very well: she will give it one that never tires, one that never weeps.

She points the mannequin at the city, whispering, Go.

Child-obedient it goes, Chang'e-shaped, as she ties one end of the ladder to a roof finial. Knowing the length will not fail her, she tightens the knot until it no longer budges. Then she casts the ladder. It falls, and falls, until it stops taut.

Between the rough jagged rocks of the moon's flanks she descends. The wind slices at her, flaying-sharp, scalpels driving between her vertebrae—searing the shells of her ears—infiltrating lungs and nose. Her fingers turn numb, and freeze solid to the rope. Her skin tears. With each rung she weighs heavier.

Lunar cold recedes. She is halfway, or three-fourths of the way. It becomes very warm and, off the corner of her eye, she sees sun-struck seas, she sees fruits and treetops, a sunlit day. She sees a mountain-top nearly as close to her as her own feet.

She passes through fire. On the moon slivers of her self vibrate within their wooden cage, leaping and hissing through wooden mouths. The puppet that is her, that appears skin and hair but whose core is cherry bay, clutches itself and translates her raw flesh to amphibious pain-cries.

On the other side Chang'e is charred hair and blood fruiting on her lips, she is blisters and lymph dewing on her arms. The snow mutes and absorbs the retching of her screams. When she does stand she totters and would have pitched over again if she does not remember that she is breathing freedom, tasting it with lungs, pores, palate.

She straightens: dignity, she must have that when she does this for the first time. She has witnessed Houyi doing it without thought or effort. Back then she did not imagine she would one day gain the capability to do the same, the right of any deity. She thinks east; she thinks of bringing it close.

One step, two. Her footprints are shallow in the snow. By the fifth she's treading on sand, on the howl of tides against cliff. Saltwater laps at her waist, searing the burns on her thighs and hips. What remains of her robes drifts seaweed-heavy in the waves.

There is a little house by the shore.

Chang'e limps up the winding path she knows her wife paved: conch shells and sea-smoothed pebbles, dyed in the bright colors that Houyi loves.

The front door, double-paneled, is shut against drafts. At her touch it parts. Inside, three rooms. An enclosure for ablutions with folded screen and fish-scale tiles, an untidy workshop, and a bedroom. This last is built for two, furniture in duplicates, a pair of armoires side by side: one filled, the other empty as though in hope.

Houyi sits at the window, back straight, clad in a thin robe carelessly thrown on that leaves one shoulder bare. She turns and her breath leaves her in a long whisper. "Chang'e."

The archer spreads burn salve over her; from the familiar vegetal smell she recognizes it as the rabbit's work. When she can speak again without her face hurting she murmurs through cracked lips, "What did you do?" Her voice claws its way out a ruin, cold-wracked, fire-scourged.

"I found your family." Houyi pours her lukewarm water, keeping at arm's length as though unsure if she may touch Chang'e.

"Family." Chang'e holds her cup, presses it to her smeared cheek for relief. "I've family left?"

"Your niece had children. It took me a while to track them—they spread and went away to far lands. Some never came back; it's difficult to read their footprints." The archer brushes away what remains of her wife's hair. Charred handfuls fall out. "Her name's Julienne."

Chang'e repeats it. "What an outlandish name."

"She is of the same blood as you. Else when she burned it the ladder wouldn't have found you."

"Or let me escape." Kinship, she thinks, the surest anchor.

She looks at her wife, who has done so much, who has opened this path. "Can you," she asks uncertainly, "take me to see this girl?"

Chang'e Dashes from the Moon

Julienne zips up her jacket and chafes her hands, wishing she'd declined the invitation to the class reunion. Her schoolmates haven't gotten any more interesting than the last time, and all the women remain—as far as she can tell—depressingly straight.

At her feet night club flyers rustle, garish things heavy on neon-pink and black. Tomorrow someone is going to be fined for littering. She stops at a 7-11 for chrysanthemum tea, a bar of chocolate, sanitary pads. Ordinary items for an ordinary life.

The MTR station is quiet, dead last-train hours and closed convenience stores. She hopes that the one night of oddity in Che Kung hasn't ruined her for a lifetime of normalcy. In a way Julienne resents that woman—whoever or whatever she was, for surely she was not that Hau Ngai—for disrupting her life. She tries not to dwell on it as she waves her card at the turnstile, goes down the escalator, and into a front carriage. The only other passenger is an older man, dozing. Yesterday's issue of the Apple Daily flutters by his side.

The smartphone in his shirt pocket chirps and shakes at the next stop. He wakes groggily, disembarks, and Julienne finds herself alone.

A hand falls on her shoulder, jerking her out of the white-noise zone born of electrical glare and the ghost of her own reflection foregrounding the tunnel rushing by. Julienne looks up to find two women. One tall, in suit and slacks. The other, astonishingly, in cheongsam. Pearls in her hair, either a net or secured by supernatural means.

The goddess is known to be exquisite.

Julienne realizes her mouth has fallen open. She shuts it.

Seung Ngo cups Julienne's face in her hands. She startles to find that the goddess' palms are not velvet; they are rough, harder than her own, as though she is a woman who works with her hands. The most menial Julienne's ever gotten is with keyboards. Carefully, as if speaking Gwongdongwa for the first time Seung Ngo says, "My wife was wrong. I do see written on you my mother and Third Niece."

Finding her voice finally she says, a little irritably, "Not my parents, I hope."

The goddess—her ancestress—lets her hands fall away. "You're your own, mostly. Will you introduce me to the rest of our clan?"

Julienne splutters a laugh. "I don't think they can take the shock."

"They don't have to know everything. And you, of course, will always be my favorite."

"Do I get the thickest red envelope?"

"Insolent child," Seung Ngo says fondly. "I'll stuff yours with gold."

A cool female voice announces that the next station is the end of the Island line. Julienne tries to imagine New Year and Chingming with all their family obligations. She's refused to show up for several years now. "Next Zungcauzit my cousins in Indonesia and Singapore are coming home. You're supposed to be on the moon by then, but…"

Seung Ngo laughs. "I'll be with you, not to worry. I've never tasted mortal-made mooncakes."

"We put ice-cream in them now. All sorts of fillings. You can even buy them off-season."

"Oh, my," the goddess says.

"But until then I've got photo albums. Of—the family. Baby pictures too. Do you want to see?"

"I'd like nothing more."

The two immortals take each of Julienne's arms, clasping her between them, and somehow they exit without needing either octopus card or ticket. Julienne knows that this year she'll attend all the family gatherings. Perhaps they won't go very well. But she will have two divine aunts with her, and isn't that worth something?

Very different, if nothing else. And never boring.

"It feels like I'm continuing a story," Julienne breathes. "You might've heard of it before."

Hau Ngai tilts her head. "And which one is that?"

"On the moon," she begins, grinning, "there's a lady with a rabbit…"

Astrophilia

Carrie Vaughn

After five years of drought, the tiny wool-producing household of Greentree was finished. First the pastures died off, then the sheep, and Stella and the others didn't have any wool to process and couldn't meet the household's quota, small though it was with only five of them working at the end. The holding just couldn't support a household and the regional committee couldn't keep putting credits into it, hoping that rains would come. They might never come, or the next year might be a flood. No one could tell, and that was the problem, wasn't it?

None of them argued when Az and Jude put in to dissolve Greentree. They could starve themselves to death with pride, but that would be a waste of resources. Stella was a good weaver, and ought to have a chance somewhere else. That was the first reason they gave for the decision.

Because they dissolved voluntarily, the committee found places for them in other households, ones not on the verge of collapse. However, Az put in a special request and found Stella's new home herself. "I know the head of the place, Toma. He'll take good care of you, but more than that his place is prosperous. Rich enough for children, even. You could earn a baby there, Stella." Az's wrinkled hands gripped Stella's young ones in her own, and her eyes shone. Twenty-three years ago, Greentree had been prosperous enough to earn a baby: Stella. But those days were gone.

Stella began to have doubts. "Mama, I don't want to leave you and everyone—"

"We'll be fine. We'd have had to leave sooner or later, and this way we've got credits to take with us. Start new on a good footing, yes?"

"Yes, but—" She hesitated, because her fears were childish. "What if they don't like me?"

Az shook her head. "Winter market I gave Toma the shawl you made. You should have seen him, Stella, his mouth dropped. He said Barnard Croft would take you on the spot, credits or no."

But what if they don't like *me*, Stella wanted to whine. She wasn't worried about her weaving.

Az must have seen that she was about to cry. "Oh, dear, it'll be all right. We'll see each other at the markets, maybe more if there's trading to be done. You'll be happy, I know you will. Better things will come."

Because Az seemed so pleased for her, Stella stayed quiet, and hoped.

In the spring, Stella traveled to Barnard Croft, three hundred miles on the Long Road from Greentree, in the hills near the coast.

Rain poured on the last day of the journey, so the waystation driver used a pair of horses to draw the wagon, instead of the truck. Stella offered to wait until the storm passed and the solar batteries charged up, but he had a schedule to keep, and insisted that the horses needed the exercise.

Stella sat under the awning on the front seat of the wagon, wrapped in a blanket against the chill, feeling sorry for the hulking draft animals in front of her. They were soaked, brown coats dripping as they clomped step by step on the muddy road. It might have been faster, waiting for the clouds to break, for the sun to emerge and let them use the truck. But the driver said they'd be waiting for days in these spring rains.

She traveled through an alien world, wet and green. Stella had never seen so much water in her whole life, all of it pouring from the sky. A quarter of this amount of rain a couple of hundred miles east would have saved Greentree.

The road curved into the next green valley, to Barnard Croft. The wide meadow and its surrounding, rolling hills were green, lush with grass. A handful of alpaca grazed along a stream that ran frothing from the hills opposite. The animals didn't seem to mind the water, however matted and heavy their coats looked. There'd be some work, cleaning that mess for spinning. Actually, she looked forward to it. She wanted to make herself useful as soon as she could. To prove herself. If this didn't work, if she didn't fit in here and had to throw herself on the mercy of the regional committee to find some place prosperous enough to take her, that could use a decent weaver…no, this would work.

A half-a-dozen whitewashed cottages clustered together, along with sheds and shelters for animals, a couple of rabbit hutches, and squares of turned black soil with a barest sheen of green—garden plots and new growth. The largest cottage stood apart from the others. It had wide doors and many windows, shuttered now against the rain—the work house, she guessed. Under the shelter of the wide eaves sat wooden barrels for washing wool, and a pair of precious copper pots for dyeing. All comfortable, familiar sights.

The next largest cottage, near the garden plots, had a smoking chimney. Kitchen and common room, most likely. Which meant the others were sleeping quarters. She wondered which was hers, and who'd she'd be sharing with. A pair of windmills stood on the side of one hill; their trefoil blades were still.

At the top of the highest hill, across the meadow, was a small, unpainted shack. It couldn't have held more than a person or two standing upright. This, she did not recognize. Maybe it was a curing shed, though it seemed an unlikely spot, exposed as it was to every passing storm.

A turn-off took them from the road to the cottages, and by the time the driver pulled up the horses, eased the wagon to a stop, and set the brakes, a pair of men wrapped in cloaks emerged from the work house to greet them. Stella thanked the driver and jumped to the ground. Her boots splashed, her long woolen skirt tangled around her legs, and the rain pressed the blanket close around her. She felt sodden and bedraggled, but she wouldn't complain.

The elder of those who came to greet her was middle aged and worn, but he moved briskly and spread his arms wide. "Here she is! Didn't know if you would make it in this weather." This was Toma. Az's friend, Stella reminded herself. Nothing to worry about.

"Horses'll get through anything," the driver said, moving to the back of the wagon to unload her luggage.

"Well then," Toma said. "Let's get you inside and dried off."

"Thank you," Stella managed. "I just have a couple of bags. And a loom. Az let me take Greentree's loom."

"Well then, that is a treasure. Good."

The men clustered around the back of the wagon to help. The bags held her clothes, a few books and letters and trinkets. Her equipment: spindles and needles, carders, skeins of yarn, coils of roving. The loom took up most of the space—dismantled, legs and frames strapped together, mechanisms folded away in protective oilskin. It would take her most of a day to set up. She'd feel better when it was.

A third figure came running from the work house, shrouded by her wrap and hood like the others. The shape of her was female, young— maybe even Stella's age. She wore dark trousers and a pale tunic, like the others.

She came straight to the driver. "Anything for me?"

Astrophilia

"Package from Griffith?" the driver answered.

"Oh, yes!"

The driver dug under an oil cloth and brought out a leather document case, stuffed full. The woman came forward to take it, revealing her face, sandstone-burnished skin and bright brown eyes.

Toma scowled at her, but the woman didn't seem to notice. She tucked the package under her arm and beamed like sunshine.

"At least be useful and take a bag," Toma said to her.

Taking up a bag with a free hand, the woman flashed a smile at Stella, and turned to carry her load to the cottage.

Toma and other other man, Jorge, carried the loom to the work house. Hefting the rest of her luggage, Stella went to the main cottage, following the young woman at a distance. Behind her, the driver returned to his seat and got the horses moving again; their hooves splashed on the road.

༄

Around dinner time, the clouds broke, belying the driver's prediction. Some sky and a last bit of sunlight peeked through.

They ate what seemed to her eyes a magnificent feast—meat, eggs, preserved fruits and vegetables, fresh bread. At Greentree, they'd barely got through the winter on stores, and until this meal Stella hadn't realized she'd been dimly hungry all the time, for weeks. Months. Greentree really had been dying.

The folk of the croft gathered around the hearth at night, just as they did back home at Greentree, just as folk did at dozens of households up and down the Long Road. She met everyone: Toma and Jorge, who'd helped with the loom. Elsta, Toma's partner, who ran the kitchen and garden. Nik and Wendy, Jon and Faren. Peri had a baby, which showed just how well off Barnard was, to be able to support a baby as well as a refugee like Stella. The first thing Peri did was put the baby—Bette—in Stella's arms, and Stella was stricken because she'd never held a wriggly baby before and was afraid of dropping her. But Peri arranged her arms just so and took the baby back after a few moments of cooing over them both. Stella had never thought of earning the right to have her implant removed, to have a baby—another mouth to feed at Greentree would have been a disaster.

Elsta was wearing the shawl Stella had made, the one Az had given Toma—her audition, really, to prove her worth. The shawl was an intricate weave made of finely spun merino. Stella had done everything—carded and spun the wool, dyed it the difficult smoky blue, and designed the pattern herself. Elsta didn't have to wear it, the croft could have traded it for credits. Stella felt a small spark of pride. Wasn't just charity that brought her here.

Stella had brought her work basket, but Elsta tsked at her. "You've had a long trip, so rest now. Plenty of time to work later." So she sat on a blanket spread out on the floor and played with Bette.

Elsta picked apart a tangle of roving, preparing to draft into the spindle of her spinning wheel. Toma and Jorge had a folding table in front of them, and the tools to repair a set of hand carders. The others knit, crocheted, or mended. They no doubt made all their own clothing, from weaving the fabric to sewing, dark trousers, bright skirts, aprons, and tunics. Stella's hands itched to work—she was in the middle of knitting a pair of very bright yellow socks from the remnants of yarn from a weaving. They'd be ugly but warm—and the right kind of ugly had a charm of its own. But Elsta was probably right, and the baby was fascinating. Bette had a set of wooden blocks that she banged into each other; occasionally, very seriously, she handed them to Stella. Then demanded them back. The process must have had a logic to it.

The young woman wasn't with them. She'd skipped dinner as well. Stella was thinking of how to ask about her, when Elsta did it for her.

"Is Andi gone out to her study, then?"

Toma grumbled, "Of course she is." The words bit.

Her study—the shack on the hill? Stella listened close, wishing the baby would stop banging her blocks so loudly.

"Toma—"

"She should be here."

Astrophilia

"She's done her work, let her be. The night's turned clear, you know how she gets."

"She should listen to me."

"The more you push, the angrier she'll get. Leave her be, dearest."

Elsta's wheel turned and purred, Peri hummed as she knit, and Bette's toys clacked. Toma frowned, never looking up from his work.

∽

Her bags sat by one of the two beds in the smallest cottage, only half unpacked. The other bed, Andi's, remained empty. Stella washed, brushed out her short blond hair, changed into her nightdress, and curled up under the covers. Andi still hadn't returned.

The air smelled wrong, here. Wet, earthy, as if she could smell the grass growing outside the window. The shutters cracked open to let in a breeze. Stella was chilled; her nose wouldn't stop running. The desert always smelled dusty, dry—even at night, the heat of the sun rose up from the ground. There, her nose itched with dust.

She couldn't sleep. She kept waiting for Andi to come back.

Finally, she did. Stella started awake when the door opened with the smallest squeak—so she must have slept, at least a little. Cocooned under the covers, she clutched her pillow, blinking, uncertain for a moment where she was and what was happening. Everything felt wrong, but that was to be expected, so she lay still.

Andi didn't seem to notice that she was awake. She hung up her cloak on a peg by the door, sat on her bed while she peeled off shoes and clothes, which she left lying on the chest at the foot of her bed, and crawled under the covers without seeming to notice—or care—that Stella was there. The woman moved quickly—nervously, even? But when she pulled the covers over her, she lay still, asleep in moments. Stella had a suspicion that she'd had practice, falling asleep quickly in the last hours before dawn, before she'd be expected to rise and work.

Stella supposed she would get a chance to finally talk to her new roommate soon enough, but she had no idea what she was going to say to her.

∽

The next day, the clouds had more than broken. No sign of them remained, and the sun blazed clear as it ever had in the desert, but on a world that was wet, green, and growing. The faint sprouts in the garden plots seem to have exploded into full growth, leaves uncurling. The angora in the hutches pressed twitching noses to the wire mesh of their cages, as if they could squeeze out to play in the meadow. Every shutter and window in the croft was opened to let in the sun.

The work house was wide, clean, whitewashed inside and out. It smelled of lanolin, fiber and work. Lint floated in beams of sunlight. Two—now three—looms and a pair of spinning wheels sat facing each other, so the weavers and spinners could talk. Days would pass quickly here. The first passed quickly enough, and Stella finished it feeling tired and satisfied.

Andi had spent the day at the wash tubs outside, cleaning a batch of wool, preparing it to card and spin in the next week or so. She'd still been asleep when Stella got up that morning, but must have woken up soon after. They still hadn't talked. Not even hello. They kept missing each other, being in different places. Continually out of rhythm, like a pattern that wove crooked because you hadn't counted the threads right. The more time passed without them speaking, the harder Stella found it to think of anything to say. She wanted to ask, *Are you avoiding me?*

Stella had finished putting away her work and was headed for the common room, when she noticed Andi following the footpath away from the cottages, around the meadow and up the hill to the lonely shack. Her study, Elsta had called it. She walked at a steady pace, not quite running, but not lingering.

After waiting until she was far enough ahead that she was not likely to look over her shoulder, Stella followed.

The trail up the hill was a hike, and even walking slowly Stella was soon gasping for breath. But slowly and steadily she made progress. The path made a couple of switchbacks, and finally reached the crest of the hill and the tiny weathered shack planted there.

As she suspected, the view was worth the climb. The whole of Barnard Croft's valley was visible, as well as the next one over. The

Astrophilia

neighboring croft's cottages were pale specks, and a thread of smoke climbed from one. The hills were soft, rounded, cut through with clefts like the folds in a length of fabric. Trees along the creek gave texture to the picture. The Long Road was a gray track painted around the green rise. The sky above stretched on, and on, blue touched by a faint haze. If she squinted, she thought she could see a line of gray on the far western horizon—the ocean, and the breeze in that direction had a touch of salt and wild. From this perspective, the croft rested in a shallow bowl that sat on the top of the world. She wondered how long it would take to walk around the entire valley, and decided she would like to try some sunny day.

The shed seemed even smaller when she was standing next to it. Strangely, part of the roof was missing, folded back on hinges, letting in light. The walls were too high to see over, and the door was closed. Stella hesitated; she shouldn't be here, she was invading. She had to share a room with this woman, she shouldn't intrude. Then again—she had to share a room with this woman. She only wanted to talk. And if Andi didn't like it, well…

Stella knocked on the door before she could change her mind. Three quick, woodpecker-like raps.

When the door swung out, she hopped back, managed not to fall over, and looked wide eyed to see Andi glaring at her.

Then the expression softened, falling away to blank confusion. "Oh. Hi."

They stared at each other for a long moment. Andi leaned on the door, blocking the way; Stella still couldn't see what was inside.

"May I come in?" she finally asked, because Andi hadn't closed the door on her.

"Oh—sure." The woman seemed to shake herself out of a daydream, and stepped back to open the door wide.

The bulk of the tiny room was taken up by a device mounted on a tripod as tall as she was. A metallic cylinder, wide as a bucket, pointed to the ceiling. A giant tin can almost, except the outer case was painted gray, and it had latches, dials, levers, all manner of protrusions connected to it. Stella moved around it, studying it, reminding herself not to touch, however much the object beckoned.

"It's a telescope, isn't it?" she asked, looking over to Andi. "An old one."

A smile dawned on Andi's face, lighting her mahogany eyes. "It is—twelve-inch reflector. Century or so old, probably. Pride and joy." Her finger traced up the tripod, stroking it like it was a favorite pet.

Stella's chest clenched at that smile, and she was glad now that she'd followed Andi here. She kept her voice calm. "Where'd you get it? You couldn't have traded for it—"

"Oh no, you can't trade for something like this. What would you trade for it?" Meaning how many bales of wool, or bolts of cloth, or live alpacas, or cans full of fish from the coast was something like this worth? You couldn't put a price on it. Some people would just give it away, because it had no real use, no matter how rare it was. Andi continued, "It was Pan's, who ran the household before Toma. He was one of the ones who helped build up the network with the observatories, after the big fall. Then he left it all to me. He'd have left it to Toma, but he wasn't interested." She shrugged, as if unable to explain.

"Then it actually works?"

"Oh yes." That smile shone again, and Stella would stay and talk all night, to keep that smile lit up. "I mean, not now, we'll have to wait until dark, assuming the weather stays clear. With the roof open it's almost a real observatory. See how we've fixed the seams?" She pointed to the edges, where the roof met the walls. Besides the hinges and latches that closed the roof in place, the seams had oilskin weatherproofing, to keep rain from seeping through the cracks. The design was clever. The building, then, was shelter for the equipment. The telescope never moved—the bottom points of the tripod were anchored with bricks.

Beside the telescope there wasn't much here: a tiny desk, a shelf filled with books, a bin holding a stack of papers, and a wooden box holding pencils. The leather pouch Andi had received yesterday was open, and packets of paper spread over the desk.

Astrophilia

"Is that what you got in the mail?"

She bustled to the desk and shuffled through the pages. "Assignment from Griffith. It's a whole new list of coordinates, now that summer's almost here. The whole sky changes—what we see changes, at least—so I make observations and send the whole thing back." The flush in her brown face deepened as she ducked away. "I know it doesn't sound very interesting, we mostly just write down numbers and trade them back and forth—"

"Oh no," Stella said, shaking her head to emphasize. "It's interesting. Unusual—"

"And useless, Toma says." The smile turned sad, and last night's discussion became clear to Stella.

"Nothing's useless," Stella said. "It's like you said—you can't just throw something like this away." This wasn't like a household that couldn't feed itself and had no choice but to break up.

Three sharp rings of a distant brass bell sounded across the valley. Stella looked out the door, confused.

"Elsta's supper bell," Andi explained. "She only uses it when we've all scattered." She quickly straightened her papers, returned them to their pouch, and latched the roof back in place. Too late, Stella thought to help, reaching up to hold the panel of wood after Andi had already secured the last latch. Oh well. Maybe next time.

Stella got a better look at Andi as they walked back to the croft. She was rough in the way of wind and rain, her dark hair curly, pulled back by a scrap of gray yarn that was unraveling. The collar of her shirt was untied, and her woven jacket had slipped off a shoulder. Stella resisted an urge to pull it back up, and to brush the lock of hair that had fallen out of the tie behind her ear.

"So you're really more of an astronomer than a weaver," Stella said. She'd tried to sound encouraging, but Andi frowned.

"Drives Toma crazy," Andi said. "If there was a household of astronomers, I'd join. But astronomy doesn't feed anyone, does it? Well, some of it does—meteorology, climatology, solar astronomy, maybe. But not what we're doing. We don't earn anyone a baby."

"What are you doing?"

"Astronomical observation. As much as we can, though it feels like reinventing the wheel sometimes. We're not learning anything that people didn't already know back in the day. We're just—well, it feels like filling in the gaps until we get back to where we were. Tracking asteroids, marking supernovae, that sort of thing. Maybe we can't do much with the data. But it might be useful someday."

"There, you see—it's planning ahead. There's use in that."

She sighed. "The committees mostly think it's a waste of time. They can't really complain, though, because we—those of us in the network—do our share and work extra to support the observatories. A bunch of us designate ration credits toward Griffith and Kitt Peak and Wilson—they've got the region's big scopes—to keep staff there maintaining the equipment, to keep the solar power and windmills running. Toma always complains, says if I put my extra credits toward the household we could have a second baby. He says it could even be mine. But they're my credits, and this is important. I earn the time I spend with the scope, and he can't argue." She said that as a declaration, then looked straight at Stella, who blushed. "They may have brought you here to make up for me."

Stella didn't know what to say to that. She was too grateful to have a place at all, to consider that she may have been wanted.

Awkwardly, Andi covered up the silence. "Well. I hope you like it here. That you don't get too homesick, I mean."

The words felt like a warm blanket, soft and wooly. "Thanks."

"We can be kind of rowdy sometimes. Bette gets colicky, and you haven't heard Wendy sing yet. Then there's Jorge and Jon—they share a bed as well as a cottage, see, and can get pretty loud, though if you tease them about it they'll deny it."

"I don't mind rowdy. But I did almost expect to find a clandestine still in that shed."

Andi laughed. "I think Toma'd like a still better, because at least you can drink from it. Elsta does make a really good cider, though. If she ever put enough together to trade it would make up for all the credits I waste on the observatories."

Astrophilia

As they came off the hill and approached the cluster of cottages, Andi asked, "Did you know that Stella means star in Latin?"

"Yes, I did," she answered.

∽

Work was work no matter where you were, and Stella settled into her work quickly. The folk of Barnard were nice, and Andi was easy to talk to. And cute. Stella found excuses to be in the same room with her, just to see that smile. She hadn't expected this, coming to a new household. But she didn't mind, not at all.

Many households along the Long Road kept sheep, but the folk at Barnard did most of the spinning and weaving for trade. All the wool came to them. Barnard also produced a small quantity of specialty fibers from the alpaca and angora rabbits they kept. They were known for the quality of all their work, the smoothness of their yarns, the evenness of their weaving. Their work was sought after not just along the Long Road, but up and down the coast.

Everyone spun, wove, and dyed. Everyone knew every step of working with wool. They either came here because they knew, or because they'd grown up here learning the trade, like Toma and Nik, like Bette would in her turn. As Andi had, as Stella found out. Andi was the baby that Toma and Elsta had earned together.

Stella and Andi were at the looms, talking as they worked. The spring rains seem to have broken for good, and everyone else had taken their work outside. Wendy sat in the fresh air with her spinning wheel. A new batch of wool had arrived, and Toma and Jorge worked cleaning it. So Stella had a chance to ask questions in private.

"Could you get a place at one of the observatories? How does that work?"

Andi shook her head. "It wouldn't work out. There's three people at Kitt and two each at Griffith and Wilson, and they pick their successors. I'm better use to them here, working to send them credits."

"And you have your telescope, I suppose."

"The astronomers love my telescope," she said. "They call my setup Barnard Observatory, as if it's actually important. Isn't it silly?"

"Of course it isn't."

Andi's hands flashed, passing the shuttle across. She glanced up every now and then. Stella, for her part, let her hands move by habit, and watched Andi more than her own work. Outside, Wendy sang as she spun, in rhythm with the clipping hum of her wheel. Her voice was light, dream-like.

The next time Andi glanced up, she exclaimed, "How do you *do* that? You're not even watching and it's coming out beautiful."

Stella blinked at her work—not much to judge by, she thought. A foot or two of fabric curling over the breast beam, only just starting to wind onto the cloth beam. "I don't know. It's what I'm good at. Like you and the telescope."

"Nice of you to say so. But here, look at this—I've missed a row." She sat back and started unpicking the last five minutes of her work. "I go too fast. My mind wanders."

"It happens to everyone," Stella said.

"Not you. I saw that shawl you did for Elsta."

"I've just gotten good at covering up the mistakes," Stella said, winking.

~

A week after her arrival, an agent from the regional committee came to visit. A stout, gray-haired, cheerful woman, she was the doctor who made regular rounds up and down the Long Road. She was scheduled to give Bette a round of vaccinations, but Stella suspected the woman was going to be checking on her as well, to make sure she was settling in and hadn't disrupted the household too much.

The doctor, Nance, sat with Bette on the floor, and the baby immediately started crying. Peri hovered, but Nance just smiled and cooed while lifting the baby's arms and checking her ears, not seeming at all bothered.

"How is the world treating you then, Toma?" Nance turned to Toma, who was sitting in his usual chair by the fire.

His brow was creased with worry, though there didn't seem to be anything wrong. "Fine, fine," he said brusquely.

Nance turned. "And Stella, are you doing well?"

Astrophilia

"Yes, thank you," Stella said. She was winding yarn around Andi's outstretched hands, to make a skein. This didn't feel much like an inspection, but that only made her more nervous.

"Very good. My, you're a wiggler, aren't you?" Bette's crying had finally subsided to red-faced sniffling, but she continued to fling herself from Nance's arms in an attempt to escape. After a round with a stethoscope, Nance let her go, and the baby crawled away, back to Peri.

The doctor turned her full attention to Toma. "The committee wants to order more banners, they expect to award quite a few this summer. Will you have some ready?"

Toma seemed startled. "Really? Are they sure?"

Barnard supplied the red-and-green patterned cloth used to make the banners awarded to households who'd been approved to have a baby. One of the things Nance had asked about when she first arrived was if anyone had tried bribing him for a length of the cloth over the last year. One of the reasons Barnard had the task of producing the banners—they were prosperous enough not to be vulnerable to bribes. Such attempts happened rarely, but did happen. Households had been broken up over such crimes.

The banner the household had earned for Bette was pinned proudly to the wall above the mantel.

Nance shrugged. "The region's been stable for a couple of years. No quota arguments, most households supporting themselves, just enough surplus to get by without draining resources. We're a healthy region, Toma. If we can support more children, we ought to. And you—with all these healthy young women you have, you might think of putting in for another baby." The doctor beamed.

Stella and Andi looked at each other and blushed. Another baby so soon after the first? Scandalous.

Nance gathered up her kit. "Before I go, let me check all your birth control implants so we don't have any mishaps, eh?"

She started with Elsta and Toma and worked her way around the room.

"Not that I could have a mishap," Andi muttered to Stella. "They ought to make exceptions for someone like me who isn't likely to get in that kind of trouble. Because of her *preferences*, you know?"

"I know," Stella said, blushing very hard now. "I've had that thought myself."

They stared at each other for a very long moment. Stella's mouth had suddenly gone dry. She wanted to flee the room and stick her head in a bucket of cool water. Then again, she didn't.

When Nance came to her side to prod her arm, checking that the implant was in place, Stella hardly felt it.

"Looks like you're good and covered," Nance said. "For now, eh? Until you get that extra banner." She winked.

The doctor stayed for supper and still had enough daylight left to walk to the next waystation along the road. Elsta wrapped up a snack of fruit and cheese for her to take with her, and Nance thanked her very much. As soon as she was gone, Toma muttered.

"Too many mouths to feed—and what happens when the next flood hits? The next typhoon? We lose everything and then there isn't enough? We have enough as it is, more than enough. Wanting more, it's asking for trouble. Getting greedy is what brought the disasters in the first place. It's too much."

Everyone stayed quiet, letting him rant. This felt to Stella like an old argument, words repeated like the chorus of a song. Toma's philosophy, expounded by habit. He didn't need a response.

Stella finished winding the skein of yarn and quietly excused herself, putting her things away and saying goodnight to everyone.

Andi followed her out of the cottage soon after, and they walked together to their room.

"So, do you want one?" Stella asked her.

"A baby? I suppose I do. Someday. I mean, I assumed as well off as Barnard is I could have one if I wanted one. It's a little odd, thinking about who I'd pick for the father. That's the part I'm not sure about. What about you?"

Besides being secretly, massively pleased that Andi hadn't thought much about fathers... "I assumed I'd never get the chance. I don't think I'd miss it if I didn't."

"Enough other people who want 'em, right?"

"Something like that."

They reached their room, changed into their nightclothes, washed up for bed. Ended up sitting on their beds, facing each other and talking. That first uncomfortable night seemed far away now.

"Toma doesn't seem to like the idea of another baby," Stella prompted.

"Terrified, I think," she said. "Wanting too much gets people in trouble."

"But it only seems natural, to want as much as you can have."

Andi shook her head. "His grandparents remembered the old days. He heard stories from them about the disasters. All the people who died in the floods and plagues. He's that close to it—might as well have lived through it himself. He thinks we'll lose it all, that another great disaster will fall on us and destroy everything. It's part of why he hates my telescope so much. It's a sign of the old days when everything went rotten. But it won't happen, doesn't he see that?"

Stella shrugged. "Those days aren't so far gone, really. Look at what happened to Greentree."

"Oh—Stella, I'm sorry. I didn't mean that there's not anything to it, just that..." She shrugged, unable to finish the thought.

"It can't happen here. I know."

Andi's black hair fell around her face, framing her pensive expression. She stared into space. "I just wish he could see how good things are. We've earned a little extra, haven't we?"

Unexpected even to herself, Stella burst, "Can I kiss you?"

In half a heartbeat Andi fell at her, holding Stella's arms, and Stella clung back, and either her arms were hot or Andi's hands were, and they met, lips to lips.

One evening, Andi escaped the gathering in the common room, and brought Stella with her. They left as the sun had almost set, leaving just enough light to follow the path to the observatory. They took candles inside shaded lanterns for the trip back to their cottage. At dusk, the windmills were ghostly skeletons lurking on the hillside.

They waited for full dark, talking while Andi looked over her paperwork and prepared her notes. Andi asked about Greentree, and Stella explained that the aquifers had dried up in the drought. Households remained in the region because they'd always been there. Some survived, but they weren't particularly successful. She told Andi how the green of the valleys near the coast had almost blinded her when she first arrived, and how all the rain had seemed like a miracle.

Then it was time to unlatch the roof panels and look at the sky.

"Don't squint, just relax. Let the image come into focus," Andi said, bending close to give directions to Stella, who was peering through the scope's eyepiece. Truth be told, Stella was more aware of Andi's hand resting lightly on her shoulder. She shifted closer.

"You should be able to see it," Andi said, straightening to look at the sky.

"Okay…I think…. Oh! Is that it?" A disk had come into view, a pale, glowing light striped with orange, yellow, cream. Like someone had covered a very distant moon with melted butter.

"Jupiter," Andi said proudly.

"But it's just a star."

"Not up close it isn't."

Not a disk, then, but a sphere. Another planet. "Amazing."

"Isn't it? You ought to be able to see some of the moons as well—a couple of bright stars on either side?"

"I think…yes, there they are."

After an hour, Stella began shivering in the nighttime cold, and Andi put her arms around her, rubbing warmth into her back. In moments, they were kissing, and stumbled together to the desk by the shack's wall, where Andi pushed her back across the surface and made love to her. Jupiter had swung out of view by the time they closed up the roof and stumbled off the hill.

Astrophilia

Another round of storms came, shrouding the nighttime sky, and they spent the evenings around the hearth with the others. Some of the light went out of Andi on those nights. She sat on a chair with a basket of mending at her feet, darning socks and shirts, head bent over her work. Lamplight turned her skin amber and made her hair shine like obsidian. But she didn't talk. That may have been because Elsta and Toma talked over everyone, or Peri exclaimed over something the baby did, then everyone had to admire Bette.

The day the latest round of rain broke and the heat of summer finally settled over the valley, Andi got another package from Griffith, and that light of discovery came back to her. Tonight, they'd rush off to the observatory after supper.

Stella almost missed the cue to escape, helping Elsta with the dishes. When she was finished and drying her hands, Andi was at the door. Stella rushed in behind her. Then Toma brought out a basket, one of the ones as big as an embrace that they used to store just-washed wool in, and set it by Andi's chair before the hearth. "Andi, get back here."

Her hand was on the door, one foot over the threshold, and Stella thought she might keep going, pretending that she hadn't heard. But her hand clenched on the door frame, and she turned around.

"We've got to get all this new wool processed, so you'll stay in tonight to help."

"I can do that tomorrow. I'll work double tomorrow—"

"Now, Andi."

Stella stepped forward, hands reaching for the basket. "Toma, I can do that."

"No, you're doing plenty already. Andi needs to do it."

"I'll be done with the mending in a minute and can finish that in no time at all. Really, it's all right."

He looked past her, to Andi. "You know the rules—household business first."

"The household business is *done*. This is make work!" she said. Toma held the basket out in reproof.

Stella tried again. "But I *like* carding." It sounded lame—no one liked carding.

But Andi had surrendered, coming away from the door, shuffling toward her chair. "Stella, it's all right. Not your argument."

"But—" The pleading in her gaze felt naked. She wanted to help, how could she help?

Andi slumped in the chair without looking up. All Stella could do was sit in her own chair, with her knitting. She jabbed herself with the needle three times, from glancing up at Andi every other stitch.

Toma sat before his workbench, looking pleased for nearly the first time since Stella had met him.

Well after dark, Stella lay in her bed, stomach in knots. Andi was in the other bed and hadn't said a word all evening.

"Andi? Are you all right?" she whispered. She stared across the room, to the slope of the other woman, mounded her under blanket. The lump didn't move, but didn't look relaxed in sleep. But if she didn't want to talk, Stella wouldn't force her.

"I'm okay," Andi sighed, finally.

"Anything I can do?"

Another long pause, and Stella was sure she'd said too much. Then, "You're a good person, Stella. Anyone ever told you that?"

Stella crawled out from under her covers, crossed to Andi's bed, climbed in with her. Andi pulled the covers up over them both, and the women held each other.

Toma sent Andi on an errand, delivering a set of blankets to the next waystation and picking up messages to bring back. More makework. The task could just have as easily been done by the next wagon messenger to pass by. Andi told him as much, standing outside the work house the next morning.

"Why wait when we can get the job done now?" Toma answered, hefting the backpack, stuffed to bursting with newly woven woolens, toward her.

Astrophilia

Stella was at her loom, and her hand on the shuttle paused as she listened. But Andi didn't say anything else. Only glared at Toma a good long minute before taking up the pack. She'd be gone most of the day, hiking there and back.

Which was the point, wasn't it?

Stella contrived to find jobs that kept Toma in sight, sorting and carding wool outside where he was working repairing a fence, when she should have been weaving. So she saw when Toma studied the hammer in his hand, looked up the hill, and started walking the path to Andi's observatory.

Stella dropped the basket of wool she was holding and ran.

He was merely walking. Stella overtook him easily, at first. But after fifty yards of running, she slowed, clutching at a stitch in her side. Gasping for breath with burning lungs, she kept on, step after step, hauling herself up the hill, desperate to get there first.

"Stella, go back, don't get in the middle of this."

Even if she could catch enough of her breath to speak, she didn't know what she would say. He lengthened his stride, gaining on her. She got to the shed a bare few steps before him.

The door didn't have a lock; it had never needed one. Stella pressed herself across it and faced out, to Toma, marching closer. At least she had something to lean on for the moment.

"Move aside, Stella. She's got to grow up and get on with what's important," Toma said.

"This *is* important."

He stopped, studied her. He gripped the handle of the hammer like it was a weapon. Her heart thudded. How angry was he?

Toma considered, then said, "Stella. You're here because I wanted to do Az a favor. I can change my mind. I can send a message to Nance and the committee that it just isn't working out. I can do that."

Panic brought sudden tears to her eyes. He wouldn't dare, he couldn't, she'd proven herself already in just a few weeks, hadn't she? The committee wouldn't believe him, couldn't listen to him. But she couldn't be sure of that, could she?

Best thing to do would be to step aside. He was head of the household, it was his call. She ought to do as he said, because her place here *wasn't* secure. A month ago that might not have mattered, but now—she *wanted* to stay, she *had* to stay.

And if she stepped aside, leaving Toma free to enter the shed, what would she tell Andi afterward?

She swallowed the lump in her throat and found words. "I know disaster can still happen. I know the droughts and storms and plagues do still come and can take away everything. Better than anyone, I know. But we have to start building again sometime, yes? People like Andi have to start building, and we have to let them, even if it seems useless to the rest of us. Because it isn't useless, it—it's beautiful."

He stared at her for a long time. She thought maybe he was considering how to wrestle her away from the door. He was bigger than she was, and she wasn't strong. It wouldn't take much. But she'd fight.

"You're infatuated, that's all," he said.

Maybe, not that it mattered.

Then he said, "You're not going to move away, are you?"

Shaking her head, Stella flattened herself more firmly against the door.

Toma's grip on the hammer loosened, just a bit. "My grandparents—has Andi told you about my grandparents? They were children when the big fall came. They remembered what it was like. Mostly they talked about what they'd lost, all the things they had and didn't now. And I thought, all those things they missed, that they wanted back—that was what caused the fall in the first place, wasn't it? We don't need it, any of it."

"Andi needs it. And it's not hurting anything." What else could she say, she had to say something that would make it all right. "Better things will come, or what's the point?"

A weird crooked smile turned Toma's lips, and he shifted his grip on the hammer. Holding it by the head now, he let it dangle by his leg. "God, what a world," he muttered. Stella still couldn't tell if he was going to force her away from the door. She held her breath.

Toma said, "Don't tell Andi about this. All right?"

Astrophilia

She nodded. "All right."

Toma turned and started down the trail, a calm and steady pace. Like a man who'd just gone out for a walk.

Stella slid to the ground and sat on the grass by the wall until the old man was out of sight. Finally, after scrubbing the tears from her face, she followed him down, returning to the cottages and her work.

Andi was home in time for supper, and the household ate together as usual. The woman was quiet and kept making quick glances at Toma, who avoided looking back at all. It was like she knew Toma had had a plan. Stella couldn't say anything until they were alone.

The night was clear, the moon was dark. Stella'd learned enough from Andi to know it was a good night for stargazing. As they were cleaning up after the meal, she touched Andi's hand. "Let's go to the observatory."

Andi glanced at Toma, and her lips pressed together, grim. "I don't think that's a good idea."

"I think it'll be okay."

Andi clearly didn't believe her, so Stella took her hand, and together they walked out of the cottage, then across the yard, past the work house, and to the trail that led up the hill to the observatory.

And it was all right.

Contributors

MEGAN ARKENBERG lives and writes in Wisconsin. Her work has appeared in *Asimov's*, *Strange Horizons*, *Lightspeed*, Ellen Datlow's *Best Horror of the Year*, Volume 5, and dozens of other places. In 2012, her poem "The Curator Speaks in the Department of Dead Languages" won the Rhysling Award in the long form category. She procrastinates by editing the fantasy e-zine *Mirror Dance*.

RICHARD BOWES has won two World Fantasy, an International Horror Guild and Million Writer Awards. His new novel, *Dust Devil on a Quiet Street*, recently appeared from Lethe Press, which has also republished his Lambda Award-winning novel *Minions of the Moon*. Recent and forthcoming appearances include: *F&SF*, *Icarus*, *Lightspeed* and the anthologies *After*, *Wilde Stories 2013*, *Bloody Fabulous*, *Ghosts: Recent Hauntings*, *Handsome Devil*, *Hauntings* and *Where Thy Dark Eye Glances*.

SARAH DIEMER is an award-winning author of lesbian young adult speculative fiction, including her debut novel, *The Dark Wife*, and the year long fiction project, *Project Unicorn: A Lesbian YA Extravaganza*. Sarah writes her lesbian adult fiction under the pen name Elora Bishop, including the *Sappho's Fables: Lesbian Fairy Tales* series, which she co-writes with her wife, author Jennifer Diemer. Find out more about her work at oceanid.org and muserising.com.

JEWELLE GOMEZ is the author of seven books including the cult classic lesbian vampire novel, *The Gilda Stories*, which has been in print for more than twenty years (alibris.com). Her adaptation of the novel for the stage—*Bones and Ash*—was performed by Urban Bush

Women Company in thirteen US cities. Her new book in the series is entitled *Gilda: The Alternate Decades* and is looking for a home. She is also the author of *Waiting for Giovanni*, a play about James Baldwin which premiered at New Conservatory Theatre Center in 2011. Follow her @VampyreVamp and her home page jewellegomez.com.

Kate Harrad is a London-based writer, parent and bisexual events organiser who blogs under the name Fausterella, which is also the title of her short story collection. Her first novel, *All Lies and Jest*, a gently speculative thriller almost featuring vampires, was published by Ghostwoods Books.

Claire Humphrey's short stories have appeared in *Strange Horizons*, *PodCastle*, *Fantasy Magazine*, and several anthologies including *Beyond Binary* and *Imaginarium: Best Canadian Speculative Writing*. She is a Viable Paradise graduate and an active SFWA member. She works in the book trade as a buyer for Indigo, and she is also the reviews editor at *Ideomancer*. As you'd expect, she is also working on a novel.

Jamie Killen has sold stories to several venues including *Red by Dawn 3* and *The Drabblecast*. She lives and works in Arizona.

Andrea Kneeland's work has appeared in more than fifty journals and anthologies. Her first collection, *the Birds & the Beasts*, is forthcoming from the Lit Pub.

Malinda Lo is the author of several young adult novels, including *Ash*, a retelling of Cinderella with a lesbian twist, which was a finalist for the William C. Morris YA Debut Award, the Andre Norton Award, and the Lambda Literary Award. Before she became a novelist, she was an economics major, an editorial assistant, a graduate student, and an entertainment reporter. She lives in Northern California with her partner and their dog. Her website is malindalo.com.

ALEX DALLY MACFARLANE lives in London, where she is finishing a MA in Ancient History. When not researching ancient gender and narratives, she writes stories, found in *Clarkesworld Magazine*, *Strange Horizons*, *Beneath Ceaseless Skies*, *Shimmer* and *The Other Half of the Sky*. Poetry can be found in *Stone Telling*, *Goblin Fruit*, *The Moment of Change* and *Here, We Cross*. She is the editor of *Aliens: Recent Encounters* (2013) and *The Mammoth Book of SF Stories by Women* (forthcoming in late 2014). Visit her online at alexdallymacfarlane.com.

BRIT MANDELO is a writer, critic, and editor whose primary fields of interest are speculative fiction and queer literature, especially when the two coincide. She is the senior fiction editor for *Strange Horizons* magazine and has two books out, *Beyond Binary: Genderqueer and Sexually Fluid Speculative Fiction* (a finalist for the Lambda Literary Award) and *We Wuz Pushed: On Joanna Russ and Radical Truth-telling*. Her other work—fiction, nonfiction, poetry; she wears a lot of hats—has been featured in magazines such as *Stone Telling*, *Clarkesworld*, *Apex*, and *Ideomancer*. She also writes regularly for *Tor.com* and has several long-running column series there, including *Queering SFF*, a mix of criticism, editorials, and reviews on queer speculative fiction. She is a Louisville native and lives there with her partner in an apartment that doesn't have room for all the books.

JL MERROW is that rare beast, an English person who refuses to drink tea. She read Natural Sciences at Cambridge, where she learned many things, chief amongst which was that she never wanted to see the inside of a lab ever again. Her one regret is that she never mastered the ability of punting one-handed whilst holding a glass of champagne. She writes across genres, with a preference for contemporary gay romance and the paranormal, and is frequently accused of humour. Her novella *Muscling Through* is a 2013 EPIC ebook Award finalist. JL Merrow is a member of the UK GLBTQ Fiction Meet organising team. Find JL Merrow online at jlmerrow.com.

JULIA RIOS hosts the Outer Alliance Podcast (celebrating QUILT-BAG speculative fiction), and is one of the three fiction editors at *Strange Horizons*. Her fiction, articles, interviews, and poetry have appeared in *Daily Science Fiction*, *Apex Magazine*, *Stone Telling*, *Jabberwocky*, and several other places. She's half-Mexican, but her (fairly dreadful) French is better than her Spanish.

NISI SHAWL's collection *Filter House* was one of two books to win the 2009 James Tiptree, Jr. Award. Her work has been published at *Strange Horizons*, in *Asimov's SF Magazine*, and in anthologies including *The Other Half of the Sky* and both volumes of the groundbreaking *Dark Matter* series. She was the Guest of Honor for WisCon 35, the world's premier feminist science fiction convention. She edited *Bloodchildren: Stories by the Octavia E. Butler Scholars*, and co-edited *Strange Matings: Octavia E. Butler, Science Fiction, Feminism, and African American Voices*. With classmate Cynthia Ward she co-authored *Writing the Other: A Practical Approach*. Shawl is a cofounder of the Carl Brandon Society and serves on the Board of Directors of the Clarion West Writers Workshop. Her website is nisishawl.com.

BENJANUN SRIDUANGKAEW spends her free time on words, amateur photography, and the pursuit of colorful, unusual makeup. She has a love for cities, airports, and bees. Her fiction can be found in *GigaNotoSaurus*, *Beneath Ceaseless Skies* and the anthologies *Clockwork Phoenix 4* and *The End of the Road*.

CARRIE VAUGHN is the bestselling author of a series of novels about a werewolf named Kitty who hosts a talk radio advice show for the supernaturally disadvantaged. The tenth novel in the series, *Kitty Steals the Show*, is due out in 2012. She's also written novels for young adults (*Voices of Dragons*, *Steel*), two stand-alone novels (*Discord's Apple*, *After the Golden Age*), and more than fifty short stories. She's been nominated for the Hugo Award for best short story, and is a graduate of the Odyssey Fantasy Writing Workshop. After living the nomadic childhood of a typical Air Force brat, she's managed to put down roots in Colorado, where she lives with her fluffy attack dog and too many hobbies.

Wendy N. Wagner's short fiction has appeared in *Beneath Ceaseless Skies* and several anthologies, including *Armored* and *The Way of the Wizard*. Her first novel, a Pathfinder Tales adventure, is forthcoming in 2014. An avid gamer and gardener, she lives with her wonderful family in Portland, Oregon. You can keep up with her at winniewoohoo.com.

And

TENEA D. JOHNSON is the author of the novels *R/evolution* and *Smoketown*, as well as *Starting Friction*, a poetry and prose collection. Her work has appeared in various magazines and anthologies, including the Lambda Award-winning *Necrologue*. She is also a musician who composes fiction albums and has had the good fortune to perform her pieces at the Knitting Factory and the Public Theater, among others. Her virtual home is teneadjohnson.com. Stop by anytime.

STEVE BERMAN takes much delight in discovering wonderful queer stories and helping authors share their voices. He has been a finalist for the Lambda Literary Award for his editorial efforts four times, including for his work on *Heiresses of Russ 2012*. He resides in southern New Jersey.

Publication Credits

"Introduction" © 2013 Tenea D. Johnson, original to this volume ∾ "Harrowing Emily" © 2012 Megan Arkenberg, first appeared in *Shimmer* #15 ∾ "Reality Girl" © 2012 Richard Bowes, first appeared in *After* (ed. by Ellen Datlow & Terri Windling, Hyperion) ∾ "The Witch Sea" © 2012 Sarah Diemer, first appeared in *Love Devours: Tales of Monstrous Adoration* (CreateSpace) ∾ "Saint Louis 1990" © 2012 Jewelle Gomez, first appeared in *Night Shadows* (ed. by Greg Herren and J. M. Redmann, Bold Strokes Books) ∾ "Narrative Only" © 2012 Kate Harrad, first appeared in *Glitterwolf* #2 ∾ "Nightfall in the Scent Garden" © 2012 Claire Humphrey, first appeared in *Strange Horizons*, March 5, 2012 ∾ "Elm" © 2012 Jamie Killen, first appeared in *The Future Fire* ∾ "Beneath Impossible Circumstances" © 2012 Andrea Kneeland, first appeared in *Strange Horizons*, April 16, 2012 ∾ "One True Love" © 2012 Malinda Lo, first published in *Foretold: 14 Tales of Prophecy and Prediction* (ed. by Carrie Ryan, Delacorte Press Books for Young Readers) ∾ "Feed Me the Bones of Our Saints" © 2012 Alex Dally MacFarlane, first appeared in *Strange Horizons*, July 9 & 16, 2012 ∾ "Winter Scheming" © 2012 Brit Mandelo, first appeared in *Apex Magazine*, June 5, 2012 ∾ "Nine Days and Seven Tears" © 2012 JL Merrow, first appeared in *She Shifters* (ed. by Delilah Devlin, Cleis Press) ∾ "Oracle Gretel" © 2012 Julia Rios, first appeared in a same-titled chapbook ∾ "Otherwise" © 2012 Nisi Shawl, first appeared in *Brave New Love* (ed. by Paula Guran, Running Press) ∾ "Chang'e Dashes from the Moon" © 2012 Benjanun Sriduangkaew, first appeared in *Expanded Horizons*, July 22, 2012 ∾ "Astrophilia" © 2012 Carrie Vaughn, first appeared in *Clarkesworld*, July 2012 ∾ "Barnstormers" © 2012 Wendy N. Wagner, first appeared in *Ideomancer*, Vol. 11, Issue 2

CPSIA information can be obtained at www.ICGtesting.com
Printed in the USA
LVOW08s0946280913

354551LV00002B/8/P